HATE TO LOVE YOU

SHAYLA BLACK

HATE
to
Love
YOU

SHAYLA BLACK

Steamy. Emotional. Forever.

HATE TO LOVE YOU
Written by Shayla Black

Includes:
MORE THAN TEMPT YOU © 2019 by Shelley Bradley LLC
SEDUCING THE ENEMY © 2020 by Shelley Bradley LLC
WATCH ME © 2007 by Shelley Bradley LLC

This book is an original publication by Shayla Black.

Copyright 2022 Shelley Bradley LLC

Cover Design by: Rachel Connolly
Edited by: Amy Knupp of Blue Otter
Proofread by: Fedora Chen

Excerpt from *More Than Dare You* © 2020 by Shelley Bradley LLC
Excerpt from *Seduced by the Bodyguard* © 2020 by Shelley Bradley LLC
Excerpt from *Naughty Little Secret* © 2014 by Shelley Bradley LLC

ISBN: 978-1-958075-06-7

more than
TEMPT
YOU

REED FAMILY RECKONING: BASTARDS

SHAYLA BLACK

Steamy. Emotional. Forever.

ABOUT *MORE THAN TEMPT YOU*

I romanced her for revenge…but what if she's not the enemy?

I'm Clint Holmes—hands-on business owner and a beast in the bedroom. Life was great—until fate ripped my father from my life. Now the only thing that matters is finding the woman responsible and making her pay. But beauty Bethany Banks is a Harvard-educated shark used to playing dangerous corporate games. How can a blue-collar guy like me outsmart her?

One glance, and the answer is obvious. I seduce her.

During our slow-dance of secrets and lies, I get to know the supposed ballbuster…only to discover her ambition and tough exterior hide a woman who's vulnerable and heartbreakingly alone. Instinct urges me to protect her, but I came for retribution. Night after night, I ply her with my burning touch until I drown in her pleasure. Suddenly, I'm addicted and questioning everything, especially the fine line between love and hate. But when the past comes back with a vengeance, exposing the truth, can I prove that I'm more than tempted to make her mine forever?

FOREWORD

There are infinite ways to tell someone you love them. Some of the most powerful don't require words at all. This was the truth rolling through my head when I first conceived of this series, writing about a love so complete that mere letters strung together to make sentences weren't an adequate communicator of those feelings. Instead, for this series, music was my go-to choice.

I *love* music. I'm always immersed in it and spend hours a day with my ear buds plugged in. I write to music. I think to music. I even sleep to music. I was thrilled to incorporate songs into the story I felt were meaningful to the journey. I think of it this way: a movie has a sound-track. Why shouldn't a book?

So I created one.

Some of the songs I've selected will be familiar. Some are old. Some are newer. Some popular. Some obscure. They all just fit (in my opinion) and came straight from the heart. I listened to many of these songs as I wrote the book.

For maximum understanding (and feels), I seriously recommend becoming familiar with these songs and either playing them or rolling them around in your head as you read. Due to copyright laws, I can't use exact lyrics, but I tried to give you the gist of those most meaningful to Clint and Bethany's story. I've also made it simple for you to give these songs a listen by creating a Spotify playlist.

Hugs and happy reading!

BEER RUN - Garth Brooks featuring George Jones
DON'T STOP BELIEVIN' - Journey
STRONGER (WHAT DOESN'T KILL YOU) - Kelly Clarkson
DARE YOU TO MOVE - Switchfoot
HAPPY - Pharrell Williams
SOMEWHERE OVER THE RAINBOW - Israel Kamakawiwo'ole
I WON'T GIVE UP - Jason Mraz
FORTRESS AROUND YOUR HEART - Sting
PLEASE FORGIVE ME - Bryan Adams
DIG - Incubus

prologue

Clint

"Come home."

I groan as I glance across the room at my father. Not again... "Dad, we've talked about this."

"No, you've talked about it. I haven't said my piece."

"But I know your spiel. Look, I've transplanted, and my roots are here now. My business is growing again. I'm still a newer kid on the block in the oil industry around here, so it's taking time." I lean back in my chair and grip my cold beer. "But I'm okay with that. Besides, you don't need me; you still have Bry at home."

My father huffs, then takes a drag of his cigar. "Until he goes off to college in the fall. Besides, when do you think your youngest brother is ever home? He's a seventeen-year-old boy who's just graduated from high school and has his own wheels. At that age, when were *you* home?"

He's got a valid point, but... "I know it's been hard since Mom's death. The last eighteen months have been an adjustment for everyone."

"It's not that. Open your eyes, son. The oil boom will likely bust again. Five years ago, this was a great business, and you were in the right place at the right time. Even Bethany agreed," he says of his investment advisor, whom he constantly raves about. "But now, it's time to cut your losses before they go any deeper. OPEC wants to put US oil production out of business, and they have the resources to make that happen. They did really well at choking your business last year."

I can't deny that. Twelve months ago, I was lamenting high costs and dismal profits. "This year has been better so far."

"Slightly. C'mon, Clint. Do you really want to eke out a living? Sell this thing. You'll get a pretty penny for the business, even if the industry isn't at its hottest right now." He hunkers back in my favorite leather chair and takes a sip of his whiskey. "If your mother's death taught me anything, it was that life is even shorter than people warn you. Forty-nine was way too young to die, but that didn't matter. Her number was up. Watching her go through all that breast cancer treatment just about killed me."

Me, too. I wasn't there for the worst since I moved to North Dakota at nineteen and went straight to work, eventually building my own oil services business from the ground up. But I came home for the end. Seeing her so frail and wasted devastated me. Losing her gutted my family. "I know, Dad."

When I reach across the space to take his hand, he squeezes mine. "Look, I want to retire. I want to do all the things your mother and I planned to before I pass on. We were going to get season tickets to one of those fancy theaters. We were going to drive up Pacific Coast Highway to San Francisco and see the sights. Hell, we were going to take a Hawaiian vacation. We didn't follow through on any of those plans because we had three growing boys and always thought there would be time. And now…she's gone."

When my father chokes back emotion, I squeeze his hand again. "I'm sorry."

"It's not your fault. She would have chosen keeping you kids happy over a vacation any day."

"But she worked all her life and didn't get to enjoy the quieter years. That upsets you, I know."

"Yes, but it upsets me more that I promised her I'd do all those things after she was gone. So far, I've done nothing but grieve and try to figure out how to carry on."

Guilt tugs at me. If I stay in North Dakota, I'll be following my own path. If I give that up to return to La-La Land, I'll be helping my family, yes. But I'll also be assuming a business that never interested me and putting myself smack-dab in the middle of crowds, congestion, and smog—all the reasons I left LA—again.

"What about Bret? He's going to graduate from UCLA next year with a business degree. I never went to college. Would he be better equipped—"

"You think he's ready to leave the frat house and walk straight into a multimillion-dollar-a-year business? Hell, as far as I can tell he hasn't pulled his head out of a keg in the last six months." My father sighs. "I'm not trying to guilt you. I'm simply hoping you'll see the wisdom of this idea. Your business might be drying up, depending on the price of oil per barrel. Mine is thriving, but it's too much for me to handle these days. I'm just getting too old."

"You're only fifty-three."

"After your mother's passing, I feel ancient."

He's not his usual, robust self. I know he's not sleeping well, and I guess that's age. But he seems more fatigued than I would have thought. Two years ago, he walked to my favorite fishing spot without any trouble. Today, he was short of breath on the same short trek. Even now, hours after our return, a fine sheen of perspiration beads on his forehead. Granted, it's almost ninety degrees and humid as hell outside, but it's comfortable in the air-conditioned house.

"Dad, you just got here yesterday. Enjoy your vacation. Maybe you'll feel refreshed at the end of two weeks and—"

"I've been thinking about this for months. Now I want you to think about it. Please."

How can I say no to that?

"All right. I'll consider it."

My father smiles wide. "Great. I worry about you out here, you know."

"Why?" I love the wide-open spaces and the down-to-earth people. Sure, it gets colder than a well-digger's butt and summers can be miserably hot, but I appreciate the beauty of nature—something you see almost none of in Los Angeles.

"I didn't see many pretty single girls while we drove through town. There don't seem to be any way out here, just a bunch of prairie dogs and cows. And I know better than to think they're keeping you warm at night."

Admittedly, that's one of the biggest drawbacks to living in the middle of nowhere. I've already dated all the single women within a hundred-mile radius. None of them are for me. When I want to feel a warm female, I have to go to Williston or Bismarck, hit a bar, and hope I get lucky. Most often I do, but sometimes I strike out. It happens. North Dakota is one of the few states where males outnumber females, especially in the western half of the state, where the surge of oil workers has made the odds of hitting a home run shittier.

"No. I'm definitely not into anything with four legs, Dad."

He laughs, absently rubbing at a spot under his right shoulder. "Come back to California. The timing is perfect. You can run my business. It's booming. It will make you rich. You can stop getting your hands dirty every day." He peers at the grease that seems permanently embedded under my fingernails, no matter how hard I scrub. "You can spend more time with me and your brothers. And I want to introduce you to Bethany."

"I don't need a financial advisor right now." Especially not one in a state I don't reside in.

"Maybe not. It never hurts to start investing, in my opinion. But that's not what I meant."

It takes me a minute to realize what he's saying. "You're trying to hook me up with her?"

"She's beautiful and smart and sweet. You'd like her, son. You'd like her a lot."

I know zero about this woman, and since I don't want to move to LA, I'm interested even less. "You date her, Dad. You're single."

"Oh, no. No. She's way closer to your age than mine. She's ambitious, on the quiet side, very direct. I trust her. At least let me introduce you next time you're home…"

If I keep refusing, he'll only keep wheedling. Like his entire proposition that I move back to LA and assume his business, it's better to defer than refuse. For all I know, he may change his mind again tomorrow.

"I'll think about it."

He pastes on a big smile and whips out his phone, then presses and swipes until he finds his photos. "We took this last month when we got together for our quarterly meeting. She even brought me a bottle of my favorite whiskey for my birthday. I asked, and she's single…"

To humor him, I lean in to look at the display. The smiling blonde looks chic and, I admit, stunning in a fitted, feminine gray sheath. Her rosy-pale coloring looks almost icy in the photo, but her eyes are a warm mossy green.

If I met her in a bar, I'd definitely try my luck. And I'd probably keep trying until she said yes. She's hot.

"Well, I can't fault your taste in women."

He laughs heartily, then darkens his phone. Before he can pocket it, the device rings. Thank goodness for WiFi-supported calling. Out here, the cell service is shit.

Dad glances at the display. "It's Brenda. One minute."

His secretary. Probably work. I take that as my cue to head to the kitchen for another beer. When I turn back, my dad is rubbing at that spot just below his shoulder again. Did he pull a muscle?

"Another whiskey?" I ask just before he answers the call.

"Hello?" He presses the phone to his ear and shakes his head.

As I head out of the room, I zone out from their conversation and flip on the kitchen radio. Garth Brooks and George Jones are singing a familiar, up-tempo song about a beer run. Grinning, I grab another brew from the fridge, pop off the cap, and take a swallow.

My dad has visibly aged recently, and I think it's because his business runs him. It's high demand. I guess that makes sense for insurance. But being a desk jockey would make me insane. I like spending time outdoors too much and I don't mind getting my hands dirty. Not much call for that in his line of work. I definitely don't want to talk all day about premiums and car accidents.

As I toss the little metal disc in the nearby trash can, my father's voice booms. I hear the shock. It's a tone I've only heard once—after my mother's doctors told my parents her breast cancer was terminal. This blow is every bit as gut-deep and stunned.

I flip off the radio and go running, only to find my dad sheet-white and blinking as he clutches the phone. "Everything?"

"What?" I ask.

He waves me away with a scowl and begins rubbing at the spot under his shoulder even harder. "Everything. I don't... That's thirty-five years of work. Of savings. Oh, shit. And he was arrested yesterday?"

What the hell is he talking about? And who? "Dad?"

He shakes his head again. "Keep making phone calls. I'll do the same and I'll be on a plane home tomorrow. If you find out anything else... Yes. Of course. I'm going to call Bethany right now. Thank you."

The moment he hangs up, I'm beside him. "What happened?"

"According to Brenda, Barclay Reed, the head of my investment firm, was arrested yesterday. He's been charged with running a giant Ponzi scheme, and every penny of his clients' investments is gone." He blinks as if he's in total disbelief. "I've got to call Bethany. He's her dad. Barclay, I mean. I'm not supposed to know that. She's illegitimate. It's hush-hush, but... She'll tell me what's happening. She's honest. There must be some explanation. I saw her less than four weeks ago, and everything was fine. She showed me all the reports. My money was growing. It can't suddenly be gone..."

He rises unsteadily to his feet. I ease him back down. He looks almost gray now. Shock, I suspect. But I'm worried. He's sweating more and seems short of breath.

"Dad, sit here. Rest. I'll get you packed and reserve you a plane ticket back to LA. If you get there and you need my help, I'll fly out."

"Thanks." He nods almost absently. "I'll call Bethany."

Since I want to hear this conversation, I pretend to gather our personal effects around the room. I try to stay calm, but my thoughts are racing. My father has worked his ass off and sacrificed for decades to save a few million dollars. He's well off, but he's earned it. I'm mad that thieves ever steal from anyone, but for scammers to swindle the life savings of a man nearing the end of his money-earning years? Yeah, I'm furious.

"No answer." He presses the button to end the call. "I'm going to try again."

But three attempts later, the "beautiful, smart, and sweet" financial advisor is nowhere to be found. How convenient. If Barclay is the prime suspect and Bethany is his daughter, odds are good she was involved, too. How dare that very pretty shark in a sheath look a lonely widower in the face and prey on his trust?

My father now looks waxen. He's rubbing at his chest in earnest.

"Dad, are you all right? Are you in pain?"

"Indigestion." He waves me off. "Happens all the time. Maybe Bethany isn't in the office. I'll try her cell."

I'd tell him to wait, but in his shoes, I would want to get to the bottom of this shit, too. Still, I'm worried.

I grab my phone to dial Gary, a buddy who happens to be the local family practitioner. Maybe he can tell me what's going on or prescribe something for Dad's anxiety.

"Her phone went straight to voice mail. Oh, god." He presses a hand to his chest as if he's trying to keep it from falling apart. "She's never not answered me. Ever."

His expression tells me that he's crushed. Shattered.

"I've got to… I have to get…" My dad stumbles to his feet.

I pocket my phone and rush back to his side. "What?"

Now, he looks disoriented and pasty. I'm no longer concerned; I'm downright alarmed.

As I wrap my arm around my father to steady him, he grabs his chest again, eyes flaring wide as he makes an animal sound of pain and crumples to the hardwood floor.

"Dad!"

"Hurt," he gurgles. "Ambulance."

Holy shit. He's having a fucking heart attack. The signs are all there.

And it will take an ambulance at least forty minutes to reach me.

Cold fear fills my veins with ice as I fall to my knees beside my dad. My fingers feel as if they're moving in slow motion as I fumble for my phone, trying to unlock the display so I can dial.

It seems to ring forever before a woman answers. "Nine-one-one. What's your emergency?"

I quickly fill her in and ask what I can do to help. Yes, he's lying on the floor. Yes, he's conscious—barely. No, he's not breathing.

Oh, shit.

After advising me an ambulance is on the way, she asks if I have any aspirin in the house. I do, thank god.

"Dad." I grab his hand. "Can you hear me?"

He makes a squeaking sound and grabs weakly at my hand. I try to stay calm. My head keeps telling me this can't possibly be happening. My eyes tell me in living, horrific color it is.

"I'm going to grab an aspirin from my bathroom. Stay here. Stay with me. I'll be right back."

No response. I pocket my phone and flat-out run across the house, into the master bathroom, then tear into my medicine cabinet. My hands are shaking as I try to open the bottle, but the fucking child-proof cap won't come off. Finally, I manage, spilling one tablet in my fist, then dash back down the stairs, panting, heart racing.

"Dad?"

He doesn't respond. Son of a bitch. I have to try CPR. I haven't practiced this since I did the lifeguard thing at the local pool when I was sixteen. But I do my best to screw my head on straight and start chest compressions and breathing.

I have no idea how long I press and exhale, trying to force air into his lungs and prompt his heart to pick up its own tempo. All I know is that I'm dizzy and exhausted and wondering if I'm making any headway when the EMTs pound on my front door.

As much as I hate to, I tear myself away long enough to answer the door. I can't acknowledge that my father still isn't breathing. The professionals are here. They'll get him going. He'll be all right.

He can't die here today.

A trio of uniformed ambulance attendants storm the house with bags and a rolling stretcher.

"Where is the victim?" a capable-looking African-American woman asks in a calm voice.

"Living room." I point.

The other two EMTs waste no time rushing to my father's side. I try to follow, but the woman blocks my path. "Tell me what you've done so far."

I trip over my words as I try to explain, but all I care about is reaching my dad's side. I shove my hands in my pockets. I need something to do. I can't stand here and merely watch. I come up with the aspirin he was never conscious enough to chew and swallow.

"Do you need this?" I ask her.

She glances over her shoulder. I follow her line of vision. The other two medics have hooked my father up to some sort of heart rate monitor.

The sharp, persistent sound rattles my head and pierces my calm. He's flatlined.

"No!" I take off to reach his side.

The woman holds me back. "Let them do their job."

"But…"

I'm not sure what to say. I have zero medical knowledge. Logically, I'll only be in the way, but… He can't be dying. And if—oh, god—he is, he can't be doing it with only strangers to comfort him. He needs family.

"Sir—"

"I have to be with him," I blurt. "At least let me hold his hand."

To my right, I hear one of the EMTs sigh as he rises to his feet and approaches me, regret softening his eyes. "I'm sorry."

"No." I shake my head. "No! I was talking to him less than an hour ago. We were making plans…"

In the back of my head, I realize I'm speaking nonsense, but I can't process what's just happened. I don't know what to say.

My father can't be dead.

"Can't you defib him?" I've watched enough medical dramas on TV to know what that means.

The female shakes her head. "That's not how it works. A defibrillator can't jumpstart a stopped heart. They stop a heart in an irregular rhythm and try to reset it. But your father is in asystole. There's no longer any electrical activity, so there's no tempo to restore. We're very sorry."

I stand rooted. In shock.

Dad is gone.

What the hell happened? What the hell am I going to do?

Pain rips through my chest. I can't breathe.

I have to call Bret and Bry and break their hearts. I'll have to go to

California and bury my father. I scrub a hand down my face. Oh, god. I'll have to take care of my seventeen-year-old brother, at least until he's no longer a minor.

I'll have to face my life without the man whose love and counsel I've relied on every one of the twenty-four years of my life.

I clench my fists. Something bites into my palm. I uncurl my fingers. The aspirin.

Gritting my teeth, I'm suddenly choked by grief and anger. I toss the little disc across the room and ignore the female who offers me a sedative. *Fuck that.*

It seems like hours pass before they lift my dad onto a stretcher and cover his face. It's all I can do to hold myself together. I feel so fucking brittle. And lost.

Overall, my father was in decent health. I don't understand.

I grab the arm of the male medic who first pronounced my father dead. "How could this happen? He's never had any history of heart trouble or disease. He was fit and still young and…"

The thirty-something guy with the goatee shrugs. "I don't know the exact cause." He drones on about heart fitness, medication, cholesterol, and other shit that didn't apply to my father. "Or a shock. Did something happen today?"

It did. His investments. His life savings.

Fucking Barclay Reed and his "honest" daughter, Bethany Banks.

This is her doing, and if I have to crawl to the ends of the earth, spend every minute and every last dime, they will pay.

chapter ONE

December 26 (Six months later)
Los Angeles

"You're welcome."

I know the self-satisfied voice on the other end of my cell phone, but I'm confused about his greeting. "Ash?"

"Yep."

We met in the oil fields of North Dakota a few years ago. The back-breaking work and the unrelenting winters weren't for him. After a couple of years, he succumbed to wanderlust and left, but we've remained tight. If I have a best friend, it's Asher Grant.

His tone tells me he can't wait for me to ask. "Okay, what am I thanking you for?"

"A gift. Granted it's a day late—how was your Christmas, by the way?—but I'm calling to give you one hell of a present."

Honestly, Christmas was rough. I did my best to keep it as jovial as possible, but it was our first season without Dad. Bret barely spoke, even to a gorgeous girl who stopped by and offered her condolences in whatever form of comfort he wanted. He's got one semester of college left…if he finishes. I've counseled him—coaxed, cajoled, and threatened, too. Bret seems to be majoring in booze, not so much economics. It would have crushed Dad to see my middle brother throw away his chance to be the first in the family to graduate. The youngest, Bryson, seems hyper-determined to act as if he's not grieving at all. He helped me decorate and cook. He ran from one party to another. Friends, music, revelry, and good times. I know Bry, now eighteen, wanted it to be like every other Christmas. It's simply not. And it never will be again.

"It was about as expected. Yours?" I ask.

"Tough without your dad, I'm sure. Sorry, man. My Christmas was fine. Great actually. I'm in Maui."

"Vacation?"

"Nah. I moved here about three weeks ago. I've been meaning to call you."

"I guess that explains why the card I mailed to Colorado came back to me," I say wryly.

"Yeah, the weather got too cold. You know I hate that. So when I was flipping through channels one night and I saw a show about house hunting in Hawaii, I thought…hell yeah. So here I am, tending bar."

"Like it?"

"Love it. I mean, the gig is decent, but this place has lots of pretty beaches and pretty women… What more could I ask for? But that's not why I called. Seriously, you should thank me now."

I'm betting Ash will say he's found some backdoor, barely legal way to fly me to Hawaii so I can celebrate the New Year with him. I can't do it. I hate to leave Bret and Bry now. I'm not Dad…but at the moment I'm the closest thing they've got. I'm also in the middle of selling our father's business. Negotiations paused for the last few days, but I expect them to resume shortly. My brothers and I are still talking about whether to sell the house here in LA. On the one hand, we're not sure any of us will live in it since I'm planning to go back to North Dakota this spring, and both of my brothers are away at college now. On the other hand, we all grew up here. It's the last vestige of our tight-knit family memories, even if it feels empty without our parents.

"Dude," I say to Ash, "if you've got some scheme…"

"No. You'll appreciate this a lot more. I assume you haven't made any headway in the Bethany Banks department?"

"None."

Ash knows how much I want to nail that woman to a wall because, while her father is still on the hook for the crime, she's getting off free. She had the nerve to send a flower arrangement to my father's funeral, but she only answered my calls to inquire about his money via email. Oh, she was incredibly sorry about everything, and she was looking into the situation. That was months ago. Until recently, she maintained her facade in the office. More than once since Barclay Reed's arrest, she's stated publicly how innocent her boss is and how she's sure he'll be vindicated. I kept thinking she'd eventually be charged, too. As his right hand and the face of Reed Financial, how could she not be?

Then, nine days ago, the FBI declared they had arrested all suspects in the case. Bethany is still roaming free. The woman who looked my father in the face in May and told him that his fortune was growing isn't complicit in this giant scam? I call bullshit.

After the feds' announcement, I drove to her secure office building in San Diego to demand a face-to-face explanation. I damn well intended to hold her accountable for what happened to my father. But Reed Financial was locked up tight. A security guard told me the business had been permanently shut down the previous week. Bethany hasn't been around since.

Furious but undeterred, I drove home. After some digging, I figured out where the woman lives. Early this morning I drove to her place, but her apartment was fucking empty. An elderly neighbor told me she left late on Christmas Eve with two bulging suitcases. She's collecting Bethany's mail for the foreseeable future since she has no idea when the shark will be back.

I'm livid.

"She fucking skipped town," I tell Ash. "I'll have to track her down again, and god knows how long that will take."

"Zero minutes, brother. Ze-ro."

My heart stutters. "You know where she is?"

"I'm looking at her right now."

His assertion is so crazy I can hardly grasp it. "She's drinking in a bar in Maui?"

"She's *working* at a bar in Maui. She started waiting tables here about…two hours ago."

My jaw drops. "Are you fucking kidding me?"

"I'm not."

Still, what Ash is telling me…it makes no sense. "Bethany Banks is serving drinks to tourists right now? This instant?"

"Yep."

"You're sure it's the same woman?"

"It's why I waited two hours to call. I wanted to be positive."

"The one who graduated summa cum laude from Stanford with a double major in business and finance at seventeen? The one who got an MBA from Harvard at twenty? You're telling me *that* woman is slinging beers at some island dive?"

"Hey, this isn't a dive. Well, not a total one. And I don't know about her pedigree. You're the guy who's memorized her bio. But I double-checked her face with a picture online. The woman I'm looking at is definitely her. To be honest, if I'd known the body she had to go with that face, I would have been motivated to find her sooner. Whoa…"

I grit my teeth. I give zero fucks about Bethany Banks's body. I only care about holding her responsible for her actions. "Before I chase her halfway across the ocean, I need to be sure it's her."

Ash tsks. "I figured you'd say that. She introduced herself as Beth. And I can tell she's never waited tables in her life. But if you want absolute proof, I'm texting you a picture right now. I took it ten minutes ago while I pretended to look at my phone as she was picking up drinks. See for yourself."

A few seconds later, an image pops up in my text messages. I tap on the thumbnail. My entire body flares hot at the platinum blonde with the green eyes, delicate face, and revealing-as-hell bikini top. Who cares if she's banging when she's a cold-hearted bitch?

I force myself to compare this picture to others I've snagged from the Internet. Then I turn arctic cold. "That's her."

"Like I said… You're welcome."

"Oh, my god. Thanks, man. You saved me weeks of digging and probably a few thousand dollars in private investigators. Hiring one was my next move."

"No need. Just hop on over to Maui. And bonus? Tropical New Year."

The timing is terrible. But I have to go. I can't let the little scam artist disappear again.

Holy shit, am I really going to jet on the first plane to Hawaii? It's crazy and impulsive. And my last recourse.

But once I get to Maui…then what? Somehow, I have to prove Bethany Banks is no angel. If I charge in like a bull and make accusations or demands, will she even speak to me? Or will she simply vanish when the pressure gets too intense again?

In the back of my head, I remember my father telling me how much I'd like Bethany, what a wonderful woman she is, and that I should date her. Blah, blah, blah.

I'm not sure what to do or how to handle the situation, but I shout for my brothers, both of whom are nursing hangovers. When they finally stumble downstairs and give me groggy what-the-fuck glares, I sit them down.

"I'm going to Maui for a few days. I'm trusting you two to behave and not burn the house down. No parties. Keep the loudness to a minimum so the neighbors don't freak. I don't care if you have a girl over. I don't care if you drink. But if you do, don't drive. I'll call you when I can."

I've got my head in my phone, already looking for the next available flight, when Bry stands. "You're just leaving us for some tropical vacation? It's the fucking holidays."

"This is business. I found Bethany Banks and I'm going to get some goddamn answers so that Dad can hopefully rest in peace." *And I don't have to live with the regret of failing him.*

It's after midnight when I land in Maui. Thank God there was one seat left on a flight that departed LAX just after eight p.m. I had barely enough time to throw a few things in a duffel and prod Bret into dropping me off at the airport. I raced onto the plane as the flight attendant called for final boarding.

After a long but uneventful flight, I trudge off the aircraft and into the airport that's not like one I've ever seen. It's almost quaint. And after I leave the arrival area, it's open to the tropical night air.

Ash is waiting for me in baggage claim with a wide smile and a tan that people don't usually have in December unless they're getting it chemically…or living in the tropics.

"Hey, man," he greets me with a shoulder bump and a back slap. "You look like shit."

"I feel like shit. Long-ass flight."

"You've been flying back and forth between LA and North Dakota too much, trying to juggle a pair of demanding businesses."

I nod. "And dealing with my crazy younger brothers."

"When was the last time you got drunk?"

"I can't even remember. Labor Day, I think."

"We'll have to fix that pronto." Then he leans in and drops his voice. "Do I dare ask the last time you got laid?"

I huff. "Even longer. All I've done since Dad died is work and solve a never-ending string of problems."

"We'll definitely have to fix that, too. Because I don't know how you're not going crazy or blind."

Despite the tension, I laugh. Ash has been a good balance for me lately. I can usually find the humor and fun in almost any situation. But for the last six months, I've sucked at it.

"I don't know, either." I shrug. "But you're probably right."

He glances at my duffel. "Any other bags?"

I shake my head. "No time. I figured I could pick up anything I forgot on the island."

"Totally. And like I said earlier, I don't have a big pad, but you're welcome to crash on my sofa while you're here."

"Thanks." I clap him on the back. "Really. I was willing to spend whatever time and money I needed to find Barclay Reed's accomplice. You saved me a lot of both."

"You should have seen my face when she walked up to the bar and introduced herself as Beth. She probably thought I was stupid or lust-struck because I gaped like an open-mouthed mute." He laughs at himself. "But I didn't let on that I knew who she was. I figured that would send her running."

I nod. "That's why I have to devise a plan. I'm here. To get closure, I need to be. But I'm not sure how to proceed. I can't bust in and start demanding answers."

Ash nods. "You've already done that over the phone."

"Exactly. She knows my name, so the minute I get in her face and tell her who I am…"

"She'll shut down and sneak out again."

"Yep. If she hadn't fled San Diego and left all my questions unanswered, I might have believed she'd cough up information—if not own up to her crimes—when cornered. Now? I'm sure she'll only slither away. I can't risk it."

Ash strides beside me, obviously thinking. "So you need another angle."

"Yeah, something she won't see coming. After working with her today, do you know anything about her? Did she talk about herself at all?"

"No. She was standoffish. I tried to engage her once or twice while she waited for me to mix her drinks. The only thing she divulged was that she'd never been to Hawaii and that she's staying with family."

"Family?" I try to think back through everything I know about this woman. I've studied her life. I know her history. I don't remember anything about relatives except her mother. "That's bullshit. Her mom finally married for the first time two years ago and lives in Salt Lake City."

"What about her dad?"

Barclay Reed. That Bethany is his daughter is a fact they've somehow managed to keep mostly under wraps for three decades. But I seem to remember the douchebag had kids by his wife.

I pluck out my phone and start surfing. "Okay, you're right. Her dad has three kids. And they all live on the island. Oh, shit. Her half sister is married to Noah Weston."

"The famous quarterback?"

"Yeah."

"Wow. That's cool. Think that's who she's visiting?"

I shrug. "I'll find out."

I'm not entirely sure how the knowledge will help me, but learning as much as possible about my enemy can't hurt. But to get her to confirm that—or even have a conversation with her—I'm pretty sure I only have one unpalatable option.

"How are you going to do that?"

"Paste on a smile and make nice with her. Eventually gain her trust and encourage her to confide in me."

He scowls. "Can you act that well?"

Great question. "I have to."

Ash shakes his head as we hit the front of the airport and emerge into the breezy Maui night. It's warm and slightly sultry. I've spent my last four Decembers in North Dakota, so this is a huge change. And I admit, not an unwelcome one.

He leans closer. "Maybe you should kill two birds with one stone and seduce her."

I look at him as if he's gone crazy. "I'm *not* touching that woman."

"You're going to take one look at her and want to. I guarantee it. You can warm her up faster and end your dry spell all at once. Getting your pound of flesh—literally—is a genius idea. Damn, I'm full of holiday gifts."

I want to refute Ash, but I've seen pictures of Bethany. I can't deny she's gorgeous. If she was any other woman I didn't already hate, I would relish the chance to tempt her into bed.

I drop my duffel in the trunk of Ash's beat-up sedan. "Not happening. I'll think of something else."

He shrugs like I'm crazy. "Good luck with that. She didn't want to make nice with anyone yesterday. You really should consider giving her big *O*s. Nothing opens a woman up faster."

Even if she's the most attractive female on the planet, I refuse to give Bethany Banks an ounce of pleasure. "Nope."

"Did you come this far to fail? Seriously, I don't see her cozying up to anyone. That woman is determined to succeed at whatever she does, almost like she has something to prove. Yesterday, she was terrible her first two hours on the job. Then my manager came out and gave her a few pointers. She excused herself for five minutes, came back reading her phone, then… After that, it was as if she'd been waiting tables for months. She learned *fast*."

I'm not surprised. "She's seriously intelligent. Hell, she's a Mensa member."

"Huh. So she's smart and stunning. Does the woman have any flaws?"

"Her moral character, dipshit. She swindled dozens of people out of hundreds of millions of dollars."

Ash scowls. "Are you sure? If she made all this money off of her victims, why isn't she living the high life somewhere? Why is she waiting tables?"

It's a fair question, one I've considered. One I admittedly don't have an answer for. Sure, the feds still have her legal bank accounts frozen, but if she's got the stolen cash parked offshore, why isn't she living the high life now? "I'll find that out, too."

Because if I can track down other people's money, maybe I can track down my father's. And I can prove Bethany Banks is guilty so she can go to jail—where she belongs. I don't know how or why the FBI overlooked her as a suspect. Did she somehow con her way out of prison time? I don't know, but I'm going to figure it out and right this injustice.

*chapter*TWO

*W*hen my phone rings at two in the afternoon the following day, I answer Ash's call immediately. "Well?"

"Brush off your rusty bartending skills. You're in. You start in three hours."

I let out a sigh of relief. *Game on.*

Last night, Ash and I stayed up, plotting the best tactic for me to interact with Bethany. If I'm going to win her over and be her pal, I can't pose as a customer who buys a drink or two. I need time with her. Working together seems like the smartest ploy. Since Ash is in good with the manager, he can give me the same shifts as Bethany. She and I will have being new on the job and new to the island in common. After those conversation starters, I'll figure out how to build from there.

"Thanks, man. I owe you."

"No sweat. I'll be by to pick you up in an hour. We'll grab a bite and head in to work."

"Great."

I get cleaned up, check in on my brothers and Howie, who's running my business back in North Dakota. Then pace while I wait for Ash. I try to nail down my opening approach—what I'll say to coax her into talking to me, how I'll thaw her ice.

By the time Ash arrives, I've got a rough plan in my head, and it starts with flattery. Don't most people like to be buttered up? Then I'll give her some aw-shucks, fish-out-of-water crap while I play on whatever sense of adventure she has about exploring our beautiful surroundings. By this time tomorrow, I'm hoping she sees me as a budding acquaintance who may soon become a confidant.

After a quick lunch at Zippy's by the airport, we head to Lahaina. "This place is tourist central, being near the hotels and right on the beach. We'll be busier as the night wears on. But you'll have a few hours to acclimate to the bar—and sidle up to your victim."

"She is *not* the victim." My father was, and he's no longer here to defend himself. That's my job.

Ash winces, contrite. "Sorry. Bad choice of words. I meant your target."

"I know. I'm just…" Touchy? Nervous? No, uncomfortable.

The truth is, I'm not loving any of this. Deception goes against my grain. I'm usually honest, even painfully blunt at times. I try to stay friendly about it, but I make my point without mincing words. Hell, I work in oil fields, so that wouldn't fly anyway. But I can't handle Bethany Banks as if she's a fellow oil man. She plays cunning corporate games like an expert. The only way I'll have a chance to beat her is to convince her I'm no threat at all.

I try to quell my irritation. I have to do this. For myself. For my brothers. But mostly, for Dad. He deserves justice.

When we pull up to the bar, two things hit me right away. First, despite Ash's protests, it's a dive. Granted, it's a dive with charm, but the place looks as if it's been here at least forty years, most of them without significant upgrades or improvements. Second, every single person appears to be having a great time—except the petite blonde who's carrying a serving tray, wearing a strappy white bikini top and denim short-shorts, walking in my direction with shoulders squared and strides economical.

Her wide-set eyes, surrounded by a thick fringe of dark lashes, hit me like a sucker punch of green. Wisps of platinum hair manage to soften the sharp angles of her face, but her full mouth pressing into a severe line shouts a silent keep-away. Her cleavage, however—which looks one-hundred-percent real—lures me closer. I can't help but gape as, chin raised, she strides past me, heading for the bartender on duty with purpose.

"*That's* Bethany Banks?" I whisper to Ash, fighting my instant erection.

He merely sends me an I-told-you-so grin.

Damn. She's fucking hot. Not just kind of. Not just a little. She's smokin'. She's a full-blown, five-alarm, inferno-inducing blaze. As much as I hate to acknowledge that, why lie?

Her pictures did *not* do her justice. They all made her look like a corporate drone. This woman... Whoa.

I don't stop to consider all the reasons I shouldn't. I turn and watch her walk away.

The view from the back is equally stunning. Delicate strands of her pale hair tumble from a loose bun and brush her slender nape. Her intricate bikini top crisscrosses her shoulder blades and wraps around her narrow rib cage, the white fabric emphasizing the faintly peachy glow of her skin. Her hips, wrapped snugly in well-worn denim, flare below her tiny waist and sway enticingly with every step.

"Put your tongue back in your mouth if you're not going to seduce her," Ash whispers in my ear.

I rip my gaze from her to glare at him. But why bite his head off when he's right?

"Yeah. I just..." I blow out a breath. "You warned me."

"And you didn't believe me. We need to get you laid."

I suspect Ash is right...but suddenly I'm wondering who the hell will divert my attention when Bethany so thoroughly snagged it. She's the enemy...and my dick doesn't care.

"Why don't you show me the ropes for now?" I suggest.

We head to the back and meet Andy, the manager. He's nice enough. My guess is that he runs this bar because his real passion is surfing and this pays the bills.

"Glad to have you on board. We always need seasonal help around the holidays, and I'm expecting New Year's to be a zoo. How long can you stay?"

"A couple of weeks. I'm flexible." Not really, but I have to be.

"Awesome. Glad you were able to start today. Terry is going home sick," he says of the bartender on duty now. "He claims he's getting the flu. I'm hoping he's just hungover. I'll let Ash give you the quick tour since you're buddies and he's the best."

"Thanks for hiring me on short notice." I hold out my hand. "I'll work hard."

And I will. I hate half-assing anything, and bartending is usually fun.

"Holler if you have any more questions Ash can't answer." He nods dismissively and turns back to a stack of papers on his desk, so we head for the door. "Oh, hey. Wait."

We turn to face him again.

"What's up?" Ash asks.

"Can one of you keep an eye on Beth? She's getting hit on a lot, which I told her to expect. But one creepy guy who was here last night is here again today. He seems awfully determined."

"The one in the loud Hawaiian shirt with the matching personality?" my buddy asks.

"That one. He parked his ass in her station as soon as we opened. He's been messing with her ever since."

"I'll take care of it," I chime in.

First, when I bartended on the side in the past, I saw a lot of the girls struggle with dirtbags who refused to understand that no means no. Second, coming to her rescue will be a great way to meet Bethany and start gaining her trust. I refuse to think about how excited my libido is to spend time with her.

"Thanks, Clint."

With that, Andy dismisses us. Ash and I file down the hall.

My buddy laughs. "You in the role of Bethany's protector. Oh, the irony…"

"Hey, I'm not out to hurt her. I just want justice. I have no doubt she helped to swindle those people, so she deserves to pay as the law provides."

"Fair enough. But, um…she clearly flips your switch. How are you going to keep your paws off her?"

Bethany Banks turning me on visually is fucking inconvenient. I'm sure that once I start talking to the woman, her personality will quickly turn me off. "I'll work it out."

I follow Ash behind the bar, where he claps Terry on the back in greeting. The guy turns, looking pale and clammy, mumbles that he feels like death warmed over, then drags his ass out of the place.

"I don't think that's a hangover," I mutter.

"Nope. If Terry is down for the count, the next few days are going to be insane." Ash sighs. "Ready for the madhouse?"

"Let's do it."

It takes me less than ten minutes to learn how the bar is set up, where the spare supplies are kept, and who's responsible for what. Since Ash and I have also bartended together before, this won't be hard. Then he introduces me to the other waitress on duty, Montana. She's a sultry brunette with dark eyes, golden skin, and big tits. Honestly, she's usually my speed in women.

And yet as we're chatting and she's flirting, my gaze keeps straying to Bethany. What is it about her? She's beautiful, but what else? Is it her aloofness? Maybe. I want to figure her out so I can understand why a brilliant woman, surely capable of making her own fortune, would help her father fleece people. The angry part of me wants to grasp how she managed not to get caught. Mostly, I fear the attraction is chemical and, regardless of what logic tells me, I want to nail her.

Fuck.

When a customer calls for a refill, Montana jaunts off with a wink. Ash pulls me to the front of the bar. "Are you that rusty? Montana would totally do you, and you blew her off."

I know, and the fact I'm not interested annoys me. "I'm not here for sex. Introduce me to 'Beth' and let's get this farce going."

As we approach, she sets a beer down in front of a guy who's fortyish in a Hawaiian shirt—like a lot of the tourists here. He eyes her with excruciating intensity. She meets his gaze with an arched brow raised.

Since I know Bethany's vitals, I know she's already thirty—now five years older than me—so this guy might be her thing. He's in great shape. The little bit of graying at his temples makes him look distinguished, rather than old. My gut tells me, however, she's not only *not* interested, but she's silently rebuffing him.

Now I'm glad I told Andy that I would make her customer interactions my business.

Mug delivered, Bethany turns to leave. The man grips her wrist hard, his muscles flexing, veins popping, knuckles white. When she winces and tries to wriggle free, he clamps tighter and stands, jerking her toward him.

Fuck that. Even if Bethany Banks is guilty of a multitude of sins, she doesn't deserve to be manhandled by this jerk against her will.

I barge my way between them, shoving her behind me. "Do we have a problem here, sir?"

Fury pinches his mouth. He narrows his eyes. "This has nothing to do with you. Butt out."

"You don't have permission to maul the staff. I'm going to have to ask you to keep your hands to yourself or leave."

Beside me, I see Ash ready to jump in. I'm not surprised since he's never backed down from a fight.

"Do you have your head so far up her twat that you don't see she's a fucking bitch?" The guy scoffs and rolls his eyes. "Yeah, and you deserve everything you get when she chews you up and spits you out."

With that, the asshole tosses down some money and starts to walk away.

I'm furious. In part because he accused me of wanting her when I do. But mostly I'm pissed on Bethany's behalf. "That was uncalled for. You're not welcome back here unless you apologize to her."

"Fuck you."

"I'm serious. Just because you pay for your drinks doesn't give you the right to abuse any member of the staff."

He grits his teeth, upper lip curling up with contempt as he turns to Bethany. "Fine. A thousand apologies."

The douche doesn't mean a word of that, and I want to pound his face. No, I'm not looking to become Bethany's knight in shining armor. But this kind of guy always grates on my nerves because he thinks he can treat all women like trash, and the only thing that matters less than them are their feelings. I hate pricks like him.

Unfortunately, I can't do anything else right now without ramping up the incident, instigating a fight…and probably getting fired. Instead, once he leaves, I turn to Bethany. I'm pissed all over again when I see she's gone tense, as if she's trying to hold herself together, and sporting a big red handprint around her small wrist.

"You okay?"

She nods. It's shaky at first, then she drags in a steadying breath. "Yeah. He might be the first to think he can demand something more than a drink. But like Andy said, he won't be the last. I'll get used to it. Thanks for stepping in. I'm Beth."

When she holds out her hand, I have to admit I'm impressed by her backbone. I've seen new waitresses shrink, cry, and ultimately quit when confronted with a customer that vile. Bethany simply picked herself up and now looks determined to carry on.

"You're welcome. I'm Clint. It's my first day." I shake her hand.

We touch. Heat flares and rolls through me, instant and scorching. If I wanted to fuck her before, it's nothing compared to the lust burning me now.

Damn it to hell.

As I stare, her pleasant smile fades. She stares, blinks. Is she feeling the jolt, too?

That thought makes the fire in my body rage even hotter.

She pulls her hand free. "It's my first week, too. You'll get the hang of it."

I clear my throat. "Yeah. Ash will help me. We've been bros for a long time."

Beside me, my buddy waves at her. "Hey."

She manages a muted smile, crossing one arm around herself as if she's seemingly uncomfortable.

"You want an ice pack for your wrist?" I ask.

She rolls it gingerly. "It will be fine."

Maybe but… "That dude needs his ass kicked."

"It won't solve anything. Besides, I'm a big girl. He won't surprise me again. I'll handle him next time. I've dealt with worse."

Like what? By her own admission, she's never been hit up waiting tables before this week.

"You don't have to do it alone. I'm here. Ash is here."

"Yeah," my buddy cuts in. "No one will let anything happen to you on the job."

"Thanks, but I've got it. Excuse me."

Bethany turns away to check on her tables. It feels as much like she's eager to get away from us as she is conscientious about her customers.

"And…that's exactly how she behaved yesterday. Polite but not friendly."

"With everyone?"

"Everyone. Andy, Montana, me, Terry, Samantha…"

Winning her over and earning her trust might be harder than I thought, but I won't let that deter me. "Well, the evening is young."

"Yep, but after five o'clock we'll start getting too busy for chitchat. If you're going to work on her today, you better do it fast."

Point taken.

"Anything else that needs to be done before the rush starts?"

Ash shakes his head. "I got it. You go do that."

When he points Bethany's way, I nod and look across the room to find her lifting a tray piled with empty glasses and plates above her shoulder, balancing it on one upturned palm. She clutches a folding serving stand in her free hand and heads for the kitchen, determination stamped all over her face.

"Let me." I stop in front of her and start to pluck the heavy tray from her grasp.

She swivels away from me, bristling. "I'm capable."

And clearly touchy. Did someone along the way imply that she wasn't? "Yeah. I just had a spare hand and thought I would help."

She softens. "It's unnecessary. You have a job to do, and so do I. I appreciate your help, but you can't rescue me all the time."

"How about just when you need it?" I try to joke.

She doesn't think that's funny. "I don't date co-workers."

I take a step back. "I don't, either. In no way am I propositioning you. I just don't know anyone on this island except Ash. Is there something wrong with me trying to be friendly? Did I insult you somehow?"

For a moment, she closes her eyes and hands me the tray with a sigh. "No. I'm sorry. I… Forget it. I won't let that jerk upset me again. I get what you mean about not knowing anyone on the island. I only know a few people myself."

"Exactly. Back home, I had a lot of pals and drinking buddies."

"Where's home?"

"North Dakota."

Her mossy eyes flare wide. "Being here must be a huge change for you."

"I haven't even been here twenty-four hours yet, but so far that's an understatement." I head toward the bar and set the tray down. "Back home, it would be below freezing. Our nights would be in the single digits, if not in negative territory. There would be snow, and the wind would threaten to cut me in half."

"That sounds horrible. But I grew up in California." She deposits the stand on a hook in a nearby alcove. "Other than the few years I went to school back East, I've lived in warm climates my whole life. What brings you to Maui?"

A few random details about myself shouldn't tip her off about my identity. Why would she jump to the conclusion that a guy with my name and background would be here for retribution, rather than a mere job? "I lost my dad recently, and Ash convinced me that winter here would be better than winter there."

Her face softens. "I'm sorry. Losing your father can be hard."

"Did yours pass away, too?" Will she lie to my face?

"No. We're…estranged. It's complicated." She waves off the questions she must see on my face.

Subject closed—for now. Though I can't say I'm surprised. We've only known each other for ten minutes. But it's all I can do not to scoff. Estranged? Is that how she describes distancing herself from the man who's taking the fall for her part in their crimes?

"So what about you?" I ask instead. "What brings you to Maui?"

The thaw in our conversation suddenly catches another chill. "I wanted a change of pace. Some well-meaning people convinced me to come here and give this place a try…"

She's being intentionally vague, and a million questions pelt me. I should look for the right lead-in question to steer the conversation toward her last job. But I don't because I already know she'll tense up even more and cut our chat short.

"Like it so far?"

She shrugs. "It's pretty. What I've seen, anyway. I got here late on Christmas Eve. I managed to get this job the day after Christmas. I've been working ever since. So I haven't seen much."

"Seems like a shame, to come all this way and not take in paradise."

She winces. "That's what all the people who suggested I come say."

"I have plans to see this island on my days off. My parents always wanted a second honeymoon here, and they never took it. I'm going to see it for them," I say truthfully. "That probably sounds cheesy—"

"It sounds thoughtful, actually."

"You're welcome to join me if you want. No pressure. I won't hit on you. It just might be nice not to see the sights alone."

Bethany nibbles on her lip for a long moment. The gesture shouldn't be sexy. It shouldn't make me want to run my thumb across the swell of that lower pout. It absolutely shouldn't make me want to kiss her.

But fuck, it does.

"I'll think about it."

"My first day off is Monday."

"Mine, too. I guess we're both going to work a killer New Year's Eve before we get a break."

"Looks that way. If you decide you want to come along, I was thinking about driving down to Wailea to see those beaches and maybe catch a bit of the southern end of the island."

"Thanks. I'll let you know. I'm staying with some…distant family right now. One of them has a baby due this week, so everything is a little up in the air."

I wonder who she's talking about or if her story is even true. "Totally. Like I said, no pressure. But I'd enjoy the company. It would keep me from thinking too much about the fact my mom and dad aren't here to see the island for themselves."

She nods, and I see sympathy flit across her features before she shuttles it. "I should get back to work." She glances across the room to find a couple looking for a refill. "Duty calls."

As I see more people filing in through the open-air entrance from the beach, I nod and head behind the bar. "When you need drinks poured, holler. I'm your man."

Shit, that came out wrong. Flirtier than I intended. A little flush stains her cheeks. "Thanks. I'll keep that in mind."

My feet are screaming uncle by the time the bar shuts down and we're cleaned up for the night.

"Holy shit," I mutter to Ash. "I don't remember hurting this much when I bartended a few years back."

"Eh, you've just gone soft. The calluses on your soles will come back."

I refrain from pointing out that working the oil fields is no posh job because Ash knows it and is simply yanking my chain. Besides, I haven't gone soft in any way. Staring half the night at Bethany made sure of that.

"Hey," he murmurs as he leans in. "Montana was asking earlier if we wanted to come to her place for the rest of the night."

I raise a brow at him. "Both of us?"

"I guess she's adventurous." He grins.

"No. Thanks, man. You go ahead."

"You're sure?"

The notion of sex sounds great…but I just can't get excited about this proposition or her. "Yeah, I'll pass."

Ash shrugs and yanks his car keys from the pocket of his shorts. "All right. Take the car back to my place. I'll ride with Montana and have her bring me back before our shift tomorrow."

"Sounds good. Have fun. Don't forget to glove up."

With a waggle of his brows and a flashy smile, he tosses down his dish towel and heads toward the flirty waitress. Seconds later, he slings an arm around her, and they're gone. Samantha, whom I just met tonight, shoots them an envious stare as she clutches her keys and heads out with a sigh.

I wonder if Ash knows that shy Samantha is interested in him.

Bethany emerges from the hall that houses the employee break room and lockers, slings a little purse over her shoulder, and heads for the parking lot. Instead of walking to her car, she stands under the awning and pulls out her phone. I follow her with a frown.

"You're heading home?"

She turns to me and nods. "As soon as I call for my ride."

Who is coming to pick her up at three a.m.? Family? A boyfriend she failed to mention? "I'm not sure it's a great idea for you to stand outside and wait alone. That guy who gave you a hard time earlier? I wouldn't put it past him to come back and harass you some more."

"You're right, but…" She looks behind her to find Andy locking up the bar, pocketing the keys, then sauntering toward his truck with a wave.

She can't go back inside. This is my opportunity.

"I have Ash's car if you want a ride home."

That contemplative lip-biting move tells me she's considering my offer. It's also wreaking hell on my restraint.

Why do I have to find Bethany Banks sexy?

"I don't want to inconvenience you…"

But she didn't mind "inconveniencing" people by taking hundreds of millions of dollars from them?

"Aren't you waking someone else up in the middle of the night to come get you?"

She hesitates, then nods reluctantly.

"Beth, I'm already awake. I'm already driving myself home…"

"But where I'm staying… It's not close."

"The island is only so big. How far can it be?"

"A good thirty minutes."

That would give me time to work on her, see if I can get her to start opening up to me.

I shrug like it's no big deal. "I don't mind."

She glances down at her phone, then back up at me. "All right. Thanks."

"Happy to help." I lead her to the car and hit the fob to unlock Ash's serviceable wheels. "It's messy, I warn you. Ash thinks organization is a four-letter word."

Bethany sends me a faint smile. "I'll pretend not to notice since you're doing me a huge favor."

As I back out of the parking space and exit the lot, I glance her way. Shadows cling to the feminine angles of her face. The silhouette of her long lashes curls against the night. She clasps her hands in her lap, looking nervous.

"You okay?"

She shrugs. "Fine."

Bullshit. "Beth…"

"Just tired."

I'm still not buying it but before I can say anything, her stomach rumbles. "And hungry?"

She gives me a self-deprecating grin. "Sorry."

"Don't be. I'm starving."

"I just never had time for dinner."

"Ditto. I've tended bar before but never in a place this hopping."

"I've never even waited tables, so this whole week has been a shock. It's really busy."

"Yeah? What was your last job?"

Let's see how she answers that.

Instantly, she draws up tight. "It was all paper pushing behind a desk. Something I'll probably never do again. Um, where I'm staying is past the airport. When you reach there, keep heading east."

Her change of subject isn't even subtle. I wonder why she thinks she'll never work in investment banking again. From her perspective, she got off scot-free. Why wouldn't she set up shop somewhere else, ride out a few years to let the heat die down and gain new clients' trust, then repeat her scam all over? But clearly, the subject is closed.

"No problem. Hey, we're driving past Zippy's. They're open twenty-four hours. What about a quick bite?"

"Oh, that's not necessary. You don't have to—"

"I could use the food." And the extra time alone with her. Who knows when I'll get it again?

"In that case…all right."

We're there in twenty minutes. The restaurant is small and well lit. Inside, there aren't many places to sit, but we order—she insists on paying for her own breakfast bagel—then we grab an open table and wait for our food.

The initial silence is awkward, and I wrack my brain for another conversation starter that won't get her back up. "Who was going to pick you up?"

"My oldest brother."

Maxon. I remember reading he's a real estate shark. "I thought you were staying with distant family."

Bethany doesn't answer for long moments. "I'd never met him until five days ago. It's complicated."

That shocks the hell out of me. Granted, Maxon is her half brother, but she'd never met him until this week? "Wow, I guess so. I have brothers. We're really tight."

"That sounds…nice."

Her voice is soft, almost wistful. Like she's envious? Like she wishes she had a close-knit family?

"Do you like him?" I ask.

"Yes."

No further elaboration. She's choosing her words carefully. But she's still talking, so I keep gently prying.

"Do you have other family here?"

"Two more brothers and a sister, along with all their spouses."

Two more brothers? My research indicated Barclay only had one other son, Griffin. But why would she lie?

"And you're just now meeting them?"

She nods. "On Christmas Eve, yes."

What the… "Tell me about them."

"I don't really know that much. The two oldest are real estate partners. They seem fantastic. Incredibly ambitious. They worked two massive deals right up until midnight before Christmas. Their wives are both sweet. Funny. Interesting. Perfect for them, honestly. And very pregnant. My younger brother is… I don't even know how to describe him. A genius. And incredibly driven. We all have that in common. Socially, he's a little awkward, but it's because he's always thinking about something technical. He runs a data storage corporation. He and his wife got married a few weeks ago and are officially moving here tomorrow. My sister is…" She sighs and I see the obvious admiration cross her face. "She's vivid, confident, snarky, full of life. She's pretty amazing. And she's married to a former pro athlete who couldn't be nicer. I'm just…trying to fit in with this big, loud clan." Then color splashes across her cheeks. "And I'm talking too much."

"Not at all," I assure her. "I'd love to hear more."

It's fascinating to see this woman I sense is usually self-assured feel so out of place. Clearly, this isn't a common experience for her. My head tells me I should be happy to see her squirm. Instead, inconvenient pity pricks me.

"Not much more to say," she demurs.

"How did you all finally find each other?"

She gnaws her lip again. She does that whenever she's not sure if or how she should proceed. "I actually met my younger brother in Seattle right after Thanksgiving. It was a business discussion. It didn't lead anywhere, but when I asked for his help about three weeks later, he bailed me out of a tough spot. When my siblings discovered I planned to spend the holidays alone, they invited me. Actually, they kind of insisted."

The snarky side of me wants to point out that it's no surprise she had no one to spend this season with. Who wants to spend time with a scam artist? But I'm human, too. I can't imagine spending the holidays utterly alone. It was a somber Christmas, just me and my brothers. But I would have gone batshit if I hadn't had them.

"Your family sounds awesome."

"They are, but I'm hoping tips continue to be lucrative so I can stop imposing on them and get a place of my own. I don't want them to think I'm taking advantage of their hospitality."

Is she pretending she has a moral compass? Or does she think that sounds like the right thing to say?

"You didn't have any more family left in California?"

Bethany doesn't answer for a long while. "Like I said, it's complicated. Who did you spend Christmas with?"

Just like that, she's done opening up. I count it as a win for now. I know more about her than I did when we walked into this place, and it's only day one. I knew before I started this ploy that I would have to be patient.

Even though it chafes to tactically retreat, I do it with a smile. "My younger brothers. They're in college and they're a pain in my ass, but I love them."

"So what did you do in North Dakota?"

"Besides freeze my balls off?" I joke, both to lighten the mood and to distract her from the fact I'm not answering that question.

My dad never told me too much about Bethany. He probably didn't know a lot about her personally—likely by her design. She's interesting…but not warm. My dad, on the other hand, would probably have told her all about his three sons, and probably more than once. I doubt she absorbed the information; I know her type. She would have efficiently taken notes about his family and tucked them away in his file, then peeked at them just before each meeting to make sure she appeared engaged and interested. If I mention Bret's and Bry's names, that might ring a bell. I haven't told her my last name yet—not that she's asked. If it comes up, I'll lie.

She smiles. "Besides that. I assume you tended bar?"

"Some. I did a little of a lot of things." All oil-related. Becoming a jack of every trade tends to happen when you own your own business. "Since my parents are both gone, I've been running their company, but I'm selling it. Not what I wanted to do with my life."

"Then what? Will you give up bartending?"

"I don't know what's next. I should get back to North Dakota, but…" Let her think I'm torn and lost and could use a friend.

"But maybe you'll wait until spring? To preserve your balls and all," she teases me.

"Which will damn near be Memorial Day, but maybe."

As she nods, silence falls again.

Our food is ready, and an employee kindly brings it to us. I grip my hot coffee and study Bethany as she plucks a napkin from the dispenser and lays it across her lap. She's avoiding my gaze now. She's nervous.

"What's wrong?"

Her startled stare bounces up to me. Is she surprised that I can read her? "I'm just out of my element. When I lived in California, work kept me really busy. I never had time for friends or…"

Dates. Boyfriends. Lovers. That's what she means. I frown. Her claim makes no sense. She has to be lying. A woman as sexy and intriguing as Bethany must have had men crawling after her since puberty.

"Anyway…" she goes on. "It's nice to talk to someone. Thanks."

I'm going to have to decipher her statement later in detail, figure out how her assertion is even possible. For now, I smile. I'm making progress. And I need to set her at ease. "You can talk to me anytime."

She takes a delicate bite of her sandwich, chews, then swallows it down with some water before cocking her head at me. "Why are you being so nice? If you were hitting on me, the answer would be obvious. But you haven't—thank you for that—but I'm confused."

By the fact we're relative strangers chatting amicably? Or because we're people who have no particular agenda in mind except getting to know each other? "Why? My motto is that you can never have too many friends. When we first met, that guy hounding you pissed me off. And I guess it's the protective older brother in me—"

"I'm pretty sure I'm older than you."

"Doesn't matter. Maybe it's the man in me. Either way, I don't like bullies. I especially don't like bullies who prey on women."

She smiles softly. "Your parents raised you right."

"I like to think so. Speaking of parents, where were yours this holiday?"

"My mother married not long ago, and I'm giving her and her husband some space." Bethany looks away and shuts down. "My father and I…"

Nearly a minute passes before I resign myself to the fact that she doesn't intend to finish that sentence. "You said it's complicated?"

"Very."

"Do you know where he is?" I know he's out on bail, but where is he living until the trial?

"Not exactly."

They aren't in contact? After being his accomplice for years and scamming their clients with him, now that he's been implicated and arrested, is she cutting him loose? If so, that's cold…

"Did you speak to him at all?"

"He left me a voice mail."

"And?" I want to demand an answer right now, but she's stiff and definitely uncomfortable. We'll come back to this line of questioning later, when I've gained more of her trust, made inroads. I can't expect that she'll spill all her secrets to me after a few hours.

"And that's it. How's your burger?" she asks.

Another dead end. I fight not to grit my teeth and nod instead. "Good."

She sends me a little smile, and I chow down a bit more, give her time to relax. I even volunteer to fetch her more water after she empties her cup.

When I return, I realize she's almost done with her sandwich. So am I. My limited time is ticking by too quickly. I need to try to push again, this time from a different angle.

"So I hear that barfly bugging you yesterday has been hounding you since you started working at the bar. Is he just trying to get you into bed? If so, calling you a fucking bitch isn't going to win him any brownie points."

"He's a jerk." She sidesteps my question.

"Absolutely. I wanted to punch him in the face." I can say that with all honesty.

When I glance at her wrist, I'm a little shocked to see bruises forming in the shape of his fingers. I don't think twice before I reach across the table and take her hand in mine.

There's that fucking jolt of awareness again. Across from me, I hear her smother a gasp.

I swallow down my hot rush of renewed lust. "Beth, this looks horrible. You should have let me get you some ice."

With a shrug, she tugs her hand free. "I'll be fine. I'm getting really tired and I'd like to get home."

In other words, I finally crossed the line and shoved her out of her comfort zone. She's done for the night.

Fuck.

"Sure."

Silently, she rises and cleans up after herself, then lifts her purse onto her shoulder. She looks nervous again.

I send her a smile I hope has some charm and motion her to the door. "This way…"

Bethany heads to the parking lot. I wish she hadn't thrown a baggy

T-shirt over her bikini top. I wish I didn't notice her smooth, firm legs and her gorgeous ass sway with every step. Weirdly—and not merely because I need information—I wish she'd stop shutting me out.

In the car, she settles into the passenger's seat and closes her eyes with a sigh.

"Tired?"

She turns to me. "Confused."

I start up the car and head east down the road. "Why's that?"

"I know Montana propositioned you tonight."

She does, huh? "Why would you think that?"

"She told me she was going to. She asked me what I knew about you."

Oh, this is interesting. "So why are you confused?"

"You turned her down, but you're driving *me* home? I don't get it. She was willing to…"

"Have sex with me?"

And Bethany isn't. That's her subtext as she nods. We're both fully aware of that fact, so why bring it up? Because, maybe, she's thought of me as more than a potential pal? If so, maybe refusing Montana will earn me more of Bethany's trust.

"I know. The truth is, I'd rather drive you home," I say.

Honestly, I'm not sure why I said no to Montana. She's fun, easy on the eyes, and even easier to get into bed. What's not to like? Back in North Dakota, she would have been the blessed cure for a blah Friday night. But now? Maybe I'm too into justice to give a shit about an uncomplicated lay.

Bethany blinks at me. "Thanks for making the sacrifice. You didn't have to."

"It wasn't a sacrifice." Spending time with Bethany is way more important than mindless sex. "I'm here on the island for a reason, and it's not to get laid."

"Wow. That's a refreshing point of view," she says, sounding even more surprised. "Can you head down Highway 36?"

"Sure," I murmur. "Refreshing, huh? Someone in your life a man-whore?"

"You could say that." Under her careful reply, there's a story. I want to hear it. But her demeanor tells me this is another closed subject —for now.

She spends the rest of the drive giving me directions until we pull up at a place that's seemingly in the middle of nowhere. I see a sign that reads Sunshine Coast Bed and Breakfast.

"You're staying here?"

She nods. "This is Keeley's business." I must look confused because she rushes to add, "My oldest brother's wife. She's got a whole yoga, organic food, and happy times approach to running this place. I think what sells most people on coming here, though, is the killer view and the charm. They haven't been open long, and she's already attracting some famous people. My sister and her husband, Noah Weston, were married here, which put it on the map. Since then, one of President Hayes's best friends, Dax Spencer, and his bride, Holland, honeymooned here. Rumor has it Shealyn West, that TV actress, and her new husband are coming here for their honeymoon, too. Keeley is really excited."

"That's great." It's impressive, but I'm more interested in the fact that Bethany is perfectly happy to chat—as long as the subject doesn't get too personal.

I make a mental note to broach "safe" topics next time we're together, lull her into letting her guard down.

"I'd give you a tour, but…"

It's dark, and everyone is probably asleep.

"I'd love that." Especially if it means locking her into spending more time with me so I can work her over. "Another time?"

As I pull up to the front and put the car in park, Bethany immediately opens the door like she can't wait to escape. Then she pauses. "Thank you for the ride. I'm sure my brother thanks you, too. He already has to be up in two hours, so I have no doubt he appreciates you letting him catch as many Z's as possible."

"Really, it's no problem. I'll be happy to do it tomorrow, too." I hope Ash will lend me his car again.

"Bethany," I hear a man call somewhere past my left shoulder.

I turn my head to find a figure standing on the lanai. He's tall. Even in silhouette, I can tell he's well acquainted with the gym. I can't make out his expression since he's in shadow, but the warning vibes he's sending my way are hard to miss.

She stands. "I'm here, Maxon. I'm sorry if we woke you up."

"When I didn't hear from you somewhere around two, I got worried. I sent a couple of texts…"

Bethany pulls her phone from her small purse. "Sorry. I didn't hear them."

Maxon steps into the light. Now I can read his expression. He's wondering what I've been doing to his sister that precluded her from hearing her messages ding.

True, I don't know this particular guy, but I know how most brothers think. Even if Bethany is new to their family dynamic, brothers—especially older ones, which Maxon is—are protective. He can either be my ally or my roadblock, depending on how I handle him.

I kill the engine of the car and step out, approaching Bethany's brother, hand outstretched. "I'm Clint." Shit. I need a last name. Obviously, I can't tell her it's Holmes. So I pull my mother's maiden name out of my ass. "Clint Dietrich. Beth and I work together. I offered to give her a ride home."

The expression I shoot him is designed to assure him that I would never hurt her.

He shakes my hand, takes my measure. I meet his gaze. He visibly relaxes. "Maxon Reed."

"Nice to meet you. Great place."

"Thanks."

A redhead with a little ponytail and a big, pregnant belly waddles onto the lanai, shielding her eyes from the headlights. "Maxon?"

"Everything is okay, sunshine." He turns to kiss her forehead. "Go back to bed. Bethany is home."

"Oh, hi." Then she frowns and looks my way. "You brought her home?"

"Yes."

Bethany cuts in, "Keeley, this is Clint."

I give her a friendly wave, less because she's several feet away and more because I have a suspicion that Maxon doesn't want me anywhere near his wife when she's only wearing a slinky bathrobe.

"Great to meet you," she says. "Thanks for saving Maxon the trip to town. Want to come in for some coffee?"

I'd love to talk to these people, see if I can get them to fill in some of the blanks Bethany is refusing to. I don't think Maxon will be too forthcoming, but I'm hoping cheerful little Keeley will be. But now isn't the time. Maxon is scowling, and Bethany looks displeased by her sister-in-law's offer.

"Thank you, but I'll take a rain check. I'll see you tomorrow, Beth. Let me know if you want a ride home then."

"Thanks again." She shuts the car door, then tucks her hair behind her ear, looking a lot more like a schoolgirl than a grown woman who's scammed people out of their fortunes.

Again, I can't escape the fact she looks nervous. Why is that her nearly perpetual state around me?

Interesting question… One I definitely need to figure out soon.

chapter THREE

*T*wo nights later, Bethany sets her tray on the bar with a clatter and leans on the hard surface with a sigh. "Andy said we'd be busy on New Year's Eve. He wasn't kidding."

"I'd say we're in hell, but I'd be insulting the underworld," I quip. "I've been mixing drinks so quickly for the last hour and a half, I'm not even sure I've taken more than a breath or two."

"Same, brother," Ash chimes in beside me.

"Terry really isn't coming?" That possibility distresses me.

Ash shakes his head. "He went to urgent care this morning. It's definitely the flu."

"Shit," I groan. "The next few hours are going to be like the seventh circle of hell."

Bethany gives me a grudging smile. "My feet already feel like they've traversed rings of fire. I don't know how I'll last another four hours. At least the tips are good."

In part because she's gotten really proficient at waitressing. But also because she looks absolutely stunning with her pillowy lips painted red and a spaghetti-strapped black dress that ends mid-thigh. It isn't low-cut or flashy like Montana's bright red number. But it hugs her perfectly, and I've spent half the night staring at her. So have most of the guys in this place, including loud-Hawaiian-shirt dude. He's back —for the fifth day in a row. His behavior is borderline harassing again, so I've been trying my best to watch over Bethany. I can't deny, though, that I simply like looking at her.

I also can't deny that I'd like to do more than look. In fact, the raunchy fantasies saturating my brain are both making me angry and making it tough to concentrate. I need to snap out of my NC-17 daydreams and focus.

"You doing okay with Mr. Asshole?" I ask.

She shrugs. "About like every other day. He wants another Bud on draft. The honeymooners a few tables over both want Sex on the Beach shots and a fishbowl of the rum punch to share. Then I need a whiskey neat and a dry vodka martini for the two guys at the front who told me they're looking to ring in the near year with a meaningless fling and asked if I'd be interested."

I hope like fuck she said no.

My knee-jerk reaction is a kick in the balls. It's one thing to want her admittedly gorgeous body, but to be jealous?

Fuck.

I'd love to tell myself that I'm simply concerned she'll be distracted by a couple of tourists and stop focusing on the rapport we're building —the one that should soon start netting me the information I need. But I know better.

What the hell is wrong with me? I've known Bethany for a handful of days. We've only talked a few times. I certainly haven't touched her. And I'm not going to. Sure, the horny guy in me would love to peel off her clothes, lower my body over hers, and press her to my bed before I find some relief deep inside her. Even if I don't want to want her, she's attractive and I'm a guy. Lust is easy.

But this feels uncomfortably like more than mere desire.

God, I can't pleasure someone who hurt my family so much. I'm here to give Bethany her just desserts, damn it, not orgasms. But to covet her? No. Absolutely fucking no.

"They sound like douches. What did you tell them?" I do my best to sound nonchalant. "Interested?"

Logic tells me she's not. In fact, she doesn't seem interested in any man, me included. Because some other guy who apparently couldn't keep his pants zipped burned her, so she finds me "refreshing?" Maybe. But one thing I do know? Since we met, Bethany hasn't acted like a duplicitous criminal mastermind. She works hard, does her job, and refuses to fraternize. Then I take her home alone because Ash seems glued to Montana these days. During the drive, I try to coax her to open up to me...but it's as if the bit she confided the other night scared her from revealing more.

I'm hoping tonight will be different.

The last hour leading up to midnight is particularly grueling. Everyone wants a fresh round to toast the new year. Champagne bottles come out of the chiller, bubbly gets poured, glasses get raised. As people start the last ten seconds of the countdown, accompanied by a tape-delayed feed on the TV from Times Square, Bethany drops her tray on the bar, grabs herself a glass of water, and takes a sip.

"Five, four, three, two, one. Happy New Year!" the crowd shouts.

Beside us, Ash leans across the bar to mack on Montana. I look away—and my stare locks on Bethany. Around us, everything is pandemonium. Everyone is kissing, their lip locks somewhere between joyous and passionate. Between us, the air is suddenly and completely still.

The urge to lay my mouth over hers storms my brain. Can she read my thoughts? I don't know. She just gazes back, unblinking. What she's not doing? Putting distance between us.

I swallow. My blood surges. My cock flares to life.

Yes, I want this to be the year I get retribution for my dad. On the other hand, what if Bethany is innocent?

Is that even possible...or is that simply my libido negotiating with my head because I want her?

"Happy New Year," she murmurs softly.

"Happy New Year."

Ash elbows me. "Ring in the New Year right. Kiss her!"

I don't dare. If I start, I'm afraid I'll back her against the bar and seduce her into wrapping her legs around me so I can unzip, and we can get busy.

Finally, I settle for cupping her shoulder. It's friendly without being flirty, right? It's also not enough. Not nearly. Without conscious thought, I shuffle closer, lean in. I'm shocked when Bethany does the same. My heart kicks my ribs. Holy shit, is this going to happen?

Breath held, I bend to her, my face inches above hers. She bites her lip, clearly wavering and unsure. But breathless. Damn it, she looks as if she wants me to kiss her. How can I? Yet how can I fucking refuse when I want to so badly?

Her pouty, rosy lips lure me closer. My body is on autopilot. I keep leaning in, moving closer and closer, heart thundering. Anticipation buzzes under my skin.

I close the distance. But just before I brush my lips across hers, she turns her head. My lips glide across her soft cheek. I inhale her light, sugary scent, then jerk away in disappointment. In frustration. I'm full of recriminations, even though not kissing her is for the best.

Fuck, I need to get my head together. I also need to lighten the mood between us.

"Back to work for me," I quip as I somehow find the will to step back. "I'll get those drinks you asked for."

"Thanks," she murmurs, then gulps down the last of her water nervously before bustling to a nearby table to pick up empty glasses and cash out their tab.

Over the next two hours, the crowd thins quickly. A little after two a.m., Andy locks up while the staff collectively groans in exhaustion.

"Good job, everyone. Beth, Clint, Samantha? I'll see you guys on Tuesday. Enjoy your day off."

"See you." I wave at him.

Predictably, Ash tosses me his car keys and disappears with Montana again.

When I look for Bethany, she's standing at the far end of the over-hang and tapping on her phone.

"Ready to head home?"

She hesitates. "I'm sure you're way too tired to drive me. Maxon volunteered—"

"Are you bailing because of what didn't happen between us tonight?"

For a moment, I think she's going to demur, but she finally nods. "I didn't mean to…"

Get that close to me. As much as her last-minute cold shoulder grated on me, I'm glad now it happened. I don't need my head clouded by Bethany. I still have a million and one problems. Fixating on how much I want to fuck her won't help.

"It's cool," I downplay our almost-kiss. "Look, we're friends, right? It would have just been a friendly New Year's peck in the moment. It wouldn't have meant anything."

A little frown steals across her face. "Sure. And nothing personal, but I have a lot happening in my life right now. I don't need anything romantic. Not that you see me that way. I'm older than you, after all."

"Not that much."

"Enough that we probably shouldn't be a thing."

Five years is nothing, and if Bethany were the target of my lust rather than my retribution, I wouldn't give a shit how much older she was. She's crazy if she thinks that matters to me one bit. But if that gives her some false sense of security, fine by me.

I give her a noncommittal shrug. "How about that ride home? There's no reason to wake Maxon when I'm already up."

"Actually, they're awake. All my siblings and their spouses gathered to celebrate the New Year, so…"

"Beth…" I give her my best let's-be-reasonable tone. "You'd have to wait at least thirty minutes until Maxon arrives, and I'd have to stand here and wait with you. I'm not leaving you alone so Mr. Asshole can find you and harass you some more." Then I notice she's sporting fresh finger-shaped bruises on her other arm. Instantly, my temper explodes. "Did he do this to you?"

"It's all right. I elbowed him in the ribs and told him to keep his hands off me or to get the hell out. He backed off."

Maybe, but for how long?

Damn it, I wish I hadn't somehow missed seeing him grabbing her again. What the hell does this douche want? He must know Bethany is not going to sleep with him. "It's not all right. Did you tell Andy?"

Suddenly, her phone dings, then she looks my way with a sigh. "Would you mind taking me home after all? Keeley is having contractions for the third night this week. Maxon can't leave her."

Fate is smiling on me. "Let's go."

Once we're in the car, I crack the windows to let the sultry Hawaiian air caress me. I've got thirty minutes to recover from my earlier slip. But how can I continue to be "just a friend" when it's getting tough to keep my hands to myself? If I tried to kiss her again, would she let me? Maybe. If I did, how much more betrayed would I feel if I proved her wide-eyed behavior is an act and she's fucked me over, too?

On the other hand, am I getting anywhere by being her pal? So far, no. I've been in Hawaii nearly a week and I'm no closer to proving she's a lying, stealing bitch than I was the night my plane touched down. I can't stay here indefinitely…

"Thanks," she says as I pull onto the highway. "As much as you've been driving me lately, at least let me give you some gas money."

When she reaches into her wallet, I stay her. First of all, I've made a few million dollars of my own, and if we ever find my father's money, I'll have another million or so on top of that. Second, I'm a little old-fashioned, thanks to my dad. Even if we're not dating, I wouldn't take money from a woman simply for doing her a favor.

"No need. I got it."

"I insist. Gas on the island is expensive."

True. But why would a thief be so adamant about repaying me? I don't have an answer for that, just like I don't have an answer for why someone who's just stolen hundreds of millions of dollars is working like a slave at a dive bar rather than enjoying the spoils of her scam. Is it a ploy designed to throw investigators off her scent? But if the FBI has publicly stated they've already arrested everyone they intend to, does she really need to be duping them?

"Nope. But if you want to give me something, talk to me. I like conversation with you."

It's probably shitty to assure her she's not beholden to me, then use her feelings to get closer. But I have to step up my game, work faster. If I don't, if I can't prove who Bethany Banks is and what she's done quickly, I have a terrible feeling life will pull me away from Maui before the job is done. Or…I'll get weak, kiss her, get her naked, and stop caring about her past. I can't live with either outcome.

"I don't know why." She shrugs. "I've said nothing interesting."

"I get the feeling you run deep. Honestly, I don't find that often."

She looks uncomfortable with the thought that I might be digging into her psyche. "I think almost everyone who reaches of age of thirty has had experiences, some that have left scars. I'm not unique in that."

No, she's not. But since I need her to open up fast, maybe if I offer something up personal she'll feel like reciprocating.

"I hear you. I've got scars, too. Do you know how awful it is to live with guilt?"

Bethany falls very quiet and drops her stare to her folded hands on her lap. "Yes. Every day."

Oh, now we're getting somewhere... But now what should I share to encourage her to open up?

"My mom died of cancer, and I was away from home for most of her illness," I blurt. Once I realize what I've said, I'm horrified...but I'm stuck. I have to roll with it. "Up until the end, I kept telling myself she wouldn't die, that she was too young and too healthy. That she would beat this. She'd always been such a go-getter. She tackled everything in life, so I convinced myself this was just a bump in the road. She was always upbeat when I talked to her on the phone. My dad tried to tell me it was serious, but I didn't hear him." I pause, frustrated that I'm choked up. "It wasn't until I came home to surprise Mom for her birthday that I saw how much the cancer had ravaged her and I realized I'd pissed away most of our remaining time together with my denial. I stayed another three weeks. I told her I loved her as she took her last breath." Tears sting my eyes. *Jesus...* "Burying her just about killed me. Even as they lowered her casket in the ground, I couldn't believe she was gone."

Bethany turns to me, tears shimmering in the dark as she reaches for my hand and squeezes it. "I'm sorry. Have you ever told anyone that?"

I can't speak, so I just shake my head and squeeze her hand back.

"Not your father or your brothers?"

"Dad was going through enough. My brothers were dealing with their own grief. I listened to them. I knew they needed it, but..." I couldn't unload on Bret and Bry.

"You don't have to be that strong for everyone. You don't have to be alone." She bites her lip as if debating the wisdom of her next words. "I'll listen."

"Thanks. I'm sorry for bringing up something that's so fucking personal." I sniffle back the threat of tears that just aren't manly. "I'm supposed to be driving you home, and here I go, bringing up a downer of a topic. If I keep talking about it, I'll embarrass myself."

She squeezes my hand again. "Then I can sit here while you get yourself together. You've done a lot to help me. This is the very least I can do."

I give her a tight smile. "Tell me about your mom."

"She had me young and raised me as a single mother. A couple of years ago, she married a great guy—a widower—and they moved to Salt Lake. It's been good for her."

"You two close?"

Bethany doesn't answer right away. "Not as much as I wish we were. She was twenty-one when she had me. I think she resented me a little bit for forcing her to adult before she was ready."

"No one held a gun to her head and made her have sex with your dad, I presume."

She shakes her head. "I just don't think she realized how much responsibility being a mom would be until I was in her life. When I was a kid, she always looked for ways to ditch me so she could party. I spent a lot of time with neighbors, babysitters, and my dad. He's older. And wealthy—or he was." She turns pensive, frowns. "I think from the time I was little I knew that she enjoyed extorting money from him to pay for my upbringing. Dance lessons, piano lessons, and lots of private schools. Dad wasn't warm, but at least when we were together he wasn't looking for ways to get away from me, so I kind of resented her for being a bitch to him."

Wow. For a woman who's barely opened up, she's suddenly shared a lot. And since we're skirting the topic of her dad, I urge her to go on. "So you're closer to him?"

She shrugs. "Yes and no. He encouraged me growing up. He made me believe I was smart enough to learn everything I would ever need to do great things in life. Up until the last few years, my mom thought the most valuable skill she could teach me was to squeeze money out of a man's balls. Apparently, I was a miserable failure at this. Anyway, I think falling in love finally brought her some peace, because she's a lot better to be around now. She's tried in subtle ways to make my childhood up to me, but I needed a mom when I was three, not so much now that I'm thirty."

That's pretty fucking sad. Through no fault of her own, Bethany paid for her mother's mistakes. She tries to shrug the pain off as if it's in the past, but I see it still haunts her.

I caress her hand with my thumb and squeeze her fingers. "I'm sorry. You and your mom have a lot to work through, it sounds like. You have time, though. You can still do it."

"And you can't. My whining sounds insensitive."

"That's not what I'm saying. I'm giving you the silver lining. She's still here for you to mend the rift. You said the other day that your dad left you a voice mail. Have you called him back? You guys still in touch?"

She shakes her head. "Which also makes me sound terrible because your dad isn't here anymore, either. Honestly, I don't know if we'll ever work our differences out."

"Did you fight?"

Bethany falls really silent. I hold my breath, wondering if she's going to tell me something helpful. Guilt niggles me for luring her into this conversation, but now that we're here, it's raw and stark and real. And I feel as if I'm beginning to understand her in a way I just didn't during our previous conversations.

"Let's just say that I recently came into contact with his unpleasant side."

Like she didn't know he was a douchebag all along? How is that possible? I want to press for more, but Bethany appears to be struggling to hold herself together.

"And you didn't like it," I finish for her. "I'm sorry."

"It was...a shock. I grew up thinking he was so proud of me. He always pushed me to succeed. I was in a gifted and talented pre-K program by the time I was three. I was reading and doing simple math at four. I never went to kindergarten, just jumped directly into second grade. I also skipped fourth grade, eighth grade, and did concurrent high school and college course work as a senior. School was really awkward. I was so much younger than everyone. I used to cry. Dad did his best to convince me that everyone was simply jealous that I was so much better than them and that I should ignore their crap. But the truth is, to those kids, I was a freak."

Shit, the picture she paints of her childhood is bleak. Against my will, I feel sorry for her. I wonder if that's why she had so little compunction about stealing from others. People showed her no compassion or empathy, so she merely returned the favor? Maybe. Is it possible she's bullshitting me altogether? Sure...but it seems unlikely. She'd have to be a really good actress. Not saying it's impossible, but how could she so realistically fake the guilt and sadness pouring off her? Then again, maybe that's how she scammed her clients in the first place.

My gut rejects that.

What if her father was the one responsible for the theft and she was swept up in the scam?

"You're fantastic, not a freak," I assure her in soothing tones.

"I'm pretty sure that, other than my siblings and their spouses, you might be the only person who thinks so. But...thanks." She smiles at me with forced cheer and extracts her hand from mine to wipe away tears.

Real fucking tears.

"You don't have to front for me."

"I appreciate that, but wallowing is no way to start a new year. Besides, we're almost to Maxon and Keeley's place and I'd rather not have them see me upset."

Good call. "Your brother seemed pretty intense."

"Maxon is protective. Griff, too. We might not have known each other long, but they slipped right into family mode. It's been...kind of nice. In some ways, they're a lot like my father. But in the ways that count, they're not."

"So was your dad married when he had an affair with your mom?"

"Yeah. Over the decades, he's had a lot of affairs with a lot of his assistants. I'm not his only illegitimate child. My youngest brother, Evan, came a few years after me. Dad even has a newborn by his last assistant, the daughter of a friend—who's predictably now an enemy." She shakes her head. "I think I overlooked a lot of his behavior for a long time, made excuses for why his wandering penis had nothing to do with his true character. But in the end, it did."

And she's disillusioned. That fact rings in her voice. So not only was her mom not someone to look up to, now she has to deal with the reality of her dad being a tomcatting, defrauding asshole.

The implications of everything she tells me have my head reeling. I need to think.

"Well, at least you have your siblings in your corner now."

"Seemingly, yeah. They've been way better to me than I would have believed or probably deserve. I'm grateful for that."

As we pull up in front of the bed-and-breakfast, her siblings, their spouses, and a few guests all spill out. The lights glow above the lanai. Tiki torches are lit. People laugh. Couples embrace. I see a lot of happiness.

"Speaking of…" she drawls. "Thanks for the ride."

"You're welcome. Looks like they're holding the party for you. Have fun."

She shakes her head. "I'm going to bed. They've got a few guests here this week, and I'd really rather not stay and be the sad third wheel. Again."

I get that. Even at a glance I'm envious of the cheer I see among the small group of people milling around the inn. "I'm sure you're not."

Bethany grips the door handle. "It's fine. They're all happily married, and that's something I'll never be. I've made peace with it. I'm good to let them enjoy their party." She opens the car door. "Thanks for the ride. Good night."

Before I can say anything, a big hunk of a man saunters over with his beefy arm slung around a gorgeous brunette's waist expanding with pregnancy. "Bethany! How are you? I saved you some champagne." Then he peers at me through the windshield. "You're Clint? Maxon told me about you. I'm Noah Weston."

I debate giving Bethany privacy and peace versus making inroads with her family and gaining insider information. It's no contest.

With a smile, I exit Ash's sedan and stick out my hand. "Nice to meet you. I'm a fan. You're killing it with the color commentary this season."

"Thanks. Other than that, nothing to be a fan of these days except the dad bod I might be working on." He pats what appears to be a flat, hard stomach. His arms definitely bulge in a tank top that leaves me little doubt he's stronger than fuck.

The brunette laughs. "You're so full of shit. You're working out harder than ever—and dragging me with you. My thighs hurt after yesterday."

"Hey, watch your language around the baby." Looking slightly tipsy, he presses a hand to her rounded belly. "We don't want her picking up on bad habits. Besides, if you want, I'll really give your thighs a reason to hurt."

When he winks lasciviously her way, the brunette laughs. She turns to Maxon. "Don't give him any more to drink."

"What?" Noah protests. "The night is still young! You want a drink?" he asks me.

"Sure," I say, then I turn to Bethany.

She looks torn.

I take her hand. "I won't stay long. I just…Ash is going to be with Montana, and I'm not ready to be alone if that's okay." I press my lips together and confess something that, even if it's manipulative, has been paining me all night. "This will be my first whole year without my parents and…I'm not sure how mentally ready I am for that."

Her face softens. "I didn't even think of that. I'm sorry to be wrapped up in my own crap. Come on in. Meet everyone."

Within minutes, I've officially met Noah's wife and Bethany's half sister, Harlow. She's just like Bethany described her—confident and full of life. I like her instantly. I can tell she's good people. Maxon shakes my hand, seemingly thawing toward me. Keeley pauses her pregnant walk to hug me and tell me glumly that the labor pains have stopped—again. Griff shuffles up next, seeming to take my measure. As we're introduced, he shakes my hand a bit too forcefully as if to let me know he's watching me and he's got teeth he has no problem using if I mess with his sister. I give him my friendliest smile to assure him that's not a problem.

By the time I've gotten the evidence I need from Bethany and turned it over to the authorities, I'll be long gone and none of these people's opinions will matter.

As unwanted guilt twinges me, Griff introduces me to his blond wife, Britta, who is also very pregnant. She's very sweet, too.

A tall, intellectual guy saunters up next. He might be smart, but he's clearly logged a lot of hours at the gym, as well. He introduces himself as Evan Cook. I've heard the tech genius's name. I had no idea he's Barclay Reed's son. Then he wraps a long arm around a beautiful African-American woman and introduces me to his wife, Nia, whom he says is also pregnant. Apparently, all these newlyweds decided not to waste any time before starting their families.

Next, I meet a few of the inn's guests just before they thank Maxon and Keeley for a great time and head off to bed. Single dad Trace, Noah's brother, picks up his sleeping son in his infant carrier, waves at us, and heads home.

Last, Evan's friend and CFO, Sebastian, comes out of the house with a cold one and passes it my way. "Beer?"

"I have to drive home," I say with a shake of my head.

"Just one," he says. "If you don't feel comfortable driving, someone will take you or let you crash on a sofa somewhere."

I hesitate. I probably shouldn't stay long. I don't know how Bethany will handle it. But I need to make inroads, get information. Plus, the idea of going back to Ash's crappy apartment to spend the rest of the night alone really does sound depressing.

"All right. Thanks." Then I scan the lawn for Bethany and see she's talking to Keeley and Harlow, but she's empty-handed. "What does Beth drink?"

He raises a brow. "I don't know. We've only met once."

"It's cool. I'll figure it out." I take a swig of the ice-cold beer, then sidle up to Maxon. "What does your sister drink?"

"Sauvignon Blanc. I've got a good one from New Zealand chilling in the fridge for her."

"Mind if I grab her a glass? She's had a rough night. It was killer at work."

Maxon nods as we head inside, toward the white, bright kitchen. "I told her she didn't have to take the first job that came along when she got here. She's so damn determined to earn some money so she can 'get out of my hair,' as she puts it and get her own place. I've

told her there's no rush, but she's so damn stubborn and independent."

"That sounds like Beth."

"Beth, huh?" He frowns. "Look, I appreciate you giving her a ride
home after her shifts, but man to man? She's not in a good place right
now. If you're cozying up to her simply to bang her—"

"I'm not. We're…friends."

"I see the way you look at her."

That's not good because if Maxon can tell I'd like to fuck his sister,
what else can he read from me? "I won't deny she's beautiful. But she's
already let me know that she's not into dating right now and that I'm
apparently too young for her."

"Pfft." Maxon rolls his eyes. "It's not as if you're sixteen, but like I
said, she's not in a great place mentally to be dating…or anything
else."

Personally, I think that's Bethany's decision and I wonder if she'd
appreciate Maxon butting in. But I don't rebut him since I'm not actually looking to hook up with her, just make her pay for whatever sins
she might have committed against my father.

Her oldest brother shows me where the wine tumblers are and
opens the fridge to extract a bottle of vino when Griff walks in. He
looks over his shoulder and spots his petite wife talking to Keeley and
rubbing her back helpfully.

Then he focuses all his attention on me again, brow raised. *Cue the
interrogation.*

"You're not trying to scam Bethany into bed, I hope."

I choke on my beer.

"Dude." Maxon rolls his eyes. "I already asked and I was way more
subtle."

"Fuck subtle. I want information. And what's with the bruises
around her wrists?" He sends me a pointed glance.

"That's not me. There's a persistent, handsy patron who keeps
coming back to the bar. I've tried to intervene when I can, but it was so
busy tonight that I missed his latest stunt."

"Why hasn't anyone thrown this guy out?"

"I'm going to talk to Andy about it on Tuesday because it's not right. But I gotta ask, why does Beth seem reluctant to stand up for herself?"

Maxon and Griff exchange a glance before the older takes over with what I assume is the more carefully crafted reply while he pours her a glass of wine. "She's in the middle of a rough patch now. She needs to work through a few things."

As answers go, it doesn't tell me much, but we're talking. It's a start. "Beth mentioned that she and her dad recently had a falling-out."

They look stunned by that admission.

"That's one way of putting it," Griff snorts.

Maxon hands me Bethany's glass, then elbows his brother. "Yeah. Our old man is a massive, bleeding asshole. It was just a matter of time before she figured that out the hard way, too. We should get back to the others."

Clearly, they aren't going to divulge more, but it's interesting that these two have an even less glowing opinion of their father than Bethany. Of course, I never assumed Barclay Reed was a great guy. He's been arrested, and the victims' stories circulating online of the clients who had trusted him for decades are heartbreaking. But he's going to get what he deserves, so I'm focused on Bethany.

"Whatever you do, though, go easy on her," Maxon murmurs. "She may not seem like it, but Bethany is fragile right now."

Griff grabs my arm. "And if we find out you've hurt her, we'll be all too happy to rip your balls off. Are we clear?"

chapter FOUR

With that warning pinging around my brain, I head outside toward the people spilled across the lanai. Evan and Sebastian seem to be deep in an office-related conversation. Noah opens another bottle of beer, takes a swig, then wraps his arm around Harlow, who is talking animatedly with Keeley, Britta, and Nia. Bethany hovers in the periphery, hands clasped in front of her. The women do their best to draw her into the conversation. She smiles, clearly listening, but says nothing. I think that's less because babies aren't her thing and more because she feels out of place.

"Hey." I approach with a cold drink in each hand before I extend the glass of wine her way. "Have a drink. You've earned it."

"Thanks. I've got to sit. My feet are still killing me."

I wouldn't mind that, either, so I let her lead me to some patio furniture clustered on the corner of the lanai. She sinks onto a love seat, probably because it's closest. I ignore the chair a few feet away and sit beside her, following suit when she props her feet on the low table.

"Hell of a night," I say.

"I have a whole new respect for waitstaff. It's a hard job."

"It is. Bartending is also tougher than I remember. Or maybe I'm just rusty."

"It might feel that way, but you have the right touch. I heard nothing but compliments on the drinks tonight."

I smile. "Good. Since I started again, I've been telling myself that it's like riding a bike."

A smile floats across her face. "Probably. Like a lot of things, I guess."

"Yes." The first thing that comes to mind is sex. In fact, whenever I get close to Bethany, it's always on my brain.

It sucks being so suspicious of the woman I'm dying to fuck.

As she sips her wine, I scoot closer—until she stiffens.

Biting back a curse, I settle back against the cushions and remind myself that I should be focused on what to say next to Bethany, how to get her to open up like she was on the drive over. I have to stop fixating on how to get into her pants. Something has raised her reserve again, damn it, and I need to relax her.

Thankfully, I know just how…

"Let's play a drinking game."

"Like we're at a frat party?" She raises an arched brow at me.

"Like we're trying to forget our problems, be silly, and have a little fun."

Bethany glances around the gathering. "The rest of the women are all pregnant. They can't play."

"I meant just the two of us. We've got our cozy corner and some fresh drinks. Why not?"

"Or we could just call it a day and get some much-needed sleep." She sighs tiredly.

"Where's your New Year's spirit?"

With a shake of her head, she laughs. "All right, but only because it's New Year's and only because I graduated college at seventeen, so I missed all the usual party stuff."

"Excellent. We're going to play a game called Drink or Dare."

"I've never heard of that."

Because I just made it up. "It's like truth or dare, but if you don't tell the truth, you're daring yourself to take a drink."

She shrugs. "Sounds simple enough. But I'm going to bore you. I've led a pretty sheltered life."

I haven't, so this should be interesting. "I'll ask you a question first so you get the gist of it. Um…drink or dare. Have you ever had a one-night stand?"

Bethany presses her lips together. "I'm pleading the fifth."

I shoot her a grin, but wonder why she won't answer. "Then you have to drink."

She lifts her glass in salute, then takes a dainty sip of the vino before setting it on the table again. If I let her play like this, we'll be here all night.

"Nope." I hand her the wine glass again. "You have to drink all of it."

Her eyes flare wide. "Are you kidding?"

"Hey, every time I defer I have to drink a whole bottle of beer." And after a few, I'll probably be drunk as hell. But I'll cross that bridge if and when I come to it.

"I'm a total lightweight," she pushes back. "This is going to be a short game."

That definitely skews the odds in my favor, along with the fact that I probably outweigh her by nearly a hundred pounds.

With a little frown, she lifts the glass to her lips and starts imbibing. At first, the sips are small and controlled. But when she eases the tumbler from her mouth and sighs at how little she's managed to drink, she tries again, this time gulping the wine until she manages to drain every last drop.

"Fantastic. Wait here!" Before she can ask what I'm doing, I dart into the kitchen, past Maxon and Griff, who are strolling out to meet up with the others, then grab the bottle of Sauvignon Blanc from the fridge. When I return to the lanai, I refill her glass and set the half-full bottle on the floor beside the love seat. "Now you're ready for the next question."

She narrows her eyes at me. "Isn't it my turn to ask you a question?"

"Sure."

Her jaunty little smile surprises me. "Hmm… Drink or dare. How old were you the first time you got drunk?"

She's keeping things light, which makes this game easy on me. Me? I'll be pressing hard, but she probably won't figure that out until it's too late.

"Thirteen. I went to a cousin's wedding, and when the adults all got busy socializing and dancing, I dipped into the punchbowl. No one told me it was spiked. My mother was so pissed when my dad had to pull me out of the men's bathroom because I'd gone in there to pee but I was too drunk to find my way out."

Bethany laughs out loud, an artless smile brightening her face. She's always stunning, but this expression makes her beyond beautiful. The tinkling sound of her amusement is light and feminine, and for the first time, she's responding to me without first thinking. Right now, she's natural. She's real. This is *her*.

It's arousing as hell.

"I can picture you as a bleary-eyed teenager stumbling around to find the exit. Oh, that's hysterical."

"When I recovered from the horrible hangover the next afternoon, I found the humor in it. When my dad was explaining what had happened to my mom, he was trying really hard not to chuckle. But he wasn't terribly successful." I take a swig of my beer. "Now it's my turn. Drink or dare… Have you ever stolen anything?"

Instantly, her face closes up. I grit my teeth, mentally berating myself. That question was too much, too fast. Damn, I need to be more patient.

"That's a terrible thing to ask."

"Sorry. It was just random," I lie. "I'm usually better at this, but it's been a long day."

"Then why don't we end it?"

I take a risk and grab her hand. "Please. I'm enjoying my time with you. Would you rather have another question?"

"No, it's fine." She waves me away. "I need to stop making assumptions and being insecure."

"About what?"

"Nothing." She shakes her head. "You asked me about stealing. I'd rather drink."

Because she's guilty and she doesn't want to admit it?

"Living dangerously?" I taunt.

"That's one way of looking at it. Bottoms up." She lifts her wine and downs the entire glass in seconds.

Coupled with her almost nonexistent dinner, I wonder how much longer before she's feeling the alcohol.

As soon as she sets the empty glass down, sinks back to the cushions, and shoots me a slightly unfocused glance, I have my answer. The booze is hitting her. Now we might get someplace.

"What did you steal?" I whisper conspiratorially.

"I never said I stole anything."

"You drank to avoid answering me."

"Which means I'm not talking about it."

I slip into flirt mode. It's not conscious. I can't help but *want* to flirt with her. "Did you steal someone's heart?"

Instantly, she scoffs. "I wish. I've never really been in a relationship. I always put work first—and I was fine with that. Hell, I was great with that since my dad was my only real example of what marriage was. If that was supposed to be happiness, I wanted no part of it."

"Never?"

She shakes her head.

"You've never been anyone's girlfriend?" I can't fathom that. She's beautiful and obviously smart and surprisingly easy to be around.

"In high school, I was the age of an average freshman when I was a senior. The upperclassmen ignored me. The underclassmen were intimidated by me. When I got to college, all the guys referred to me as jailbait. No one wanted anything to do with me." She shrugs. "As soon as I finished my MBA, my dad put me to work. I wasn't about to date clients and I didn't have a lot of opportunities to meet other men. I didn't have any girlfriends I could go barhopping with, either. And online dating never held any appeal. Besides, I was too busy."

"But you've had sex?"

"Yes." She glares at me.

I want to know how old she was, who with, why she gave her V-card to someone she didn't even have a relationship with. But my last too-fast question taught me that I need to slow down. So I'll keep a lid on my curiosity—for now.

"What about you?"

"I've had sex," I assure her, tongue-in-cheek.

"A lot of it, I'm sure. You're smooth. You look like the kind of guy who knows what to do with a woman. One of my first thoughts when I saw you was of your hands."

"My hands?"

"They look capable of stroking a woman and making her very happy."

Okay, that's the booze talking, but it's interesting to know that she's thought about me, even in passing, as more than a friend.

"Oh, yeah. What else did you think?"

"Hey, it's my turn to ask you a question. And since you sneaked in a few extras, you can answer me. Ever been someone's boyfriend?"

"Not since high school, but yeah."

"Why not since then? Why not now? Did something happen to swear you off relationships?"

Good question, one I haven't given much thought, to be honest. "No, nothing happened except I got busy with work and figured I had all kinds of time to find the right woman. And I want what my parents had. They were married for twenty-eight years, and I never saw two people more in love. A couple of my buddies put a ring on the first piece of steady ass they got, and now they barely talk to their wives because they have nothing in common and they're miserable. I want more."

She nods slowly. "I want what all my siblings have. I didn't know that until I saw the way they care and compromise. They tease and help each other and share everything." She sighs. "But I'll never find that. I grew up warped and I'm not sure I'm wired for relationships. Damn it, how did we end up talking about me again? No." She shakes her head. "Drink or dare. Who was your first girlfriend?"

"Well, if you mean the very first one, that would be Reah, whom I met in church camp when I was thirteen." I lean in and whisper, "We kissed behind a tree when we were supposed to be working on a camp production about the Nativity story. Then we got caught…and we both got sent home. My mom was pissed. That was a running theme during my teen years. But if you mean my first semi-serious girlfriend, the first one I had sex with, Demi and I dated our entire sophomore year. Over the summer, she took Driver's Ed and ended up falling for some douche of a football player from our rival school and broke up with me. I was pretty crushed for a while."

"But you rebounded, I take it?"

"Yeah, I did. With one of Demi's friends, Catherine. That was ugly for a while, but a couple of months into our junior year, I figured out I was dating her as a fuck you to Demi and let her go. I dated another girl while I was a senior, but when she got accepted to a college on the other side of the country and I decided to move to North Dakota to tackle a whole new way of life, we decided mutually to end things." I shrug. "That's it. She was my last 'girlfriend.' Now it's my turn. Who was your first sexual partner?"

"That's personal!" she protests, her voice slurred, her eyes glazed.

She's definitely well on her way to drunk.

"All our conversation tonight has been pretty personal, don't you think? I'm not asking you to share anything I haven't shared myself." I brush my mouth against her ear and have to restrain myself from letting my lips linger on her neck. "Don't worry. Your secrets are safe with me."

As I pull back, her eyes are closed. She shivers delicately. Am I getting to her? Is she thinking about having a relationship—sexual or otherwise—with me?

I shouldn't like that thought. But suddenly I'm hard as hell, so I do.

Bethany shakes her head. "I'd rather drink again."

"You passed on the last two Drink-or-Dare questions. The rule is that you can't pass on three in a row."

"You're making that up."

Totally. But I manage to keep a straight face. "Seriously, you have to answer…"

She frowns. "Fine. His name was Dalton. I was twenty and fresh out of grad school. My father set us up."

The tense way she's suddenly holding her body tells me it wasn't good. "Did you like it at all?"

"No."

Her answer is so quick and sharp, I'm worried. "Did he hurt you?"

She takes a long time answering. "Doesn't the first time always hurt?"

That isn't what I asked, and now I'm downright suspicious. "Did he force you?"

"No."

But something about the way she utters the word tells me it wasn't exactly her choice, either. I'm dying to know what the hell happened, but even as I sit beside her, Bethany starts pulling into her shell and putting distance between us.

I squeeze her hand. "I'm sorry if I brought up bad memories."

"Not your fault. You didn't know. I just...try not to think about it."

"We all have those moments in life we'd rather not remember."

Like my dad dying on my living room floor and me being wholly unable to save him.

Fuck. I need to get my head back in the game.

Still, the next thing that comes out of my mouth is way flirtier than it should be. "Have you ever found a lover who made you feel good?"

Bethany extracts her hand from mine, tosses back another glass of wine, then crosses her arms around her middle. "I'm passing on that question. Can we talk about something else?"

"You know what, sweetheart? We don't have to talk at all. Come here."

I extend my arm to curl it around her shoulders before easing her close. She's stiff, but she doesn't protest, merely sits beside me in oddly companionable silence as I drink the rest of my beer.

To my surprise, she lays her head on my shoulder with a tired sigh.

"You okay, Beth?"

"Yeah."

That's good. As much as I need the information and I wonder constantly if she's guilty, I feel so reluctant to hurt her. Or believe the worst about her. What seemed like such an open-and-shut case of criminal activity when I was packing my suitcase in LA to hunt her down in Maui now feels a lot less obvious.

Is there any chance the scheme to steal all their clients' money was purely her father's? That she somehow didn't know? Or am I hoping so because she's shown me her fragile side and I feel this irrational urge to protect her, even as I'm dying to take her to bed?

I don't know.

Still, I can't stop myself from opening my big mouth. "Sex should never hurt, sweetheart. It should only make you feel like the goddess you are. And if you've never found the right man to prove that to you...I'm here if you want me."

Silence.

Is she trying to decide what to say to me? How she feels about my offer? Is she shocked? Upset? Or intrigued?

After a few dozen tense seconds slide by, I risk a peek at her face—and realize she's fallen asleep.

Damn…

When I look up, I realize that everyone else has gone to bed. The lanai is empty. The house is dark. We're totally alone. And I don't want to leave Bethany's side, so I curl her closer, lay my head back, and shut my eyes.

Slowly, I become aware of sunbeams dancing on my lids. My neck is bent at an odd angle and propped against something hard. I try to move, but I'm too damn stiff to do anything but wince. On the plus side, someone soft—definitely a woman—is curled up beside me, her head on my chest. My arm wraps around her small waist as I press her to my side. At the feel of her, my morning wood becomes more than automatic and nothing less than insistent.

I risk opening one eye, my fuzzy brain scrambling to remember who the hell I spent the night with and where. The sound of the waves crashing on the nearby beach registers at the same time I look down to find Bethany plastered against me. We're still on the lanai, where we apparently spent all night cuddled together. And even though the sun is up, I'm in no hurry to let her go.

Except…I'm wondering if getting so cozy with her is a giant tactical mistake.

On the surface, I should be pissed at myself for sleeping with the enemy. After all, when I boarded the plane to Maui, I had no doubt Bethany Banks was guilty and needed to pay. Now, nothing is that simple or obvious anymore. Nothing is black and white. She's human. She's real. She's been abandoned, ostracized, and hurt. Some people might use that as a justification not to care about anyone else—and as a rationale to commit crimes. It's still possible Bethany did that. But the stories she shared about herself and the compassion she showed me last night after hearing about my mom…

Fuck, I'm torn. Who is she really?

I study her as if staring will answer my question. All I see is her pale hair tumbling from its messy bun in a silken cascade down to her plush breasts. Dark lashes lay curled against her rosy cheeks. Soft lips are gently parted in slumber. Her face looks so at peace, she appears guileless, like a sweetly mussed female, not a criminal mastermind.

Appearances can be deceiving.

Still, the Bethany I'm coming to know seems too human to treat hardworking people so inhumanely by scamming them out of their every last dime. For the first time, I'm giving serious consideration to the possibility that she might truly be innocent.

I don't like this indecisive gray area. My head keeps telling my libido to back the fuck down and stop trying to make it okay to want a criminal. My gut tells my head to stop being so quick to judge.

It's frustrating to be this unsure what to think.

Maybe it's time to examine the facts again. I first convicted her mentally because she was my dad's financial advisor. It seemed logical that she knew where his money had gone and how it had been stolen. But the feds arrested and charged Barclay Reed, not Bethany. She admitted last night that she'd recently encountered her dad's "unpleasant side," even admitting she'd made excuses for him. Yes, in the context of his wandering penis, not clients' financial transactions. Did she really mean both? I don't know.

It's possible Bethany was Reed's accomplice and that she escaped jail time because she's a cooperating witness. If so, that doesn't change anything. Helping to commit a crime still makes her responsible. But I keep wondering if she, too, was somehow duped by her father's scheme.

No clue.

And I'm right back to the beginning of this argument with myself.

Beside me, Bethany stirs, rolling toward the sun as her lashes flutter open. She turns to me, brows knit in confusion before her eyes flare wide with a gasp. "We spent the night out here?"

"Looks that way. I only figured that out when I woke up a few minutes ago."

"Oh, my god. I had too much wine. I never get drunk and—"

"It's okay." I cut into her panic. "You were tired, it was New Year's, and I twisted your arm into playing that drinking game. How much do you remember?"

"Some…"

Does she recall telling me about her first lover? About the first thing she thought when she looked at me?

"Don't worry. You didn't embarrass yourself."

"If you have to assure me of that, I probably did." She winces.

"You hungover?"

"No, thank goodness. And I know you're not because you barely drank. Have you seen anyone else this morning?"

"Not a soul."

She cocks her head as if she's listening for sounds from inside. "The house seems awfully quiet this morning. I wonder where everyone went… Do you want coffee?"

As she rises to her feet, I follow suit, scowling when she won't meet my gaze. Is she embarrassed that she spent all night pressed against me? Does she suspect on some level how personal last night was?

"Sure. That would be great."

Without even thinking, I drop my hand to the small of her back and guide her inside. She bustles away from me, almost running for the kitchen.

Yes, she knows exactly how personal last night was. She's feeling cautious again. Her walls are up.

As she turns on the coffeemaker and retrieves a pair of mugs from the cabinet, she looks decidedly nervous. I lean against the island and regard her with a considering stare. "Beth, in case you're wondering, we spent last night together platonically. I'm not going to jump on you this morning."

"I never said you were."

"But you act as if you're worried I might."

She retrieves the cream and sugar. "It's just…I don't make a habit of spending the night with anyone. Maybe waking up next to someone you've only known a few days is normal for you. For me, it's not."

I wonder how much sex she's actually had beyond Dalton the First, who apparently sucked in bed. Is it possible her experiences have been few and far between?

As sexy as she is, that possibility blows my mind.

"It's not normal for me, either," I admit. "But this isn't a big deal. We're friends."

"We are."

The quick snap of her agreement makes me think she's also thought about us being more. My cock perks up again at the thought.

Ignoring it, I lean closer and murmur softly, "I won't touch you if you don't want me to, I promise."

She shoots a skittish glance my way. I see the wary question in her eyes.

But what if I do?

"Thanks." She turns her focus to the brewing java instead. "I'm sorry. I'm handling this badly. I'm not a morning person, especially before coffee."

"And you're not looking for someone right now. Neither am I."

But the suggestion is between us now. I know we both feel it.

Her face softens. "Clint, it's not you."

"No worries. After coffee, I'll leave you to enjoy your day off."

I'll use the time to regroup and figure out how to approach her from a different angle, one that skirts the sexual tension brewing between us. I don't have a choice.

"No rush." She hands me a cup of steaming joe, then sets about making her own.

After a few sips in the awkward silence, she sets her mug down and scans the bottom floor of the house. "Hello? Anyone home?"

No answer.

"Maybe Maxon is at the office and Keeley went somewhere?" I suggest.

"It's New Year's Day. He and Griff both planned to take the day off. Keeley isn't going much of anywhere these days since she keeps having labor pains."

I shrug. "Did they text you? Leave you a note?"

"Good question." She goes in search of her purse and retrieves her phone. "Oh, they're at the birthing center! Keeley's water broke at six this morning. They want me to come when I wake up so I can be there when their daughter is born and I become an aunt again. That's so sweet." Tears fill her eyes.

There's no faking how genuinely touched she is that they included her.

"Finish your coffee, and I'll take you where you need to go."

"It's your day off…" And she clearly hates to impose.

"It's okay. This is more important than random sightseeing."

"Let me grab a quick shower and… There's an outdoor facility if you want one, too. I can get you a towel. Maxon has some clothes you can borrow."

A shower would clear my foggy head, and I need to be at the top of my game around Bethany. "I'll take the towel. I stashed some clean clothes in the gym bag I keep in the trunk."

A few minutes later, she's putting herself together in the cottage out back, which they call an ohana in Hawaii. That's where she's staying. I wish I could get into the place to search her personal belongings, maybe find proof of her guilt…or innocence. But there's no time now, so I enjoy the hell out of the hot spray and the morning breeze on my skin.

When I finish putting myself together, I wait for Bethany in the kitchen. A few of the inn's guests mill in for pastries someone left on a plate on a nearby buffet table.

When I hear the back door open, I turn to see Bethany enter. She's wearing a lacy white tank and faded jeans that hug her sleek thighs— and make me want to be sure she knows I'm a man. She's arranged her hair into a loose braid that tumbles over one shoulder. Platinum wisps surround her face. She's tossed on some mascara and lip gloss, and she looks amazing.

I don't realize I'm staring at her until she frowns. "Is this the wrong thing to wear to a birth?"

"No. You look great. Just marveling at how fast you were," I lie to cover my reaction. "My mom used to take forever, change clothes four times, redo her hair, paint her nails… We waited a lot when I was a kid."

She smiles and slings a small pink purse over her shoulder. "I've always been busy, so I learned how to make the most of the minimum. Ready?"

"Sure."

I lead her outside and we get on the road. The drive to the birthing center takes twenty minutes, and she fills most of the time by texting Harlow and passing the updates along to me.

"Keeley is dilating quickly. They think she'll be delivering in another hour or so."

Bethany looks worried we may not make it in time, so I drive a little faster.

"Is your whole extended family going to be in the waiting room?" Maybe I can use some of the time to discreetly talk to them.

She shakes her head. "In the delivery room. Keeley picked a midwife who believes that families should welcome babies together. So that's what she wants us to do."

"Wow." Thankfully, Bethany said family, which excludes me. I'm happy I won't be witnessing a virtual stranger give birth today.

"It's great that Keeley and Maxon want you there. Did you expect to be treated like family when you first arrived?"

"Hardly. I expected to be grilled at the least. Maybe even blamed and reviled. But they've been amazingly inclusive and understanding."

They seemingly have. Which brings up another question... Would these people really welcome a criminal with open arms? What are the odds she conned all of them, too?

"When did you first find out about your siblings?"

"I've always known. Dad never tried to hide them from me." She frowns. "Of course, he described his children by his wife as useless and ungrateful, so I never had any desire to meet them. I wish now I hadn't taken him at face value about Maxon, Griff, and Harlow. Well, about a lot of things, really."

"Evan, too?" I know she purposely didn't include him, but maybe since I tossed out the question, she'll take the bait and give me more information.

Bethany shakes her head. "Dad knew of Evan, called him 'the weird kid,' but they didn't meet for the first time until last summer, at

Harlow's wedding. He always told me that Evan's mother was a money-grabbing whore and that if he paid any attention to his son, she'd try to extort him for more. I didn't learn until recently that Evan's mother died when he was five and, instead of claiming him, my father allowed Evan to be a ward of the state and shoved into foster care until he turned eighteen."

Her carefully arranged expression slips. I see glimpses of her disillusionment. She looks so much like she's hurting…

I steel myself. I need facts, not feelings.

"Beth, did you two have a falling-out because he lied to you so much?"

She nods. "You have no idea."

Before I can ask her to elaborate, Bethany's phone dings again. "It's Harlow. They've revised the timeline up. Keeley might be delivering in thirty minutes!"

"We'll be there in less than ten," I promise.

Bethany seems distracted for the rest of the car ride, so I don't pry anymore. I make a mental note to come back to the subject of her father, try to find out whether it's possible he lied to her about the scam, too. Now just isn't the time.

As promised, we pull up to the birthing center in eight minutes. I drop her at the door and thankfully find a prime parking spot close by. Not long after, I run inside the pseudo-medical facility, asking a maternal woman behind a desk where to find the Reed birth. She points, and I catch up to Bethany just before she disappears behind a set of double doors with Harlow.

"Thanks for bringing Bethany here—and so quickly," the pregnant brunette says.

"My pleasure. Where can I wait for Beth? I'm happy to take her home whenever she's ready."

Beside Harlow, Bethany's expression softens. She's surprised I'm willing to wait around? I don't mind. Sure, I have other things to do on my day off, but Keeley and Maxon may well spend the night here. It would be out of everyone else's way to take Bethany back to the inn. The logistics of the situation help me take every moment I can get with her.

"I hate to inconvenience you," she murmurs.

"You're not," I assure her. "Go be with your family. I'll find some-where to wait."

"Harlow!" Noah sticks his head out the door. "You're here, Bethany. Good. It won't be long now…"

"No time," Harlow shrieks. "Come with us!"

She grips my wrist and gives me a surprisingly strong yank before she starts sprinting toward the open door, swelling belly leading the way. Bethany follows, shooting me a wide-eyed stare and a shrug. I start to sweat. Am I really about to witness a woman I've only met a couple of times give birth?

When we round the corner, the obvious answer is yes.

With one eye open, I wedge myself against the back wall on one side of the room. Thankfully, a discreet sheet covers everything I'd rather not see. Maxon holds Keeley's hands. Harlow scoops ice chips into her mouth. Britta gives her last-minute advice.

Over Keeley's rhythmic pants and the monitors she's hooked up to, the atmospheric music overhead abruptly goes quiet. Journey's "Don't Stop Believin'" takes its place seconds later, suddenly blaring from the overhead speakers.

"Who changed the music?" the redhead demands with a scowl between contractions.

"I did," Maxon offers. "That meditative crap wasn't working—"

"It's supposed to help me focus."

"Screw that. Journey will help you push like a champion. And it won't put the rest of us to sleep while we wait."

Keeley grips his hand tighter and leans in with a scowl, teeth bared. "So this is about you?"

"No, sunshine." He backpedals. "Of course not. But you're always making mixes for everyone else to encourage them. I've been putting this one together for a while. To show you that I'm thinking of you and our daughter. To tell you both that I love you."

Another contraction hits. The pain seems to ramp up. Keeley groans and sobs at once. "That's wonderful and terrible. I practiced my breathing to the other music."

"It sounded like whales humping."

Everyone erupts into laughter, including me. Before it dies down, Keeley bows as the contraction seizes her. She grips Maxon's hand with all her might and screams.

The midwife, a Hawaiian woman in her fifties who looks both efficient and calm, rushes in and makes a beeline for the mother-to-be. "I'm going to check you now, Keeley. You're probably close."

The redhead nods. "I think so."

Journey's rock anthem slides into the Kelly Clarkson tune "Stronger (What Doesn't Kill You)." It was one of my mom's favorite songs. She worked out to it while she could. She fought death to it. At the end, she told me that even though cancer was getting the last laugh, the tune had definitely helped her stay as strong as she could during her last days. For that, she was thankful.

I really wish she was still here. She would be able to read Bethany so much better than me…

"Nine centimeters," the midwife says happily.

Suddenly, Keeley tenses and squeezes Maxon's hand in a death grip once more as she growls out in agony. "Are you kidding me?"

"No," the midwife assures. "You're almost there."

"I meant my husband. What were you thinking with this song?"

I can't see Maxon's face but I swear I can hear him swallow audibly. "Giving you encouragement, sunshine. From one lady to another. Kelly has had kids. Birth didn't kill her, just made her more badass."

Keeley rolls her eyes, and I'm thinking Maxon made a decent save of the situation—until he opens his big mouth again.

"Of course, Kelly didn't wait until January first to go into labor and bypass a whole year's worth of a tax break…" he grumbles.

Harlow leans across the distance and slaps her oldest brother upside the head. "You just keep digging yourself a deeper grave, fidiot. Shut up while she's still letting you breathe."

Griff nods. "I admit that I can sometimes be oblivious, but—"

"You mean insensitive," Harlow cuts in.

Britta represses a smile and nods, sending her husband a fond glance.

"Whatever." Griff waves her away. "But even I wouldn't say something that douchy."

"But you thought it," Maxon contends.

When Griff doesn't answer right away, everyone laughs again.

Keeley giggles, too—until another contraction wracks her, her entire body jolting.

Maxon leans in. "Breathe, sunshine. You got this."

"You fucking breathe! I'm trying to—*ahhhh!*"

"You're doing great," the midwife encourages. "I see the top of the baby's head."

Evan pokes Maxon in the back. "Don't lock your knees. You've lost the color in your face. Medically speaking—"

"Save the explanation, babe." Nia caresses his arm, then turns to Maxon. "Breathe, buddy."

Evan frowns. "But if he understands what he's doing that may cause him to faint—"

"Don't you *dare* faint on me!" Keeley shouts, huffing in between her words. "Do you hear me, Maxon Miles Reed? If you pass out, I'm going to—" She jolts again. "*Oooh!*"

"One more good push, Keeley." The midwife nods enthusiastically. "One more, and you'll be a mother."

"And I'll be a father," Maxon mumbles. "This is really happening. Oh, shit…" He loses more color.

"What doesn't kill you makes you stronger…" Griff parrots the song still playing overhead.

"Bite me," Maxon growls back.

"How about you hold my hand?" Keeley demands of her husband.

"I am. Sunshine, could you let up a bit? I think you're about to break it."

"Giving birth is breaking my vagina!"

It's taking everything I have not to howl with laughter. Britta doesn't even try to stop herself. Neither does Harlow or Nia. Even Evan looks as if he's repressing a roaring guffaw.

Noah starts to sweat, then leans over to his wife. "Is this how you're going to be when you give birth?"

"No." She shakes her head. "Keeley is much sweeter than I am. You probably ought to wear protective gear the day I have this big boy. Especially a cup."

Half the color leaches from his face. "You wouldn't really kick me in the balls. Right?"

"I can't guarantee what I'll do if you get too close. That looks painful."

"It is," Britta put in. "My labor with Jamie felt so long I barely knew what day it was by the time I pushed him out."

"Are you kidding me?" Harlow looks terrified, then turns to her husband. "If that's the case, that's a definite yes on the cup."

He nods adamantly, then no one speaks again because Keeley wails out in a primal howl of pain that makes me wince and feel really damn sorry for her.

"Did anyone give her drugs?" I ask Bethany, who's beside me, looking wide-eyed and stunned by the birth playing out live and in color in front of us.

"Keeley wants to do this naturally." She swallows and clutches my arm like she needs help balancing. "I'm thinking she's crazy."

"Don't remind me!" Keeley snaps between contractions. "If there's a next time, I want *all* the drugs."

"You'll forget about the pain," the midwife assures.

Maxon scowls. "Of course there will be a next time. Sunshine…"

"Now isn't the right time to talk about having another baby…" Britta shakes her head at him.

The midwife motions Maxon to get behind Keeley and help her brace.

"Ha! I won't forget an instant of this," the redhead hisses out as she grits her teeth and bears down.

"That's it!" the midwife coaxes. "Just one more push and—"

Keeley keens out an ear-piercing shriek that bounces off the walls and fills the room. It's low and pained and seems to last for fucking ever. I tense and hold my breath. Bethany eases toward the bed, still gripping my arm. Suddenly, she gasps and squeezes my hand, too.

Personally, I can't see much of the birth—and I'm happy with that. I get peeks of the midwife's profile, since the Reed clan has all gathered around Keeley in front of me. I've got a glimpse of some sheet, the mom-to-be's left calf and foot, along with her forearm and damp, flushed face.

Suddenly, the midwife pulls and tugs, then lifts the infant above the sheet, little by little, until her entire body is nestled in the woman's arms.

"Oh, my god…" Maxon breathes, seemingly fixated on his daughter. "She's…"

"Beautiful," Keeley finishes, staring at the infant like she's a miracle. Then the new mother bursts into tears.

"Amazing." He bends to his wife as the baby starts to cry in protest. "Thank you. She's perfect. God, I love you."

The redhead looks at him with absolute worship in her eyes. "I love you, too. We did it."

Then she buries her head in her husband's shoulder. He wraps his arms around her and strokes her damp hair as she sobs. I have absolutely no doubt how strong their marriage is. They're committed the way my parents were. I feel the love, thick and tangible in the room, which now includes the child they made together.

"Would you like to hold your daughter?" the midwife asks after wiping her down and briefly checking her out.

"Please." Maxon sounds choked up.

I am, too. I never realized that witnessing a birth and being surrounded by this much joy would impact me.

Suddenly, the overhead song switches and a male vocalist croons, "Welcome to the planet. Welcome to existence…" As Switchfoot fills my ears, the love in the room swells even more, including the baby's sniffling aunts and proud uncles. I can't remember the last time I've been around a family that functioned like a family. I'm doing all I can to hold my brothers and me together, but I'm not Dad. We all miss him and Mom. But they're both gone, and this—right in front of me—is the circle of life.

What's in front of me is something I really want someday—real family.

Bethany turns to me. Tears run down her face. I crowd in to stand beside her and comfort her. She cries harder when Maxon and Keeley invite her closer to see the infant.

"She's beautiful," Beth whispers. "Congratulations."

Then Nia and Evan step in to get an in-depth glance at the

newborn, and Bethany approaches me, chin trembling, wonder and envy all over her face. It seems like the most natural thing in the world to open my arms to her. It feels even more natural when she walks in and I enfold her against me.

Without hesitation, she lays her head on my chest. I cradle her neck and press kisses to her crown. We don't speak words, but I know we've both been touched by what we've witnessed together this morning. She's lowered more of her walls and shown me her softer side. I can't unsee that. It's impossible to unknow how caring she can be.

In the span of a few hours, for better or worse, everything between us has changed.

chapterFIVE

When we reach the inn a few hours later, we're alone. Maxon, Keeley, and baby Kailani, whose name was chosen because it's Hawaiian for sea and sky, will be home sometime tomorrow.

Bethany has been quiet since we left the birthing center. Not sad, just contemplative. Judging by the fact she's barely let go of me since Kailani made her way into the world, Beth is as impacted by the infant's birth as I feel. I wish I knew what was going on in her head.

"It's midafternoon, and you never got breakfast. I'm sure you're starving," she says as we enter the bright kitchen at Maxon and Keeley's place. "At least let me cook for you before you go. I owe you that much."

"You don't owe me anything. I was happy to drive you there."

"But you stayed. That was above and beyond. I'm already cooking for myself. So unless you have someplace to be…"

"I don't." My mission is her.

She grabs a few things from the pantry, then opens the fridge. "Allergic to anything?"

"No."

"Hate anything?"

"My palate is pretty open-minded."

She turns and smiles at me. "Perfect."

I try not to let the warmth on her face affect me. No such luck.

In a few short minutes, she's diced an onion, sliced off some soft white cheese I can't identify, chopped sweet cherry tomatoes, then grabbed a couple of skillets from the drawer beneath the stove. She's proficient, methodical, and strangely fascinating to watch.

"You're good in the kitchen. I can, um…boil water."

"Seriously? Then what do you eat?"

"A lot of stuff that's frozen or out of a can. Where I live in North

Dakota, there aren't many restaurants nearby, so I learned to fend for myself...but it wasn't pretty."

"Your mom never taught you to cook?"

"She liked taking care of 'her boys,' as she called me, my dad, and my brothers. I never imagined a time she wouldn't be here to do it." Thoughts of my parents and years we should still have together always drag me into a pensive mood. I can't go there right now. This is my alone time with Bethany. I have to take advantage of it. "In fairness, she did teach me some basics before I moved out of the house, so I can scramble an egg, make tacos, even toss together a no-frills lasagna. That's about it. Who taught you? Your mom?"

Bethany shakes her head. "Since Mom wasn't around much, an older neighbor taught me. Patti lived alone since her jerk of a husband left her for a friend of their daughter's and the other kids had moved away. She and I spent a lot of time together when I was in junior high since she loved to cook, and I enjoyed learning. She was kind. It was nice."

Though their mutual loneliness tossed them together, I can tell Bethany was genuinely fond of the woman. "Where is Patti now? Still in your old neighborhood?"

For a long moment, she doesn't answer. "My freshman year of high school, I went to her house to tell her that I'd been invited to a slumber party by this really popular girl and to ask if she'd help me bake awesome brownies to take. When I knocked, she didn't answer, even though her car was out front. I waited a few minutes in case she was in the shower or something, then I let myself in with my key so I could check on her."

Dread tightens my stomach. "Was she dead?"

"Yeah." Sadness mutes her expression.

"Heart attack?"

Losing my dad decimated me, and I'm a grown-ass man. I can only imagine how traumatic losing a maternal figure as a kid must have impacted Bethany.

"No. She'd hung herself."

Oh, shit. Being left behind sucks. So does the hurting, grieving, and clinging to happier times. But to lose a loved one to a death so preventable?

"How old were you?"

"Eleven."

"You must have been devastated."

Bethany nods as she sautés the onions. I can't see her face since she's focused on the stove, but my money is that, on top of an already emotional day, she's fighting tears.

"I'm sorry, sweetheart."

"The worst part was, she didn't leave a note. She didn't say good-bye. She just…"

The squeak in her voice tugs at my heart. As much as my head tells me I shouldn't empathize with her until I figure out how guilty she is, I can't be unmoved. At the moment, I can't even bring myself to care whether she scammed clients' money or not.

Maybe the big picture I've been missing is that Bethany Banks endured a childhood full of disappointments, thanks to the adults around her. How was she supposed to learn to care about others when she had almost zero examples to follow? How was she supposed to truly understand the trauma she'd leave in her swindling wake if no one ever showed her empathy or compassion?

I vault to my feet and cross the kitchen, wrapping my hands around her delicate shoulders. "Beth…"

She sniffles. "I'm okay. I just haven't let myself think about Patti Robbins in years. And watching Kailani's birth this morning was…intense."

"Totally."

"So I'm just emotional. It will pass."

She scoops half the onions onto a spoon and drops them to the heating skillet on her left, then cracks two eggs in each pan. They sizzle. The savory smells begin to meld. My stomach growls. But all my thoughts are with the complicated woman I'm holding in my arms.

"You must think I'm pitiful." She dabs at her eyes. "Every story I tell you about my past is sad. I'm not an unhappy person."

Maybe, but she's not exactly filled with joy, either. I'm trying to decide what to attribute that to. Guilt? Or events far more tragic?

"You don't have to pretend to be all right for me."

"I'm not. I promise." She sets thin slices of the cheese down around the firming eggs and throws the cherry tomatoes into another pan. "It's just that I haven't had time to reflect on anything in…well, pretty much a decade. Until I came here, I worked constantly and moved fast. Yesterday's events quickly became irrelevant. My focus was always on tomorrow. Now that everything has changed and I'm…I don't know, getting in touch with myself?…all these memories and feelings are flooding back." A self-deprecating laugh follows. "I promise, I'll get myself together."

"You are together," I assure her, caressing her shoulders. "Can I do anything to help?"

"You are, just by being here and listening to me."

I'm glad that's how she sees the situation, but if she's actually innocent and figures out I've been hanging on her every word simply to gain her trust and use whatever she divulges against her? I'll be another asshole in a long line of them who have used, hurt, and mistreated her.

But I'm here for justice, not to exploit her.

Another nagging voice in my head asks, if Dad knew I felt this much empathy for the woman who may have, even inadvertently, caused his death, would he be rolling in his grave?

That's a question I'd rather not answer. I need to stay on task.

"Beth, something happened to you recently, didn't it? Why did you come to Hawaii?"

She pops two pieces of sourdough in the toaster, then removes the cherry tomatoes from the third pan before dividing them equally between the first two. "We always talk about me, and I never get a chance to ask about you. Why did you move to North Dakota?"

Hard change of subject. I'm not surprised. Bethany doesn't let many people inside her life or thoughts. Learning who she really is— and deciding what she's capable of—is going to require more time.

The one commodity I'm running out of.

Negotiations for my dad's business will probably resume tomorrow since the buyers seem eager. I'll have to head back to California to sign the papers soon and move the last of Dad's stuff out of the offices.

While I'm there, I'll visit Bret at UCLA, then try to slip up the coast to check in on Bry in Santa Barbara.

"You'll laugh," I tell her. "I went to North Dakota because I wanted to make money, and I read on the internet—which makes me sound really stupid in retrospect—that I could earn a lot of cash doing industrial work there. I like jobs that require both brains and brawn, and it was a drastic change of pace from where I grew up. I was determined to be independent. At first, everything was great. I have to admit, though, that after the first couple of snows, the novelty of the white stuff wore off."

And the house I built there seems tainted by the ghost of tragedy. Every time I walk in, I see my dad lying dead on the floor. And on the rare occasions I'm there now, I can't wait to leave.

"Still think you'll go back in the spring?"

Though I'm beginning to wonder if that's the right move, where else would I move? "Yeah."

"But no girlfriend back there? I remember that from last night." She gives me a little smile as she plates the toast, slaps on some butter, then sets a bit of spinach on top of our sizzling scrambles. "Can you do your job anywhere besides North Dakota?"

"Not really." I could move to Texas or Alaska or a few other oil-producing states, but I'd only be starting all over again in a business where it's hard to gain a foothold.

"Do you still like your job? Is it what you always wanted to do?"

"I like it, but I'm not sure I see myself doing it forever. The hours suck. It can be backbreaking. And it's hard to find reliable people." I laugh at myself. "Growing up I really wanted to be a rock star. Unfortunately, when I tried to sing…the feedback wasn't super positive. So I had to give that up. What about you? I know you haven't always been a waitress."

"No."

"What was your last job? You said you were a paper pusher…"

"Pretty much. I was good at it, too, but…" She trails off with a regretful shrug. "When I was a kid, I wanted to be a chef when I grew up. My father told me it was a waste of my intelligence."

And never mind what she wanted to do? "Seriously?"

She nods. "My IQ is why everyone I went to school with thought I was a freak."

"Just how smart are you?"

Sliding hot skillets across the stone countertops as spinach leaves curl with the heat is a stall tactic. "Enough to get me into the Harvard MBA program at seventeen."

I already knew that, but when I think about what a feat that is, she amazes me. "Wow."

"So…yeah. Dig in. I hope it's good. High protein, a few veggies, some healthy fat."

"It looks as spectacular as it smells," I praise her in all honesty.

"Thanks. Tabasco? Salsa?" She plucks both bottles out of the fridge before sliding two forks and two napkins in my direction, then settling onto the stool beside me.

"Maybe." I watch her pour a liberal amount of Tabasco on hers. "Are you going to be able to feel your tongue later?"

Bethany laughs. "I like things spicy. What can I say?"

I like things spicy, too. Maybe not food, but women? Yes, please. The one beside me has so many facets, and the longer I spend with her the more of her personality I glimpse. The more I find myself liking her…despite the fact it isn't smart.

"All right." I sprinkle a little on to be adventurous, then I take my first bite. The combination of flavors hits my tongue. I don't even think about what I'm saying before the words slip out. "Mmmm… This is amazing. We should get married."

The light trill of her laughter fills the air. "I'm glad you like it, but marriage seems a bit drastic for food. How about, since we're friends, I promise to feed you if you're hungry?"

"Deal."

Parts south love the notion of her sating all my hungers. But that's lust talking. It would be dangerous to get in any deeper right now.

We eat in silence that feels thick with awareness. She's so close that with every lift of her fork, her elbow brushes my arm. Whether I want to feel it or not, desire simmers in my blood. Why can't I get my head and my body on the same page?

"What are you going to sightsee today?" she asks.

I glance at the clock on the microwave. "The sun will be down in a few hours, so it's probably too late. I'll do it another day."

Bethany places a hand over mine. "I'm sorry you missed out."

"I didn't. I got to spend the time with you."

Her cheeks flush as she looks up at me from beneath the fringe of her lashes. "I'm really glad you were here today. I felt less like a third wheel. And you're really easy to talk to. Thanks."

I quash my guilt. I enjoy talking to Bethany—way more than I should. And I hate feeling disingenuous. "You're welcome."

She bites her lip like she's gathering her words and her courage. "If you don't have plans, I'd like it if you stayed a while."

She's going out of her way to ask for time with me. That's a first. Because she's starting to trust me? Because she's ready to open up?

"I'd like that. It would be more entertaining than going back to Ash's place to warm his sofa alone. He's working tonight. After that, he'll probably spend more time with Montana. What did you have in mind?"

"Would you mind helping me do something for Maxon, Keeley, and baby Kailani?"

"Sure. What are you thinking?"

"They've been so gracious, opening up their house to me when they didn't have to. They're letting me stay in the cottage—sorry, ohana—out back for free, which is the most lucrative room on their property, just so I can have some peace and privacy. It's really sweet, but I feel bad about taking advantage of their hospitality. I've been making my way in life for a long time, and I'm not about to quit. Since I'm saving my money to move out—hopefully next week—I can't buy them anything. They seem to have everything a newborn could need anyway. But I can whip up some dinners for them to reheat next week while I'm at work. That way, they'll only have to focus on the baby."

There's her thoughtful streak that confuses me every time she shows it. Bethany is willing to use her lone day off, stand on feet that surely feel overtaxed, to make the lives of the people around her better. Could this same woman have stolen millions from her clients?

"That's really sweet of you."

She shrugs. "I wish I could do more, but I want to help my brother and his wife in some meaningful way so they know I'm thinking of them."

"Then I'm happy to stay." I swallow down another bite and try not to moan in pleasure. "I don't know how much help I'll be since I suck in the kitchen…"

"How are your furniture assembly skills?"

"Much better."

"Good. That's where I'm terrible. Maxon didn't get time to put together the baby's changing table. It was backordered for weeks and it just arrived. So if you don't mind helping, I'd like to surprise them."

"No problem."

We finish up our meal in minutes, then rise from the breakfast bar and head back into the kitchen.

"You start the food. I'll do our dishes," I offer.

"You sure?" She seems surprised.

"Yeah. That's one thing my mother taught me really well."

With her melodic laughter in my ears, I tackle the dirty plates and pans with a grin. Then it hits me that I enjoy making Bethany smile.

That's so dangerous…

When I've finished loading the dishwasher, I turn to find several casseroles in progress. Lasagna, I recognize. Everything else? I have no clue.

I watch in awe as Bethany tosses together seven dishes without once glancing at a recipe. She makes it look effortless, and she manages to slide lasagna, baked ziti, black bean enchiladas, butternut squash and spinach ravioli, a gumbo bake, and chicken Alfredo pie into the refrigerator ninety minutes later with minimal help from me.

"That was impressive, woman!" Even my mother would have been amazed.

She waves me away. "It was fun. And now all they have to do is heat the casseroles up when they want to eat. Should we tackle this changing table before it gets too dark?"

"Lead the way."

Bethany and I hit the garage and find Maxon's tool stash, then we head for the baby's nursery. I stop in the doorway. Soft grays and cheerful white fill the space, accented with a touch of pink and topped off with a chandelier. Everything looks plush and inviting and ready for the arrival of their newborn—except the changing table still in pieces.

We find the instructions. They're written in pseudo-English that's almost impossible to follow. After a lot of confusion—I hate cam bolts—and laughter at the puny Allen wrench included, we finish assembling the changing table. Together, we move the piece to the blank wall by the window and complete the task by filling the appointed cubbies with stacks of tiny diapers and packs of baby wipes.

Clean-up takes less than five minutes. The sun is just setting. Our timing is perfect.

"Everything looks great. They're going to be so happy." Bethany looks my way, wearing a smile. "I couldn't have done it without you. Thanks."

"My pleasure. This baby is going to be so loved, I can tell."

"Yeah." She sounds wistful.

I turn to her. "You okay?"

She shrugs as she flips off the light and leads me back into the great room. "Still emotional, I guess. Since we left the birthing center, I've felt jumbled and I've been trying to put my finger on what's bugging me. My life is a mess. I have no one to blame but myself for that. But this is something else." She tilts her head and regards me with solemn eyes. "Have you ever believed something deep down, then been stunned when you've realized it wasn't true?"

"Can't say I have."

She sighs. "Then what I'm thinking probably won't make sense."

"Try me. Doesn't mean I can't listen." Is she somehow realizing that stealing would, in fact, hurt people? Is she grasping that by swindling her clients with her father she did wrong?

Bethany manages a hint of a smile. "You're a really amazing guy, you know. Tell me again, why aren't you taken?"

"I haven't been looking. What about you? You're smart, kind, and hardworking. Why aren't you taken?"

"I haven't been looking, either."

"So what's bugging you, Beth?"

She sighs. "I hate to dump this on you, but right now you're my only friend. I mean, that I'm not related to."

She sounds as if she's apologizing for having feelings. Or for wanting to share them. That disturbs me. So does hearing that she has almost no one in her life to talk to. Her admission should make me happy because I can exploit her loneliness to my advantage. Instead, I have to fight the urge to wrap her in my arms and assure her she's not alone anymore.

"Go on."

"It's hard to put into words." Bethany shrugs. "Maybe this will sound odd. But I'm still stunned and in awe from witnessing Kailani's birth."

"I feel the same," I admit. "But mostly stunned. I wasn't expecting *all* that."

Her light laughter surrounds me. "I'll bet. Sorry you got way more than you bargained for."

"Yeah, but it was…profound. It's something I'll never forget."

She nods. "The way it made me feel is a lot to process."

"Because?"

"I spent so long thinking I'd never have what Maxon and Keeley or any of my other siblings have. Marriage and babies were for someone else. I had a world to conquer. I had a glass ceiling to raise. I had an empire to learn. Nothing else really mattered. If I ever felt twinges of wistfulness for more, I always had plenty of work to squash them. All that was fine until I came here. My brothers and sister have these great marriages. And to hear them tell their stories, none of them reached this point without overcoming a lot of hardship, conflict, adversity, and fear."

"Fear?"

The curl of her lips is nothing short of self-deprecating. "Apparently all the Reeds are born with an innate aversion to emotion. Well, Maxon, Griff, Harlow, and I probably have growing up with our father to thank for that. But Evan struggled not to reject feelings, too. We've discussed this phenomenon and shared some about our upbringings." She shakes her head. "But I've been intentionally trying not to think about where I'm at in life or where I'm going, long term. Right now,

I'm focused on putting one foot in front of the other until life makes sense again. And so far—"

"Hang on. It sounds like your life fell apart. Are you sure you don't want to talk about that?" I try not to fire the question at her, but I'm dying to know if she'll admit the real reason she's in Hawaii.

She shakes her head. "It's a long story full of family drama, and I won't bore you. But today made me realize that feelings aren't wrong. There are more reasons to let someone close to you besides figuring out how you can use them."

"Yes," I confirm, instantly wondering what she means. How did she use people?

Again, she gives me an ironic smile. "That probably sounds obvious to you—and to most people. But it's a new way of thinking for me. If Maxon hadn't listened to his heart, Keeley wouldn't be his wife. Kailani wouldn't have been born today. Griff would still be a miserable bastard who hated Maxon and didn't know his son, Jamie, existed. He wouldn't have Britta or another baby on the way. Harlow would have kept her relationship with Noah to a fling. Evan would have stayed in Seattle, grieving the loss of a wife who didn't love him, rather than letting himself fall for Nia. But every one of my siblings made the choice to open themselves up to new possibilities, and their lives are all better for it. I can't help but wonder if I've been blind and I'm missing out."

Her speech is both a jolt and a gut punch. Did she really tell me all this because she's just now realizing that using people is wrong? Or is she trying to tell me she's receptive to more than friendship because she's fishing to find out how I feel about her?

My heart starts pounding. Hooking up with Bethany would be the most expedient way of getting closer to her. It would allow me intimate access into her psyche and her life. But I'm so conflicted about going there... Sex—even if I haven't stopped thinking about having it with her for days—would muddle my thoughts even more. And I hate the idea of screwing her literally merely so I can screw her figuratively.

On the other hand, if she's willing to open up about anything at all, I need to play along.

"Does the possibility of falling for someone scare you, Beth?"

"Scare? No. It terrifies me. What if they're not everything I think they are? Or need them to be?"

I try to shrug off my remorse. If she's innocent and if she wants me, I'll be the most thoughtful, attentive lover she's ever had. If she's guilty…then she should get what she deserves.

"What if they are?" I murmur.

"I don't know." She shrugs. "And what if I'm not enough for them? I've never stopped to think about what it would require to make a significant other happy."

"Are you thinking about it now?"

"Yes."

I shouldn't ask but… "Are you thinking about it with me?"

"We've only known each other for a few days."

Though she hedged, her face tells me that's exactly what she's thinking.

"That isn't what I asked. Have you thought about it with me, Beth?"

She hesitates, gnawing on her lip. "Yes."

I lean closer. God, this is so dangerous. My heart pounds and throbs. I'm aching to touch her. She has no idea how badly I want to give in…

"Even though you said you don't date co-workers and aren't looking for romance?"

An even longer hesitation. "Yes."

"What exactly are you thinking about, Beth?"

"Stop asking me questions and kiss me."

chapter SIX

*H*er whisper pelts my brain, heats my blood, stops my heart—stiffens my cock. "Are you sure, Beth? I think we should talk about this."

But talking is the last damn thing my body wants to do.

"Look, if you don't want to…" She ducks her head in mortification and turns away.

I pull her back to face me. "Oh, I do. But…" I scramble for an excuse to explain my reluctance. "You and I both need a friend right now. Let's make sure neither of us is mistaking loneliness for attachment."

"It's a kiss, not marriage."

"You're right. But once we cross the line…" *There's no going back.* Frankly, that's one of the few things stopping me from backing her against the wall, laying my mouth over hers, and stripping off her goddamn clothes.

"Really, just forget I said anything."

"Now that it's out there, I can't. So we need to work through this, especially since you're not the only one who's been thinking about it."

"Oh." She looks taken aback. "Well…the inn's guests will start wandering in here shortly for the evening wine and appetizers Keeley usually sets out. Britta's mom is taking care of it today, but if we want to talk privately, we should head to the ohana."

"Let's go."

As I press my hand to the small of her back—mostly because I can't keep my hands off her—Beth and I make our way out the back door, following the stone path to the cottage on stilts that's adjacent to the main house. Under the structure is a fenced-in lanai with a quaint table and chairs. Bethany makes her way up the stairs and opens the bright turquoise door.

Once we're inside, my gaze sweeps over the cozy space. A plush sofa invites a duo to snuggle. Windows all around provide both mountain and ocean views to enjoy. Exposed ceiling beams and tropical colors relax and soothe. A little kitchenette supplies sustenance when needed. But it's the big bed dominating the place that tells me this room was made for romance.

It's impossible not to picture Bethany lying across the white sheets, half-dressed, breathing hard, and waiting for me to peel off all the rest. I do my best to push the vision aside and focus, but it's not happening. All I want is her.

"This is really nice," I manage to say.

"They've done a great job with the place. Have a seat. Want a beer? Keeley keeps a few up here."

"Sure. Thanks."

As she opens me a cold one and pours herself a glass of white, I scan her room again. It's meticulous. Other than the suitcase on the luggage rack and another standing in the open closet, I would swear the room is vacant. I'm not surprised Bethany keeps the place neat and orderly. It fits her. My personal space is always a little more…relaxed.

Finally, she hands me the chilled bottle, then sinks beside me nervously, clutching her glass. "I'm sorry I pushed you to kiss me. I shouldn't have."

"I'm glad you did. It was bound to come up sooner or later anyway." I sip my brew and set it on the tray across the nearby ottoman. "Because like I said, I've been thinking about kissing you, too, Beth. I've been thinking about it a lot. I know your life is complicated now. So is mine."

"That's another reason I should never have said anything. I don't want to drag you into my problems."

"You're not dragging me. I'm willing to help you work through whatever's bothering you. We're friends, right? That's what friends do."

When we first met, lines like that were a necessary evil, and I had no problem saying whatever would get me into Bethany's good graces. Now? Unless she asked me to help her carry out the Reed Financial scheme, I think I'd do just about anything to ease her load.

Because I don't simply want her; I like her, too.

Fuck.

That inconvenient truth aside, I can't let my questions about her role in Dad's death go unanswered.

What the hell am I going to do? If I refuse Bethany tonight, I doubt she'll give me a second chance to touch her. If I give in, there's no way I'll be able to stop at just a kiss. Either way, she's going to tie me up in knots.

Fucking no-win situation.

"Thanks for the offer. But some things I need to work out myself. They're big and complicated."

I frown. "And I'm too young to understand?"

"No. I'm too scared to share, all right?"

Because of what she'll admit? Or what I'll think of her?

"Okay." I squeeze her hand. I can't push her any more now. "But I'm here for you."

"Thanks."

Suddenly, we're sitting in shadow illuminated by only the faintest hint of dusk eking through the windows. Her green eyes look so wide and uncertain. Her pale skin gleams. Her rosy lips and the way she nibbles that bottom one eat at my restraint.

"If we're really going to talk about this, I should turn on some lights and grab us a snack from the main house."

I suspect she's stalling, but that's okay. It gives me more time to think. "That would be great."

With a quiet nod, she rises and flips on a cozy table lamp before letting herself out of the cottage. She descends the stairs and disappears inside the inn.

The moment she's gone, I realize that I'm alone in her personal space and this may be my only opportunity to search it for clues. I have five minutes—tops—to figure out whether I need to put on the brakes with Bethany...or whether I can give in to the endless fucking need burning me to take her to bed.

I hate this. I wish I had a choice...but I can't pass up this opportunity.

Shoving down my niggle of reluctance, I fling open her suitcases, checking the side pockets and zippered compartments first to avoid ruffling her carefully folded clothes. They're empty. Other than a collection of shorts and T-shirts, I find nothing of note in the rest of her luggage. A few dresses and a couple of light sweaters hang from the overhead rack.

Next, I yank open the dresser on the far side of the bed. Panties in muted colors—some lacy and downright sweat-inducing—line the bottom. Delicate matching bras are nested and stacked beside them. The rest of the drawers net a collection of bikinis, socks, scarves, and tanks. No papers. No thumb drives. No files of any kind. Of course, it doesn't help that I don't know what I'm looking for other than something that tells me whether Bethany Banks is guilty.

She doesn't have a computer that I can see. Maybe she left it in San Diego. Maybe the feds confiscated it. I don't know. But damn it, the clock is ticking, so I keep moving.

Quickly, I sweep the bathroom. She keeps the counter clear of personal items. In the cabinet, I find nothing out of the ordinary— makeup, deodorant, shampoo, shower gel, and the like. There's no incriminating evidence, unless you count tampons and birth control pills.

Darting back to the main room, I visually sweep the cottage again and spot her purse on the kitchenette counter. The display on my phone tells me she's been gone four minutes.

Stop or keep searching? I don't want to be caught, but if I quit now, will I get another chance to inspect her personal space again?

Biting back a curse, I reach for the magnetic closure on her quilted pale pink purse. The golden logo across the front proclaims the bag is Chanel. Inside, there's one main compartment containing mints, a mini hairbrush, a few tubes of lipstick, and a compact—but nothing incriminating, nothing that gives me a reason to mentally convict her.

I also find a small ring with two keys. One I saw her use to let us into this unit. The other… I don't know what it opens, but I know what it doesn't: any sort of safe deposit or strong box. My best guess is that it unlocks her apartment in San Diego.

Next, I troll through her matching Chanel wallet, feeling guiltier by the moment for invading her privacy because it's seeming more and more like she's done nothing…except make me second-guess everything I thought I knew.

Her driver's license, ATM card, and credit cards galore take up all the slots. She doesn't have a lot of cash on hand—mostly small, wrinkled bills people have left as tips, but her posh purse tells me she must have money somewhere. Same with all the plastic. But I keep coming back to the fundamental question: why the fuck is she working as a cocktail waitress when she's way too educated for the job? Either she's hiding here while maintaining a low profile to ensure people cool down and look the other way before she hits up her stolen stash and starts living her bougie life, or she's innocent, the feds and her father have stripped her of everything, and she's just trying to survive.

Which fucking possibility is the right one?

Tucked inside a compartment I nearly missed is a card from an FBI agent, Trevor Forsythe. I've never heard of this guy, but I whip out my phone, take a picture of his digits, then slide it back into place. I'll pursue that later. But there's nothing else of note here, and I have the same damn questions I did before I invaded her personal belongings without her consent.

Finally, I reach for her phone. It's password protected, no surprise. Bethany isn't stupid, and I'm at another dead end.

When I hear soft footsteps making their way up the stairs, I shove everything in her bag once more. I'm not going to make it back to the sofa in time, so I'll have to lie to her. Again. This is really bugging the shit out of me.

Behind me, the door opens. Wincing, I peek in the nearest cabinet. "Hey, I was just seeing if there was a glass I could pour the beer into. Found one."

When I turn, she's looking at me suspiciously. I don't blame her. What self-respecting beer drinker wants their cold beer poured into a room temperature mug?

"Let me put it in the freezer for you, at least for a few minutes." She takes it from my hand.

There she is again, thinking of others. "Thanks."

As I settle back onto the sofa, she handles the mug, then sets a plate of cheese and crackers, along with some fresh pineapple, grapes, and mangos, in front of us. "Help yourself."

I'm not hungry, but I've already been an impolite bastard. I can choke down a few bites to make her effort worthwhile. "Thanks. You should eat, too. You've worked hard the last couple of hours."

She gives me a wan smile as she plucks a grape between her fingers. I reach for a cracker and watch her, shoving down guilt and grappling for conversation, when she sucks the fruit between her lips, closing her eyes as she bites.

Watching her is a sexual experience that makes me instantly hard. And when she lets out an unconscious moan, the urge to kiss her, strip her down, and fuck her hits me even harder. Feeling like a heel, I drag in a shuddering breath.

Jesus, what am I going to do?

She swallows and lifts her wine. "You know, you're the first man who's ever wanted to discuss whether we should kiss before we actually did. I'm not sure if I should be flattered you're taking this so seriously or feel rejected because you put me off."

I need to decide how to proceed, but my head is at war with my gut. Both keep tangling with my libido until I'm one giant clusterfuck. But everything boils down to two increasingly obvious facts: One, the desire I feel for this woman isn't going away. The more I get to know her, the more I want her. Two, though my quick search of her ohana is hardly comprehensive, I haven't seen a single shred of evidence that Bethany is guilty…and everything about her behavior so far says she's not.

It's possible the feds didn't arrest her is because she really is innocent. It's possible she's been through a lot, and I've just been an asshole on a witch hunt. It's possible the quiet, caring woman I've been trying to resist these last few days is the real Bethany Banks.

It's also possible that's what I want to believe because I'm falling for her.

Fuck, I could talk myself in circles all day. I have to make a decision now, so I'm going with my gut. The Beth I've come to know isn't the kind to steal from anyone. So I'm going to stifle my suspicions and believe she's innocent…unless I prove her guilty. Until then, I'm going to treat her not like a suspect but like a woman.

Like my lover.

"When you put it like that, I sound like an idiot," I quip. "If you still want me to kiss you, I'm beyond happy to do it."

Five seconds slide by as she sends me a considering stare.

Whether she means to or not, she's making me wait. Anticipation screams through my blood. The thought of finally touching her is so fucking turning me on.

"If you're sure you want to…"

"Yeah, Beth. I *really* do."

I can say that with all honesty.

With a nervous nod, she tilts her head up to me. Her eyes slide shut as she waits.

My heart thumps as I cup my fingers around her nape and stare. God, she's going to be a sensory treat; I can already tell. Her skin here is ridiculously soft. Her braid caresses the back of my hand in a silky graze. I'll explore every inch of her eventually. Right now, I'm fixated on her delicate jaw in my palm as I caress her pouty lower lip with my thumb.

As I lean in to kiss her, she surprises me by staying me with a palm on my chest. "But Clint? One thing… I've never been vulnerable to a lover. Ever. I'm trusting you. Please don't make me regret it."

Her plea gouges my conscience. "Beth…"

Shit. Maybe I should come clean here and now, explain everything, and give her the opportunity to tell me the truth in turn.

As I'm weighing the pros and cons, she wraps her arms around my neck, pulls herself against my body, and slants her lips across mine.

Then I forget everything.

Her kiss is an instant jolt of lust. My heart stops, then starts to thud dangerously. I drag in a breath to control the hot surge of lust, but it's useless. Desire pours through my veins like lava, scalding every inch with need.

I yank her closer, fastening my mouth over hers, and tumble her back against the arm of the sofa. As my body covers hers, I revel in her indrawn gasp. Impossibly, my desire notches up again. Impatiently, I part her lips with my own and sink into her.

Oh, hell yes.

Against me, Bethany melts, tilting her head to admit me deeper.

Groaning and greedy for more, I give her exactly what she silently begs me for.

Fuck, she smells so sultry and sugary sweet. She fits against me, every curve and swell, like she belongs here. She kisses like she's hungry, and I'm her dessert. The way she tastes is something I've fantasized about a hundred times, but now that I *know* her shy, sweet-tart flavor? I'm going to crave it every time I don't have my mouth on her.

The endless kiss goes on. Our tongues caress in a fevered frenzy. I get dizzy. She makes me sweat. Ache. Need. What little restraint I have goes up in flames.

A warning voice in my head reminds me that Bethany merely asked me to kiss her. I should probably leave it there until our situation is less complicated. But now that I've got my mouth and hands on her...I don't have the will to stop.

"Beth, what do you want?"

"More," she breathes.

Her reply goes straight to my dick.

Taking her face in my hands, I angle my mouth over hers again and sweep inside, plunging deeper. God, everything about her is flipping my switch in a way I've never felt. A week ago I would have said this woman wasn't my type. Too quiet, too delicate, too controlled. Now? Every fantasy I'm having is about mussing her up and making her scream.

"Beth... Fuck, yes." I pant as I drag my lips across her jaw to whisper against her ear. "I've wanted to do this since the moment I saw you."

A little smile curls the corners of her lips. "I wasn't sure why you were staring. It unnerved me, so I looked past you."

"All that made me do was want to look more." I kiss her again because I can't help it, but I nearly lose myself when I taste more of her sweetness. "You're the reason I said no to Montana. Even when you were barely speaking to me, I wanted you. There was no way I could think of her. You crowded everyone else out."

She looks stunned. "You said we were friends."

"We were. And we are. But I've always wanted more." I may have been dishonest about the reason I sought her out, but I can't not be honest about that.

"Even though my life is such a mess?"

"You're not the only one."

"Does it bother you that you're younger than me?"

Is she actually hung up on that? "Why should it?"

She considers that for a long moment. "You're right. These days, my dad never seduces a female older than half his age. Why shouldn't I be with whomever I want?"

"He can have all those girls." I take her face in my hands. "I want a woman. I want you."

When I lunge in and crush Bethany against me again, she meets me in a rough, breathless tangle of lips and arms. Beneath me, she unfurls, opening to me, luring me farther inside, sliding her tongue against mine. I'm kissing her as deeply as I can, but I still crave more.

I haven't taken Bethany to bed yet, but I already know that one night with her isn't going to be enough.

Admittedly, over the last decade, I've had a lot of sex with more than a few women, so I know my usual response to a hookup. This isn't it. Hell, this doesn't even feel sane. Right now, I'll do anything to sate the gnawing need to sink inside Bethany and know what it feels like when she's mine.

My hands wander down her back, molding to her sides, clutching her hips, before I cup her ass and lure her against me. Her snug denim is in my way, and I hope she lets me peel it off soon so I can feel the woman underneath. But I have to take this at her speed. As revved up as I am, she might not be ready for more than a blistering kiss or two. And maybe me going back to Ash's place to take a long masturbatory shower to thoughts of Bethany would be for the best. It certainly wouldn't be the first time.

Suddenly, she tears her lips from mine, harsh breaths filling the air as she grabs the hem of my shirt and jerks it halfway up my torso. "Take it off."

She doesn't have to ask me twice.

With one fist, I yank it from my body, then toss it across the room.

With another, I grip her hair and angle her mouth beneath mine so I can kiss her deeply again.

Bethany moans and meets me halfway, her fingers digging into my shoulders. She kisses me back as if nothing in the world matters more to her right now than being with me.

I can't keep my hands off her. They roam under her lacy tank, traversing the soft skin of her back. When I reach her bra strap, I want to pry it open so fucking bad. But I hesitate. Is she ready for this?

"Do it," she whispers as she rains kisses on my neck.

"You're sure?"

She cocks a brow. "Would you rather I keep it on?"

"Hell no. I want you totally bare. I want to see your breasts—touch them, suck them, torment them." When a shiver wracks her body, I press on. "I want to watch you writhe for me, hear you scream for me."

"Ambitious?" she pants.

"Confident."

Bethany reacts like a woman who hasn't been touched enough lately. Or maybe ever. Then again, when I'm with her, I feel as if I'm ravenous—and she's my ideal banquet. Our electric, erotic chemistry is no joke. Whatever happens between us is going to be more than explosive.

With a shake of her head, she gives me a shove and peels off her delicate tank to reveal a lacy beige strapless bra. The swells of her breasts rising above her slender waist and her smooth, peachy skin have my eyes bulging and my mouth watering.

Yeah, the bra needs to go—now.

Clutching her hips, I drag her closer, my lips falling automatically to claim hers again as I wrench the hooks of her bra open. The second the garment is free, I toss it in the vague direction I lobbed my shirt. Then I press our chests together, bare skin to skin.

She gasps. "Clint…"

My palms roam the soft flesh of her back. Fuck, she feels like warm velvet. I'm dying to know the weight of her breasts in my palms, in my mouth.

"Yeah?" My voice sounds rough.

She looks into my eyes. "Are you going to do more than kiss me?"

Hell yeah, I am. "I would never keep a lady waiting."

When she sends me a lazy-lidded smile, my heart chugs. Fuck, she's sexy when she's flirting with me. Bethany is usually so serious, so her little tease is a thrill.

Desperate now, I drag my lips down her neck and ease back onto my knees. The sofa isn't going to work for what I have in mind, but I'll worry about that in a minute. Right now, I'm fixated on her breasts.

Holy gorgeous nipples. I like boobs. No, I *love* boobs. They're my thing on a woman. When I first meet an attractive female, I look at her eyes, glance at her mouth, then see what God or her plastic surgeon implanted inside her chest. It's not very evolved, I know...but I'm a guy.

With Bethany, I'm perfectly happy with quality over quantity. I've seen better-endowed women topless, but her breasts might be the most beautiful, symmetrical pair I've ever laid eyes on.

"Oh, sweetheart..." I cradle one in each hand.

At my touch, she jolts, and when I rake my thumbs across the tips, she inhales sharply.

I smile like the ravenous bastard I am. "Do you like your nipples sucked?"

"I guess." She sounds breathless but hesitant. And slightly confused.

Does she not know the answer to my question? The possibility that every man she's ever slept with has been a bumbling dipshit in bed weirdly thrills me. I love the idea of being the first to blow her doors off.

I can't resist toying with her. "Is there any part you don't you like?"

She bites her lip and wriggles as if she's unnerved by the way I'm cupping her breasts and staring. "The part where they lick them like I'm a lollipop. Or when they blow on them. What is that?"

"Ineptitude. Let me try, Beth. If you don't like it, stop me. In fact, any time I do something you don't like, I expect you to let me know."

The sideways glance she shoots me tells me she's surprised. "And your ego won't take a nose dive?"

"No. Every woman likes something different. That's cool. I can adjust because I already know sex between us is going to be amazing. I want to make sure you find it amazing, too."

Her body relaxes. "Okay."

When I focus on her curves rather than the conversation, she tenses. I bet she's expecting me to pounce on her tits, do something that doesn't stimulate her, and ignore the rest of her until I decide to thrust and grunt and come.

Balancing my hands on the arm of the sofa, I lean in and brush a kiss against her lips. Instantly I realize I'm going to need another. But a second buss becomes a long melding of lips. After that, I have to taste her again, see if her flavor is really as addicting as I recall.

The second my tongue slides against hers, I know the answer is yes. I groan and lean in, kissing her in heated sweeps, searching every last corner of her for untapped flavor.

She clings to me, whimpering. I don't know whether she's conscious of her legs gently parting around me or not, but crouched in front of her, I sure as hell am.

Finally, I manage to break the spell of her kiss to trail my lips down her neck, licking and nibbling on the way. I nip at her collarbone, earning an excited little gasp. My thumb brushes one taut nipple before I lave my way down the swell of her breast, then lift her straining tip to my mouth.

I tease her with a hot exhalation before I close my lips around the point and kiss it softly. It beads tighter, the surrounding flesh crinkling and flushing darker. I smile.

"Like it so far?"

"Uh-huh." Her reply is breathless.

"What else?"

"I'm anxious. Waiting. My stomach is in knots. My heart…"

"Is racing?"

She gives me a shaky nod. "The closer you come, the faster it gets."

"Good." I pet her, then press another kiss to the side of her breast. "Let's try more."

"Hurry."

Her answering plea is a rushed breath that makes me grin. Holding her pleasure in my hands, suspending it for my own dirty thrill, makes sweat bead at my temples and my cock throb in need.

"Remember, tell me if you don't like this…"

As aroused as she seems now, there's almost zero chance of that. Vaguely, I wonder if her past lovers haven't bothered much with foreplay or just didn't care about her experience. Then the hard bead of her nipple is against my lips, and I don't care about anything but pleasing her.

Slowly, I open my mouth and ease her breast inside. Her ragged inhalation as I close my lips around the hard crest and give it a gentle pull almost undoes me.

She gasps. Her entire back goes taut. Whether she means to or not, she thrusts her breasts toward me. "Yes…"

I moan in understanding, reveling when she closes her eyes and sinks into the moment.

Then I tug harder, the suction stretching her nipple against my tongue, pulling on it with friction.

Bethany braces her hands on my shoulders, her eyes flaring wide. "Oh!"

So she likes her nipples stimulated and she likes a little edge. We're going to get along so, so well…

Lifting her free breast into my other hand, I pinch the hard point. "I don't want this one to feel neglected."

"N-no. Oh…yeah." Her head falls back, over the arm of the sofa, and she reveals the vulnerable arch of her throat to me. She's trembling and flushing—and she's not doing a single thing to hide it.

God, her reactions are everything I could have wanted—visible, honest, and arousing as fuck.

I give the nipple in my mouth one last hard tug before I release the other from my grip, swirl my tongue around it, and watch her shudder.

She digs her fingers deeper into my flesh. "Clint…"

I give her taut crest a firm, almost savage pull before releasing her. "Something you want to say?"

She gives me a slow, dazed shake of her head. "Just…more."

"Keep doing it? Or do it harder?" I coax. I think I know the answer, but I love the idea of her telling me exactly how to undo her carefully buttoned-up facade.

"Both," she manages to whisper.

"Yeah?"

I nip one tip with my teeth and delight in her indrawn breath. Then I switch to the other, laving it in long, luxurious strokes, prepping and priming it until she's squirming and arching her back in a silent plea.

"Hm-huh." Her affirmative cry is almost incoherent because it's damn near a wail.

Am I the first man to actually arouse her? The way she responds, as if she's surprised by her body, suggests that's the case.

This time, I don't hold back. I give her tender breast a little squeeze, then lift it directly onto my tongue before I close around her. She pants. I take a long draw of her, one suckle after another. She writhes. I nip down with the edge of my teeth. She keens, parts her legs wider, and wraps her hands around my neck to force me closer.

"You're so sexy," I mutter against her flesh. "I want to do this to you half the night. I want to see how swollen and hard I can make your nipples. Then I want to use my fingers and tongue to find out just how wet I make your pussy."

"I'm already drenched," she admits. "I'm aching."

"Good." I keep thumbing her nipples, alternately gliding and pinching. "You ever felt this aroused while your pants were still on?"

She blinks at me, mossy eyes bright, wide, and hazy. "I've never felt like this at all."

Is she actually admitting she's never, ever been aroused?

Holy shit. That's terrible…and yet it turns me on like nothing else.

I brush away a strand of hair clinging to her lips, then kiss her rosy mouth, tasting her sweetness even as I keep toying with the taut peaks of her breasts.

"Still want me to give you more?"

Bethany hesitates for a mere instant. "I don't know whether I'll go up in flames or just explode, but…don't stop."

"Good. I wasn't planning to."

The second my words are out, Bethany surges up, collides into me, then tumbles me onto my back before straddling me. Her lips burn across mine with feverish need. Mashing her breasts against my chest, she sighs into me as her fingers walk across my skin, exploring with inquisitive brushes here, a teasing drag of her fingernails there. "I can't seem to get close enough to you."

Shuddering, I caress my way down the sleek line of her spine. "I can't get close enough, either."

Bethany sits up and slides her way down my body until her ass is perched on my thighs. I gotta say, the view is spectacular. Plush pink breasts sit high above her narrow rib cage and the long, lean line of her torso. Her cute little belly button peeks above the waistband of her jeans that cling to every dip and curve.

But she doesn't notice my perusal. She's too busy gaping at me. "How much time do you spend in the gym? I thought abs like these were for celebrities and bodybuilders."

I laugh. But before I can answer, her finger traces the line bisecting my abdominals from stern to naval. Her jolt of a touch makes my flesh quiver with electricity.

My breaths pick up speed when her fingers wander south of my waistband. Slowly, she drags one curious finger past the button fastening my jeans, then down to my fly, until she's tracing the ridge of my aching cock.

I buck as if she burned me. I'm so aroused that my skin feels as if it's on fire. How can she undo me with one itty-bitty touch? "Fuck…"

"Do you want to?"

When she drags her finger back up my engorged shaft, I can't follow her question. "Want to what?"

"Fuck." She bites her lip, and I can tell she's nervous. "Me, I mean."

Does she think there's any way at all this doesn't end with me on top of her, plowing deep inside her, making her feel every inch of me?

I grab her wrist to stop her wandering fingers. "Oh, yeah. I want you naked, panting, and wailing for me."

With a shaking breath, she wrenches free and attacks my fly, practically tearing away my button and clawing at my zipper.

After my last trip to the gym, I wore my spare pair of clean underwear, so once she yanks my fly open, my bare cock all but springs into her eager hands.

The feel of her fingers wrapping around me is mind-bending, spine-melting. Incredible. "Oh, my god…"

She strokes every bit of my length she can reach, fingertips skimming the sensitive head. A tremor quakes me. I know it's been a long while since I had sex, but even after my longest dry spell, the sensations were never this intense.

"What are you doing to me?" I groan.

"Trying to make you feel good."

"You're succeeding."

Bethany's fingertips dance up my cock again as she gives me a bad-girl grin that makes me shiver.

Shit, no matter how much I'd love to let her have her way with me, I have to take control of the situation. I can't think of another time or another woman who's undone me so thoroughly and so easily. It's a little terrifying.

Gathering my resolve, I wrap my arms around her and haul her closer.

She yelps in surprise, wrapping her arms and legs around me as I stand. "What are you doing?"

"Getting you someplace more comfortable, where I can spread you out and fuck you." I flip off the light by the sofa and make my way to the bed. "Lose the pants."

She licks her lips nervously. "And the underwear?"

I send her a wolfish smile as I kick off my shoes and jeans. "Leave those to me."

With a shaky bob of her head, she complies while I fish a condom from my pocket. I only have two. *Damn it.*

I forget my problem as I watch her shimmy out of her denim. I've seen those sleek thighs in shorts, and the sight is mighty nice. But getting to view the whole package almost fully unwrapped? I swallow. Stare. She's even hotter than I thought.

And her strappy, pale-pink panties are nothing short of a visual sin. Two sets of thin straps crisscrossing under her naval reveal tantalizing glimpses of her flat abdomen. Under those little bands of silk, the garment plunges to a lacy vee, intersecting just above her pussy to—barely—cover the essentials.

My tongue belongs there.

"Say something," she begs. "You're just staring."

It seems impossible that she's feeling insecure, but I hear it in her voice. "Oh, sweetheart... You are sexy as hell. I'm going to eat those panties off your body."

A flush steals across her skin from head to toe. Time to get busy.

After tossing the condoms on the nightstand, I lift Bethany and drape her across the middle of the bed, shoving tropical-colored pillows out of my way and onto the floor. Then I crawl above her, looking down at her gleaming like a pearl in the evening shadows. She's focused completely on me, on us, on what will happen next.

She stuns me when she trails her fingers down my chest, over my abs, and wraps hers fingers around my cock again. "I'm waiting."

"Are you trying to rush me?"

"If you're still wondering, I must not be doing this right." She strokes my length again, harder, faster.

Somehow, I resist the urge to let my eyes roll into the back of my head and lose myself. "You're doing more than fine, sweetheart. Trust me."

In fact, the longer she's got me in her hand, the more I feel my skin go damp and my system buzz with need. If I don't stop her, this is going to be over way before I'm ready.

I twist away from her, tangle my fingers in hers, and pin her wandering hand to the bed. "But I'm a gentleman. Ladies come first."

Her lips part in a soft, open-mouthed *O* as I work my way down her body, pressing kisses to the undersides of her breasts, her abdomen, and between the sexy crisscrossed straps of her panties before I open my mouth over the pink lace covering her pussy.

Bethany wasn't lying; she's drenched. Through the fabric, I smell her. I taste a hint of her essence that only leaves me hungry for more. I feel how swollen and juicy she is.

"So fucking sweet," I moan.

She shudders and cries out as I drag my tongue up the lace, then prod her clit through the lace. "Oh!"

"If you're at all attached to these panties, you should take them off now. If you leave me to do it, I can't guarantee they'll be wearable tomorrow."

"Okay." She wraps her thumbs around the straps at her hips.

Though I want her naked, I resent having to take my mouth off her and I'm even harder-pressed to give her the space to strip. With a curse, I ease up and flip on the closest light so I can see every inch of her, especially her face when I thrust deep and fill her up.

I turn just in time to see her wriggle her panties down her thighs and into a puddle on the floor. Then I get my first view of her completely naked. "Oh, sweetheart… Give that pretty pussy to me now."

I back her onto the bed and wedge myself between her legs. She falls to her elbows, watching me, eyes dark with desire. I prowl closer until I flatten her onto her back. It takes all my restraint not to fit my hips between her spread thighs, probe for her wet opening, and plunge my throbbing length inside her.

Instead, I lave her hard, juicy nipples and draw each, one after the other, into my mouth, eliciting another catch of breath from Bethany. Then I let my lips trail down her body once more until the Shangri-La of her pink, neatly trimmed sex is right under my lips. She's wet and swollen. Her clit peeks out from between her folds, begging for attention.

I cup her with my hand. Her entire body shudders as her eyes close. She lets out a long, agonized breath. "Clint…"

"Hmm, I'm here. And I'm staying here for a good, long while. Spread your legs wider."

She trembles as she complies. "I-I don't need to be more aroused for sex. Believe me, I'm more than ready."

"We're going to get there, I promise. First, I need this perfect peach of a pussy in my mouth."

Thankfully, she doesn't protest.

With a growl, I rake my tongue up her center, lapping at her sweetness and reveling in her shocked little moan, before I settle on her clit.

Her fingers find their way into my hair, and she tugs, hips wriggling, as I work the hard bud.

"Oh, my…" Her back arches. "Oh. *Oh…yes.*"

The sound of her pleasure resonates through every nerve and cell in my body. Once, I swore I'd never give her an orgasm. Now I can't fucking wait. There's something so kittenish and sensual about Bethany. If I had to bet whether any of her former lovers had ever gone down on her, I'd gamble everything I owned the answer is no. Being her first is turning me the fuck on.

Happily, I redouble my efforts. I'm glad now that I've always enjoyed being oral with females. It won't take me long to learn what stroke of my tongue will send her over the fastest. And I'll definitely enjoy figuring it out.

Soon, I settle into a slow, draggy rhythm, teasing her with long strokes before I lazily suck her clit into my mouth and pull, taunt her with a little nip, then release her to start all over again. Soon, she's tensing, holding her breath, squirming and panting and begging.

"Clint... Oh, please. Please. I..." Her next breath trembles, along with the rest of her body. "You're killing me."

"Hmm," I drawl, unwilling to take my mouth off her succulent flesh.

I love the way she swells and blushes and grips my hair, trying to pull the short strands. The sting of my scalp spurs me on, makes me want to taste her on a deeper level.

With my thumbs, I part her rosy folds and peek at all her sweet pink flesh. She's beautiful all over, but hell, this must be the most perfect pussy I've ever seen, especially when I'm watching her whole body twist and writhe with the pleasure I'm giving her. And maybe I only think she's so ideal because I'm in the moment. Maybe she's really not any better put-together than any other woman. But I don't remember similar thoughts ever crossing my mind.

I dip my tongue deep in her well, drawing from the source of her flavor. Fuck, I want her everywhere—on me, around me, under me. Arousing her is pushing me close to the brink. I need to send her over and end my self-torture.

I've got to get inside her.

As I curl my tongue deeper, I circle my thumb around her distended clit in slow circles. She wails in agony, back contorting. Her skin is rosy all over. She struggles to breathe. And she looks so goddamn beautiful in pleasure I can hardly remember why I ever refused to give her any.

"I-I'm…so close."

Fuck, yeah, she is. I can feel it, taste it, sense it.

I grip her hips, sweep my tongue back over her clit, and lap my way into the rhythm I know will undo her. Seconds later, she digs her nails into my scalp, thrusts frantic hips up at me, and saws air in and out of her lungs before she screams like I've devastated her with the kind of pleasure that's changed her definition of the word. And I'm loving every second of her orgasm, the smooth flow of honey, the undulating roll of her body as she tries to wring every last moment of ecstasy out of her climax and share it with me.

Finally, she falls limply to the bed, breathing deep and fast, legs lax. Beautiful satiation transforms her face.

I drink her expression in as I grab a condom before making my way up her body, kissing one hip bone and dragging my tongue over the soft valley between her breasts. Then I settle on top of her.

"Am I alive?" she asks with a loopy grin.

"You are," I assure her. "In about two minutes, I'll happily prove it again."

She shakes her head. "In two minutes, I'll still be lying here with my eyes closed, trying to comprehend what just happened."

I laugh as I peel open the condom and roll it down my aching cock. "Not a chance. Come here, sweetheart."

When I gather Bethany in my arms, she shifts to her side with me, soft and instantly willing to cuddle. It feels good to have her against me, trusting me enough to hold her close when she's vulnerable.

Stroking my palm across her skin, I glide down her back, over the cheek of her ass, across her thigh. Needing more of her nearness, I lift her leg over my hip and press kisses across her shoulder, up her neck, take teasing nips of her lobe. Her eyes flare wide with surprise and rekindling arousal.

I send her a knowing smile before I brush her lips with a kiss. "Hi."

"Hi."

I press my mouth to hers again, this time nudging her open. As soon as she parts for me, I invade deep, fusing our lips together as I roll her to her back and align my cock with her opening. I probe her, gliding inside her—one slick, tight inch at a time. She wraps her legs around me, gasping as I slowly submerge myself all the way.

Oh, damn… Being buried inside Bethany is almost a sacred experience. A shudder wracks me from head to toe. A groan tears from my chest. My hands tighten on her hips. I want to keep her pinned under me for each thrust as much as I want to feel her in my grip and be assured that she's mine.

I tear my lips from hers. "Hold on, this is going to be hard and fast."

"Yes…please."

That's all I needed to hear.

Like a man possessed, I grip the far edge of the mattress and use it as leverage to fuck her in deep, rapid-fire strokes. Her lips trailing across my jaw and her arms wrapped around me like she hopes I never let go does something to me. But the way her pussy grips me is magic. With every retreat and surge inside her, I swear she melts my muscles, ignites my skin, and fries my brain.

"Yes!" I use every bit of my strength to pull myself up and into her, even deeper than before. "Fuck…"

"Clint!" Her lips move in a flurry of frenetic need across my shoulder. "I ache again. How?"

Around me she tightens, wails, fingers digging desperately into me. I can't last much longer. Bethany is destroying my self-control. Being inside her and hearing her climbing cries of passion juices my bloodstream with pure, dizzying euphoria. I can't stop myself from plowing into her one hard, pounding stroke after another.

"Come for me," I growl out. "Come…"

It's my last coherent thought before bliss rolls me. The sensations only grow more intense when Bethany tosses her head back and clamps down on me with a violent, shattering scream. As she comes apart in my arms, I unravel. Blood rushes. My heart pounds. My body grinds, churning closer and closer to a climax that I swear feels cataclysmic and unlike anything I've ever termed an orgasm in my life. It's stripping me down, ripping me up, fucking rooting me to this woman. I should be terrified. Instead, it can't get here fast enough.

When the peak finally hits, it seizes my whole body. My rhythm falters. I try to get impossibly deeper inside her. Even though it's hopeless, I still sweat and growl and charge ahead, pouring out every ounce of need into her. Something thick and unfamiliar backfills its place. I can't identify it, but it's sweet. It attaches me to Bethany in a way I've never felt. It makes me grip her harder, spill the last drops of my soul into her, and cling as if only she can somehow save me.

As if, regardless of who she is or what's happened in the past, with her is where I belong.

chapter SEVEN

*D*awn is a promise on the horizon when I slip out of Bethany's cottage and tiptoe to the main house. She's still sleeping, wrapped in the limp sheets and cozy blankets we shared last night.

Other than Bethany, I can't remember the last woman I actually slept beside for more than an hour or two. I usually don't like touching a lover in my sleep. But, as seems to be the case with a lot of things, she's different. All night, Bethany kept curling away from me on the far side of the bed. More than once, I rolled closer and dragged her body against me, wrapping my arm around her waist and burying my face in her neck. I woke up to her scent, to the feel of her backside against my cock, which stood hard and eager to pleasure her again after a peaceful, uninterrupted night's sleep.

Since Dad's sudden death, that's unusual, too.

I let myself in the main house's back door, hoping not to see anyone, and promise myself I'll start mentally unpacking last night after coffee.

As the brew drips into a spare carafe, I rummage around to find some fruit and a few pastries Keeley keeps on hand. As I toss everything onto a tray I find in the pantry, my phone buzzes. I almost ignore it—until I see the display.

"Bret?" I answer my middle brother. "You okay?"

"Yeah. Just checking in, making sure you're okay. Happy New Year, bro."

"Sorry I didn't call yesterday. Tending bar the other night was a bitch. I think my feet are still recovering," I try to joke, all the while wondering why Bret is calling so early…and what I'm going to tell him about Bethany. I know how he'll view the situation—and that he'll see what's happening between her and me as a betrayal.

"It's cool. I would have called sooner myself, but man, was I hungover. I'm so glad class doesn't start for a couple of weeks."

"Yeah. Listen, not to nag, but it's time to lay off the booze and start focusing on the future again."

He's quiet for a very long time. "Yeah, I know. And I know you've had it way worse than me, watching Dad die and being helpless to stop it. But I keep realizing that I'm twenty-one, and both of my parents are already gone. Basically, I'm an orphan. And every time I think about doing things like finding my first job, buying my first house, or getting married without them giving me advice or cheering me on, it scares the shit out of me. I've got no safety net."

I understand exactly how he feels, but he's wrong. "I know it's not the same, but you've got me. I'll always be here for you. I don't profess to know everything, but I promise I'll help you figure it out as best I can."

He sighs. "Yeah, and I appreciate it. I'm aware that I need to adult and to stop leaning on parties and vodka to get through this shit. I'm just trying to figure out how. It will be easier once you nail that fucking bitch. How's it going, by the way? Get anything from her yet?"

I wince. What the hell do I say? Bret is convinced that if I pin Dad's death on Bethany, his pain will vanish. Looking back, I pretty much thought the same.

"Listen… Now that I'm here and looking into all the facts, I think we may have gotten it wrong. She's not who you think."

"What does that mean?"

"Based on what I've been able to find, I don't think she was involved with the theft of Dad's money."

"What? How is that even possible?" he shoots back hotly. "She was his financial advisor. She had the pulse on his investments. According to you, she fucking lied to him, didn't care that he died of a massive heart attack after he got the news, then skipped town. What suddenly changed?"

"Bethany and I work together, so I've spent some time actually getting to know her. She doesn't have a greedy or vicious bone in her body. I even had the chance to search her place and found nothing incriminating. I just don't think she did it." When he answers me with shocked silence, I feel compelled to fill the void. "Bret, there are two sides to every story. I don't know all of hers yet but—"

"Oh, my god. You fucked her, didn't you?" my brother growls.

I swallow. "The situation is more complicated than—"

"Bullshit! You got some from her and decided that her pussy is more important than Dad's justice. I can't fucking believe you."

Shit, Bret is pissed, which makes him almost impossible to reason with. Still, I have to try. Yeah, I admit the cynic in me still harbors niggling doubt about Bethany and wonders if I'm being played by a maestro. But I can't admit my reservations to my brother. Innocent until proven guilty, right? Ninety-nine percent of me is not sorry about what happened last night, and I won't let him guilt me into regretting the intimacy Bethany and I shared.

"Stop. Think. Do you want to know what happened to Dad and the money or not? I'm not going to get whatever information she has about the criminal operation at Reed Financial by being an asshole. She may be the only person who can tell us, so don't judge. You're not here. You don't know what's happening. You don't know her. And you don't know what she's been through."

"Whatever. I hope you can live with putting your dick above your family. Just don't cry to me when she fucks you over, too."

Suddenly, I hear three beeps in my ear and scowl. The little shit hung up on me? I shouldn't be shocked. Bret has always been a rash hothead. I wish like fuck he would think things through before he acts.

Gritting my teeth, I shove my phone in my pocket. Now isn't the time to reason with him. Sure, I know why he's upset. I understand what my actions look like on the surface, but he shouldn't judge without the facts. Once I can answer the questions we've all had since the day I told him Dad was gone, he'll come around. For now, I'm going to focus on Bethany and earning her trust so she'll tell me her secrets. No, we probably don't have a future. That sucks because I actually like her, and we seriously had the best sex ever. But someday —soon—I'll have to come clean with her. Hell, she doesn't even know my real last name. And once she figures out who I am, she might even hate me.

Unless we're stronger before I confess… Unless the feelings between us genuinely grow and she's willing to forgive…

Because lying and deceit are totally the ways to persuade her not to lump you in the douchebag category.

Okay, I'll have to try plan B, then—once I figure out what that is.

But what if Bret is right? that annoying voice asks me. *What if she is guilty?* Nope. I can't let myself think about the fact I could be falling for the woman who contributed to my father's demise.

The coffee finishes brewing, and I balance it all on the tray before I head back to Bethany's cottage. Inside, I set everything on the kitchen counter, then tiptoe to the bed.

At my approach, she rolls over and opens her eyes.

The sight of her is a gut punch. Her pale hair splays across the sheets. Her half-closed eyes look slumberous and sexy as hell. But the little smile curling up her lips makes me want to strip down and persuade her to repeat last night right now.

"Morning," she murmurs, voice husky.

Just like that, I'm hard again.

I clear my throat. "Morning. I found some food and coffee at the main house."

She moans, something between acknowledgment and pleasure, then hides a lazy yawn behind her hand. "Thank you. That's really sweet. Would you mind grabbing my robe off the back of the bathroom door?"

It's on the tip of my tongue to remind her that I've already seen it all, but if that makes her feel comfortable, I'll do it.

"Sure." I grab the pale blue satin garment and hand it to her.

"Thanks."

"Want me to pour you some java?"

"Please. Can you add a splash of cream from the fridge and a stevia packet from the cabinet to the left?"

"You got it."

By the time I've done that, Bethany rounds the corner to claim her steaming mug, robe securely belted around her small waist…which only accentuates the fact she's not wearing a bra. I can see the points of her nipples. I remember what they felt like, tasted like. I remember how she responds to my touch.

She clutches the mug, blowing on her brew to cool it, not quite meeting my gaze.

I swallow down a scalding sip of my own and try not to seduce her, at least not before caffeine.

With a sigh, I set my java aside and grab her by the waist. "Come here."

Bethany is stiff until I nestle her against me and press a gentle kiss to her lips. Finally, she blinks up at me. "You make good coffee."

"You make good everything else. Last night was…" I grin at her. "Let's just say I wanted to blow your doors off, but I'm the one dazzled." When she blushes, I can't help but laugh. "We're good together. How are you feeling about it?"

She frowns. "You actually want to talk about this?"

"You don't?"

"I guess we could. It's just that I expected…"

"What? For me to roll you on your back and do you again without saying a word? Or for you to wake and find me gone because I decided to skip out?"

"Either."

I can only imagine she expects that because someone taught her to. "Was Dalton the morning-after jackass?"

"He was one of them." She nibbles on her lip nervously, gaze not wavering from the brew in her mug. "But he was the one who hurt the most."

I tuck a stray strand of hair behind her ear. "Want to tell me about him?"

She shakes her head. "He's not important."

"I'm not trying to make you uncomfortable, Beth. But I need to know what you want to happen between us next."

"I don't know."

"Now that we've had a night of fun, are you having thoughts about kicking me to the curb?"

"I wouldn't have said yes in the first place if I didn't like you enough to want more than a hookup. But I don't have any expectations," she's quick to assure me. "I just appreciate you being so…kind."

I'm not following. "Kind?"

A soft blush stains her cheeks. "Caring about my pleasure. I've only had that once before, and even then—"

"Seriously?"

"That's weird to you, huh? Sex was just never that important. Now I see the big deal." She gives me a nervous laugh.

It's shocking to hear Beth confirm the suspicions I had last night. It blows my mind that a woman as gorgeous and responsive in bed as Bethany has only had one sexual partner before me who gave a shit about her pleasure. I'm not going to ask if she's picked up all her exes at Douchebags R Us. And I'm not listening to that voice in the back of my head—the one that sounds a lot like Bret's—telling me I shouldn't be giving her orgasms now. Because what really matters is what happens next.

"It was a big deal for me, too." And while I'm being honest, I might as well admit something else. "It felt special."

In fact, I'm not only relieved that I need to spend more time with her to find out what she knows about the Reed Financial scheme, I *want* to spend time with her. If she were any other woman, I'd already be thinking this relationship might turn serious.

Instead of smiling, she nods pensively. "It's almost too bad we can't have more than sex."

Frowning, I sit and pull her onto my lap. "Why can't we?"

"Like I've said, there's a lot going on in my life. I don't know how long I'll be on the island. Or how long you'll be here, for that matter. Still…" She squirms. "It's only fair of me to tell you that…I'm not exactly who you think I am."

I try to act completely casual, as if I'm not thrilled she might be on the verge of admitting something useful. "What do you mean? You're not Beth?"

"You've heard my family call me Bethany."

"Yeah, I figured you liked using your nickname at work or something."

"It's…more complicated than that." She presses her lips together. "Remember I told you that my dad and I aren't speaking, that our relationship is messed up?"

"Yeah."

"He's done some illegal things and he's probably going to prison for a long time. Before you ask, yes, I'm shocked and I'm saddened. But all this has put me in a really awkward position. People who knew and trusted me have turned on me. Even those I've worked with for years suddenly seem to have their pitchforks in hand, and they're coming after me."

"Guilt by association?"

"Pretty much. The guy in the loud Hawaiian shirt who keeps hounding me? He's a former client. I've known him for a decade."

The asshole's behavior makes more sense now, but it's still not okay. He doesn't get to verbally or physically harass Bethany for answers.

Is what you're doing any better?

I shove aside the nagging voice. "What does he think you can tell him? Do you actually know anything about what your dad was busted for?"

She sighs and rises, clearly uncomfortable with the conversation. "I can't really talk about it."

I try to tamp down my disappointment. It was unrealistic to hope that after one night she was going to spill all her secrets. But I want like hell to end this subterfuge, tell her who I am, admit my unexpected feelings so we can move past this. Maybe she cares enough about us to stay with me.

"I'd like to help you, but I can't if I don't understand."

"I appreciate that, but there's nothing you can do now. I just thought you should know I'm kind of off-balance and I have been since my professional life fell apart. I'll figure it out, but everything happened so recently. It's been a lot."

"Off-balance in what way?"

"Men who once worked around or under me used to call me ball-buster and ice queen and all the other unflattering, misogynistic terms for a smart, confident female. That's how I see myself. This shy, stuttering, uncertain person you know? I'm not her."

That explains the hints of assertiveness she showed me last night. And I feel good about that because she wouldn't have demanded anything she wanted sexually if she didn't feel comfortable with me. "I think you're awesome, even if you are feeling a little uncertain right now. If you ever want to talk, I'll listen and help you however I can."

Bethany smiles gently. "Thanks. I just wanted you to understand. I should also tell you that I might have to leave suddenly."

That makes me panic. "Leave?"

"I'll be called to testify, but I have no idea when. It could be next week or two years from now."

"As a witness for the prosecution? Or the defense?"

"Either. Both." She shrugs. "Anything is possible. Can we change the subject?"

I grasp all her reasons for being secretive, but I can't stay in limbo. I need answers. I'll need to deal with Bret's shit soon. I also need to get back to my life. I'd like to stop lying to Bethany. And I'm going to have to deal with the unexpected attachment I'm feeling to her somehow.

"Sure. Just…if you leave, don't forget me." I caress her face. "I'm not going to forget you anytime soon."

"Believe me, I won't." She bites her lip, this time to suppress a smile. "You have another condom, right?"

Despite all the problems, I grin. "Yes, ma'am. I do."

"And we don't have to be to work until four this afternoon."

"Yes, ma'am, that's right." I clasp her hips and drag her closer.

"I promised I'd help Britta's mom serve breakfast for the inn's guests, but I've got an hour or so. What do you say we put that condom to good use?"

I love the way she flirts—and lets me part her robe to see all her naked skin underneath gleaming in the morning sun. "I always like to make a lady happy…"

After breakfast in bed that was way more bed than breakfast, I leave Bethany's ohana with a big smile on my face. Unfortunately, during the drive back to Ash's place for a shower and a change of clothes, reality intrudes.

Bethany is slowly opening up to me, but at this rate it might be weeks or months before she divulges everything. I don't have that long. Sure, Howie, who's running my business back home, is reliable and capable. But I'll have to return to North Dakota and oversee operations again soon, or the reputation of the oil services business I've spent more than five years building will all swirl down the toilet.

That means I need to start digging around to see if I can uncover any dirt myself.

From the console of Ash's crappy sedan, I grab my phone. While I'm idling at a stoplight, I scroll through the device until I find the picture I took of the card I uncovered in Bethany's wallet. Trying not to register the tremor in my hands, I dial the FBI agent's digits. I'm almost positive I'm going to get voice mail.

Trevor Forsythe answers on the first ring. "Hello?"

"Agent Forsythe, my name is Clinton Holmes. My father was one of the victims of the Reed Financial fiasco."

He pauses. "I'm listening."

"I'm calling for some information. I know Barclay Reed was arrested and is currently out on bail…"

"Yes."

"I read an official statement a few weeks back that you've arrested all suspects in the case. Is that still true? Do you have any additional suspects you're now pursuing?"

As soon as the words are out of my mouth, I wince. This guy doesn't know me at all. He can't even verify that I am who I say I am. He's not going to tell me a fucking thing.

"I'm not at liberty to discuss this case beyond the statements we've already issued."

Of course not. "Look, my father only ever had contact with Reed's daughter, Bethany Banks. I understand she was his right hand for a decade. She kept a full list of clients and supposedly managed their money, yet all their funds—in addition to those of Reed's own clients—disappeared. I watched my father fucking die of a heart attack the day he realized all his money was gone…" My voice is getting louder, and have to choke back the desperation in my tone. "Sorry. I'm personally impacted by this case, so I'm trying to understand her involvement and if there have been any inroads in recovering the money. And I'd like to see *all* the perpetrators brought to justice."

Getting Dad's savings back would at least be a consolation prize. But I'm far more focused on Barclay Reed—and anyone else responsible—going to prison.

"I'm not at liberty to discuss that either, sir. Parts of the investigation are still ongoing."

"But you've already determined Ms. Banks is innocent?"

"Mr. Holmes, I really can't say anything beyond the statement we've already issued that indicates Ms. Banks won't be charged with a crime. When the case goes to trial, the prosecution will lay out its case. Then you and the rest of the public will hear the details. Until then, I'm afraid I can't offer you any other information."

"But—"

"No. You want answers. I don't blame you. But I have a lot of victims to look out for," he points out. "I'm sorry for your loss."

The line goes dead.

With a snarl, I smash the button on my phone and resist the urge to hurl it into the windshield. I don't need another goddamn dead end.

The next twenty minutes of traffic, coupled with an impromptu rain shower, don't brighten my mood. Sure, I had a great night with Bethany. I'd like to have more. But I'd like to do it with a clear fucking conscience. I don't know how or if I can make that happen.

I shove the key in the lock, surprised to find Ash standing in the kitchen, chowing down on some Cheerios.

"Hey! Have a good night?" he asks with a waggle of his brows. "Since you didn't come home, I figured something good happened."

I pocket my phone, rake a hand through my mussed hair, and intentionally ignore his question. "I didn't expect you to be here."

"After work last night, Montana and I came here for a while. But early this morning, we decided that we've scratched our mutual itch, so she left about seven, waved sayonara…and we're done."

"You cool with that?"

"Yeah. She was fun, but there was nothing else between us."

I get that. "You know Samantha likes you, right?"

Ash looks surprised. "Why would you think that?"

"Are you kidding? Every time you left with Montana, she gave you longing looks as you two walked away."

"Huh. I totally missed that. I must be off my game." He shakes his head. "But now that I know… She's cute, not my usual. I might be interested. So what's going on with you and Beth?"

With a frustrated huff, I plop down on the cheap living room sofa. "Dude, I don't even know. I'm being pulled in so many different directions… What if she's guilty? What if she's not?"

"None of that would matter if you didn't like her."

I nod. "I more than like her. I think there's something real between us. As much as I've fought it…"

"You didn't expect to give a shit about the enemy."

"Yeah, and she's not at all what I expected. Besides being fucking sexy, she seems really sweet."

"Got any ideas what to do next?"

"Keep searching for information wherever I can, I guess. But it looks like I have to be patient until something gives."

I hate this plan, especially since I worry what Bret will do. He's not going to let our fight this morning go. And what happens if Bethany finds out I've been less than honest? She's been burned. She finds it hard to trust. She'll hate me if she learns the truth before I'm ready to tell her.

"Wish I had something brilliant to say, but you're right," Ash says.

I nod. "Maybe day drinking is the answer. Vodka is sounding wise right about now."

He barks out a laugh. "I don't know, man… I've asked tequila for advice, and when I've listened, it's been shitty."

"Good point."

With that, Ash tosses on a clean tank, says he's out to the gym, then disappears. I spend most of the day either Googling, napping, or pondering. Finally, it's time to head to the bar. After a quick text to Bethany, she assures me that Griff is giving her a ride to work since he's already headed in that direction. I arrive a few minutes before our shift. Despite all the doubt and uncertainty, the anticipation of seeing her again is way stronger. Excitement tightens my gut.

Right or wrong, I want to be near this woman. I want to see her smile. Hell, I want to give her reasons to smile—and not just for the sex, though that's amazing, too. I want her to smile because she's with me.

God, I have it bad.

When I duck into the bar, I expect to see Bethany setting her purse down, grabbing a tray, and wiping tables clean as she gets ready for what's sure to be another busy night of tourists partying their way through a holiday week in paradise. Yesterday's hangovers are a memory now, and a lot of these visitors know they only have another day or two here, so they're likely planning to make the most of them.

What I don't expect to see is Bethany sitting in the quietest corner of the place, holding hands with a stranger.

I stop. Stare. Scowl.

Who the fuck is he?

"That's a development I didn't see coming," Ash mutters in my ear.

A million things run through my head. Bethany said she wasn't into relationships right now. She said she'd only had one decent sexual experience in her life, so the odds of her reconnecting with an ex seem slim. I've already met all her siblings. Even if I hadn't, these two aren't looking at one another like family.

What pisses me off even more? She's crying.

Clenching my fists, I charge toward the far end of the bar.

Ash grabs my arm and holds me back. "Don't march over there and throw around accusations. It won't end well."

"Who is this fucker? Why is she letting him touch her?" I hiss. "And why the hell is he upsetting her?"

"I don't know, but you need to calm down. Did Beth promise you exclusivity?"

"No, but—"

"Then there is no but. You two spent a night together. That's it. That entitles you to nothing."

He's right, but that only pisses me off more. "I can't let him upset her."

Or put his hands on her.

"I get that. So why don't you make your way over there and ask in a friendly-like way if everything is all right. Anything else is likely to sound like an accusation and upset her more."

"Fine." I jerk my arm free and suck in seething breaths, trying to calm myself as I head closer.

It's a long twenty seconds, and they seem so wrapped up in their conversation—and each other—that neither even looks my way.

Until I clear my throat.

Bethany blinks up, spots me, and jerks her hands from the other man's. She looks pale. Though she's wiped away her tears, I still see the hint of wetness on her cheeks.

Whatever the fuck is happening, I feel like ripping this dude's head off.

"Clint." She jumps to her feet. "Hi."

This other guy is practically crawling across the table to put his hands on her, and that's all she says to me?

Maybe Ash is right. Maybe there's some explanation. I can't act like a jealous, overprotective prick…even if I feel like one.

"Everything okay?"

She lets out a shuddering breath. "Yeah. This is Stephen Lund." Then she turns to the tall, rangy guy with blond movie-star looks and a placating smile I want to punch from his face. "Stephen, this is Clint Dietrich. We…work together."

I shake his hand and glare directly into blue eyes a few shades lighter than mine. "Nice to meet you. Just to be clear, we're also dating."

Lund busts out laughing. Not exactly the reaction I was expecting… He's not surprised? Or pissed? Or wondering what the hell is going on? I sure am…

"I kind of guessed that. Bethany has always had a habit of keeping her personal life and thoughts private. I learned long ago to read between the lines." His grin widens. "But let's just say you made it a lot easier."

She rolls her eyes and slaps at his arm in a gesture that almost looks brotherly. Now I'm confused. What *is* their relationship?

"Glad we cleared the air," I say. "How long ago?"

"What?"

Since you fucked her? "Did you learn to read between the lines?"

"Oh…" He nods. "About two decades ago. I probably would have learned sooner, but we were just kids."

They grew up together? But they're not together?

"You two can stop talking about me as if I'm not here." Bethany scowls. "I'm going to clock in. I haven't done that yet. Stephen, be nice," she admonishes. "Clint, I'm fine. Don't worry."

With that, she disappears into the employees-only area.

I turn back to her supposed pal. "So you've known Beth a long time?"

He nods. "Her whole life. You haven't, and my guess is you'd like some dirt?"

Obviously, he can read me. I hate that, but it's not going to stop me from asking questions and hoping I get answers. "That would be helpful."

"How long do we have?" He glances toward the hallway where Bethany disappeared.

"Maybe three minutes."

"How serious are you about her?"

"It's new, but I definitely have feelings I didn't expect."

He flashes me a wide smile. "Good. She deserves some happiness."

"She told me there's a lot going on with her father." I fish for information.

"Yeah, it's a shit show. Look, I'm just here to talk to her. I've been on the island for a couple of days, staying with Harlow and Noah— where she would have crashed if she hadn't found out I was coming. It's a long story; I'll let her tell it. Bottom line is, she knows I'm not mad. Nothing is her fault."

Was he somehow impacted by the Reed Financial scam? I can't ask. If Stephen mentions the question to Bethany, it will give everything away. Instead, I bite my tongue.

"What's she like?" I ask instead. "I've only known Beth for a few days, and she says she's not herself right now. She's had some reservations because of her situation and the fact I'm a few years younger. I'm falling fast," I admit. "So I'd appreciate some help."

His eyes narrow. He's assessing me, gauging my authenticity. "I think she's figuring out who she really is. She's lived a very structured life until recently. She's always had a lot of expectations heaped on her shoulders. She was constantly overloaded and had to shove aside her personal life. Now, she's feeling her way through a new reality. But underneath all that, she's caring. Sensitive." He frowns. "She needs friends, and I'm trying to be here for her. So don't fuck with her. She's had enough of that to last her a lifetime."

I open my mouth to ask him what the hell that means. How is he trying to be here for her?

But Bethany appears beside us, a little frown knitting her brow. "You're not still talking about me, I hope."

"Maybe a little." He winks. "Like I was saying, I've got a car on the island and when I find a rental I like, you can crash with me if you want. In a spare bedroom," he adds hastily. "And I'll be happy to drive you home tonight to save Maxon the trip."

"I got it," I cut in.

Yeah, I don't exactly have a car of my own, just like I know who she rides with is her choice. I also understand she and Lund are "friends." But I don't know anything about this guy except that he's roughly her age, he cares about her, and that I see some sort of intimacy between them I don't like.

"You sure you don't mind?" she asks me. "It's so far out of your way."

"No problem." I'll figure out the details later.

"All right." The other guy shrugs. "Call me if you change your mind."

"Sure. My next day off is Sunday. If you still have time for dinner then, I'm up for that."

"Let's do it. I'll call you." He gives her a dazzling grin, then enfolds her in his arms and kisses her cheek like he has every right to touch her. "Good to see you again, shorty. Nice to meet you, man." He waves at me. "Talk to you."

Then he's gone. I don't dislike him. He seems okay. But he knows far more about Beth than I probably ever will, so in that moment I despise him.

Still, I can't do anything except grind my jaw, count backward from a hundred, and try not to sounds like a possessive asshole. I've never felt this way. I don't even know where this animosity is coming from.

"Hey, guys!" Andy shouts across the bar, and all the waitstaff comes running to the hallway.

Trying to shove down my annoyance, I follow, then listen as our mostly absent manager regales us with crap about a stopped-up toilet, a fraudulent string of credit cards, the wine shipment that's late because of the holidays, and the fact that Terry is still out with the flu.

I can't even grab a word with Bethany before an unexpected rain shower becomes a downpour. Drenched tourists rush in and the crowd suddenly goes from easily manageable to utterly insane.

By the time I look up again, it's nearly ten p.m. Hours have passed in a blur. I've seen Bethany, but I haven't been able to focus on where she is and if she's all right.

A quick glance tells me she's bustling from one table to another, dropping off the drinks I just mixed, before she wipes her hands on a dishtowel hanging from her waistband, grabs her tray like it's a shield, and heads to the back corner.

Mr. Loud Hawaiian Shirt is waiting, and she looks nervous as she approaches.

I can't hear them, but I can see he's agitated, and she's defensive. My gut says this is going to get out of line fast.

"I'll be right back," I tell Ash as I storm out from behind the bar.

Stephen's drop-in agitated me, but this guy's bullying is sending my temper over the edge.

As busy as we've been, Ash doesn't argue. Or maybe I don't hear. Whatever. Former client or not, this guy isn't manhandling or bruising Beth anymore.

"—the fuck happened," he spits. "I'm entitled to—"

"Beth…" I put a protective arm around her. "Go. I got this."

She turns to me, startled. "That's okay. I can do this."

"You can, but you don't have to."

There's that indecisive little nibble on her lip again. She's weighing the situation, probably her sense of responsibility, which is great, versus her fear and loathing, which seem pretty mighty, too.

"You sure?" she says finally.

"Oh, that's it," snarls the asshole. "Run away. Get your knight in shining armor to protect you. He must think you're a helpless little damsel in distress. Ha! He doesn't know the teeth and claws you have. He doesn't know that pretty facade he probably likes to fuck holds an ugly bitch inside."

"That's enough," I growl at him, urging Beth away from the confrontation. "Tell me what you'd like to drink or leave. Beth is a waitress, not a punching bag."

The guy slams his beefy fist on the table. "You don't get it. You look at her and you see a pretty piece of ass. I see a hustler. I see a criminal. Watch your money, pal. If you have any, she'll fuck it out of you, too."

He scrapes the chair across the floor and lurches to his feet, almost knocking the table over.

My heart freezes in my chest. What is he saying? That Bethany has had sex with him? When? Why?

Before I know what I'm doing, I'm chasing him to the exit—and barely keeping my hands off his throat. "What the hell does that mean?"

"Exactly what it sounds like. That sweet little thing you keep defending? I got ten minutes of pleasure out of her. And nothing but endless shit in the last six months."

He's talking about *my Beth* like she's one step above a whore. "Who the hell do you think you are?"

"If you have to ask, you might try paying attention to the news, kid."

I resent this guy on so many levels right now. But he's a former client. He has a story if he's here night after night, trying to get some sort of restitution or pound of flesh out of Bethany.

"I'm not a fucking kid. And I'm a lot more familiar with the news than you think. What the hell do you think she can give you at this point?"

Surprise bounces across his face, then he stares back in speculation. "She can return the money that belongs to me."

I swallow. I have to be careful here. I can't let on too much in case he says something to Bethany, and he's hardly an ally. But there are two sides to every story. I can't ask my dad his side anymore. This fortyish windbag is the only other client of Reed Financial I've ever met face to face.

"What if she doesn't know where it is?"

"She damn well should. I trusted her with my money for five years. Hell, I handed her a check for seven million dollars two days before Barclay Reed was arrested. She promised to personally see to it. You keep thinking she's innocent if it makes you feel better about fucking her. But I'm telling you, she's not the sweet thing you think."

Then he's gone. And I'm so angry I'm shaking.

Yes, this guy was a victim of the financial scheme, just like my dad. Instead of succumbing to the shock, he chose to fight back. He's entitled to be angry. Seven million is a lot of money. And I get that he's looking for someone to blame. I was once, too.

But what he's doing isn't cool.

This asshole will be back, I have no doubt. He wants his money, of course. But he's full of righteous, pent-up rage and seemingly desperate for revenge. I need to protect Bethany because I have a feeling he's capable of far more destructive things than hurling insults.

Why did she ever let this man touch her? He might not be terrible to look at, but he's an angry, vile misogynist. The way he talks about her, as if he sees no value in her... She *is* smart and kind. He thinks I don't know her? Ha! He's the one who doesn't.

That knowledge is my only consolation, because I don't understand anything else that's happened in the last ten minutes.

The only other thing I know is that I need to talk to Bethany ASAP.

chapter EIGHT

"You're quiet," Bethany remarks on our drive back to Maxon and Keeley's inn.

As I steer through the inky night, away from civilization, I tap my thumb against the steering wheel. The silence during our ride feels sharp. It's ratcheted up my tension. I don't want to hurl accusations at her, and I don't want to argue while I'm driving. But waiting hours to get this off my chest has pushed my mood someplace ugly.

"A lot on my mind," I say finally.

"You're wondering about my relationship with Stephen."

"Among other things, yes."

He's not the first problem on my mind. I'm also deeply disturbed by everything her former client spewed. But since she brought Lund up, maybe I've cooled down enough to talk about him. The asshole? How do I deal with the knowledge that she had sex with someone who feels nothing but contempt for her? How do I even ask why?

She sighs. "When you walked in and saw Stephen holding my hands, you probably thought we seemed cozy and romantic. But it's not like that."

"So you've never been to bed with Lund?"

I'm hoping like hell she says no. Instead, a flush steals across her face.

"He's been a good friend my whole life. His father and mine were cronies and golfing buddies. Sometimes, all of us spent weekends together and had barbecues... He's comfortable."

I grip the wheel harder. There's a whole lot she's not telling me, including the fact they—at some point—fucked. No, I don't own her. But I want to understand what's going on between them now.

"Then why did he think you weren't speaking to him? Why did you stay with Maxon and Keeley to avoid him at Noah and Harlow's place?"

She rolls her eyes. "Of course he told you."

"He said you would explain."

"All right. Remember I said that my father had gotten a friend's daughter pregnant? I was talking about Douglas Lund. Amanda is Stephen's younger sister. That wasn't the only terrible thing my father did to his supposed bestie, but it definitely started the bad blood between them."

"Why would you assume Stephen would blame you for your father's sins? Because everyone else is?"

She nods. "I knew the affair was going on. I knew what my father is like. If I had said something... But I didn't because, despite the age gap, they're both adults and seemed happy, and I never thought he'd treat her like a piece of ass. But maybe I could have stopped it if I'd made my father's business my own." She gives a bitterly ironic shake of her head. "Then again, that's true of a lot of things."

"What do you mean?" Is she talking about the financial scam, too?

"Long story."

One she's not ready to tell. Another dead end.

With a frustrated sigh, I pull up at the inn. It's dark except for the light shining from the window in the nursery. So unless Bethany invites me in, the evening—and my chance to get answers—is over until tomorrow.

I stop the car and put it in park. "I know you and Stephen dated at some point."

She unbuckles her seat belt. "It's late, and I'm not up for this conversation, Clint."

When she opens the door, I grab her arm to stay her. "Please."

With a sigh, she settles back in her seat. "All right. We didn't date. He understood my life and he comforted me when I asked him to. I needed to know what sex with someone I actually cared about would be like. I needed to know if I could feel anything for someone I wasn't screwing for the wrong reasons. He was the only decent sexual experience I had until you. I'm not going to apologize for it. I'm thirty. I've made choices you'll probably never understand. My past isn't up for negotiation. If that's a deal breaker for you, then it's better for me to know now. I'll find another ride home tomorrow."

Her words ping in my head. I don't like her answer, but...she's right. I have no moral high ground. In the past, I've taken women to bed for way less righteous reasons than needing solace or affection. Hell, my intentions with Bethany are definitely less than pure. Or at least they started that way. Some people would argue that I'm fucking her for the truth. That I'm using her. While that might be a smarter choice for my heart, that's not what's happening at all.

"I'm sorry, Beth. Your past is yours, and you owe me nothing. I was…" *Jealous as hell.* "Out of line."

Under the sedan's overhead lights, she bounces a soft gaze my way. "Honestly, I didn't think it would matter to you until I saw your face. I'm—"

"Annoyed with my behavior? I don't blame you. I'm pretty fucking annoyed, too."

"No. In an odd way, I'm flattered. What I did has never mattered to any of my past lovers. I'm not looking for a caveman, but it's nice that you care."

Thank god she's not totally pissed. "Is it asking too much to not let someone else touch you while we're together?"

"Would that work both ways?"

Right now, I can't imagine being interested in anyone else. And I definitely don't need any more complications. "Yeah."

"Don't you want to think about whether you'd like to be exclusive?"

"No."

She glances over at the dark ohana beside the house, then back to me. "Is Ash expecting you back at his place tonight?"

"I think he's trying to see what's between him and Samantha."

"Do you want to stay with me tonight?"

The smart choice would be to walk away until I have my head screwed on straight. Until I've got some perspective. Until I'm not jealous that someone else gave her the comfort I want to shower on her. But I need every moment with Bethany. I need her trust. And I need her attention. The truth is, I wonder if I'm coming to need her.

Jesus, I put myself in the stupidest, shittiest position.

Still, there's only one answer. "I would love to stay with you. I'd love to get those clothes off you, my hands on you, and hear you scream my name again."

A blush steals across her cheeks again. "Now that Maxon and Keeley are back, we might have to be a tad quieter than last night."

Fuck that. "They have a newborn, so I think they know all about sex."

"They just don't need to know my business. No one does."

Not even me. Bethany isn't going to make getting information from her easy.

Together, we cross the yard and traverse the stone steps to the little cottage. She opens the bright door and reaches for the light switch inside.

I grab her wrist. "Don't bother. We're not going to spend any time in the kitchen."

Her breath catches. I can't see her face in the dark but I hear her excitement. It probably shouldn't and I wish it didn't, but her gasp sets my blood on fire.

With a tug, I pull her body against mine. We crash together. I lower my mouth to hers and shove her lips apart with my own. I'm not patient. I *need* this woman in a way I don't understand. I want to be the one to give her pleasure and comfort and whatever else she requires.

When Bethany melts against me and surrenders herself to the kiss, I wrap my arms around her and lift her from the floor, urging her legs around my waist. She all but climbs my body, tightens her grip on me, and deepens our kiss.

Fuck yes.

The minute we reach the bed, I set her flat on her back, crawl onto the mattress above her, and strip away my T-shirt. "All I could think about all evening was replacing the memory of Lund's touch with mine."

She pauses unbuttoning her short-sleeve sweater to caress my face. "I wasn't thinking of him at all. I only want you."

Her admission does something to me that I can't ignore or fight.

Swallowing, I shove her sundress up her thighs, press my entire body onto hers, then grip her hips and lift. I strain to get closer, my cock notching against her sex. At the feel of my erection against the soft pad of her sex, I toss my head back and groan. *So, so good.* And she's already damp. I saw the little wet spot on her panties. I swear I can almost feel it through my strangling jeans.

With a snarl, I stand and tear into my fly, yanking a few condoms from my pocket and slapping all but one on the nightstand.

Around us, the sounds of the night—frogs, insects, and waves—resonate in the distance. But my breathing is the loudest. It tangles with her gentle pants, which ramp up to a little gasp when I rub my fingers directly over her lace-covered pussy.

"Take them off."

Bethany doesn't argue, simply shimmies the silken undergarment off her body and lets it fall to the floor. She peels the sweater off, too. The only things between me and her naked body are two spaghetti straps and the soft gray dress they're holding up.

"Does this zip in the back?" I tug at the cotton.

She shakes her head. "It stretches."

Even better.

I flip the strap off of one shoulder. As she shrugs out of the other, I'm aware of her bare pussy inches away. My entire body's imperative is to be there now—and never leave. But I want to see her nipples, too. I want her breasts bare for me.

I jerk down on the bodice. The soft cotton strains until her breasts spring free and the dress gathers around her waist. She's not wearing a bra. I suspected it the second she ditched the sweater. Now that her taut, candy-sweet nipples are inches from me and her naked pussy is even closer, I'm not sure where to start.

Decisions, decisions…

I roll the condom on, ignoring my shaking hands, then dive onto the bed beside her, latching onto one of her hard pink crests at the same time my fingers find their way to her clit.

Bethany whimpers under me, fingers tugging at my hair, hips moving in needy wriggles.

Her arousal spikes my bloodstream with savage triumph. I'm driven not just to give Bethany pleasure but to surround her, to make her feel wanted and adored. Vital. I want to fill her up so thoroughly that she'll never seek out Stephen Lund or any other man for comfort.

She won't find it in their empty touches. And I will make damn sure she thinks twice about having a meaningless fling with a client—or anyone else—again.

Yeah, that's lofty and irrational. I know. But I can't control my urges right now. I'm not even going to try.

"Beth…" I breathe against her skin before I pluck her other nipple with my lips and teeth, then follow that up by sliding excruciatingly slow circles around her clit.

"Clint…" Her breath hitches. "Oh… What are you doing to me?"

"Making you feel good. Do you like it?"

"Yes."

She sounds breathy, aroused. It turns me on more.

"Good. Tell me when you're close to coming."

"I'm almost there," she admits. "I don't understand."

"What?" The explosive chemistry between us?

"I hardly liked sex before you. But today, I thought of almost nothing else."

Oh, fuck if that doesn't flip my switch even more. "I thought about you, too, sweetheart. Your lips, your soft skin, the way you toss your head back when you're trying to fight the rising need to scream, the way your eyes turn so green before you come. Like now."

I can see her under the moonlight streaming in. The silvery beams illuminating her also show me how dilated her pupils are and how hazy her expression has turned.

"Clint!"

"I'm here. God, you're so fucking sexy." If my brain could focus on something other than arousing her, maybe I'd be more eloquent about the soft, slick pad under my fingers and her nipples stabbing desperately in my direction. But all my body knows is that she's ready for me to sink into her. "I want to put my hands and mouth everywhere."

"No." She shakes her head frantically, nails digging into my shoulders. "Inside me. Now."

I'll never turn down that invitation.

I vault over her thigh, between her legs, and grip her knees, settling them around my hips. Then I'm pushing my way inside her. The hot, slick walls of her pussy threaten to dissolve my self-control. But I'm spellbound by more than the physical pleasure of sex. Her arms encircle me, opening to me, welcoming me. Wanting me. As I penetrate her, Bethany presses kisses across my jaw until she catches the corner of my lips with her own.

All bets are off then. I slant my mouth over hers and slide deep inside as I surge forward the last few inches and take complete possession of her body. She arches up and cries out, legs spreading wider under me, silently begging me for more.

I clutch her hips, hoping like fuck I won't leave bruises, then I crash into her in every way possible, stroke after long, rapid stroke. My skin is burning. My libido is lit up. Every part of me is utterly on fire for this woman. I hate to put a name to what I feel for her...but I'm more than a little worried I've fallen in love.

Seconds later, she's tightening and bucking underneath me, clutching me as if she can't get close enough, and calling out to me in shrill cries that send shivers skittering across my skin. With a growl, I grip her hair, force her to stare into my eyes.

As I watch her come, ecstasy implodes me.

With a chest-deep groan, I bury my face in her neck and let go of everything, especially my sanity. I ride her through an agonizing, clawing climax that's the most fucking intense thing I've ever felt. My head is swimming, my senses reeling. And still I pound and press my way deeper, shaking and growling and holding her like I'll never let go.

When it's over, I'm panting, blinking. Stunned.

Son of a bitch.

I look down at Bethany—and freeze when I see tears seeping from the corners of her eyes.

"Sweetheart?"

She squeezes her eyes shut and shakes her head. "I'm fine."

"You're crying."

"You make me feel things..." She gives me the most heartbreaking smile. "You don't know how amazing and confusing that is."

I don't.

Swallowing, I smooth the hair back from her face. "Tell me."

"Don't you want to get up, get dressed..."

And put space between us?

"No." I'm still inside her, still connected to her. "Is this too intimate for you?"

She hesitates. "I'm not used to it. I'm not used to any of this. Where have you been for the last ten years?"

The humor she tries to inject into her question is unmistakable, but I hear it for the plea it really is. Something is going on in her head. In her heart. If she's half as caught up in me as I am in her… Yeah, that makes me want to celebrate. But it also terrifies me. What happens when she finds out why I sought her out in the first place?

"Wishing I knew you," I tell her softly. Until I can find a way to be honest about everything else, I can be honest with my feelings.

Her smile that turns into tears rips at my chest. "If I'd known you all this time, it would have saved me a lot of pain."

Bethany is so open right now. She wants to tell me things. The yearning to share is on her face. I feel guilty as hell for even encouraging her. On the other hand, if I had zero agenda other than to love this woman, I would still be coaxing her to spill everything to me.

"You keep saying these things that break my heart. Tell me why. Let me take some of the pain."

She shakes her head. "It's not your problem, and you don't want it."

"I do." I press a soft kiss to her mouth. "Tell me what hurts you. I'll hold you. We'll work it out."

"I don't want you to look at me differently afterward."

"Beth, you aren't your past. You are your heart."

As soon as the words are out of my mouth, I stop. My world tilts on its axis in a dizzying sway before slowly righting itself. What I just admitted to her—and myself—is that I no longer measure her by what happened before we met. Whatever she was involved in previously doesn't define my feelings for her. I might not know every single thing about Bethany Banks, but I know her on some deep level that I'm not sure many do. Past transgressions, if she's even guilty in the Reed Financial scheme—that wasn't her. This woman who's still holding me and doing her brave best to fight tears is.

Gently, I withdraw from her, dispose of the condom, then return to gather her in my arms.

"You're amazing," she whispers. "You're the first man I believe genuinely wants to know how I feel."

"You're so warm and beautiful, and I'm struggling to understand how every man you've ever spent time with didn't see that and didn't care."

"It's...complicated. Dalton? My first..."

"Your father set you up on a date?"

"It wasn't a date." She swallows. "It was a business transaction. I was fresh out of grad school. Dalton was thirty-five. A new tech billionaire. Dad sent me to dinner with him, told me to be friendly, give him whatever he wanted, and not to come home until he agreed to invest with us. I was naive. I thought Dad meant let the man order lobster and for me to laugh at all his jokes. I thought he meant to be persistent."

Sick, roiling nausea slides through me. I know exactly where this is going.

"Your own father pimped you out?"

Her tiny nod is full of shame. "I felt flattered by Dalton's advances. Well, at first. I had a crush on him when Dad introduced us. The fact that someone obviously well-respected and urbane liked *me*? I was thrilled. When I say it now, I sound stupid, but I grew up sheltered."

"It's not your fault. He took advantage of you."

"Maybe, but I let him. After all the wining, dining, and conversation, he took me to his hotel room. The sex was horrible. It hurt. He thanked me for my virginity, then rolled over and called my dad to give him the account. Even then, I didn't get it. After that, he dialed his wife, told her that he loved her, turned out the lights, and rolled over. I was so stunned. I didn't know he was married."

"What a dirtbag." I'm completely furious on her behalf.

"As soon as he fell asleep, I cried. I eventually slept. But when I woke up, he was gone. The next time I saw him was at a big holiday bash we threw for our clients. He brought his beautiful wife and shook my hand as if he barely knew me. I was so humiliated."

Forget furious. I want to kill this guy. What an absolute prick. But he's a symptom, not the problem.

"I'm so sorry, sweetheart. What did your father say?"

"That I did a good job. In fact, he patted me on the back for being smart enough to know that business and sex mix just fine. He chastised me for letting silly emotions get in the way, of course. Then I got the speech about how there was no such thing as love, just power and control and having the balls to use the weapons at your disposal to wield them."

What kind of man uses his daughter's innocence and self-respect to make a buck? "He sounds like a goddamn monster."

She gives me a little shrug. "He is who he is, driven and detached. Since Dalton brought a ton of prestige and cash to the organization at a time we needed it, it was hard not to see Dad's point. So I buried how I felt and carried on." She closes her eyes. "Dalton was the first. Unfortunately, he wasn't the last."

Oh, my god. How many random VIPs did her father coerce her into getting naked with? How has she coped? I can't imagine what letting people use her did to Bethany's psyche. No wonder she never felt real pleasure. I'm also not surprised she sought Lund out. Who could blame her for wanting sex on her terms? Or wanting to know if being with someone she at least liked would be different? I'm thrilled she responds so totally to me. That must say something about her feelings, right?

If I don't find the gentlest way possible to explain why I pursued her and why I've completely changed my mind, the enormity of my betrayal… *Fuck.* It will crush her. And I doubt Bethany will never forgive me.

"What do you mean? There were…others?"

"Yeah." And she doesn't sound proud of that. "Dad occasionally asked me to close deals with other reluctant investors. Anytime I hesitated, he would tell me how much he needed me and how proud he was of me. So I didn't always say no when I should have." She winces. "It sounds horrible. I never wanted you to know because I didn't want you to lose respect for me. I swear, it didn't happen often. And it's been years since a client touched me. After a while, I became less naive and more savvy. I figured out ways to persuade a potential investor to sign without crawling between the sheets."

"Oh, my god…" I'm astounded by all the ways this man used his daughter. And I hate that she ever let him get away with it because it's clearly taken a toll on her. It's also probably why she developed a thick outer shell that I've had trouble cracking—until now. "Oh, sweetheart."

"I hope that also explains why I had sex with Paul Daniels," she murmurs.

"Who?"

"Mr. Loud Hawaiian Shirt."

"He didn't tell me his name," I say numbly.

"But he told you we fucked, I'm sure." She wrenches out of my arms and rises to pace. "He was a big prick when we met. I knew my dad was going to ask me to 'finesse' him. Turned out he had a little prick when it counted. But he also had hundreds of millions of dollars. That's all the reason my father needed to unleash 'his secret weapon.' That's what he called me, you know."

Dumbfounded, I sit back. "Your father deserves to die."

"He'll probably spend the rest of his life in prison. That's some consolation."

"That's not enough for the shit he put you through."

"Well, I should have refused, and I'm hardly the only one he hurt. In the last couple of weeks, I learned he's heaped misery on all my siblings. I don't know if prison time will be justice, but at least he'll be away from us. Hopefully, we'll all find solace in that."

She sounds torn and a little sad.

I don't understand. "You're not going to miss him?"

Her hesitation shocks me.

"I miss the man I thought I grew up with. He seemed to nurture and praise me. I was so starved for attention as a kid that I soaked him up like a sponge. Looking back, I see that he cultivated my intelligence because he always intended to put me to work. He was just waiting for me to grow up and finish school so I could be another tool in his box to expand his wealth and power."

The way she describes him, I can't imagine that she knew or had anything to do with his financial scheme. It sounds as if he was perfectly capable of screwing any and all of the people around him. No doubt he was happy to have a variety of pawns, including his own daughter, to shuffle in whatever way benefitted him most. The anger and disillusionment she must be feeling… It's no wonder she's been closed and guarded. It's a shock she's opening up to me at all.

And I feel like an utter shit for not being honest with her in return.

I've got to be. Now isn't the time. It will sully this moment where she's finally allowing herself to purge her hurt. She won't remember that I'm trying to console her or that I'm in her corner. She'll just hate me—with good reason.

Could this situation get any more fucked up?

I gather Bethany against me and hold her protectively, silently telling her that I'll be her buffer from her dad and the users who took advantage of her for a moment's pleasure. "I'm so sorry, sweetheart. I can't imagine what you've been through. I was always close to my dad, so to wake up one day and realize he's not who I thought… How did it not shatter you?"

"The one useful thing he taught me is how to compartmentalize. I've cried. I'm sure I'll cry again." She sniffles. "Maybe now if you don't stop making me so mushy. But I won't let him prevail. That's the other valuable lesson I learned from him. The last person standing wins. This time, that's going to be me."

"You're so strong. I'm proud of you. Never forget, you're better than that son of a bitch. I have no doubt you'll beat him. And I promise I'll be beside you."

"Thank you. I needed to hear that. I was so afraid that if you knew the truth, you would judge me." Her voice drops. "That you would rebuff me."

For the first time, she initiates affection by throwing her arms around me. My heart wrenches. Fuck the past. From now on, I'm going to take care of her. I'm going to live up to my word. And when I tell her the truth, I'm going to hope that she'll show me understanding and empathy. Then I'll tell her what I've been suspecting all day.

I'll tell her that I'm in love with her.

Two days later, I stand across the kitchen from Maxon, who's glaring at me. For the third morning in a row. I'd like to believe he's just grouchy because he's suffering from new-parent sleep withdrawal, but I'm pretty sure he's pissed at me. After all, I disregarded all his warnings about Bethany's fragility and took her to bed anyway.

If he knew the truth, he'd probably punch my face. And I feel so shitty about deceiving Bethany I would let him.

"You doing okay?" I venture. "Surviving fatherhood so far?"

"Yeah. You stayed over again last night, huh?"

I nod. "Beth is still sleeping, so I thought I'd bring her coffee." It occurs to me that maybe Maxon thinks I'm freeloading off of his sister —and therefore, off of him. "Look, I can pay for the room if you'd feel more comfortable."

Her oldest brother scowls. "I don't want your money. I gave my sister a place to crash. She can do whatever she wants while she's here. Have you thought about what you'll do when she moves out?"

"Technically, I'm staying with a friend." Hell, if I wanted to get a place of my own, I could. "But I know Beth has plans to move out. She'll find the right place eventually."

Maxon raises a brow. "She told me yesterday that she'll be leaving on Sunday."

No shit? Where is she going? Why didn't she tell me?

"She didn't mention that."

He gives me a judgmental arch of his brow. Since he's not happy with me, I'm sure he thinks there are at least a dozen good reasons why Bethany didn't loop me into her plans. But I can't think of a single one. Despite telling me her secrets, is she pulling away?

Clearly, we need to talk.

I'm about to gather a carafe of coffee for Bethany, along with a plate of fruit, when Keeley enters the kitchen holding baby Kailani, who's dressed in a white onesie that reads I FOUND MY PRINCE. HIS NAME IS DADDY. She's also wearing a pair of pink pants and a matching flowered headband.

"Morning," I say to break the tension. "She looks precious."

Keeley smiles. "Isn't she?"

Maxon kisses the baby's head, then looks at his daughter with an adoring grin. "You would be cuter if you'd sleep more at night, but I love you anyway."

His wife laughs. "Good luck, buddy. Britta assures me we have weeks, if not months, of two a.m. feedings in our future."

"That sounds terrible." But Maxon doesn't look upset. He's still wearing that loopy grin that says he loves his baby girl.

"Well, you signed up for it, big guy." Keeley winks, then turns to me. "Would you mind holding her for a minute? I haven't had a chance to say good morning to my husband yet."

"Sure," I mumble before Keeley hands me the infant and shows me how to support her fragile head. Once we're good, the redhead wraps her arms around her husband and kisses him soundly.

They're in love. It's obvious she's ecstatically happy with her life. Maxon looks damn smitten, too.

I want what they have. I mean, I always knew I would want a wife and kids eventually, but I saw that in my thirties, when my business was more established and I felt ready. Looking at the two of them, I feel the itch for that future now. I was ridiculous for imagining love would wait until it was convenient for me to fall.

Could Bethany ever let herself fall for me? Is happily ever after something she's even ready for?

I stare at the pink-cheeked baby who peers at me with slitted blue eyes. She's soft and smells good. She yawns as if she's already ready for a nap her parents won't be getting. She sticks her tongue out, lunging toward Keeley as if she's seeking her mother for some breakfast. But she wraps her little fingers around one of mine. Her nearly translucent fingernails are sharp as hell but she's absolutely adorable. I've never spent much time with a newborn. Suddenly, I'm fascinated —and a little envious.

Does Bethany want children someday? And why am I thinking about this before I even know whether we could possibly have a future?

Keeley ends the kiss with a squeeze of Maxon's biceps and a saucy grin, then picks up a little remote on the kitchen counter. Suddenly,

Pharrell Williams's "Happy" floods the room. Bethany's older brother gives his wife a smile full of devotion. My parents used to look at one another like this.

When Keeley cradles her daughter in her arms again, I load up a tray with the hot coffee and bites of breakfast.

"Want some vegetarian quiche to take with you? I can also whip you up a watermelon-kale smoothie that's amazing."

She means well, but that sounds terrible. "No thanks. This will be plenty for now. We'll grab something more substantial before we head into work."

"Okay. Well…if you change your mind—"

"He won't, sunshine." Maxon wraps an arm around her. "Just like I'm not going to. Most men want more than seeds and sprouts for breakfast."

"You're just stubborn and have the palate of a four-year-old." She looks my way. "Come on. Back me up. You like kale, don't you?"

I wince. "Sorry, no. I have to side with your husband."

She gives me a mock huff. "Then out of my kitchen. Both of you! Neither of you are welcome back until you try my smoothie."

"Does that mean I don't have to do the dishes anymore?" Maxon teases. "Hot damn."

As I head for the back door, I see Keeley swat Maxon with her free hand, then both of them dissolve into laughter as their daughter falls asleep, cocooned between them safely.

Yeah, I definitely want that. Bethany and I need to talk.

At the top of the stairs, she surprises me by opening the door, wearing that robe that keeps me from her naked body too often. Not that I didn't enjoy her last night—more than once. But every time I'm with her, it's like I've never had her. Or like I'll never have enough of her.

"Coffee. Thank you!" She pours two quick mugs. After doctoring hers up in seconds, she sucks down half the mug in big, caffeine-deprived swallows.

Her moan of enjoyment is almost comical.

"Like that, I take it?"

"I *need* it. Someone kept me awake half the night."

"Are you complaining?"

"Not right now. Ask me how I feel at midnight."

We'll both be dragging ass then, but being with her was totally worth it.

Since I like my java black, I start gulping it down, savoring the hint of bitterness and burn on my tongue. "So…Maxon says you're moving on Sunday?"

She quickly turns sheepish. "I forgot to tell you, didn't I? My bad. Stephen called me yesterday morning. While he was looking for a rental on the island for himself, he found one within walking distance of the bar. It's not what he wants, but he sent me pictures. I checked it out yesterday on my way into work." She searches around until she finds her purse, then digs inside, finally pulling out an envelope. "I'm going to sign the lease today. It's only a three-month term. Granted, it's not a great place, but if I'm frugal, I should be able to afford it. I hope. But Maxon and Keeley will have their inn back. I can't impose anymore."

Everything she says makes perfect sense. But I'm not happy. I don't like that she intends to walk to and from work alone. And I don't like that she intends to live there without me. I want to be closer to her, both for my investigation and our future. If I'm with her nearly twenty-four seven, she'll keep feeling closer to me and open up even more, right? It should also give me the perfect opportunity to tell her the true reason we met. After that…I'm hoping she'll be able to forgive me.

But if, like the cynic in my head suggests, she's actually guilty of playing a role in stealing her clients' money… Well, if I'm living with her, she'll be hard-pressed to hide it for long. Then I can figure out how to make sure justice is served—without hurting her more than she's been hurt.

"What if we pooled our resources and moved in together?"

"Seriously?" She looks stunned. "Y-you want to live with me?"

"Hell yeah. I mean, first off, I need a place to crash, too. When I'm at Ash's apartment, my bed is his sofa, which could double as a torture rack. Making rent on your own in Maui can't be easy. Hell, I remember months in North Dakota when I was first starting out. Despite working multiple jobs, I could barely afford rent there, where it's way less expensive. We both need a place to crash, and it would be good to save some money." I set my mug down and approach, wrapping my arms around her and brushing my lips over hers in a kiss of good morning. "And I'd get to spend a lot more time with you. That's a bonus in my book."

"Are you sure?"

After everything she told me about her past, that's what she's asking. Does she somehow think that whatever her dad conned her into doing makes her less worthy or less desirable?

"Yeah. Admittedly, I've never moved in with anyone, but I think we'd do better than all right, Beth." I stroke her cheek and stare into her eyes, hoping she sees my sincerity. "In case it's not clear, I'm falling for you."

She sucks in a shocked breath and stares mutely.

I understand. It's the first time we've said openly that what we have is more than a fling. That there's more involved than our bodies.

"I'm falling for you, too," she finally murmurs. "Hard. Fast. It scares the hell out of me. But I don't want to stop."

Smiling, I draw her closer. "Good. Don't. I'm right here. I'm not going anywhere."

The tremulous smile that lights up her face enflames my body. An hour later, our coffee is cold, but I don't care. In the most eloquent way possible, she said yes.

In the back of my head, I know our cohabitation will be good for a lot of other reasons I haven't already considered. I can watch over her in case Paul Daniels comes around again, because the asshole still hasn't let up. Of course, once we move in together, I'll have to figure out what to tell my brothers. It's been three days since Bret hung up on me. I need to deal with that soon, and he'll flip shit when he finds out that I'm doing more with the "enemy" than sleeping. But I can't live my life to make my brother happy, and he doesn't know Bethany the way I do.

I've got so many reasons why this move is a great idea. But if Bethany found out who I actually am, would she see it as anything other than an epically underhanded betrayal?

No.

Shit, my subterfuge is getting deep and difficult. I'm not sure I know how to dig my way out anymore. I'll have to figure it out soon. I don't have a choice because, for us to have any sort of future, I'll eventually have to tell her the truth.

chapter NINE

My feet ache like a bitch. I've worked five straight days slinging drinks, each day seemingly busier than the last. Finally, our Saturday night shift is blessedly over. So is the New Year's rush. Most people who lingered this holiday week will be flying home later today.

In a few hours, Bethany and I will be moving in together. Despite all the secrets and lies between us, I can't wait to be closer to her.

"Hey." Ash slaps me on the back as I make my way out of the bathroom, shaking my hands dry because Andy has been too busy playing Candy Crush to order paper towels.

"Hey." I nod his way. "Crazy night, huh?"

He falls in beside me as we trek down the employees-only hall. "Yeah. I'm really hoping next week isn't so insane."

"I'm with you on that, man. You heading out with Samantha for the night?"

"Yep."

"How's that going?"

"Well, I'm not getting any, but—"

"Really? Even though you've spent the last few nights with her?"

He nods. "Crazy, right? But we talk. A lot. About anything and everything. It's not like being with Montana. She only wanted to fuck. I actually like that I'm getting to know more about Sam than her erogenous zones."

This is the first time I've ever heard Ash say that waiting for sex isn't a deal breaker.

"That's cool. So it's going well?"

"Yeah. Once she got past the shyness, I found out she has this quirky sense of humor I dig. Her mental Wikipedia of movie knowledge is damn impressive, too. What about you and Beth?"

"We're moving in together today, so I'll be off your sofa. Sorry I haven't had a chance to tell you before now. It happened fast."

He turns and blocks my path, stopping me. "Are you getting information from her? Or falling for her?"

I can't bullshit Ash. He'll see right through me. "Dude, I already fell. I never realized what I wanted or needed in a woman until her."

"How does she feel about you?"

"She says she's falling, too. I think she feels something. We haven't put labels on it yet." I blow out a breath. "I sound crazy, don't I?"

"Sound?" He barks out a laugh. "We both know you are."

I give him a good-natured grin. "True enough."

"I've known you awhile, bro. You wouldn't have feelings for Beth if she wasn't worthy of them. Does she know…everything?"

"Who I am?" I shake my head. "I need to figure out how to tell her without killing her trust. She's been through a lot."

"What happened to finding your dad's money and figuring out her role in the scam?"

"I don't know anything right now." And I need to for our future. For my brothers' sanity.

"You can't just forget about it. I get that you're really into Beth, but she's your only hope of learning—"

"The truth. I know, and I'm not letting that go. But if I don't handle this situation right, I'll lose her." I rake a hand through my hair. "I've wedged myself between a rock and a hard place, and I don't know how to get out. Any ideas?"

"No. Just be sure you know what you're doing. But if it turns out she's innocent and you want a future with her, my advice is to be as honest as possible—quickly. Every day you wait is just another day she'll think you've betrayed her."

I hate it, but he's fucking right.

After he sends me an apologetic shrug, he turns to find Samantha, purse in hand, waiting by the back door.

As Andy shoos everyone out, I notice Montana looking cozy with a buff tourist. Apparently, he'll be filling Ash's vacancy beside her tonight. Terry is finally back at work, but his energy flagged as the evening wore on, and he spent the last couple of hours in the back, rather than behind the bar.

I don't see Bethany anywhere.

With a frown, I poke my head into the break room. Her locker is open and empty, so she probably grabbed her purse and went outside. Sure, it's a nice evening, but I've warned her that Paul Daniels is likely coming back for his pound of flesh. Andy finally addressed the issue today and forced Montana to wait on him, but I worry that roadblock only motivated Bethany's former client more.

She shouldn't be alone outside.

Fishing my buddy's car keys from my pocket, I jog out to the sultry night. Ash and Samantha are already in her car and heading out of the lot. Andy locks up behind me, then makes a beeline for his truck. Montana and the tourist have disappeared already, probably on foot to his hotel nearby. Terry slumps to his beat-up VW, looking nearly ready to fall over in exhaustion.

No sign of Bethany.

Alarm sets in. I'm just about to shout for her when I hear her voice drift around the corner of the building. "What do you want?"

"To see you. I've been trying to find you for weeks. Why did you come to Maui?"

She's talking to some guy, and it's definitely not Paul Daniels. I've never heard this low, polished voice before.

I creep closer, careful not to alert them I'm listening.

"You're here, aren't you?" Bethany responds, her voice sounding as hard as armor. I've never heard her talk in this assertive, rapid-fire tone. "Besides, I had to get away from the bad press back home. Too much negative attention."

"And I guess you're working in this shithole to lie low. Good cover."

Is that why she's working here? I've been wracking my brain for an explanation that made sense…

"Where are you staying?" he goes on.

"With a guy I met last week."

Technically, she's spent her nights with me, but we're not staying at my place. Did she misunderstand the question or is she trying to mislead this guy?

"And saving your money since your accounts are still frozen. Good.

You've always been the smart one. Now I need you to do something for me."

"Tell me."

"We've taken a lot of damage. But you can put a stop to Reed Financial's bleeding and make this whole case against me go away now."

I freeze. Is she talking to Barclay Reed? He's *here*? Holy shit. Why does he think he has any right to talk to Bethany? He must have balls the size of fucking Jupiter.

Since he knows what happened to the money people invested with him, I have no compunction about eavesdropping. Besides, if Bethany needs me, I'll be here to protect her.

"What's your plan?" she snaps.

"Bring me that video, Bethany. You know the one I mean. It's critical. Tell me you were thinking ahead and got it out of the office before the feds descended."

"Where's the money?"

"Safe. I can't get to it now, but you know me…"

Is that supposed to be some kind of assurance? From a man who would cheat his clients and use his own daughter for profit?

"But it's accessible?"

"Are you second-guessing me?" he snarls. "I'm your *father*. I paid for your very private, expensive education, including that Harvard MBA. I gave you a position as my right hand in one of the most profitable organizations of the last decade. I've never doubted you. Don't you dare repay me like this. Do you have the video or not?"

God, he just laid an ugly fucking piece of manipulation on her. I want her to give him a verbal beatdown or, better yet, punch his damn face. She doesn't.

"Of course," she assures.

His sigh of relief is audible. "This is why I handpicked you to work by my side. Brilliant, brilliant girl. I need you to make a copy of it, then return to San Diego and deliver it to the AUSA."

"Timeframe?"

"What kind of question is that? Tomorrow. Hell, now. And I don't mean pop it in the mail, Bethany. I mean deliver it, along with a very personal reminder. You've never disappointed me. I know you won't start now."

My jaw drops. Is that asshole really insisting that she give her body to some other dude in order to save his ass? I hope she tells him to go fuck himself.

"I have no money for a plane ticket," she points out.

"Here's two thousand dollars." I hear the rustle of bills. "It should get you to the mainland and back."

"All right, but let's talk this through. We have to be smart. We can't overplay our hand."

Our hand?

"We're not," he insists. "You play a royal flush when it's time to crush the opposition. Now's that time."

"It's not. The case isn't going to trial for a while, but rumor has it our mutual friend will be promoted up the food chain in the next couple of months. If we wait until just before his new position is announced, he'll have far more incentive to heed your demands."

Bethany is *helping* her father? She's plotting with him?

I stagger back against the wall of the building. Please fucking tell me I'm misunderstanding this conversation.

But logic tells me I'm not.

Has she been lying to me all this time?

"Clever…" Reed praises. "You have a point." He sighs. "I don't like the idea of waiting. It inhibits our ability to start investing again, but it's all for nothing if the charges aren't dropped. All right. I'm relieved you're monitoring the situation, but I expected nothing less. Keep up the good work. I'll be in touch soon."

The click of his dress shoes as he walks away resounds in the night. His cadence steady, confident. I prop myself up against the wall since disbelief threatens to take me down.

I can't move. Hell, I can hardly breathe. What the fuck am I going to do?

Suddenly, Bethany appears around the corner. When she spots me, she gasps, palm pressed to her chest. Her whole body goes tense. "You're here. You heard."

"Yeah." I try to keep the accusing note out of my voice even though

I'm livid that she's apparently conspiring with her asshole of a father. And like the possibility of that isn't ripping me to shreds.

"It's not what you think. Please, please believe me."

Under the overhead lights in the parking light, I see the vulnerable plea on her face that I hear echoed in her words. The confident ball-buster I heard only moments ago is gone, replaced suddenly by the shy, withdrawn Beth I first met over a week ago.

Who is the real Bethany?

"Then tell me what's going on."

"Can we please not talk about it here?" Her voice trembles.

When I look at her closely, I see that her body is, too.

She genuinely looks rattled. Whether I want it to or not, my anger softens. But confusion still has me reeling. Will whatever explanation she gives me really make everything okay?

"Fine. I'll take you back to the inn."

I'd rather head to Ash's place since he won't be there and it's so much closer. But doubt about her—and about our future—creeps in. If she can't explain everything I overheard away, I'm not going to want to be in the same room with her. I'll want to be alone, where I can wonder how the fuck my heart got everything so wrong.

On some level, I hate fresh mistrust creeping in. But maybe I shouldn't be surprised. She *is* her father's daughter. It's possible she's conned me in a different way than she conned my dad. It's also possible I was snowed by her sob story and so blinded by lust that I didn't see the truth.

"Thanks," she says quietly, then doesn't speak again until she's in the passenger's seat and we've left the lot.

As I drive down the mostly empty road, Bethany surprises me by wrapping gentle fingers around my arm. "Everything you overheard must have been confusing."

"That's putting it lightly."

"Will you listen to my side of things?"

That takes me aback. Does she think there's any way I don't want to hear this? "Of course."

"Thank you. That's all I ask."

Her fingertips drag slowly across my skin, as if she's reluctant to withdraw her touch. Once she does, she clasps her hands in her lap again, not saying another word until we reach the inn.

When I roll into the parking lot and shove the car in park, I turn to her expectantly. "Go ahead. I'm listening."

"Come upstairs with me? Please. The explanation is long."

I tap my thumb against the wheel, but what is there to decide? I want to hear how she'll talk her way out of this. I need to hear her side of the story I've been chasing for weeks. Now that she finally seems willing to give it, I'm anxious it will change everything between us. I'm dreading she'll tell me she's guilty...and I'll realize it doesn't matter as much as it should.

Because I'll still be stupidly in love with her.

Regardless, I can't run away. This is my responsibility. She might be a cheat and a liar, but I doubt she's capable of doing me bodily harm, so I've got no reason to decline.

"All right."

In silence, I follow her up the stairs. I hear her keys rattling as she inserts hers in the lock with trembling fingers and enters the dark ohana. She doesn't bother with the lights.

Instead, she turns as I shut the door behind me and throws herself against me, barreling me against the portal. "Clint?"

Her nearness throws me into a tailspin. My head tells me to watch myself, but my body is seemingly wired to respond to her. All she has to do is brush against me and turn her face up, stare at me with those wide green eyes, and I'm more than aching for her.

Fuck.

"What, Beth?" I manage to get out gruffly. "Spit it out."

"I know what you heard sounded awful, but my father is a manipulative bastard. I told him what I had to in order to get away from him. I'll explain more. Everything. I promise. Just… Would you make love to me one more time? In case you hate me after I've told you all I know. Please."

I should say no. Her assurance helps some. Still, I shouldn't let sex cloud our discussion. But Bethany rarely asks me for anything, especially closeness, affection, or sex. And like her, I'm afraid of how the truth will change us. I don't know what I'll think or believe after I hear her side of the story. I also don't know where we'll stand after I tell her my secrets.

This may be the very last time I touch Bethany.

Swallowing down my desperation at the thought, I cup her nape, urge her body closer, and plaster every inch of her against me, then slant my lips over hers. She meets me halfway with a cry, clinging to me.

Under the press of my mouth, she opens eagerly. As I dip inside, I taste the need in her kiss and I can't help but groan.

In the past, she's always been more assertive in bed than in conversation, almost like she felt compelled to perform for my pleasure. Given what I know now about her corporate sex life, that makes sense. But what we have feels different. Real. Not like she's trying to coax or dazzle me, but more like she simply wants to be close to me.

Right or wrong, smart or not, I want the same.

Time turns meaningless when I pull her T-shirt over her head. The yellow bikini top she wore all evening distracted me each time I caught a glimpse of the strappy, suggestive thing. Now it's just in my way.

When I tug on the string at her back, the two triangles of fabric fall away from her breasts. I break the kiss long enough to pull the rest of the bathing suit top over her head. Bethany barely has a moment to gasp before I'm back her mouth again, eating at her like I'm starved, and cradling her perfect breasts in my hands, thumbs stimulating her nipples.

She encourages me by deepening the kiss and dropping her hands to my fly. With a few snaps of her deft fingers, she opens my shorts, shoves my underwear aside, and wraps her fingers around my aching length.

"Beth." I can't stop the moan. "Fuck, you do this to me…"

"What?" she whispers as she presses her lips up my neck and dusts them across my jaw.

"Turn me on and inside out. No woman has ever done to me what you can."

Shit. I'm giving her power over me, handing it to her on a silver platter. If she's only taking advantage of me for cover or merely having a fling for her amusement, I shouldn't make using me so easy. But her touch is like that favorite song I'll never stop wanting to hear. It calls to me, excites yet comforts me. It gets stuck in my head until I'm unable to think of anything else.

"I never really enjoyed sex until you," she admits. "And now all I want is to spend time with you, block out the rest of the world, and learn every part of you. I want to know how much better it feels when I pleasure you because *I* choose to."

What is she saying? My muddled mind can't quite untangle her meaning while her fingers glide up and down my cock.

My flesh is on fire. I can't stand clothes between us. I don't want anything separating us—especially not the dubious past or our uncertain future. I only want right now and the two of us naked.

"Jesus, Beth…" I hiss when her fist pulls its way down my length again. Her free hand tugs at my shirt in impatience.

As soon as I yank the cotton over my head and cede my bare torso to her, her lips are all over me. She nips at my shoulder, strokes my arm, laves my nipples. Her every touch makes me shudder. There's no stopping this or worrying about sanity. It's as if we both want to wring every ounce of pleasure possible out of this moment.

In case it never comes again.

When I reach for her shorts, Bethany dodges my grasp by sinking to her knees. I feel her hot breath on the crest of my cock, now aching and straining for her. The cynic inside me tells me she's offering me a blow job to distract me. She's sucked other schmucks like me to make them compliant, not to make love.

Then she takes me in her mouth, cradling my dick on her tongue, then draws her lips around me in a slow, sensual tug. An electric zap charges up my spine with primal need to have her—possess her—in every way possible. God, this *feels* like it means something.

"Oh…yeah." I tangle my fingers in her hair, tug away the elastic band holding it up, then grab the silky skeins by the fistful. "Beth!"

As I ride her mouth, she hums around me, seemingly greedy to have all of me. I hold nothing back because nothing else happening between us matters in this moment—not my suspicions, my worries, or my fear of heartbreak. Our connection matters. The woman I've fallen for is touching me, and I swear I feel her giving me something far beyond a mere blow job. She's giving me all of herself.

The nagging cynic inside me shouts that I'm romanticizing this moment because I want her to be innocent and every swipe of her tongue feels so good that my eyes are rolling in the back of my head. Yes, what she's doing to me feels epic, but that's not why I'm refusing to listen to that nasty voice in my head right now.

I'm choosing to listen to my heart. It urges me to pull her closer, melt into her, give her every bit of me.

I do.

With another surge, I sink more than my cock into her mouth. I surrender to the worship of her tongue and the devotion of her lips. I silence the argument in my head to focus on her alone.

Her fingers dig into my thighs, then curl around my hips to pull me even closer. She eases back to heap pleasure and adoration on my sensitive crest, then slips down my length in a dizzying, suction-filled glide. I feel her nose against my abdomen, her hot breath against my skin. Through the shadows, I watch her, an open-mouthed siren, staring at me like she'd do anything to make me love her.

Bethany repeats the process, picking up speed until I'm gasping. I watch her lose herself in the moment, see her seemingly let go of all her inhibitions and focus on exalting me.

Not going to lie, getting head is always great. But the way she showers me with bliss and simply gives herself is the biggest turn-on of all.

"Beth…" My strangled yelp is all the warning I can give. I'm about to lose it.

She doubles her efforts to touch me everywhere, seemingly dedicating herself to my ecstasy. I know I'm not the only man who's ever been in her bed—or in her mouth—but right now I feel like the most important.

And I have no doubt this is going to be the most cataclysmic orgasm of my life.

Seconds later, it crashes down on me. I'm helpless to do anything but growl out as need overtakes me, jolts my body, then sends me hurtling into a euphoria that's the closest thing to nirvana I've ever experienced. I lose myself in its crushing throes, forgetting all sense of time, place, purpose. Of anything but her.

When the massive orgasm comes to its devastating end, I blink and pant, swaying on my feet, heart pounding. Somewhere along the way, I melted against the wall. I'm still holding Beth's silky hair in my fists, just as I did while she wrung every bit of pleasure from my body that I had to give.

Holy shit. What the hell has she done to me?

With a soft pop, she releases my cock from her lips and slowly stands, looking shy as she kisses my shoulder, my pectoral, my cheek. "Clint?"

"Beth." I manage to pull her closer, even though my legs threaten to stop supporting me. "Oh, my god…"

When she lays her head on my chest, I feel a hint of her smile. "Finally, I get the chance to make you feel half as good as you've made me feel. I've wanted to do that for a long time. It's the first time I've ever wanted to do that at all."

Really? "What else have you wanted to do?"

She blinks up at me. "Honestly? Give more than my body to you."

Does she want to be open and honest with her body before she's the same with her story? Or is she hoping to butter me up with what she thinks I want to hear so I'll be so happy and sated and, of course, believe whatever she tells me?

Fuck, I hate this suspicion and indecision. What if the truth pulls us apart?

"How?"

She peels off the rest of her clothes to stand before me in the dark. "I've never, ever surrendered complete control of my body to any man. I was always in charge. I pulled the strings and held myself separate, despite the physical closeness. You're different. I don't want to manipulate you by doing things *to* you. I want to do them *with* and *for* you. I want to yield myself and give you whatever you desire."

Fuck, I want to believe her so much the ache is a physical pang. If she's serious, then I'm staggered and humbled by how much she's allowed herself to become vulnerable with me in less than two weeks. On the other hand, she might be telling me what she thinks I want to hear. I can't discount that…no matter how I'm dying to.

Either way, I'm not turning her down.

After kicking away my flip-flops, shorts, and underwear, I take her hand and lead her through the darkened ohana, through the kitchenette, and beyond her bedroom. I fling open the doors to the little balcony that faces the ocean and urge her outside.

Immediately, the night air caresses our skin. It's cool, but not chilly. The wind is like a soft caress. Palm trees sway. Ocean waves break.

Her breathing grows choppy and loud. "Clint?"

I turn to her. "No one will see us. The inn's guests are asleep. If Maxon and Keeley are awake, it's because they're with the baby, so they'll be too busy to care about us."

"But—"

"You asked me what I wanted. I want your trust. I want you to believe that I will treat you exactly as you deserve."

Whatever that might be.

And maybe after she's divulged her story, it will seem like the perfect time to tell her exactly who I am and why I pursued her. Maybe I'll even believe her enough to confess how much my feelings have changed since we met. In a perfect world, she'll believe me in return and admit she loves me, too.

Or everything will blow up in my face, and I'll wind up both empty-handed and alone.

"All right." Her murmur is so soft the wind almost sweeps it away.

I drop an approving kiss on her shoulder. "Lean forward. Put your elbows on the rail."

She does, looking back at me over her shoulder with trembling trust.

The acceptance on her face revs me up again. "Are you on the pill?"

"Yes."

Even if I hadn't seen evidence of that myself less than a week ago, I would have believed her earnest tone. "Have you ever had sex without a condom?"

"No."

I spread kisses up her spine as I reach around her body to cup her mound. She's drenched, as she always seems to be for me. At my touch she gasps, then melts with a moan.

My hand shakes as I align my crest to her entrance. "I've never had sex without a condom, either."

Dad drilled the notion of safe sex into us, and I never wanted to be that guy who got a random girl pregnant, then paid for my careless-ness for the next eighteen years. But I'm not asking her about this simply because I left my condoms on the other side of the cottage. I want this because everything inside me is driving me to take Bethany without any barriers between us. Am I daring her to prove that she trusts me? Am I trying to get as close to her as possible?

Probably. Yes. And I'm done questioning it. Right now, I'm just feeling.

Despite the orgasm I had a few minutes ago, my cock is hard and my body is primed. I want her. I want to imprint myself on her. No matter what happens, I'm never going to forget this woman. I'm going to make damn sure she never forgets me.

"Do you want me?" I nudge my bare cock against her so she knows exactly what I'm asking.

For a moment, she hesitates, then she nods—slowly at first. Soon, she's looking back at me with something desperate in her eyes. "Please."

"Fuck," I hiss, then drop my mouth to the sensitive spot between her neck and her shoulder. "I want you so goddamn bad."

"Take me." Her voice is a whisper in the night. "Don't stop."

I know a dozen good reasons why I probably should walk away, but none of them compel me more than the connection I feel with Bethany right now.

I grip her hips, bend my knees, then surge inside her in one long, rough thrust.

She gasps and tosses her head back. The sight of all her platinum hair spilling down her narrow back and flirting with my hands at her waist turns me the fuck on. The feel of her, hot and silken and without a single barrier between us, almost undoes me where I stand.

It's *so* good. I groan and surge deeper before I settle into a slow, grinding rhythm that has her gripping the railing like a lifeline and writhing with me in a silent plea for more. I give it to her as I settle my fingers over her clit and rub in soft circles. I've paid attention and learned her body. This is how she likes it best. So even though it's killing me to put the brakes on my cadence, it feels totally worth it when she tightens around me and her needy bud turns to stone under my touch in seconds.

"Clint…" she keens.

"Right here," I mutter in her ear. "Wanting you to feel so good."

"Oh, god." She clutches the rail like her legs are threatening to dissolve beneath her.

Eventually, I'll speed up and send her careening toward orgasm, but I want to make this moment last as close to forever as possible. So I keep it slow, each bareback stroke of my cock a steady press inside her, a nudge against that sensitive spot high inside her, coupled with a lingering touch of her pouting clit. The friction sizzles me with so much sensation I swear I'm going to lose my damn mind. But I keep it up. For her.

"No. No!" she begs. "More."

"I will, sweetheart. Eventually…" I taunt. "First, I want to feel you, see you, listen to you beg."

"Please," she pants. *"Please!"*

Loving the knowledge that I hold her satisfaction in my hands probably makes me a caveman, but there's nothing better. Sure, I love orgasm. Who doesn't? But I derive a thrill out of knowing she's lowered her defenses and allowed me as deep inside her body and soul as a man can get. I never really understood the importance of that until this moment. But her honest responses to my touch are totally doing it for me, even as they're turning me inside out.

I nip at her shoulder as I fuck her deeper…and lift my fingers away from her pussy.

Instantly, she wails. "Clint!"

With a grin, I slip my slick digits in my mouth. "Hmm. You're so sweet on my tongue."

She only manages to answer with another toss of her head and a high-pitched whimper.

Moving the cascade of her hair aside, I press my lips to her ear. "I want to lay you across the kitchen table and have you for breakfast. Coffee and your pussy—the two best things in life. I would never need sugar or cream for my java if I had you spread out in front of me."

Maybe that's over the top, but it fits my mood.

And Bethany likes what I'm saying if that heavy-lidded look she sends over her shoulder is any indication.

Fuck, this is so hot, and I'd love to drag this out endlessly—just stay with her—but unfortunately my restraint has limits. And this slow, flesh-to-flesh seduction is killing what's left of mine.

Settling my thumb above her clit again, I strum it in rhythm with my quickening thrusts. She moans and grabs my arm, nails sinking into skin as her walls grip me tight.

She's close—so, so close. I can't resist pushing her even closer to the edge.

"Your orgasm is right there, isn't it?"

With a choppy, indrawn breath, Bethany nods and jerks back against me, as if she's trying to speed up my thrusts.

"You want it?"

She nods more emphatically.

I grip her hip in warning. "Then stop trying to control my pace. Beg me for it. Give all of yourself to me."

Again, she whimpers. Not a protest, but as if the idea of relinquishing the last bit of power is terrifying. Still, she syncs up with my rhythm, softens against me, and allows me to take her exactly where I want her to go.

In seconds, her breath begins to hitch, her body tenses, her cries turn keening. She freezes for a long moment, then her entire body shudders with an involuntary spasm. The jerk of her clit against my fingers and the hard grip of her pussy match her hoarse groan of ecstasy as she gives herself over to me without an ounce of reluctance.

Her total surrender undoes me like nothing else, and I lose all semblance of mastery and coordination. I can't stop myself from pouring into her, becoming one with her. Falling even more in love with her.

A small eternity passes before my head stops swimming and I catch my breath. The second I withdraw from the swollen clasp of her body, she tears away from the railing and whirls to me, throwing herself into my arms. She presses an inexpert, anguished kiss to my lips. I feel wetness on her cheeks.

Worry kicks me in the gut. "Sweetheart?"

"I'm fine," she croaks.

I know she isn't. Nothing about this situation is, either. "Tell me what's wrong."

She nods. "I'm worried. I need to tell you everything. Just…please don't think the worst of me."

Bethany fears I won't like her confession, and maybe I won't. But the irony of this situation doesn't escape me. She's definitely not going to like what I have to admit in return. But I can't lie to her anymore. If she's really decided to share her truth with me for the good of us, I need to do the same.

By mutual agreement, we shower. We kiss slowly, heaping affection on each other as if we're both anxious about what will happen next. When the water finally turns cool, I reluctantly cut it off. Dread churns in my belly. What if this really is the end? What if she tells me a story that perfectly explains away all my doubts…but she can't forgive my deception?

After she tosses on a thin blue nightgown, she climbs into bed. I'd rather have her naked, the way we've been sleeping the past few nights, but I sense the garment is the security blanket she needs right now.

When I ease onto the mattress beside her, I resist the urge to close my eyes. Sure, I'm exhausted. No surprise after a long, busy shift and two killer orgasms, but what happens in the next ten minutes might decide the rest of my fucking life.

"Come here." I open my arms to her, glad for the opportunity to hold her. "Talk to me."

She slides in willingly and lays her head on my chest. "Please try to keep an open mind, okay?"

"Of course." Will she do the same when it's my turn? Or if she says she's guilty, will it even matter to me anymore?

"Have you ever heard of Barclay Reed?"

Here it comes… Everything inside me tightens. "Yes."

She doesn't look surprised, probably because this story has been all over the news. "He's my father, and he's probably going to prison for scamming people out of something close to a billion dollars. No doubt, Paul Daniels told you that." She draws in a quivering breath as she tries to brace herself.

I shrug. He didn't, but I don't want to derail what she has to say with a technicality that's not important now.

"Did he also tell you that I was Barclay's right-hand woman?" She nods. "I was the face of Reed Financial. Dad kept a few clients of his own, like Douglas Lund. Clients who had a lot of money and predated me joining the firm. But most he had shifted onto my plate. I managed the investment strategy for the entire organization. I looked at every client every week—sometimes every day—and made recommenda-tions about what to invest, as well as when and where. I said when to buy, when to sell, and when to get out of the market and take shelter in bonds or other low-risk investments."

I gape. She was in charge of *everything?* "People trusted you with their money and… Are you telling me you had a hand in taking it?"

"No. God, no. I'm trying to explain how everything went so wrong. Our organizational roles are what allowed the theft to happen. I have a securities' license, but my father insisted on maintaining control of all actual transactions. He said it kept him familiar with where his clients were in their wealth-management plan and allowed us to have a system of checks and balances, which was especially important when I was fresh out of school and my knowledge about managing people's money was still mostly theoretical. So my job encompassed more of the day-to-day operations—client meetings, risk assessment, and trade planning. He managed the organization itself and handled the execu-tion of the clients' investments. I could check the balance of any port-folio simply by logging in to the software we had built about three years ago. I didn't *see* the funds, just tracked their growth or loss electronically. So I had every reason to believe they were exactly where I suggested he invest them."

Is she saying her father duped her, too?

"So…you advised clients, took their capital, and recommended the strategy, but your dad actually handled the money?"

"Exactly. But ten months ago, I was working late one Thursday evening. It was, maybe, eight o'clock. Dad poked his head in my office and told me to leave. Not like he gently urged me to go home because it was past dinnertime, and I'd been working killer hours for months. He literally ordered me to get the hell out of the office. He looked nervous."

"So you left?"

She nods. "Even if I was his 'favorite' offspring, as he liked to call me, he never quite let me forget that I was the illegitimate one. Most of his clients saw me as his brilliant investment strategist, whom he was probably banging. A few knew the truth, the ones I liked and trusted. Some of them, I really miss. They felt like friends."

Does she count my dad among those few? If so, why didn't she answer her phone that fateful day?

Her expression turns sad. "But I knew how most people viewed me. Sure, it irked and upset me. Sometimes that perception even undermined me, but my professional life was tied to Dad's. Until I truly proved my worth in financial circles, no one was going to believe I wasn't his something-something at the office since he had a reputation as a man-whore and I couldn't prove my ancestry. It would have been my word against his. And I knew he could be a real bastard…but he was my father. I never thought he'd stab *me* in the back." Tears well in her green eyes. "He did. And I didn't see it coming because some part of me always wanted his approval, was always trying to overcome being his bastard daughter, even though that was his fault, not mine." The silvery drops fall down her cheeks in wet paths in the moonlight. "I sound pathetic, like a stupid girl with Daddy issues. But I was accustomed to him and I thought I knew him well enough to believe that, on some level, he cared." She drags in a breath. "Anyway, since bad moods were nothing new, I didn't question him. I just picked up my things and left. After that, things started getting weird."

"In what way?"

"He told me to cool down on the trades for a while, said he was flipping some funds around so he could protect them during what he thought would be a turbulent time in the market. When I pressed him, he admitted that he was moving money around because his wife was threatening to divorce him, and he didn't want Linda to have half of his wealth. It wasn't until a few months later, and only after he installed a safe in my condo and stuffed it full of his most incriminating files, that I realized he was actually offshoring not just his personal funds but the whole organization's. He'd moved ninety-five percent of it to the Caymans without anyone knowing. He was positioning himself to take the money and disappear. But then Linda tried to serve him with divorce papers before he could finish what he started. He fled to Maui to evade her. Somehow, the FBI got suspicious —I think Douglas Lund had something to do with that—and they started investigating." She laughs bitterly. "I defended my father for so long. I knew he was a selfish asshole, but even I was surprised he had so little compunction about stealing from clients. It hurt that he lied to me. But the worst part was that everything he put in my safe made it look as if I was the guilty one. He tried to set me up to take the fall."

Her voice trembles. Her face looks so solemn. Maybe I'm a stupid schmuck, but I want to believe her.

If she's telling the truth... God, the enormity of Barclay Reed's dirty deception hits me square in the gut. It's so horrific it almost doesn't compute. My father would have done anything to make me happy and help me succeed. I was stubborn and I didn't always want his advice. Sometimes I refused to do something his way without first trying my own, but he would never, ever have plotted to throw me under the bus to save himself.

The cynic in my head reminds me again that she could be lying... but if she wanted to con me into believing how innocent she is, wouldn't she would have spoon-fed me an elaborate story up front? Why would she have waited days and sobbed through the explanation that seemed equal parts blunt and self-critical?

I have a choice to make. But right now, I only see one. I'm putting my faith in Bethany. I'm choosing her.

As I hold her shuddering body against me, the implications of her tale hit home. He used Bethany's brain, pimped out her body, and took advantage of her need for his attention and approval—for a fucking decade—then tried to throw shade her way so he could escape both his wife and prison in one fell swoop.

Barclay Reed left a lot of victims in the wake of his appalling scam, but Bethany was the ultimate one. He betrayed her as a human being, a boss, and a father.

I wish I hadn't merely eavesdropped on their conversation earlier. I wish I'd killed him.

"Oh, sweetheart. I'm so sorry. That must have hurt so damn much. But the FBI cleared you, right?"

"They wanted to arrest me on principle, but the feds declined to file charges. It was touch-and-go for a while. I spent so much money on attorneys… Finally, they stopped viewing me as a suspect, but everyone else is still suspicious. *Everyone.* Paul Daniels? I can't convince him that I had nothing to do with his money disappearing because I was the face of Reed Financial. Whenever he'd call in the past, I could tell him at the touch of a button what was happening with his money. So in his mind, I not only knew the funds had been swindled, I was in on it. No amount of logic has convinced him otherwise. It's been that way with so many of my clients and their families…"

Including me. I'm part of the reason she's crying now. Paul Daniels approached Bethany head on. He demanded information and repayment…and yeah, he was an absolute insulting douche about it. But at least he didn't lie to her.

I did.

"I can't tell you how many desperate calls and emails I had to ignore on advice from my attorneys since anything I said could and would be used against me…"

Which probably explains why she never answered any of my questions or accusations.

"It's been a lot to handle. But I tried to do the right thing. An attorney friend of mine, Kathryn, helped me set up a nonprofit corporation for the victims and their families. I donated a hundred thousand dollars to the fund. I had to do something. The victims have suffered so much at my father's hands, and I didn't see what was happening in time to stop it. The money I gave isn't much in the face of what Barclay stole, but was all I had to offer. I'd love to give more once the feds unfreeze my accounts, but I don't have much liquid cash left."

I'm stunned. Despite everything Bethany has been through, everything she probably realized she would go through in the future, she gave up the financial security she had to help others. How many people would do that? How many would bother while they were having to work so hard to simply survive?

"That's an amazing gesture, Beth. Incredibly selfless."

"I had plans to do more, like fundraising with corporations I've worked with over the years. When I started soliciting donations before I left San Diego, I quickly realized that everyone viewed my attempts to help as either a stunt to deflect my guilt or another greedy money grab. So I stepped aside and let Kathryn manage the fund." She closes her eyes, looking as if she's fighting tears. "The investments are growing nicely since I'm quietly managing everything in the background, but donations have become a lot brisker without my involvement."

And Bethany feels rejected. I hurt for her. She's been used, betrayed, and snubbed at every turn. And still, she chose to give back to others. I'm not convinced I would have been half that altruistic.

I wish like hell I could erase all that for her and make her happy. But I don't have a magic wand, so I simply hold her tighter. "I'm sorry, Beth. Nothing has been easy for you."

She shrugs. "The fund is growing. That's what's important, not my feelings. Believe me, no one wants to hear that I had to leave everything and everyone I knew behind, rely on strangers I share blood with, and take a job where I can't use my education. The victims have been through worse. I get it. I live with the shame that all this horrible stuff happened on my watch. And disillusionment because the father I thought I knew didn't live up to the pedestal I put him on as a kid." She caresses my face. "But I'm bouncing back. This won't beat me. He won't because I won't let him. And some good has come out of all this.

I've gotten to know my brothers and sisters. I feel like I'm actually a part of a family now. That's something I've never really had. And you…you're the brightest spot in my life. Thank you for listening and understanding. Thank you for believing me. I *need* the solace of a safe place, and I'm so blessed that I've found it in your arms."

Stab me in the heart. She couldn't have made me feel any more unworthy and guilty if she'd tried.

I can't confess now. She needs reassurance, comfort. I have to show her I'm someone she can believe in. If I tell her that my father was one of her clients and that I came after her for "justice," I'll only add to her sense of betrayal and disillusionment. I'll hurt her—maybe beyond repair. But I can't go on keeping the truth from her forever, either.

What the fuck am I going to do?

I'll work on that—after I've reassured her.

"I'm here for you. Whatever you need, sweetheart… I want to help you." I kiss her, a tender press of my lips to hers that's so bittersweet, and hold her tighter when she cuddles into my arms. "Will your dad be back for that video he wants? What is it?"

She tenses. "That's another way he used me, and I didn't want to believe it—until the obvious stared me in the face. Shortly after his arrest, he came to me and said Lund was being vengeful and bribing people to pin this crime on him. He swore his old crony had fabricated evidence, drummed up false witnesses, and poisoned the FBI against him. I believed it because after the man found out that Dad had gotten his baby girl pregnant, Douglas came screaming into the office and threatened to get my father back if it was the last thing he did. So, still believing Barclay was innocent, when he asked me to dig up blackmail material on the federal prosecutor, I should have said no…but I didn't. The video was supposed to be the backup plan to the backup plan. He swore we'd only use it if *nothing* else worked. But I know now that Dad's own actions have put his ass in boiling water, and he wants me to take that video to James Braden, the prosecutor"—she clarifies—"and deliver it…ahem, 'personally' to let him know we mean business."

"I can't believe he has the audacity to assume you'd lift a finger to help him, much less sleep with someone."

"Well, like you heard him say, I've never let him down. And Dad never likes a task done halfway." After an acid smile, Bethany turns quieter. "It doesn't matter, though. I don't actually have the video."

"Why did you tell him you did? And why didn't you cuss him out for everything he's done to you?"

She sighs. "Because if I told him I didn't have the video, he'd only berate me for failing him and hound me until I fix his problem. I don't want to deal with him, and since he never bothered to tell me the truth, I don't feel that I owe him any semblance of honesty in return. And I didn't cuss him out because, first, he wouldn't have heard it. Sociopaths don't feel guilt. They can pretend to, but they don't actually empathize with anyone else's emotions, you know? And second, I've been called a man-eating shark. Which I can be."

"I heard you talking to your father. You were so…snappy and forceful, almost commanding."

"With Dad you have to be, or he runs you over. But I can't outshark him when he's the one I learned from, so I didn't even try. Instead, I went with misdirection. By the time he realizes I lied to him about the video and about James Braden's upcoming 'promotion'—which will be an utter shock—it will be way too late."

And Bethany will have gotten a bit of revenge of her own.

I'm proud of her. She's slaying her dragon in her own clever way, and I love that.

I love her.

After another gentle kiss, I hold her close. Soon, I'll tell her the truth, when the time is right. She deserves that. For now, I'm going to support her and believe in her the way her father should have. Once we get past the inconvenient truth about how we met, I will never give her a reason to doubt me again. Then I'm going to ask her to spend her future with me. If she's happy here in Maui, I'll give up my business in North Dakota. I'll also find some way to make my brothers accept her. I'm so in love with her I'll do just about anything to keep her by my side.

*chapter*TEN

"Help me," I say to Ash later that morning.

He and Samantha stopped by our new place to lend a hand, and now the ladies are in the kitchen, checking out the appliances. She's really different than Ash's usual squeezes, and they seem comfortable together. Vaguely, I wonder if the sex is happening yet. Interestingly enough, my guess is no. Sam is going to make him wait after the way he chased Montana's tail, and I kind of respect her for that. But that's not what I wanted to discuss when I dragged my pal outside to grab the last of Bethany's clothes.

"What's going on?" Ash frowns. "Did you tell Beth who you are?"

"No, and before you say anything, I know I've got to soon. But I have to find some way to make sure she doesn't completely hate me afterward. Yes, I created this stupid-ass mess, but I'm in love with her."

"I know. Do you think she's innocent?"

"Yeah." Mostly. I still have a few niggling doubts, but they're really unanswered questions. Things she was too raw to answer last night. Probes that would have killed the feels between us when we needed them. "She told me pretty much everything. She's been through a lot, man. It's beyond awful. So when I'm done confessing everything, I need her to know that I've really, truly fallen for her. There's nothing more important."

"All right. We can work on that. But I've been thinking since we last talked about this. Let me play devil's advocate for a minute."

"Okay, but Bret is already doing a damn good job of that."

He smiles grimly. "In his shoes, I would, too. Look, you've known this woman for…how long?"

"Ten days." Admittedly, it sounds crazy.

"I see you wincing. You get what I'm saying." He leans in and drops his voice. "Personally, I think she's a good human being. A really hard worker, too. But you told me yourself that she's used to playing corporate games and winning. She has to be at least a little bit good at crafting and floating cover stories or she would never have been able to swim in the same chum-infested waters as her father."

"She has a good poker face," I admit. It's still not easy for me to read Bethany. "But once she opened up, she was brutally honest about her past. It's not pretty. Everything she told me jibes with what I know about Barclay Reed and the events that led to his arrest. I even called an FBI agent assigned to the case and he reiterated that the feds have no intention of charging Bethany with anything. Besides, she has no idea who I am. Why would she bother to BS me?"

"That's a valid question. I don't have an answer, unless she's simply covering her tracks in general. But what I'm saying is, your brothers are going to suspect she played you. So will everyone else. I understand you don't want to alienate her when you tell her the truth. But I also want you to make *really* sure she hasn't duped you before you divulge your identity and lay your heart at her feet."

"Demanding proof before I tell her how I feel isn't a good way to start a relationship that requires trust."

He nods as if conceding my point. "There is that. And you've got your mind made up. Since I'm not going to sway you—and I'm not even sure I should—tell me what you want to do."

"Besides get the two-ton gorilla of guilt off my chest so we can figure out how to have a future together?"

"Yeah." He laughs. "What did you have in mind?"

"The whole picket fence, man. She's the first woman I've met who I can see myself with long term. She's smart as hell. Like you said, she's not afraid of hard work. She's gorgeous and surprisingly compassionate. We...click. Something in my gut tells me not to ever let her get away."

"Is that your motive for moving in with her? You're done digging deeper into her life and her past?"

"If I find out more about those things along the way, that's great. But exposing her isn't the reason I want to live with her. I'm sure it sounds crazy. If you were telling me you'd fallen in love with someone after ten days, I'd probably check your temperature, too. But everything I've done in life I did because it felt right, like moving to North Dakota and starting my business. Both decisions turned out good. I think the same might be true of my relationship with Beth. We just need to get to an honest place. So help me figure out how to do that, huh? In time, we'll convince my brothers. But I keep feeling like the stolen money isn't what's important. Bethany is."

"Then like I told you before, you just gotta do it. Rip off the lies like a Band-Aid."

I shake my head. "It can't hurt. She's had enough of that."

"What if tonight, after you're all moved in, you open a bottle of wine, sweet-talk her into bed, then tell her you have feelings for her and that you might have gone out of your way to meet her for the wrong reasons, but you're all in now. She's either going to believe you or she's not."

True, but that's asking a lot of someone who's been betrayed by a parent she idolized for most of her life. In fact, she's been disillusioned by men for a decade. Had her trust burned. She needs me to give her more than platitudes to believe that revenge is now the last thing on my mind.

"You're on the right track, but I think I have the perfect idea."

"Good. I hope it works out. I'd like to see you happy."

After lifting the last suitcase from Ash's car, I lug it toward the front door, where I hear the women chatting and the sports channel in the background informing me that the Jaguars beat the Bills in the first Wild Card game of the playoffs.

I glance over and notice the way Ash is looking at Samantha. "I'd like to see you happy, too. Any chance?"

A sly grin crosses his face. "When I first got together with Sam, I was thinking no-strings sex. But she's successfully—and creatively—put me off and forced me to get to know her. I'm digging the way she has this fun approach to life, but it's serious, too. And you know I've never taken anything too seriously. Her? She's different."

"I totally understand."

Ash claps me on the back, then drops his voice. "You got this. Just convince Beth that being with her has changed your mind."

I also have to convince her that being with her has changed my heart, that I came to Hawaii prepared to make her pay because I hated her. Now all I want to do is love her forever.

"Yep. I'll let you know tomorrow how it goes."

Late that night, I'm about to drop over from exhaustion, but Bethany and I are settled into our new apartment. In truth, it's just shy of a train wreck right now. It's a studio apartment with less than five hundred square feet. I've never lived in a place so run-down and cramped. It came unfurnished, so after Ash and Sam left to start their shift, we spent the afternoon at thrift stores buying a second-hand futon, a coffee table, and a couple of folding chairs, along with some mismatched dishes. At a big-box store, we bought some must-have small appliances and groceries, then lugged it all back here to organize.

Finally, after hours of sweat-inducing work and a takeout pizza, we're settled in. It's a definite step down from the ohana Beth has been staying in. But our new place has a quirky charm I don't hate. And most important, it's ours—together.

While we were at the big-box store, I slipped two doors down to another store while she was perusing a small table and chairs for the dining area. In less than ten minutes, I found the one thing that should convince her I love her and, despite our twisted past, I seriously want to spend my future with her.

A gorgeous two-carat engagement ring. It's simple and elegant and looks exactly like her.

Hopefully, when I propose, she'll say yes. Then, thank god, I should be able to come clean so we can start our future together.

I'm also glad that will mean the end of my poor bartender act. I'm exhausted. Then again, who wouldn't be after a few hours of sleep, thanks to our late-night discussion and our early-morning lovemaking, followed by hours of lifting heavy shit and carting it up two flights of stairs—no elevator—all day? Bethany looked somewhere between weary and catatonic when I shooed her into the shower and told her I'd toss some of the new sheets we laundered in the communal facility downstairs onto our crappy little futon mattress.

And I will. Right now, I feel glued to my chair. I'm trying to muster the energy to move while staring at the black-velvet ring box in my grip, nervous as hell. Israel Kamakawiwo'ole's chill ukulele-rich version of "Somewhere Over the Rainbow" plays in the background, assuring me that dreams I dreamed of really do come true. I hope so. If all the clouds were actually far behind me right now, I could believe it more easily. When I close my eyes, I can picture Beth and me, hand-in-hand, under the swaying palms, all smiles living an amazing life here together. I believe it…almost.

But what if she doesn't say yes? What if she can't forgive me?

As I hear the shower spray turn on, my phone buzzes. Who the hell is calling this late? I glance at the display. Why is Bret ringing me past midnight his time? I shouldn't complain. At least he's calling me after hanging up, hopefully to listen to what I'm saying about Bethany.

"Hey, bro."

"Are you sitting down?"

"Yes."

"Don't be mad, but I did something. I needed to. I *had* to know."

That sounds ominous. "What?"

He hesitates. "I drove to San Diego and broke into Bethany Banks's apartment."

I vault to my feet, nerves and exhaustion forgotten. "What? Why the hell did you do that?"

"To prove you're wrong. She may give you good pussy, but she's a lying, thieving snake. I needed you to see that. And now I can prove it."

Foreboding gongs in my chest. I force myself to take a deep breath. He can't be right. Bethany told me herself that her father left incriminating evidence at her place for others to find, right? Bret simply fell for it.

But I have to hear my brother out. He doesn't understand how I feel and he doesn't know Beth. I have to prove that I'm listening and that I care. "First of all, are you fucking crazy? You could go to jail for breaking and entering. A conviction like that could be attached to every résumé you ever float for the rest of your life."

"Relax. I didn't take anything of value. And no one saw me."

"How do you know? Where are you now?"

"I'm heading out of San Diego now. I drove to a mall, then waited until well after dark to hire a taxi. I paid cash. No one should be able to tie me to anything. But I got two hours alone in your girlfriend's place."

I do my best to tamp down my fury. "You have no right to invade anyone's privacy. You don't see me snooping through your shit."

"Yeah, okay. So it's underhanded. I get it. But what's really important is the shit I found."

"And what is that?"

"Admittedly, nothing at first, except the fact her apartment is almost all white. It's so devoid of color that it's weird. Like she has no personality."

"I promise you she does." But Bethany definitely prefers neat and organized. She likes lines that are simple, colors that are crisp and unfussy. White suits her.

"Well, the place gave me the creeps."

I refrain from pointing out that Bret was predisposed to not like anything about Bethany. "Her decor isn't a reason to convict her of anything. If it was, I would have locked you up a long time ago for violating good taste with all those skateboard posters and bikini shots."

"Ha ha," he returns acidly.

"I'm serious. You don't know her. I do."

"Boning her doesn't make you an expert, either," he spits back at me. "You *think* you know her, but your dick is not the most logical part of your body. Stop being a chump. I saw the evidence of her guilt tonight."

He's clearly dying to tell me all about whatever "smoking gun" he's found. He's convinced it's going to change my mind. I'm not sure how. Bethany has already told me so much, probably more than going through her apartment ever would. But I'd pretty much figured out that truth when I searched the ohana. At the time, I thought prowling through Beth's stuff was simply being thorough and smart. But I didn't start understanding the woman at all until I opened my ears and my mind.

"Bret, look... I'm tired. It's been a long-ass day, and I have to work tomorrow night. I'm pissed as hell at you for taking a chance that might have flushed your future down the toilet, especially for a vendetta. As much as we hate it, Dad is gone. So is the money. But think about this: he was the last person who would ever want you to risk yourself, especially for revenge. Despite what you think you saw, Bethany has told me everything. And I mean *everything* about how the money disappeared. I get why she had nothing to do with it. Which is also why she hasn't been charged with a crime."

"Whatever she told you was bullshit. She wasn't charged with a crime because she fucked the federal prosecutor. I saw the video, bro. I found it tucked away in her apartment. I'll cut you some slack for being bowled over by a pretty face and a centerfold body. She looks like she'd be fantastic to bang. But get the right head in the game, bro. She's responsible for Dad's death. How can you let your dick get in the way of that? How are you living with yourself? Sleeping at night?"

The bottom drops out of my stomach. I gape. Is this the video Barclay hit Beth up for? "How do you know the identity of the guy in the video?"

"His name, James Braden, was on a sticky note in the envelope with the flash drive. All I had to do was Google."

The box containing the ring—the symbol of my future with Beth—drops from my numb fingers.

She fucked the prosecutor? Funny how she never mentioned that part… In fact, she lied and told me she didn't have the video at all. Did she film herself fucking the prosecutor to save her glorified sperm donor from prison, as Barclay seems to think? Or did she whore her body out to save herself?

It's an ugly fucking question, one I don't want to answer.

For months, I've been trying to fathom how she wasn't charged with embezzlement and theft. When she confessed everything and put her spin on it, I believed her. Her explanation sounded so real and she seemed so guilt-ridden and torn. But if I take emotion out of the equation, I gotta be honest…Bret's suggestion makes a lot more sense.

I let out a rough breath. God, this can't be happening. Please tell me it isn't. I close my eyes and try to process Bret's words away. The agony in my chest insists my brain find some other explanation. There must be a perfectly rational one, right?

Like what? And why didn't she tell you the truth about the video?

I have no answers.

Still, I refuse to jump to conclusions. I need to talk to Beth, hear her side.

See how she'll squirm out of this one.

"What did you do with the video?"

"Made a copy. I left the original there, in the envelope she used to mail it to herself. You want to check out the fine piece of blackmail for yourself?"

Do I want to see the woman I'm in love with fuck someone else to avoid being charged with a crime? Even the thought of it cramps my gut.

"Send it." No matter how much I don't want to, I have to watch. I have to see if anything on the footage indicates why she hopped into bed with James Braden.

"I'll do it when I get home." Bret sighs. "I get that you're really vibing with this chick, and she's obviously smart enough to feed you a believable story. But it's better to know the truth now, before you're in even deeper."

Like after we were engaged?

It feels absolutely shitty, but my brother is right.

Behind me, the bathroom door opens and Bethany walks out with a towel wrapped around her clean hair—and absolutely nothing else.

My jaw drops. My blood races. Guess what my cock is doing?

How stupid does that make me?

"Um, thanks. I gotta go."

Bethany sends me a catlike smile and revs my libido even more.

"Call me tomorrow, after you've seen the footage," Bret says. "Then we'll talk about how to nail the bitch to the wall."

"Later," I mutter, staring at the woman who seemed to be every-thing I needed and wanted in a wife…and staggering because my happy vision from mere minutes ago is now falling apart.

"I'm serious, Clint."

Bret is, and he has every reason to be.

"I know you're trying to help. I'll take it from here. And…thanks for looking out for me."

"I've always got your back, bro. Get your head out of her pussy and do the right thing."

With that, we hang up, and Bethany sways toward me. "Who was that?"

"One of my brothers."

"Everything okay?"

No. It's a fucking disaster. I want to confront her, but on the off chance Bret somehow got everything wrong, I don't want to accuse her before I've seen the video. Besides, I'm tired. I'm stupidly fucking emotional. And I also haven't found a way to be honest with Beth myself.

I can't deal with any of this right now.

As I hurtle myself out of the chair, I swoop down and clandestinely scoop up the little ring box before pocketing it. Then I turn to her. "Fine. I'm ready to call it a night. You?"

"Well…" She sidles up to me, pressing her naked body against my bare chest and dusting kisses up my neck. "I'm ready for bed."

If I take what she's offering, she'll only cloud my head. And if she lied to me, I can't let myself want her anymore.

Somehow, I manage to grab only her shoulders and ease her away. "Sorry. I need a shower and some sleep."

"Oh. Okay." Bethany tries to hide her crestfallen expression, but I see her hurt. "All right. Good night."

When she turns away, I hate to end our great—even momentous— day together on a sour note. I wish she could come clean and allay my worries, put this goddamn terrible suspicion to rest once and for all…

"Hey." I grab her wrist and turn her to face me again. "I meant to ask you, what was on the video your dad is after? How did you black-mail the federal prosecutor?"

"He hooked up with a suspect."

That's all she's going to say? "Who? Anyone you know?"

She blinks away. "No one important."

Her lie guts me. I release her quickly, as if touching her burns me. Fuck, if she was so easily dishonest about this question, what else was she dishonest about?

"Gotcha. Sleep well."

Shaking, I turn away and shut the door between us. That ring in my pocket? I might as well throw it in the trash. I'm still going to sleep on this and wait for Bret's video, just in case it contains something that changes my mind. But it's wishful fucking thinking. My broken heart finally agrees with my head. Bethany has played me, and I've just been too dazzled to see her for the beautiful manipulator she is.

So unless a miracle happens, I'm going to tell her who I am…and that I have the video that enabled her to escape prosecution. Then maybe I'll get what I came here for in the first place: justice for my dad.

Now that Bethany has torn my fucking heart out of my chest, ripped it to shreds, and spit on it, nothing else matters.

chapter ELEVEN

The following afternoon, we drive into work. We've barely spoken since we woke on opposite sides of the bed.

I received an email with the video from Bret late this morning, along with apologies that he came home and fell asleep almost instantly because the drive was long and, because of a freak accident on I-5 in Santa Ana, traffic was a bitch. The footage is still on my phone, unwatched. I can't bring myself to open it and see beyond any doubt that Bethany has betrayed me. To know that I fell for someone and I now have the power—and the responsibility?—to destroy her because maybe that's what she deserves.

But I also can't bring myself to stop looking at her, wanting her, wishing she'd explain everything away so I could go on blissfully believing her.

What a fucking fool. I knew before I met her that she played corporate games to win. I thought if I didn't pit myself as her foe, if I approached her instead as a friend and a lover, that she would be human and honest. But no. Maybe she never learned integrity since her father used—and warped—her for his gain. Unless none of that is true, either.

Or maybe I'm letting suspicion get the best of me because it seems crazy that I could fall so hard and fast for a habitual liar and a heartless criminal.

I'm at a decision point now. What I choose next will either make or break us.

"You okay?" Beth asks softly as she stashes her purse in her locker at the back of the bar.

She's asked me at least ten times today.

"Fine," I lie.

"Do we need to talk about something?"

Everything. Make all this confusion go away so I can believe in us again...

But odds are, that isn't going to happen.

"I've just got a lot on my mind after my brother called last night. I need to sort it out. We'll talk after the shift, okay?"

She looks reluctant to let the matter go. "Sure. If you need some space to think, that's understandable. But if you want to talk, if you need a sounding board… You've been so good about that with me, I'd be happy to return the favor."

Because she means that or because she wants another opportunity to gather info and figure out a way to use it so she can keep screwing me over?

God, I hate this fucking uncertainty.

I nod her way, and she clocks in before leaving the break room. I can tell she's worried. Vaguely, I wonder if I actually matter to her or if pretending to give a shit is all part of the act.

Ash told me I had to rip the Band-Aid off and be honest with her. He was right; I do. I've got to force myself to sit down with the footage, take it all in—no matter how hard it is—then man up and let the chips fall.

"How did last night go?" my pal asks as he saunters in, low-voiced. "Did you tell her?"

"No." I close my eyes. I have no doubt he can see my misery all over my face. "I think she played me after all."

He rears back in shock. "What makes you think she's guilty?"

"Everything I was too busy falling for her to see."

"I'm sorry, man. Really." He claps me on the shoulder. "If you need an ear or a sofa, you know where to find me."

I nod, and he clocks in. Before he leaves the break room, he pauses. "I don't know if it matters to you, but as I came this direction a minute ago, I noticed the dude in the loud Hawaiian shirt with the even louder mouth is back. He's already drunk. I think he's unstable."

Great. I don't need Paul Daniels adding another wrinkle to this mess. I'll keep an eye on him. Whatever Bethany's sins—and they might be plenty—she doesn't deserve his violence.

"Thanks."

With a nod, Ash leaves.

Finally, I'm by myself. And I'm out of excuses. I have to watch the video.

My hands shake as I shut the door. No one else should come in here since our shift is about to start. If I gave a shit about this job—or anything but the truth—I'd be out there helping Ash set up. But he'll cover for me since he knows I need a few minutes.

Finally, I launch my email, ignoring everything but the attachment from my brother. Before I see a single image, I already know this is going to hurt like hell.

Four sickening minutes later, I close the app, darken my phone. After watching Bethany use her moves on the suit she seduced, there's a gaping hole in my chest where my heart used to be. I'm in danger of throwing up what little lunch I managed to choke down. The emptiness of my future without her stretches out before me. Her perfidy is going to leave a scar for decades. God, she's an amazing liar. I believed everything, all the way down to the boo-hoo stories about how her father used her.

This video proves she's more than capable of using someone for her own ends without anyone coercing her at all.

I feel so fucking gullible and stupid.

But I've got to detach myself from her and turn over this evidence. It may burn her—if the feds choose to open the investigation against her again. But if I won't be walking away happy, then I should get the justice for Dad that I came to Maui for.

Slowly, I rise. Weariness beats me down. Fury bubbles under it all, simmering dangerously. I put a lid on it. Sure, I could be mad at her, but I'm far angrier with myself. Bethany was only being who she is deep down. I'm the dumb ass who fell for it.

When I make my way out of the break room, Andy is standing in the hallway, looking all too ready to point out that I wasn't behind the bar at four o'clock, which makes me late. Instead, he takes one look at my face and frowns.

"Do you need the night off?"

I drag in a breath. Even that's excruciating. My whole body feels ready to crumble. Goddamn it, I hate this thousand-pound weight of defeat crushing.

"I think…I need to quit. I wasn't really here to work. I was here for Bethany."

Andy heaves a sigh. "I kind of figured. You look like shit so I hate to ask, but can you stay for this shift? I'll get Terry to cover you tomorrow. He owes me some extra time after being so sick. After that, I'll find a replacement."

I'd like to help a guy out, and I hate to think I'm too whipped by one lying bitch to perform a function as simple as pouring drinks with a smile, especially when the bar isn't particularly busy, but I don't know if I have it in me tonight. "I'll do my best."

"Thanks. I actually came back here to tell you that the tall blond guy who visited your girlfriend—or maybe ex-girlfriend—the other day is back. And whatever he said made her cry. She ran down to the beach. He followed. They've been gone a few minutes."

I don't care what Stephen said to her. Well, I try not to care. Did she bamboozle him, too? Or are they in on this scam together? It would be a sly but clever move for her to take advantage of the fact that her father has a vengeful enemy determined to see him locked up. Once Barclay was in prison, then she could make off with her lover and all the money. And that would conveniently set them up for life. *Nice.*

I murmur a thanks to Andy, who nods and wanders off. When I look up, Ash motions me over with a frown.

"What?"

"You look terrible."

"It's even worse than I thought."

Watching Bethany work James Braden over with her mouth, then her lithe little body… Granted, she didn't look as if she was enjoying being naked with the pompous windbag. But that's neither here nor there. She's not the prey wrapped up in her father's web. She's the fucking black widow.

"Jesus. I'm sorry. What are you going to do?"

I shrug. "What I should have a long time ago. She's on the beach?"

"With that Lund dude, yeah. He came in all full of righteous anger and acted super protective of Beth. He murmured a few words to her in the corner, showed her something, then she fell apart."

The smart thing to do would be to leave. Turn and walk away from her drama and her lies. Not give her another chance to sink her hooks into me because I have this terrible feeling I'll take one look at her and my heart will ache to make excuses and I'll be too fucking weak to resist her. I can't let that happen. And I can't let her have the last word. I want to look at her, face to face, and tell her what she's done to my family. I want her to understand what an amazing man her greed killed. I want to show her pictures of my brothers so she'll know the faces of boys orphaned before they were ready to be men. I want her to feel some fucking guilt for once in her life.

Is she even capable?

That anger brewing in my belly starts spewing as I march outside the bar and spot Bethany pressed against Stephen Lund. Her entire body shakes with supposed sobs. He's holding her and stroking her hair, as if he's comforting her.

Is any of it real? Or has she conned this poor sap, too? After all, why take the money from the Caymans and split it with a lover when she can have it all to herself?

Vaguely, I wonder why she even bothered to make this pit stop in Hawaii and why she worked in this nowhere bar doing this dead-end job if she had nearly a billion dollars waiting for her in the Caribbean. Some part of her cover? An elaborate ploy to keep the feds off her trail? But doesn't she already have the perfect get-out-of-jail card with that video? James Braden won't want to lose his position of power. I'm sure he'd do almost anything to keep this secret buried.

Whatever. I'm done trying to figure out how Bethany's mind works. Time to confront her and end this.

"Hey," I call out to them.

She wrenches out of his embrace, nose red, cheeks wet with tears—and eyes blazing with betrayal. "Clint Dietrich, huh? How long were you going to feed me that bullshit, you son of a bitch?"

So she knows my identity? A glance over at Lund, sharp brow raised, tells me he's the snitch.

"Until I got the truth, which I apparently never did," I spit back. "But congratulations. Now you have the real name of the latest guy you fucked over so you can add me to your long and distinguished list."

Gaping, she lunges my way. "What the hell are you talking about? I believed in you. I told you some of the ugliest, most shameful details about my past. Things I've never really told any other human being because I loved you—"

"Aww, my heart is bleeding."

Her eyes flash rage, but her sniffles offset the menace in her expression. "And you never even told me your real fucking name. When you came on strong day one, hot and gorgeous and so focused on me, I should have known it was too good to be true, that all your talk about wanting to get to know me was just lies. You only wanted information. You wanted to use me." She shakes her head in self-recrimination. "I was the idiot who fell for how caring you seemed, how perfect we felt together. I'm genuinely sorry about your father, Mr. Holmes. I really liked your dad a lot. He was one of my favorite clients, one of the few who knew who my father really was. He told you, didn't he? You came here knowing. And you blamed me, like all the others, because I was the face of Reed Financial."

Is she really going to play the victim until the bitter end? "I watched my father die on my living room floor because *you* didn't call him back when the news broke."

Bethany recoils. "I didn't know that. I'm sorry. I feel terrible about his passing—"

"Save your empty platitudes, *Beth*. You were never going to call because you were complicit in stealing the money he'd earned with his life's work." It feels both good and horrible to finally say that. The rage growing and growling inside me pats me on the back for laying that at her feet.

But my stupid heart is still breaking.

"What? No! I couldn't call your dad—or anyone—back that day. The FBI was *interrogating* me. They thought I was complicit, too. I eventually proved them wrong."

"No, you proved calculating and cunning after you fucked the federal prosecutor. Congratulations. Did you do it to save your dad's miserable ass? Or were you planning all along to take the money and run by yourself?"

Bethany's jaw drops. She blinks, seems to reel, then shakes her head, looking beyond hurt. "Is that what you really think of me?"

I've got to hand it to her. If I didn't know the circumstances and hadn't seen the evidence, her crushed expression would convince me that I've got everything wrong and that my lack of faith is breaking her heart.

"That's what I *know*. And don't think I won't use it against you."

"Then we have nothing left to say. For the record, I slept with James Braden at my father's request—something I hadn't done to help him in over four years. Something I'd told him I would never do again. But I demeaned myself because, at the time, I thought Barclay was innocent. He'd convinced me the feds were on a witch hunt at Douglas Lund's request because the man knows big people in high places. The father I'd looked up to my whole life was seemingly being framed for a crime he didn't commit. His business—hell, *my* business—would undoubtedly crash down. Everything I'd ever poured my energy or soul into would be gone. First, I tried to talk to Braden, convince him using every other method I could. In the end, he told me he would look the other way, but only if I fucked him. You see, he was six weeks post-divorce after his wife left him for another man, and he was looking for revenge sex. He said I would do. So I let him use me. I wanted to cry the whole time. But what choice did I have? What would you have done, if you could, to save your dad?"

I think of the exhausting thirty-plus minutes of CPR I tried to perform—to no avail. I would have done anything, of course. Would I have let someone I didn't love use me? Yeah, without hesitation. I also took Bethany to bed way after it was too late to save my dad. Does that make me worse? No. By then I was falling for her...

What, if anything, does she feel for me?

Nope. I'm not asking myself any more questions where she's concerned. Every time I do, I just give myself mental wiggle room to let her fuck me over again, and she's way too good at covering her ass. I can't let myself believe a word she says anymore.

It's over. We're done.

"When all else fails, spread your legs and dazzle the poor schmuck, huh? You got that act down, sweetheart."

"Are you serious right now? I paid Braden for his silence with my body. I made love to you with my heart. But since you lied to me from day one, I don't expect you to understand how genuine my feelings were. And for your information, I had *no* idea my father filmed my encounter with Braden. When he told me later he had so he would have an 'insurance policy,' I was horrified. Oh, and he gave me pointers on how to improve my performance. You know, for the next time he needed my 'help.' I still didn't find out for months after that my own father was both lying to me and ready to let me take the fall for his crimes."

"Why did you lie to me about what was on the video and whether you had it?"

"I didn't tell you the contents because I was ashamed," she says as if it's obvious. "I whored myself out to help a man who will never know the meaning of love and never gave two shits about me except for the money I could make him and the favors I could do for him. And I didn't lie about the location of the video. I thought it was gone. How did you find it?"

"Why would I give you any clues to help you talk your way out of this one?"

She rolls her eyes. "I'm not trying to talk my way out of anything. I'm genuinely trying to understand how you got your hands on it. I found the video on my dad's laptop. I saved a copy on a flash drive in case I ever had to explain myself, then did my best to erase it from his machine. But Dad was paranoid at that point. He was having security monitor all emails and searching everyone's purses and briefcases before they exited the building. He told me it was because there was a corporate spy in our midst selling our secrets. I know now that he wanted to make sure no one could help the feds build a case against him. So I physically mailed the flash drive to myself. As far as I knew, no one was checking the mail room. But the flash drive never came to my apartment, so I assumed it was lost. Barclay destroyed his computer as the feds were rushing in to raid our offices. I'd mailed myself the only remaining copy—that I knew of. How did you find it?"

Bret didn't mention where in Bethany's apartment he found the video or how he located it. But he did mention an envelope... Coincidence? Shit, if there's any chance Bethany is telling the truth...

No, I can't let myself hope that. It screws me every time.

"It's irrelevant. I've seen the footage. And from my viewpoint, it sure looks like you took Braden to bed to avoid being charged with a crime."

"Well, you'd be wrong. And how do you think for one minute that you have any moral superiority? Everything you ever said or did with me was a lie." She huffs. "You know, I shouldn't be surprised that the first time I let myself fall in love, you turn out to be no different than most every other man. You used me. You never cared about me. You just wanted revenge. Well, you got it. I hope you're happy." She turns to Stephen, who stepped back and silently watched our exchange. "Can you take me somewhere? Anywhere." She sends another glare at me. "Away from him."

That shouldn't cut me to the quick. It does.

"Sure, shorty." He eases forward and moves to wrap a protective arm around her.

I step between them and clutch her arm. "It wasn't an act. Oh, it should have been. I wanted it to be. But if anyone is the idiot here, it's me. I loved you, and I have no reason to lie about that now. I was going to fucking propose to you." I grind out the words in fury. "I had the ring in my pocket last night when I found out about the incriminating video."

Why am I defending myself? Why do I think it will even matter to her?

She shakes her head, clearly fighting off new tears. "Stop! I can't handle more of your bullshit. Yes, I probably deserve this heartbreak for all the wretched things I've done in the past. Fine. I'll heal. I'll learn from this mistake and move on. At least I can live with the knowledge that I was genuine with you. But you know the really terrible part? If you had come to me and told me your actual name and said that you'd once wanted payback but had changed your mind, I would have believed you. I would have forgiven you. I still would have loved you. But that's my fatal flaw: blind loyalty. No more. I'm done being lied to and used. Fuck off." She wrenches free. "And don't come back."

I stand numbly as she dashes away and disappears into the bar. Through the open awning, I see her disappear down the hall. She appears a moment later under the bright lights, wiping her cheeks, purse on her shoulder. Samantha hugs her. Andy says something that has her shaking her head. Then she disappears out the back door.

"I fucking want to break your goddamn face right now."

Zipping around, I glare at Lund. "Because I fucked your girl, too?"

It's a nasty swipe, and I wish I could take the words back the minute they're out of my mouth. What if Bethany was being honest and Stephen really is just a friend? What if she genuinely gave all her body not to keep herself—but her father—from prosecution? What if she really loved me?

What if I was too fucking suspicious to listen?

That seems to break his calm. "No, because you fucked her over, just like I suspected you would the minute I started digging into you and nothing added up. You broke a good friend's fragile heart. Did I take Bethany to bed once? Yeah. She'd never known what it was like to have sex with someone she liked and trusted. So I tried to be there for her. It wasn't passionate. It never happened again. I tried to be good to her. And you're being an absolute shit for not grasping that the multi-millionaire scumbags her father hooked her up with were strangers who saw her as nothing more than a piece of ass. Believe me when I tell you Barclay didn't give two shits what Bethany had to do to make his life better. He expected it of her, and she tried so, so hard to please that terrible son of a bitch. She had no one else. The worst of it is after Braden finished with her, she felt so dirty and terrible and worthless. She admitted to me years ago that's how she always felt after sex. I hated Barclay for putting her in that position. But you know what? I loathe you even more right now because you just made her feel a hundred times worse than her father ever did."

I flinch, but his words still flay me open. "Don't lecture me."

"You need to hear the fucking truth," he roars back. "Finally faced with overwhelming evidence that her father had swindled all their clients, Bethany did the bravest thing she could, you righteous mother-fucker. She took everything Barclay had stashed in her safe, prowled through every bit of it, including his electronic records she accessed via his password records. Then she made sure it all reached the FBI. That woman you think took everything from you, including your father? When they first arrested Barclay, the FBI only had circumstantial evidence. Bethany changed that. She's the only reason Barclay Reed will be going to prison."

I stagger back. Stare. The words repeat themselves in my head.

Oh, my god.

"How do you know that for sure?"

"Suspicious till the end?" He shakes his head. "My half sister, Nia, told me. Her husband, Evan, confirmed since Bethany asked him to provide the feds access to Barclay's files on his private storage servers. I came to Maui because, like her, I'm having to deal with the sins of my father. And there are a lot of them, some I may never be able to forgive. But I also came because I knew Bethany was here and because I suspected she'd be hurting and need a friend. I intended to convince her that I didn't blame her for Barclay getting Amanda pregnant. I'm pissed, but my sister is an adult. She knew exactly who he was. At least half this shit is her fault. My dad wouldn't hear any of that. He went all *V is for Vendetta* on Bethany's father. And now we're in this fucking mess." He shakes his head in disgust. "But I'll take her from here. You go back to North Dakota, though I'd rather you burn in hell. And stay the hell away from Bethany. I'll take care of her until the real Mr. Right comes along."

When Lund turns and makes his way across the sand, I barely notice. It's all I can do to stay upright and process the bomb he just dropped on me.

Maybe she's duped him, too. It's possible Stephen has all his facts wrong. But if he was too smart to buy my act, it stands to reason that he wouldn't buy any Bethany put on, either.

And what if Lund is right? What if Bethany is telling me the truth? What if I screwed up by letting my "logic" deep-six the gut instinct that told me she's innocent?

Fuck. Right or wrong, stupid or not, I've got to talk to her before Stephen takes her away. Before it's too late. Before the woman I once swore was the best thing to ever happen to me leaves me for good.

I dart up the beach and into the bar. Inside, Andy looks less than thrilled. Samantha glares my way. Ash is giving me a what-the-fuck side-eye. Lund is nowhere to be found. Ditto for Bethany.

"Where did they go?" I look at my pal. If anyone will understand my need to find her and unearth the truth, it will be him.

"Out the back door, to the parking lot."

I pull his keys from the pocket of my shorts as I take off in that direction. "If she comes back, keep her here and text me."

"Dude, I don't think she's coming back—ever."

Samantha's glare only turns more glacial. "I don't know what you said, but she looks absolutely devastated, you asshole."

If Bethany has been honest with me from the start, that makes perfect sense. If she hasn't, why would she bother to put on an act to convince my pal and his kinda-sorta girlfriend that I've broken her heart? The obvious answer: she wouldn't.

Oh, fucking hell. Tell me I didn't screw up this badly…

But I can't deal with Ash, Samantha, or any of the others right now. I have to see if I can catch Beth and Lund in the parking lot before they leave.

Shoving my way out the double doors, I stumble onto the porch, under the rusting overhang. It doesn't take more than a few seconds to scan the nearly empty lot. I never paid attention to what kind of car her guy pal drives, so I don't know whether Lund has already taken her away. But I don't see either of them hanging around.

But I hear a sudden groan of pain. What the hell? I can't see anyone, but it sounds as if it's coming from around the corner of the building.

"Shut up, Junior."

Barclay Reed. I'd know that patronizing voice anywhere.

What is the fucker doing here? Even if only half of what Bethany told me turns out to be true, he's a horrible father and an even worse human being. Ultimately, he had at least some hand—if not all—in swindling money that belonged to my father and all the other Reed Financial clients. I hate him. He deserves full punishment under the law. Since I came to Maui for justice, I should start with him.

I'll figure out how to feel about Bethany later.

"Oh, my god!" She sounds horrified. "What did you do to Stephen? You could have killed him."

"So what? Listen to me, you ungrateful bitch. I gave you half your blood. I raised you. I educated you. I gave you valuable life lessons on a silver platter. And how did you repay me?"

The wooden boards of the patio creak with someone's every step. I try to ease closer silently.

"Dad, put the bat down." Bethany's voice trembles.

My eyes flare wide. Is the son of a bitch threatening her?

"Don't you back away from me," he snarls. "I'm not going to use it on you unless you make me. Lund Junior just needed his mouth shut. Stupid prick. He's soft and he's weak if he thinks his father's greatest sin is in not recognizing his illegitimate black daughter. As if anyone gives a shit about Nia… Stephen would be stupider than hell to disown his father and walk away from his inheritance because of one irrelevant female. If he does, that only proves he'll never make it in the real world, and I'd certainly be doing everyone a favor by offing him. But that's not why I'm here. You better explain why my attorney called me today to tell me the evidence the feds have against me is all the shit I stashed in your safe. Did you fucking turn me in?"

"You planted that evidence in my apartment so the FBI could find it on my property and think I was guilty," she returns incredulously. "What did you expect me to do?"

"I had to have a backup strategy. I would have gotten you the best lawyers on the planet. At the very least, you would have only served a few years. You're young. You could bounce back. I'm an old man."

"You're not even sixty."

"That's still too old to go to prison."

Holy shit. I won't even ask what's wrong with Barclay Reed. Obviously everything. Sure, he's seemingly confirming everything Lund told me on the beach. But one thing is crystal clear—and far more important—right now: Bethany is in danger.

I don't care about the rest of the conversation. Sure, I have more questions. Eventually I'll want to understand. But now I only care about keeping Bethany alive.

Barclay having a baseball bat concerns the hell out of me. I can't let him whack me unconscious like Lund or I'll be no good to Beth. I need the element of surprise. Or I need help.

Suddenly, I feel a heavy hand on my shoulder.

Startled, I whirl and find Paul Daniels and his loud shirt behind me, holding a finger to his lips.

He wants me to be quiet? Fuck that. I can't leave Beth to Barclay's mercy. He clearly has none because, just like she said, he's a sociopath. He cares only about himself.

I wrench from Daniels's grasp, ready to charge forward, focused on how I'm going to stop Bethany's father. This time, her former client wraps his beefy fingers around my arm and hauls me back and shoots me a silent, thunderous scowl before motioning me to be quiet again. Why? Is he looking to use the element of surprise against Barclay? Or Beth?

Then he withdraws a 9mm pistol from his pocket and flashes me a terrible smile. My blood runs cold.

Emphatically, I shake my head. He can't hurt her. He can't snuff Bethany Banks out of my life.

I'm not ready to live without her.

That realization blows me away, but I have to compartmentalize it for now and deal with the threat in front of me.

"Run, Beth! Go!"

Hoping like hell she can escape her father, I turn to face Daniels, prepared to stand between her and his bullet.

The shorter man pushes me out of the way with a snarl. "Stupid son of a bitch."

As I hear pounding footsteps thundering off the porch and into the dusk, my shoulder bounces against the wall. I whirl toward Daniels, as Barclay comes around the corner with a killing glare all over his face—directed at me.

Until he sees his former client holding the gun.

He pales and holds up both hands, shaking his head. "Paul... I'm glad you're here. You can help me make that little blond thief pay for all the pain she's put us all through. She wants everyone to think I tried to frame her but—"

"Fuck you, Reed. It's over. I overheard everything you said. If anyone was set up, it was her. After all, you had no problem offering her to me as incentive to invest. Everything you've done is even more appalling now that I know she's your daughter. What kind of father tries to destroy his own kid? And what kind of asshole steals the fortune a dying man wants to leave to his children? You deserve to rot in hell, you motherfucking scumbag." Daniels raises the gun.

"No!" Barclay pleads.

"Don't!" Suddenly, I hear Beth's voice and look up to find her standing ten feet past her father's shoulder. "He's done terrible things, I know. And I'm sorry about your cancer. But we can't take justice into our own hands."

The way I did.

"Believe me, I thought about it," she goes on. "Once I realized what he'd done to me, there were times I *really* wanted to, but his fate isn't up to you. Or me. I didn't want to throw away the rest my life for him. Do you? Honestly?"

"My life is already over," he growls.

Daniels is going to pull the damn trigger. I can hear it in his voice.

In that split second, I see Bethany lunging toward her father like she intends to do whatever it takes to save him. I can't let her. Daniels isn't going to mete out justice, but cold-blooded murder.

I have a single instant to choose, but there's no choice at all. I have to protect Bethany, even if that means her father dies. She must live.

With a roaring leap, I tackle her out of harm's way just as Barclay's former client pulls the trigger.

His shot shatters the quiet paradise. Nearby birds squawk and fly to the safety of the skies. Tourists in the bar scream. People charge out. And Bethany's father crumples to the concrete in a bloody heap.

chapter TWELVE

"Are you all right?" I ask Bethany.

It's been hours since the shooting. Since her father died right before her eyes. Barclay Reed was a callous son of a bitch who died faster and easier than he deserved. After all, he's the reason my own father is gone, and I'm fucking glad to see the justice I came to Maui for has finally been served. But that barely registers now. I'm focused on Bethany, on the horror and wrenching sadness she's struggling through after watching the man she looked up to her entire childhood unexpectedly and violently take his last breath.

"Fine," she murmurs, not meeting my gaze.

It's a lie. She's not fine. She's not merely exhausted. She is emotionally spent.

Besides Barclay Reed lying on a slab at the morgue, Stephen Lund suffered a blow to the head that resulted in a concussion. He's in the hospital for observation, but should recover in a day or two. The police arrested Paul Daniels for murder, interviewed Bethany and me at length, then left with assurances that they'll be in touch. I'm hoping she finds some consolation in that.

A glance at my phone tells me it's almost ten p.m. Through the evening, Ash brought us bottles of water. Samantha followed up with salads and appetizers, even a couple of scoops of ice cream, trying to tempt Bethany into eating. She refused every morsel and now looks ready to fall over. I'm worried about her.

The woman has been through hell. In the span of an hour, I broke her heart and she lost her dad. Despite all that, she answered the detectives' questions clearly and concisely. Her voice trembled, but she never succumbed to tears. I see them lurking now, needing release. Normally, I would put my arms around her and lend her my strength, encourage her to give me all her troubles. In fact, I'd love to. I'm desperate to. But she refuses to lean on me. Hell, she's barely speaking to me.

I have no one to blame but myself.

I fucking wish I had a do-over on this entire afternoon. If I could go back, be honest with her about my identity, then ask questions before I accuse her of playing me, remind myself there are two sides to every story… None of that would save her father, of course. Paul Daniels was determined to have his pound of flesh and, once he heard the truth from Barclay Reed's own lips, he was willing to go to prison to get it. Maybe that's not a surprise since his days are numbered anyway. But I compounded her sudden loss with my lack of trust and utter betrayal. I thought I understood the situation, so I opened my big mouth and said all the worst things. I was so fucking wrong.

How do we come back from this? Or can we? Did I destroy us forever?

Despite those anxieties, I can't not help when she looks so ready to fall over. "Sweetheart…"

When I cup her elbow to lead her toward a chair, Bethany twists away. "Don't touch me."

Sighing, I release her and step back, somehow managing to keep my hands off her. But it's a fight. Touching Bethany, comforting her, feels so right.

"I'm sorry for your loss," I say instead. "I know you and your father had a difficult relationship at the end, but it's always painful to lose someone you love."

She wraps her arms around her middle as if she's trying to give herself the fortitude to press on. "More than I probably should have. But he was a positive influence in my childhood. He made sure I never wanted for anything, he educated me well, and spent time with me. For that, I'll always be grateful. I'm just in shock now. I'm sure I'll grieve him and eventually accept that he's neither the man I thought nor here with me anymore. Forgiveness for everything he did—to everyone—will take time."

True. It's a small blessing that she's already considering absolving him. If I'd forgiven sooner, I wouldn't have been stupid enough to pursue Bethany under false pretenses. And I wouldn't have gotten my heart ripped out. I'm probably only getting what I deserve… But if she can eventually find mercy in her soul for her father, she'll find peace.

Of course, part of me can't help but wonder if she might find it in her heart to forgive me someday, too.

"The healing will happen when you're ready," I murmur. "And I know it's a small consolation that he won't be able to hurt you anymore—"

"But an important one. At least now there will be no trial. Not having my name dragged through the mud anymore will be a relief. The truth can come out, and I can walk free from his shadow and move on with my life."

"Eventually, those will feel like positives."

Bethany turns to glare my way. "Yes, but don't act like you care. I've already heard enough of your lies. I don't need more."

"Sweetheart—"

"Don't call me that."

I sigh. "I'm really sorry, Beth. For everything I accused you of. For every lie I told you. For—"

She holds up a hand. "It doesn't matter now. You got the answers you came for. You got the justice you wanted. The will my father updated weeks ago in anticipation of his divorce becoming final leaves me everything. So hopefully, I'll be able to track down what's left of the victims' stolen funds and return them to everyone, you included. Beyond that, you and I don't have anything else to say. It would be best if you didn't contact me anymore."

Oh, fuck.

But I need to tell her so many things. That I feel like the most stupidly righteous idiot on the planet. That I regret not being honest with her. But most of all, that I love her. Bethany isn't ready to hear any of that now. I understand. I won't give up on us, though. I may have fallen for her because I orchestrated this giant lie to ferret out her "crimes," and I regret that like hell. But I don't regret a moment of the time we spent together.

"Did you call your siblings?"

She shakes her head. "I don't think the news of Barclay's passing is something I should deliver over the phone. It would be better to gather everyone together and tell them face to face."

"You're right. Grab your purse, and I'll take you—"

"No, I'll find my own way. I don't want to see you, spend time with you, or even be in the same room with you. I'm moving out of the apartment, so you can do what you want with the lease. It's over, Clint. We're done."

Her words hurt like a physical blow, but arguing is pointless now. I fucked up and all I can do is give her the time and space she needs while hoping I'll someday have the opportunity to put us back together.

"You don't have a car, and even if they've discharged Stephen from the hospital, he's in no condition to drive. I'll get you to Maxon and Keeley's place. I'll even help you tell your siblings what happened so you don't have to live through it again by yourself. Then, if you still want me to go, I will." I can't resist cupping her face. "But I'll be back. I meant what I said when I told you that I fell in love with you and I had every intention of asking you to be my wife."

Bethany hasn't cried all day, but now my words reduce her to tears. "Don't. Just…don't."

I'm pushing, and she can't take it.

Slowly, I drop my hand. "Okay. We won't talk about it any more tonight. Just let me get you to your brother's house safely."

She hesitates, then nods. "Only because it's the fastest way there, and they deserve to know what's happened."

We make our way out the bar's back door, probably for the last time. I already told Andy I wouldn't be back. No need to work this job now that my cover story is moot. I doubt Bethany will be back, either. She needs to grieve. And just like I can't stand to be in my North Dakota home anymore, I doubt she'll want to work in the place where she watched her father die.

The drive to the inn is tense and quiet. She texts Maxon and tells him to gather the family at his place. It's important, but she refuses to say why. He agrees, then she darkens her phone and zones out. Whatever she sees of the dark night out her window seems to hold her attention. Or maybe that's just her way of avoiding me.

We're drawing close to Maxon and Keeley's bed-and-breakfast, and

I have this sense of a clock ticking away the last of my time with Bethany. I try to rationalize. She'll still be on the island tomorrow. I won't let her get too far from my side. I'll find small ways to let her know I love her and that I'm here for her without pushing too hard. She thinks she doesn't want me now, but someday she'll realize that she wants a lover who will care for her, who will devote himself to her. I'll be waiting. I'll be ready to prove that I'm sorry and that I'm worthy. I'll beg her forgiveness. Then I'll do whatever it takes to convince her that she's it for me. She's the only woman I'll ever love.

Still, what if that day never comes? What if these are the last moments I ever spend with Bethany?

Panic eats at my gut. If I don't say something, will she leave thinking she meant nothing to me except revenge? Will I regret staying silent in these final moments for the rest of my lonely life?

I reach for her hand. "I was proud of you tonight, Beth."

For once, she doesn't wrench away. She also doesn't reply.

Into the silence, I go on. "I know from personal experience that what you went through tonight with your father was one of the hardest things to deal with—ever. A father's death stays with you, and you constantly wonder what you could have done to save him."

Finally, she turns to me with a little frown furrowed between her brows. "I've already wondered that."

"The answer is nothing. Paul Daniels was on a mission, and you couldn't have stopped him. Just like I couldn't do anything to prevent my dad's heart attack. Your father made enemies. My father didn't take care of his health. Sometimes accepting that things are out of your control is the most difficult lesson of all. It's a lesson I wish I would have accepted before I lost you."

Bethany pulls her hand free. "Don't."

I back down. I have to. "You handled the police and their questions with poise and perfection. I'm not surprised. You're strong, Beth. Hell, you had the spine and the independence weeks ago to realize you had to cut ties with your dad. You'll carry on professionally now that he's gone and I have no doubt you'll succeed."

Slowly, she nods. "I'm not going to let my father take my future from me. He's already tainted too much of my past. I'm damn good at investment counseling, and I love what I do. Multimillionaires and Wall Street bigwigs may never trust me again, but that's okay. I'll face the future on my own terms. That's something I should have done all along."

"Where will you go?" I ask as we pull up at the inn.

My time with Bethany is almost up—and it's killing me.

She shrugs. "I don't know. There's nothing but terrible memories in San Diego. I'll probably sell my ridiculously expensive condo I can't afford anymore and find someplace else to call home. You?"

I'll be wherever Bethany is, but she isn't ready to hear that. "I'm going to leave North Dakota. The guy who's been watching my business back there wants to buy it. I'm going to let him. The sale of my dad's insurance agency should be complete in the next week or two. Both of my younger brothers are away at college. So I guess I'll be looking for someplace to call home, too. And a new job to go with it." Then I take a risk and grab her hand again. "But wherever that is, Beth, I'll be thinking of you. And only you. You may never believe me because I know I didn't show you the way I should have, but I love you. I love the way you make me think. I love the way you challenge me to understand you. I love it when you finally let me behind your walls and smile. I love that, when you give your body to me, you do it completely. Most of all, I love your strength and courage. I love the way you didn't let your father or anyone else defeat you. I love that you're real and true and that you taught me so much about ignoring my assumptions and listening to my heart."

She doesn't say anything, just continues to look down, occasionally swiping at her wet cheeks with a shaking hand.

"Beth…" I tilt her chin to face me.

Her big eyes, the pain twisting her mouth, and the silvery paths running down her face all rip me apart. She didn't let her asshole father break her, but I just might. I hate that—and myself for hurting her—more than anything.

If Bethany never gives me a second chance, I have no doubt she'll be my biggest regret.

She closes her eyes as if she can't take the intimacy of our stare anymore. I want to lean in and kiss her passionately, convince her I mean every word I say. We're only inches apart… But that's not what she needs now.

Instead, I press my lips softly to hers—a breath, a brush. A good-bye.

When I ease back, I see Maxon, Griff, Noah, and Evan all hovering on the lanai, looking grim. Just beyond, I spot the women gathered in the great room, heads bent together, hands clasped. I hazard a glance Bethany's way. She looks relieved to see everyone and yet more than nervous now that the moment is upon her.

"I'm here if you need me," I vow.

She shakes her head. "I've got this. It's something I need to do. It would be better if you left and didn't come back."

I'm hurt but not surprised by her answer. "Take care of yourself. If you need or want me for anything—ever—all you have to do is call."

"I'm done being blindly loyal. And you've proven that I can't trust you."

Before I can reply, Maxon and Noah are at my door, opening it. Bethany exits the car on the other side, and Griff pulls her straight into his waiting arms.

"We know," her oldest brother says somberly. "News travels fast on an island this size."

At least Bethany won't have to break the news or explain everything again. Instead, Griff and Evan lead her inside the house. All the women rise and greet her, Harlow the first to hug her and offer both affection and condolences. I'm so relieved that Bethany won't be alone tonight.

"Thanks for being here for Beth," I tell the other two men. "She's really broken up."

"We know she is," Maxon assures me.

"Not only is he gone, she watched the son of a bitch die…"

Noah winces.

Maxon lets out a curse. "I'm sorry for her. I hated my father, and I'm neither surprised nor upset that a former client offed him. But I wrote him out of my life to preserve my mental health long ago. Bethany only realized his true colors a few weeks back, and before she could even reconcile the reality with the fairy-tale father she thought had raised her, he's gone."

Exactly. "She's grieving. She needs people who care."

"She's got us. And she's got you, too."

I shake my head. "It's…over. I'll let her explain if she wants to share. I can't do anything right now except respect her wishes and go."

Noah scowls. "You're walking away from her?"

"Not by choice." And not forever. "She wants me to. And…I deserve to suffer."

"Whoa. Slow your roll." Harlow's husband looks at me as if I've lost my damn mind. "You're giving up? When she needs you most?"

I open my mouth to explain, but Maxon waves a hand in my face. "I get it. You're doing the altruistic thing for some reason. It's a mistake. Maybe that's my perspective because ruthless is bred into my veins. It's a Reed trait…along with not knowing your heart. That's where Bethany is at right now. If I had only listened to my head, I wouldn't be married to the best woman in the world and I wouldn't have a beautiful baby girl."

"Same for Harlow," Noah cuts in. "I can't tell you how often she tried to put distance between us. I'm damn glad I was pushy and tenacious."

Their admissions surprise me. I thought they'd always been deliriously happy. Nice to know someone overcame their differences and found happiness. Just not sure that's ever going to be Bethany and me…

"Did either one of you deceive your wives?"

Their identical scowls might have been comical if I was in any mood to laugh.

"No," Noah admits.

Maxon shakes his head. "But I did plenty of other shitty stuff. Trust me. Do you love Bethany?"

"Yes." I came for my pound of flesh…but I'm the one who lost my heart.

"Then we'll help you."

"Why?" It's a passing curiosity. His help or lack thereof isn't going to change the outcome. Bethany has to decide on her own that she wants me. "When we first met, you didn't like me much."

"I didn't. But the more time my sister spent with you, the more she came out of her shell. None of us had managed to get past her defenses. You did. If you give up on her now, she'll only retreat into herself. And since I've gone this route—so has Griff—she'll turn brittle. If you love her, don't let that happen."

I look up at Beth. The wives are reaching out to offer their comfort and support…and already I see her pulling away.

"Believe me, I have no intention of walking away forever, but she needs time to grieve. And she needs time to figure out if she can forgive me. I'm not going far, though. And she'll have to tell me that she'll *never* love me before I give up on her completely."

Maxon smiles his approval and claps me on the shoulder. "Perfect. Keep working on her. We'll help. She'll come around."

I can only hope.

Noah nods. "Why don't you crash for the night and come back in the morning when she's fresh. Right now, she's in no shape to make lifelong decisions. Things may look a lot different tomorrow."

I doubt it, but I nod and exchange digits with the guys. "I'll be back. Take care of her for me until then, huh?"

Maxon nods. "You got it."

As I climb in my car, I'm grateful to see the two men join the rest of the family to exchange condolences and hugs. They're not letting Bethany shy away from their comfort or support. As much as I hate leaving her now, I know she'll be in good hands until I can wrap my arms around her again and begin proving that I am the man she can count on. Until she believes deep down that I'm the same man she fell for.

I stop by the apartment we moved into only yesterday, when the day was bright and the possibilities were seemingly endless. But everywhere I look I see Beth now. I can't stay here. It's too haunted. I can't miss her this much without losing my mind. Instead, I grab a shower and a clean change of clothes, then head to Ash's, who welcomes me with a beer and an ear.

It's close to dawn when I finally find sleep on his lumpy piece-of-shit sofa. I wake up a few hours later, feeling less than rested but beyond ready to start winning Bethany back.

When I reach the inn a little before ten, Maxon greets me with his mouth pressed in a grim line. "She's gone. I'm sorry. We tried… She's leaving the island. And honestly, I don't know where she's going or if she's coming back."

chapterTHIRTEEN

Three months later
Los Angeles

Bethany

$\mathcal{M}$y hand trembles as I smooth my skirt, then press my fingers across my jittery stomach to calm it. Above me, the sunny spring sky wraps me in California blue. Behind me, my car door hangs open. Stay or go? But I know the answer. It's now or never. Do or die.

I'm a woman on a mission. This is it.

I shut my car door, press the fob to lock the vehicle, and stare straight ahead at the gorgeous but unfamiliar home in front of me. The now-familiar strains of Jason Mraz's "I Won't Give Up" float through my head, crying out that, although we have a lot to learn, we're worth it.

Today, I'll find out if that's true. I'll figure out once and for all if anything Clint Holmes claims he felt for me in Maui was real.

Would he have sent me the ballad about persevering, along with the handful of other songs encouraging me to give our relationship another try if he wasn't? It seems unlikely. He now has all the answers he sought about the Reed Financial scam. He got justice, too. What else could he want from me...except me?

No, Clint didn't compile the song list he sent a few weeks ago. Keeley did; he admits that. But he swears he feels all these sentiments.

I never thought of music as therapy, but apparently it's Keeley's way of navigating difficult emotions. It seemed silly at first, but I see why now. I've picked every song apart. Sting's "Fortress Around Your Heart" tells me he understands that he invented the battle between us inside his head and that he's well aware his lies caused me to raise my defenses. Bryan Adams's "Please Forgive Me" just melts my heart. How can I refuse a man who asks for forgiveness for loving me too much? Yesterday, "Dig" by Incubus was on high rotation. Yes, we all have a weakness that cleverly attaches and multiplies. I'm guilty, so I can't blame him for not being perfect.

But do I dare trust him again?

Do I dare not try?

I haven't been ready to tackle that question until now because the last three months have been hell. My final morning in Maui, I left Maxon and Keeley's place with tears and hugs and promises to keep in touch, then I took a taxi to the hospital, helped Stephen through the discharge process, and settled him into the temporary rental he's found. He had to be feeling better because he was already eyeing the property's caretaker, a pretty blonde named Skye. Before I hopped on my red-eye back to LA that night, he told me I was crazy to run from Clint because that man loves me. I was too shell-shocked by everything that happened the night before to hear it.

A week after my father's death, he was buried in San Diego. The service quickly became a nightmarish media circus. Thank goodness my siblings came, except Griff, who stayed behind with Britta for the birth of their second beautiful little boy, Grayson. But Maxon watched over me protectively. Harlow held my hand. Evan fended off the press.

My siblings came not to pay their respects to the man who sired us but to support *me*. I was beyond touched—and they haven't wavered since. If one silver lining has come out of the multitude of Barclay's lies and indiscretions, it's my family. We've grown closer over the last few months, despite me being back in California now.

But I miss them. A lot.

During the funeral, Maxon also made sure that Linda, Barclay's vengeful wife, didn't get too close to me. Once she found out I had inherited everything remaining in Barclay's estate and her boy-toy Marco left her for a wealthier sugar-mama, the woman threatened to kill me. Last month, she was found guilty of all charges in the Reed Financial scandal—conspiracy, aiding and abetting, money laundering. She's going to prison for the rest of her life. None of my siblings seemed surprised or broken up about it. How sad that the woman who met this tragic end was such a horrible human being that none of her children even shed tears. Then again, being married to Barclay for thirty-five years probably warped her into someone as twisted and self-serving as he'd been.

Clint came to my dad's funeral, too. That was the first—and only—time I've seen him since our breakup. I hoped laying eyes on him wouldn't affect me. After all, he lied to me. He betrayed me. He coaxed me into laying my soul bare when he didn't love me. But his expression as we stared at one another across the thirty feet that separated us said something very different. I felt him there, full of concern and remorse—and devotion I wanted to believe so badly it tore at my heart.

Still, how could I after his words and longing looks in Maui were all lies?

He sent a beautiful sympathy bouquet for the service. We talked afterward, but he didn't press me. He didn't touch me, either...though I secretly wished he had. Instead, he told me that if I wanted or needed him, he would come right away, no questions or expectations. Then he whispered that he loves me.

I wasn't ready to hear it. Though Barclay's passing no longer upset me, I left the funeral in tears.

Not long after, I flew to the Caymans. My trip there to retrieve the victims' stolen funds was long and frustrating. Weeding through all the documentation, bureaucracy, and legalities took weeks. Finally, the bank relinquished the funds to me—all seven hundred eighty million dollars of it. It took another few weeks for me to clear my plans with the feds.

And the entire time I was in the blue-ocean, palm-tree paradise, I couldn't stop thinking about my time in Maui with Clint. Was any of what we shared real? Did he fall for me, despite wondering if I was guilty? Does he really love me?

I don't know, and the battle between prudence and hope seems never ending.

Since returning stateside two weeks ago, I've dispersed all funds back to the victims and quietly let them know I'm here if they ever need a resource or help in understanding their investments. I recommended other well-respected advisors to them, of course. I was stunned that a handful of former clients insisted on sticking with me.

Though maybe I shouldn't be surprised. After Barclay's death and during Linda's trial, the facts of the case hit the news. I was exonerated in the court of public opinion when it became clear that I had no knowledge or hand in the scheme. The one day I had to testify, I barely held myself together as I described the moment I realized my father had utterly deceived me—and all our clients. Maybe those people now feel sorry for me. Maybe they believe in second chances. Either way, I've retained enough of these former investors to start my own financial services firm.

Stephen Lund hired me, too. Yes, probably out of loyalty and pity, but I appreciate his friendship. He still hasn't left Maui, and he's not spilling about what he's up to, much less when—or if—he intends to return home and resume his role as his father's second-in-command again at Colossus Investment Corporation. But he sounds happier than I've ever heard him. I wonder if that pretty blonde is the reason…

Noah and Harlow hired me to manage their money, too. Ditto Evan and Nia. It's above and beyond the call of sibling duty. But I'm working exceptionally hard to make the most of their investments and ensure they never regret their decision.

The only client whose stolen funds I haven't returned yet is Clint's. This, I wanted to do in person. Because honestly, every day we've been apart, the man has done his best to ensure he's never far from my thoughts.

I need to know where we stand—once and for all.

Shortly after my dad's funeral, he started texting me. Sure, he said he was sorry a lot. Every day, he reiterates that he loves me. I've never replied. At first, I had too much happening to expend mental energy on anything except Barclay and the mess he left. Now that I've straightened it up, I've started getting perspective. I'm wondering if Clint and I could ever be an us again.

In the last two weeks, I've thought of almost nothing else. I'm still not sure what to believe.

Recently, he started texting me about more day-to-day stuff, too—

making me feel like I'm a part of his life. Bryson, his youngest brother, is apparently flourishing at college. Bret, the middle sibling, finally realized that his hate for me was misplaced. He's laid off the booze and started hitting the books again. I'm happy for them both. I've never met Bret, but I'm glad for his sake that he's moving on.

Not that I don't understand where he was coming from. Grief can bend a person in terrible ways, and while it's fresh, it's hard not to welcome any kind of comfort, even if it's wrong. Thankfully, my crutch was less destructive than alcohol. I devoted most every waking hour to the victims' fund I began, which has grown twenty-three percent in the last nine months. I'm proud of that accomplishment. I'm even happier that the funds I returned to the victims were sometimes even more than the amount they initially invested.

Clint sold his father's business, then sent me his third of the proceeds with the explicit request to add the amount to the victims' fund. To have him embrace my most near-and-dear cause touched me. It made me cry…and wonder if we could have forever.

A few weeks later, he surprised me again, this time by sending me the proceeds from the sale of his North Dakota business, along with a note asking me to invest it. Because he trusts me, he says. Because he wants to show me that he has utter faith in me. Because, despite what I think, he still loves me.

At the time, I didn't know what to say…so I've said nothing. All professional correspondence has been via certified letter or a temp I hired until I land my business somewhere and put down roots. Regardless, every single day Clint texts me his thoughts, his feelings, his hopes for our future, and his sincere apologies.

Why would he persist after three months if he didn't mean it?

In my purse, my phone buzzes. Speak of the devil… It's Clint.

`Good morning, sweetheart. I miss you. It's a beautiful day, but it would be even better if you were here. It would be perfect if you wanted to talk.`

I'm tempted to reply…but I don't. What I need to say should be said in person.

Hey, good news. I got a message from Ash last night. He and Samantha are engaged! Happy for them… He's managing the bar now but that's temporary. Sam finishes her degree in finance in May and will be looking for an entry-level position. The wedding is in June in Maui, and I'm best man! If you'd like come, I would love to see you. Because I love you. Still. That's not going to change.

There's no stopping the way my heart melts.

Right after I found out he lied and used me for revenge, I wanted to hate him. For a few days, maybe I even did. But it didn't last. He's made staying mad impossible. Now, I look forward to his daily texts. He doesn't know, of course. I've waited to see if his feelings were more absolution than lifetime devotion. But he hasn't wavered one bit since our separation.

So, it's time for me to finally figure out if we have any hope of a future. Because as much as I'd like to say I've fallen out of love, I haven't.

The phone in my hand buzzes again as I head slowly up the walkway, toward the door.

What are you up to? I'm still at home in LA, working through what my next business venture will be. I've got some ideas… I wish we could talk about them. You might be surprised. I know you're probably still angry—and with good reason. But I won't stop texting you unless you tell me to. Maybe I won't even stop then. It's the only way I have to convince you that I'm beyond in love with you and want to spend my life with you. I want to marry you.

He says that almost every day, more lately than when he first started texting. I'm finding it harder and harder not to believe him. I've questioned whether that makes me crazy. Maybe I should be holding a grudge. That might have been satisfying, at least for a while. But I've realized a few things through all of this. First, not forgiving is what started this mayhem. Second, the more I let distrust and negativity into my life, the more I risk becoming like Barclay.

That's something I never, ever want.

For the first time since our one-sided correspondence, I raise my trembling fingers to my phone and tap out a reply.

Answer your door.

As soon as the message is delivered, I shove the phone back in my bag and ring the bell.

Seconds later, footsteps pound through the house. The door wrenches open, and Clint stands there, tall and shocked and looking so good in jeans and a T-shirt, he makes me as weak-kneed as the first time I saw him.

I drag in a breath and brace myself. "Hi."

"You're here. Oh, my god. You're here! Come in."

When he lurches back, I step over the threshold and into his foyer, nervously clutching my purse. He leads me into the living room beyond. It's expansive, lined with bookcases, framed by a large sectional, comfy chairs, and a marble fireplace that's a statement all its own. This place is nice, but it doesn't look like him.

"Thanks. Did your mother decorate the house?"

He nods. "A few years before she passed, yes. Did you want to sit?"

I can tell he's nervous. Because he doesn't want to spoil the opportunity to convince me of his feelings...or is he worried I'm here to call his bluff?

"Thanks." As I perch on the edge of the sectional, he sits on the massive coffee table right in front of me.

He's mere feet away. My heart pounds. I wasn't sure if or when I'd ever be close to this man again...and now I can't think about anything else.

"I'm sorry." I assume he's apologizing to me again for what happened in Maui, but he takes my hands instead. "I can't not touch you. It's been so long. I need to be sure you're real."

When he squeezes my fingers, he squeezes my heart, too. I clutch him in return. It feels so good to touch him again. He's like welcoming warmth after three long months of emotional winter.

"What brings you here? Not that I'm not thrilled to see you. Not that I want you to ever leave," he rushes to assure me, scooting even closer. "But you haven't spoken to me since the funeral and…"

He's been trying not to give up. I see that on his face.

We have to figure out how—or if—we can put the past behind us. But first things first.

I reach into my purse and pull out an envelope. "Open it."

Clint tears into it and scans the check for just under four million dollars, then looks at me with a scowl. "You came here just to return my father's money?"

"It's something I had to do. I know money won't bring him back, but I'm hoping it gives you and your brothers some sense of peace and security."

"This is a nice gesture. Thank you for your honesty and integrity, but I haven't doubted you since you left Maui. In fact, I want you to invest this money. My brothers and I already talked about it." He presses the envelope back into my hands.

Is he for real? "You want me to manage the money he spent his life making? The money my father took?"

Clint nods. "I don't trust anyone else."

He's serious. OMG… My heart floats in my chest as if his face-to-face vote of confidence filled it with hope again. I can only think of one thing he's trying to say to me with this gesture: that he's put every reservation he ever had about me to rest. When our gazes connect, I see that same message in his blue eyes.

I smile. "You're sure?"

"Positive. What I'd like even better is to talk to you, try to alleviate your distrust in me, so we can be together again. Please don't say no."

I'm not surprised he's confronting this head on. We need to. I'm finally ready.

"Clint, what you did to me was deceitful."

"Horrible and unforgivable. But…" He slides his fingers between mine. "I'm hoping you can find some way to forgive me."

Now that I've been able to move past my own trials and reflect on what he went through, that no longer sounds farfetched. In fact, I almost don't blame him. Shock, grief, loss—they can do terrible things to anyone's psyche. And unlike my father, his did nothing to deserve a

premature death. I understand why Clint looked for someone to blame
—and I was the obvious choice. But we have to talk this out.

"You lied about everything."

He shakes his head. "Our meeting was a lie. My job at the bar was a
lie. Initially, my attempts to be your friend were a lie. Everything else
was totally fucking real, sweetheart—especially how hard I fell for
you. Even when logic told me I was being selfish and irresponsible, I
couldn't stop myself. I wanted you. I needed to be with you. I love
you. I hope you can find some way to believe me."

He's been saying these same things via text the last few months. It's
hard not to believe him now, when he has no more reason to lie.

"Tell me, in your ideal world, what would happen next between
us?"

"Hey, bro. I'm out. I'll be back—" When I turn to the other man
who just stumbled into the room, his eyes flare wide. "Holy shit.
Bethany Banks?"

Standing, I nod, absently thinking how much he looks like his
brother—and their father. "You're Bret?"

He approaches, hand outstretched. "Yeah. Hey, I'm really sorry for
being a douche and breaking into your apartment."

Clint admitted that to me, too.

"It's okay. I understand." Honestly, he didn't destroy or deface
anything. If Clint hadn't told me his brother had been in my place, I
wouldn't have known. "Water under the bridge."

"Great. Thanks. I'll, um…leave you two to talk. It was nice to meet
you. For whatever it's worth, I wish you'd put my brother out of his
misery and marry him. He loves you. Bry and I would be happy to
have you in the family."

My elation spikes. I expected it would take months—maybe years
—for Clint's brothers to stop hating me. I worried they would resist
any attempt we made to patch up our romance. But for Bret to practically beg me to marry his brother…

As Clint and his middle sibling exchange a manly shoulder bump, I
can't stop smiling. Then his younger brother nods my way and melts
out of the room.

"Sorry about the interruption," Clint says. "We're alone now."

"Your brother seems like a good guy."

"He's made progress lately. In fact, he came down from UCLA to spend the weekend with me. Bry may or may not show up, depending on whether he can tear himself away from his new girlfriend. But even if he does, I won't see him for hours yet. So let's talk about us and my ideal world."

"Please. I want to hear that."

"You would be the center of it, of course. The only part of our past we'd ever think about would be meeting and falling in love. You'd be wearing my ring. We'd be planning a wedding and finding a place to live together for the rest of our insanely happy lives. Soon, we'd start catching up with your siblings on the baby thing. I want a few of our own, and it would be great if all the kids were roughly the same age so they could play together. I'm glad you're starting your own financial services business, because I'd like to be working beside you eventually. I'm already registered to take the online classes to become a certified financial planner. Once I've completed those, I'd want to learn from you, grow our business together, while I finish my college degree. I would be your full partner—in business and in life. Most of all, I want to show you how madly I love you every day. And I want you to love me back. That world, to me, would be perfect."

I blink, utterly stunned at how far he's already gone to mesh his life with mine. More hope makes my chest swell until it's tight—but in a good way. The very best way, in fact.

"How do I know you mean it?" That's the last question I have, the one I haven't been able to get past on my own.

"Stay right here."

Before I can reply, he darts across the room and up the stairs. I hear him rummaging around up there. A curse follows, then he jets back into the living room winded, but looking surprisingly upbeat—and clutching something in his fist.

That hope expands even more until it fills up my whole body.

"You don't have any proof about me. Just like I never had any proof about you when we were in Maui. The truth is, I tried to apply 'logic.' I questioned everything and took each word you said with a grain of salt. It's what a cautious, rational person does, right?" He shrugs.

"How much better would it have been if I had simply gone with my gut and believed you were exactly the woman you seemed? That you were the only one I could ever want or need, despite the apparent 'proof' otherwise, for the rest of my life?"

He makes an excellent point. Relationships don't come with guarantees. It's not a savings account or a municipal bond. There's no assurance this romance will pay the dividends I want. Cupid isn't the FDIC, who will insure a substantial chunk of my investment in his heart.

I'm willing to trust him—and us—or I'm not. It's as simple as that.

Granted, in the past, I was blindly loyal to my father. But I put my faith in the wrong someone. Clint took such good care of me in Maui—far better than my father did, even at his best. I can't shade Clint with Barclay's wrongdoings just because they're both men who told lies. I can't fall into the guilt-by-association trap. I have to believe that Clint is exactly the man I fell for.

Slowly, I nod. "What's in your hand?"

He smiles, looking both sheepish and a bit shy. "You never saw it, did you?"

"What?" But I'm pretty sure I know.

Suddenly, he's down on one knee. "Bethany Alannah Banks, will you—"

"You dug up my middle name?"

Clint laughs. "I knew everything about you before I orchestrated our first meeting in Hawaii. The only thing I didn't know was the actual you. So, yes. Bethany Alannah Banks, I love everything about you—the kind, the shy, the ballsy, the witty, the unsure—even your middle name. Please do me the extreme honor of being my wife and making me the happiest man on earth."

When he flips open the ring box, I gasp. It's everything I ever imagined an engagement ring should be. It's not big or gaudy. In fact, it's simple. It's elegant. It's…me. The marquise-cut diamond sits on a simple white-gold band, flanked by two smaller marquise-cut diamonds nestled on either side. No other embellishments. Nothing that jumps up and screams "look at me!" Just a pure, exquisite expression of the love he's been trying to give me for the last three months.

"Can I try it on?"

He doesn't hesitate. "If it gets you any closer to saying yes, then absolutely. All day long."

After yanking the ring from the box, he insists on sliding it onto my finger.

The moment he does, my equilibrium fixes itself. Everything feels right. My world is perfect.

Well, almost.

I blink up at him. "Want to hear my version of an ideal life?"

"Yes. Please tell me we can meet somewhere in the middle, Beth. I don't want to live without you."

Finally, I reach out and touch him. "You're the center of it. The only part of our past we ever think about is falling in love and learning from our mistakes so we can have an amazing future. I'm wearing this ring, and we're planning a wedding. And buying a place on Maui, where I can be near my family, and we can live an insanely happy life together. Yes, we definitely have to catch up to my siblings in the baby department. I want our kiddos to play with their cousins. Professionally, you and I would have this great home-and-work relationship, and we'd make an amazing investment team to help the financial dreams of others come true. And most of all, I want to show you that I love you, too. And that I never stopped. That's my perfect world."

"Seriously? For real?" Clint gapes, looking sucker-punched. "You're saying yes?"

I glance at the ring, then into the face of the man I never expected to love…and now can't imagine living my life without. "I'm saying an enthusiastic hell yes."

Instantly, my reply fills the chasm between us and builds a bridge across the divide. He pulls me close, crushing me against his chest, then swoops down to claim me with a kiss that feels like a tender, passionate start on our forever.

When we finally lift our heads long moments later, we're both panting. "No joke, right?"

"I love you. I have for a long time. And I think Bethany Holmes has a wonderful ring to it."

"My dad thought the same thing. In my last conversation with him, he tried to convince me that you and I would be perfect together."

I smile. "Your dad was a wonderful, wise man."

Clint kisses me again. This embrace takes even longer to tear ourselves away from. We'd both rather find the bedroom, but there are still things to settle…

"How do you feel about moving to Maui?" I finally ask between long bouts of lip locks.

"Actually, I was thinking of heading there anyway. Bret and Bry will be okay if I go. They're men now. They're both doing great. None of us want to sell the house here since it's full of our childhood memories. Thankfully, my aunt Sandra has decided to leave Kansas after a miserable winter. So she'll be moving here in a few weeks. We're going to rent her the house. She'll take good care of it. Problem solved." He gives me a big grin. "When I was on the island, I fell in love with it and the people, just like I fell in love with you. So all we have to do is choose a date to get married and a house in which we'll live happily ever after."

I'm beyond elated. When I first stepped foot on Maui, I never imagined the journey would change my life—and me—for the better. My heart feels like it might burst from my chest—in the best way possible.

Tossing my arms around Clint, I kiss my way across his jaw before brushing my lips over his and tugging up on the hem of his very inconvenient shirt. "We'll look at a calendar and real estate listings later. Right now, I can't wait to be with you."

He cups my face in his hands. "Oh, sweetheart. You have no idea how desperate I've been to get my hands on you, how much I want to show you in every way possible that I love you. I'm thinking we should get started on the rest of our lives now. We can call the family and give them the good news later. Don't you think?"

Smiling, I flash him my engagement ring. "I do."

Get ready for a sexy AF temporary-fling, friends-to-lovers Reed Family Reckoning!

When he became a single dad, Trace Weston swore off romance. Then his sister-in-law asks him to give her bestie, Masey, a post-breakup night of pleasure neither can forget in the first steamy, emotional Reed Family Reckoning: Friends novel.

MORE THAN DARE YOU
Reed Family Reckoning: Friends
by Shayla Black
(available in eBook, print, and audio)

5 Stars! "More than Dare You...was every bit of a sexy, can't-put-this-book-down page-turner I wanted it to be." – Reading in the Red Room

I dared her to spend a hot, no-strings night with me. Now I'm determined to keep her forever.

I'm Trace Weston—recently reformed bad boy and full-time single father. My life is already complicated, but when my sister-in-law asks me to give her bestie, who just ended her long-term relationship with a cheating jerk, some hot, post-breakup pleasure, I'm game. I never expected to want Masey Garrett with a burning hunger, but she's shy, sassy, driven, and incredibly kind. Suddenly I'm falling fast...but she's only mine for a night.

What's a former player to do? Change the rules.

Now she's under my roof day and night. We're playing house...but I want a real family. Though she loves my newborn son, the skittish beauty keeps her feelings about me a secret. There's nothing I wouldn't do to win her over, but other than passion, how can I persuade Masey I'm the man for her? Sure, I could drop an *L* bomb...except that once imploded my heart. But when her past turns her world upside down, can I chance everything and dare Masey to stay with me forever?

EXCERPT

"She's just wanting a one-night thing, right?"

"Yeah. She's looking to pop her post-Thom cherry with a manwhore who can show her everything she's been missing. I told her you'd be perfect."

I try not to let Harlow's words sting. Normally, I'd grin at that description and own it. I can't deny that's who I am. Well, who I was. But being a dad has made me look at life more seriously. I have my eye on the future now. Not the endless pussy I can chase but the actual months and years in front of me…and what I should fill them with. For my sister-in-law, though, I'll do this favor and help her friend feel good.

"Sure."

She winces. "Sorry if I offended you. I didn't mean to."

"It's fine. So she wants to know what it's like to have someone other than Thom fuck her?"

"Yes and no. Yes, she wants to know what it's like for someone other than the selfish douche she dated for ten years to fuck her." Harlow leans in and drops her voice. "But when Thom dumped her for a chick who masturbates online for a living, he told Masey she sucked in bed. It's not good for a girl's confidence."

I don't know Masey and I don't know Thom, but I'm pretty sure I know who the asshole is in this scenario. "I'm sure it's not."

Ninety-nine times out of a hundred when some guy tells a girl that she sucks in the sack, it's not her issue. But Thom is probably one of those without a self-reflective bone in his body and he can't see how he contributed to their lackluster sex life. I'm not expecting Masey to be the best lay ever. But I doubt she actually needs more than a few orgasms and a confidence boost.

"Even so, she wants to know what she could be doing better."

If Masey is looking for pointers, that's easy enough. "No problem. Anything else?"

"There's a guy back home, apparently. Her hot neighbor. He asked her out right before she left home, and they plan to get together when she returns. Not that she thinks they'll hop into the sack right away, but…better to be prepared, you know. Other than that?" Harlow shakes her head. "She's not looking for more than a good time tonight, so don't worry she'll turn into a clinging vine."

Somehow, Harlow's assurance makes me even more uncomfortable. But she's merely asking me to help a friend in need, so I let it go. "Got it."

"Great. Just…be nice. I know you will. But she's been through a lot with Thom. Even though she's glued herself back together, she's more fragile than she lets on."

It's not a problem since I'm not usually an asshole. "Absolutely."

"I appreciate you doing this. If you'll send her off in the morning with a loopy grin, I'll be eternally grateful."

"One loopy grin, coming right up," I reassure her. "If you'd like, I'll make sure she's bow-legged, too."

Harlow flashes me a megawatt smile. "That would be great! I knew there was a reason you're my favorite brother-in-law."

"I'm your only brother-in-law."

"Details." She gives me a playful wave of her hand. "Anyway, she wanted me to assure you that if you don't find her attractive, there won't be any hard feelings. Buy her a drink and tell her you're busy tonight after all. Just do it gently."

At this point, I can't picture that. Masey sounds like she needs TLC, and my sudden misgivings aside, I need to get laid after a five-month dry spell. It's not a match made in heaven, but we can make it work for a night. "I'm sure it won't be a problem. I'm assuming that if she doesn't find me attractive, she'll let me down easy, too?"

"Sure." Harlow shakes her head. "But that won't be an issue."

"Why do you say that?"

She leans in with a conspiratorial whisper. "I showed her your picture. I think I had to wipe the drool off her chin."

"Well, at least she has good taste," I quip. "Got one of her? I haven't seen—"

A woman walks into my line of vision, a mere dozen feet away. Instantly, she ends my speech, stops my heart, and makes my dick jerk like a divining rod in her direction. She's got reddish-brown curls that sway around her shoulders, a delicate profile, lush lashes that fan the palest porcelain cheeks, a red bow of a mouth that nearly has me crying for relief, and curves for days under her clinging, va-voom red dress.

"Holy shit," I mutter.

Harlow turns and follows my line of vision. When her gaze lands on the brunette, she flashes a smile. "Masey!"

SEDUCING
THE

Enemy

A Forbidden Confession:
FIRST TIME

SHAYLA BLACK
Steamy. Emotional. Forever.

ABOUT *SEDUCING THE ENEMY*

Just how far will he go to take his pound of flesh from her?

I'm Jett, self-made billionaire.
I've achieved everything I've ever set my mind to—except revenge.
Eight years ago, my best friend stole my multimillion dollar idea...
After I fell for his little sister.
He made a fortune.
And she stabbed me in the back.
Now he's in financial straits, while I'm richer than I ever dreamed.
So I made Whitney a bargain: forty million dollars in exchange for a week of her body.
But now that she's in my bed, animosity may not be all I'm feeling...

Enjoy this Forbidden Confession. HEA guaranteed!

Chapter One

Dallas
4 p.m.

Jett

*S*he's late.
    Maybe she's not coming, asshole.
That's a distinct possibility.
What did you expect? You're the enemy.

I am, and she's too smart not to realize I'm springing a trap. She also knows I'm powerful enough to destroy her and all she holds dear.

But I'd rather not. Does she know that, too?

I shove the thought away. What's in Whitney Chancellor's mind—and heart—now shouldn't matter. She made a choice, and I'm going to make her regret it.

You made a choice, too. And she probably hates your fucking guts for it.

But that doesn't change anything. If she doesn't show today, I'll keep coming at her. I have ways to bend her to my will.

She *will* give me what I want.

I tap an impatient thumb on the charred wood of the handscraped bar. The faux-rustic room is designed to be a "laid-back" watering hole, but since it sits in the middle of a horribly pretentious hotel in an exclusive, five-star part of town, I'm calling bullshit.

I've been here ten minutes, and I already despise this place.

You're just nervous.

No shit. But this site is less than two miles from her house, so I'm here.

It's been eight years, and I traveled halfway around the world for this. For her.

That doesn't mean she'll come, especially since you ordered her to.

In hindsight, that may not have been my best strategy, but cushioning my approach would have been counterproductive. It's best if she understands I'm a world-class bastard, and nothing—not even her—will soften me.

Whitney has probably discerned that. After all, I've put her in a terrible position. One of two things will happen next: she'll sweetly capitulate like she seemingly did all those years ago...or she'll tell me to go fuck myself. With her, I've got a fifty-fifty shot.

I'm almost hoping she chooses the latter.

At the sound of heels clicking across the tile floors in the otherwise empty bar, I snap around.

And I nearly drop my jaw.

Holy motherfucking son of a bitch.

Why is Whitney still so beautiful that, when I see her, I struggle to string two thoughts together?

She approaches me, dark hair curling past her elbows, mouth rosy, jewelry understated, ankle-strap heels classic—and black dress instantly sweat-inducing.

A band of fabric hugs her neck like a collar. Intermittent, gradually widening strips—strung together only by a loose lacing of satin playing a daring peekaboo with her exposed skin in between—tapers down, ending with a black leather belt that cinches her small waist. Her shoulders are covered. So are her tits—barely. But I can't not see their tempting swells or the soft valley in between. The skirt ends halfway down her sleek thighs where another subtle row of crisscrossed ribbons mirrors the bodice detail just above her flirty hem.

Two things are immediately obvious: I still can't look at Whitney without desperately craving her, and she isn't wearing a goddamn bra.

This dress would make any other woman look like a whore. Somehow, she elevates it to elegant.

Clearly, she came to make me suffer.

She stops at the bar less than three feet from me, and I'd be a lying SOB if I said my heart wasn't pounding.

"Whitney."

She turns to glance at me over her shoulder, hazel eyes full of anger. "Jett. What do you want?"

A dangerous question.

"To talk." *For starters.*

"I don't have anything to say to you."

She's lying.

"So you don't want to save your brother?"

Her expression spits hostility. "You know I do. Or I wouldn't be here."

Yes, just like I know she's incredibly loyal to him. She'd do anything for him. I'm banking on that.

Whitney sets her small, chic purse on the bar, laying her left hand on top of it. She's wearing an engagement ring.

Fuck. It's not even subtle. It's a statement rock, designed to flash a warning to every other man to back the hell off.

Too bad for her fiancé nothing will make me comply.

"Congratulations." I cast a pointed glare at her ring. "Who's the lucky dick?"

"None of your business. I presume you summoned me here to negotiate?"

I nod and try to keep my cool. I'd much rather seduce her—and she probably knows that. It kills me to remember I was the first man to lay his lips on hers. The first man to possess her mouth. She was a very sweet sixteen to my horny twenty-one. I was old enough to know better but too desperate to touch her to care.

Almost.

By sheer willpower, I stopped myself short of doing something her very affluent family would have insisted I go to prison for.

In the end, my restraint didn't matter. Nearly slipping that one moment cost me everything.

That seems like a lifetime ago.

Her hypnotic eyes aren't filled with innocence anymore. Nope, when she looks at me now, I see venom.

"What's your offer?" she demands.

"In a hurry? Why don't we have a drink? I haven't seen you in a long time."

She scoffs. "Let's not pretend I matter to you."

I raise a brow at Whitney. She does matter...but admitting that would only weaken my position. "Humor me. After all, it's my forty million dollars."

"Fine." She lifts one delicate shoulder like she doesn't care, but I can read her. On some level, I get to her and she hates that. "Vodka cranberry. Make it a double."

I acknowledge her with a curt nod, then I motion to the bartender, who takes our order.

"You're not drinking with me?" She scowls.

"I never drink." I haven't since that summer.

Whitney's gaze probes me for a long moment. "Because you're a control freak?"

You have no idea.

I smile. "You can call me names and divert the subject all day. That doesn't change why we're here."

"So you're going to lend Vance forty million dollars to save his company—"

"Which should have been *our* company."

"You lost that lawsuit."

"Because your brother is a lying, thieving snake." *And you helped him, didn't you?*

She arches her dark brow at me. "Is all this charm how you've become so successful?"

Life has apparently roughed up my sweet princess and given her a stronger spine. I like it.

Breaking her will definitely be more fun.

"No. I'm successful because I'm ruthless."

She says nothing, but her silence concedes the point. She knows. That's enough for now.

When the bartender sets her drink down, she grabs the elegant tumbler like it's a lifeline. That's the only outward clue that I make her nervous.

It's the perfect time to make myself clear. "The forty million is a buyout, not a loan."

"He won't agree."

"Then I can wait for him to go bankrupt and buy it up for pennies on the dollar."

She glares at me. "How do you know we don't have other financing?"

"If you did, you wouldn't be here."

The way she purses her lips is a confession. She's out of options. "Why do you imagine Vance will listen to me?"

"He needs the money too badly not to."

"He'll never sell to you."

Does she think I'm going to give either of them a choice? "I'll make sure he has the right incentive."

That sets her on edge—as it should. "Like what?"

"Leave that to me."

Whitney tries to shrug like it's irrelevant, but I see through her. She knows she's cornered.

That does my black heart good.

"Whatever," she says flippantly. "What's your proposal? What do I have to agree to so my brother gets the money?"

"We're having a drink first, remember?"

"*I'm* having a drink. You're watching me for reasons I can only guess at."

She shouldn't have to guess too hard, especially when she's dressed like that. Then again, she's likely baiting me for a reaction. Oh, she'll get it. But not now.

When I'm ready.

"Tell me what you've been up to since I last saw you." I keep the words soft, but there's an underlying command.

Whitney feels it. She stiffens. "Not much to tell that I'm sure you didn't find out for yourself. I finished high school. Then I attended Stanford and earned my economics degree. I stayed to finish my MBA. I've been home a handful of weeks, trying to help Vance unravel this situation. And here I am."

I knew all that. She's intentionally not telling me what I really want to know. Who has she dated? Who else has she kissed? Who fucked her first? Who fucked her last? Who does her goddamn heart belong to?

Patience, I tell myself, swallowing back all my questions. I *will* find out.

"What about you?"

There's the subject change again. Why? She can't possibly believe I'm going to give her anything she can use against me.

"After the last summer I saw you? I dropped out of college so I could bartend by night and spend my days developing an even more profitable intellectual property."

It was the perfect setup for me…almost. Entire days to push myself to create an even better app than the one Vance had stolen from me. Full nights of making money and hooking up with her acquaintances. That disappointed the hell out of my dad. Even my older brother, Quint, lectured me about throwing my future down the toilet. But Whitney was always in the back of my mind, haunting me.

I had everything to prove.

"I launched the following year." To success beyond my dreams, which spawned a massive tech company that now circles the globe.

"Tell me about your mother."

I sigh. It's the one weakness I'll show Whitney because, under all the animosity, she's too human to use my pain against me. "She died four years ago. Breast cancer."

That horrible night, I sobbed and held her hand, watching as she took her very last breath. It still fucking hurts every time I think about it.

Whitney's face softens. "I'm sorry. I know you two were close."

"Yes."

And I haven't been close to anyone since. I've tried. My brother and I have a better relationship now. My sisters, Ivy and Lacey, have reached out again and again. But it's me. Something inside me is dead.

I'm almost ashamed to admit that getting beyond my grief didn't cure my toxicity. Probably because my mother wasn't the cause. The poison is all about Whitney, about the way she stabbed me in the back and left me to bleed out.

"I understand. I miss my dad," she murmurs softly.

"I heard about his car accident. I'm sorry." I genuinely mean that.

She's had a terrible few years, too. Some part of me that still gives a shit about her—no matter how hard I've tried not to—empathizes. That part wants to reach out and hold her, soothe her, and tell her I'm here for her.

The rest of me has learned better.

"Thank you," she murmurs.

Silence falls again, and Whitney clutches her purse like she's nervous as she downs the last of her drink. Next time she looks at me, she's glaring. Her shields are up once more. "So now that we've caught up and you've watched me drink, what do you want?"

"In exchange for forty million dollars to save your brother's financial ass?" I smile tightly. "You."

She swallows like my words unnerve her, but she doesn't look surprised in the least. "I'm engaged."

"That's not my problem."

Slowly, she closes her eyes. To brace herself? To hide her fury from me?

Finally, she nods. "What are your terms?"

"One week."

"For me to be your whore?"

She's trying to bait me. "You putting an ugly spin on our arrangement isn't going to make me change my mind."

She clenches her delicate jaw. "What do you expect?"

"I'll send a car to pick you up at precisely nine o'clock. Bring *nothing* with you. Anything you need, I'll provide. When you arrive, the front door will be unlocked. Once inside, you will strip. And you will kneel. Then you will wait for me. You *will* be completely mine. While you're with me, you will forget two things: any other man who's ever fucked you and the word *no*. You will do *anything* I desire with, to, or for me during our week together. Am I clear?"

"You're a bastard."

"That can't be a surprise."

"No."

"Are you refusing?"

Whitney hesitates. "No."

Triumph spikes. I lay a twenty on the bar for her drink. "You accept? You'll get in my car tonight?"

She looks down at the bar like she's ashamed. She makes me wait and sweat and worry that she'll refuse. But we both know she won't. For her brother's sake, she can't.

"Yes," she finally whispers.

I settle a finger under her chin. "Look at me when you answer."

"Yes, I'll come be your forty-million-dollar piece of ass for the week." With a jerk of her head, she pulls away. "Don't touch me until then."

I smile at her show of spirit. It's intriguing—but it won't last. I'll make sure of that.

"You have four hours to get yourself in order. After that…" I trail off into a smile.

Let her imagine the worst.

I'm sure she thinks I intend to use her horribly and cause her pain. Quite the opposite.

I'm going to give her so much pleasure she'll lose her mind.

And surrender her heart?

Since I can't afford to listen to the mocking voice in my head, I shove it aside and slide a burner phone across the bar to her.

She picks it up, then frowns. "What's this for?"

"To contact me in case you choose to back out. If not, at quarter till ten, you will text me to verify your arrival. Make no mistake, Whitney, this device only allows you to call or text *me*. So don't bother trying to use it to contact anyone else so you can tell them where to find you for the next week." I send her a cold smile. "It will be our secret."

I toss those words she uttered to me long ago back in her face.

Predictably, she blanches. "I hate you."

"I don't care. I'll see you this evening."

I force myself to walk away. The rest is up to her. But I've dangled the carrot and I've cornered her. She'll come. She'll submit.

Then I'll make her pay.

Eight years earlier…

Jett

I shouldn't put my hands on Whitney Chancellor. Really, I shouldn't… but the princess is right there, mere feet away by the shimmering pool, wearing a pink bikini and soaking in the sun. Her long, dark waves brush the swells of her pert ass as she sways to *the* sexy ballad of the summer.

For fuck's sake, I need to keep my distance. But how, especially today?

Tiptoeing across the back patio, I sneak up behind her, cover her eyes, and whisper in her ear, "Happy sixteenth birthday, Whitney."

She whirls around and flashes me rosy cheeks and a flirtatious grin. She might still be too young, but nothing about the way I want her is innocent.

I'm twenty-one. I know better. I shouldn't make a move on my best friend's little sister, especially before she's grown. But during the past two months, she's been just beyond my reach, wearing next to nothing to combat this heatwave and tossing me come-hither glances. My impatience to have her under me chafes. I'm almost beyond caring what I "should" do.

It's bad, like masturbation-in-the-shower-twice-a-day bad. Still, I can't not wish her a happy birthday, right?

"Thanks! Is that for me?" Her gaze falls on the fluffy cupcake on the nearby patio table.

"Of course." I retrieve the pink-frosting confection and hold it out to her.

Unlike Whitney, I didn't grow up with money. Despite having five dollars left to my name, I used half of it to buy her something I hoped would make her happy.

I watch as she plucks it up. She licks her way through the frosting before taking a delicate bite. "Mmm… So good."

I swallow back a groan. It doesn't matter that I jacked off not an hour ago. I'm harder than ever for her.

"Thanks for remembering, Jett," she murmurs.

I try not to focus on the way her pretty pink tongue peeks out as she licks residual frosting from her plump lips. "Yeah. Sure."

"It means a lot to me. I'm pretty sure my brother forgot. Tell me again why you're friends?"

Despite knowing she's teasing me, I'm still tongue-tied. "We're, um…going into business together."

She knows that, dumb shit.

Whitney smiles. "I remember the spiel. You've got the brains, Vance has the connections, and you're both ambitious as hell. You'll succeed. How's it going? Almost done?"

"Yeah, almost. We've logged in a ton of hours, but I've nearly finished the coding, and he's been writing up the business plan and making lists of people to contact. We should be ready to launch before we go back for our senior year. So just a few weeks now…"

Her smile dims. "I'll miss you when you're gone."

"You will?" She's always been flirty, but this is the first time she's stated her feelings outright.

"Sure." She backs up and gives me a suddenly nervous, nonchalant shrug. "It will be so much quieter when you and my brother are gone. Who will I nag about hogging the TV late at night while you play Xbox and refuse to share your tequila? Who will play Monopoly with me until four a.m. when I can't sleep?"

Maybe that's true…and maybe she's saying that in case she thinks I don't like her *that* way. But I have—from the moment I met her eight weeks ago, when I first stepped foot onto the Chancellor estate. Everything around here is ornate, too traditional. Stuffy. Perfect.

Except Whitney. She's all the beauty, but she's also a new spring breath of fresh air.

Vance would have my ass if he knew what I wanted to do to his little sister. He's protective. But the way she's looking at me proves her thoughts aren't a little girl's. They're a woman's.

"I hope that's not all you'll miss about me." I tuck a strand of hair behind her ear. "I'm sure going to miss more than that about you."

"Yeah?" She bites her lip and sends me a flirty glance through her dark lashes. "If I wanted something for my birthday, would you give it to me?"

"I'd give you the world if I could afford it." But I can't.

I hate that I wasn't raised rich, like her. I barely have two nickels to rub together. She deserves better.

Whitney sets the rest of the cupcake aside and eases closer. She looks nervous as she shakes her head. "I don't want you to buy me anything. My parents have already given me tons."

That's true, but I admire that she's not a typical spoiled little rich girl who doesn't see her good fortune.

"Then what can I give you, princess?"

"A kiss." She looks so earnest. "Please. You'll be the first."

My heart stops as I stare at her tempting mouth. "I don't know if that's a good idea, Whitney."

I manage to get the words out, but my protest is weak. How can it be anything else when I want her so badly?

"Maybe not, but I think you want to. I see the way you look at me."

It would be easier to lie and tell her she's mistaken, but I can't crush her. "I want to, but Vance…"

"He has nothing to do with us. In case you hadn't guessed, I…like you. I just want a kiss."

It's wrong, and I know it, but I thread our fingers together for one simple reason. "I like you, too. I think about you a lot. But you're underage."

"I'm not a child."

She's really not. She's actually pretty mature. God knows her body has filled out in all the right places, like a full-grown woman's.

"You have no idea how badly I want to say yes."

A new smile brightens her face. "Really?"

"Yeah," I admit roughly as I stare at the three stories of windows that make up the back of the vast house. Vance could be watching us even now. "But we can't. Not here."

I drop Whitney's hand.

"Definitely not here," she agrees. "I'll be in my room, Jett. Waiting."

Then she takes her cupcake and her music and disappears inside. I heave a deep breath as I watch her go, the tiny triangle of fabric revealing more of her ass than it covers.

God, I want her. I crave her so badly I'm shaking.

I shouldn't give in. I should stop myself from even laying a finger on her.

But she's giving me the chance to kiss her, be the first man to take her lips. That does something to me. Lights my possessive fire. Makes me want to growl that she's mine.

It's wrong and it's dangerous and I should have my fucking head examined. Knowing the feel of her will only make my lust burn a million times hotter.

But I don't care. I'm going to do it.

I'm going to kiss Whitney Chancellor.

Dragging in a breath, I push my way into the house and look around. It's empty. Her dad is at work. Her mom is out getting stuff for Whitney's party tonight. Vance is in the study, on a conference call.

It's now or never.

Resolution firing up my veins, I march upstairs. Whitney's door is cracked. I see her pacing.

I ease in, heart pounding, and shut the door behind me.

She stops and blinks up, meeting my stare. "Jett?"

Am I going to kiss her? That's the subtext of her question.

I nod and stalk across the room, every move clipped. As if I need to leave all my doubts behind. As if I can't reach her fast enough.

Finally, I cup her cheek and slide against her body. My free hand palms her nape. Willingly, she tilts her head and meets my stare. It's not merely that she's looking at me, but the way she's doing it, like she's completely open to me.

Like she's completely mine.

"Whitney…"

There's nothing else to say when the candy lips I want are so sweetly parted just inches under my own.

I bend to her, dragging my thumb across her so-soft cheek, and watch her wide hazel eyes slide shut.

Fuck, this is surreal. But it's the best dream imaginable. Princess Whitney wants *me*, and all I have to do to please her is take her mouth with my own.

Yes…

Finally, I touch my lips to hers. I hear her little indrawn breath. She tenses against me, fingers digging into my shoulders. But the way she's wriggling to get closer tells me she's every bit as nervous and eager as I am.

This means something to her. Every bit as much as it means to me?

I sink into the kiss. She puckers, and it's sweetly unpracticed. I regroup and redouble my effort until she's less hesitant. Then I nudge her lips apart. She offers no resistance, shyly softening and conforming herself to me.

Need and impatience claw at my restraint. I'm slipping.

A groan tears free when I slide inside Whitney's mouth. She welcomes me. And she's like sugar on my tongue. I clutch her tighter as I deepen the kiss.

She's with me, pucker for pucker, tongues stroking, lips clinging, breaths harsh.

Suddenly, she's sinking onto her bed. I follow her down, wholly unwilling to stop kissing her, especially when her body is under mine, we're alone, and she's so obviously consenting.

As if my hands have a mind of their own, my palms wander her curves, skating the valley of her waist, cupping her hips, clutching her thighs. Then her legs are around me. I'm pressing my unflagging erection against her damp bikini bottoms, and our bodies are moving together as one.

Fuck, I don't think I've ever been this hot.

Whitney gropes until she circles my wrist, then lifts my hand.

Suddenly, I'm cradling the tender weight of her breast in my palm. I groan. The subversive part of me needs to know just how aroused she is, so I thumb her nipple.

She breaks our kiss to toss her head back and cries my name. "Jett…"

"Oh, princess. You feel amazing." I squeeze her mound and close my eyes, letting go for this one moment. I haven't done anything irrevocable to her. I can stop any time.

Right?

Under me, she shimmies and rocks. Pleasure jolts me with every move. The minute I realize we're going through all the motions of sex with our clothes on is also the moment my hand seems to get its own ideas and shoves aside the little scrap of pink covering her breast. My mouth gets on the bandwagon and sucks the pretty dark nipple I just exposed, tonguing it until her back arches and her whimpers fill my head.

Jesus, I'm going to come.

"Princess…" I pant. "We've gotta stop."

She shakes her head, trembling when my exhalations fall on her straining nipple. "We don't. Please. I want you. I want all of you."

Whitney doesn't give me time to think, just wraps herself around me—arms, legs, lips—and wordlessly begs me for more.

I shake. The thought of being inside her nearly sends me over the edge.

Sure, I've had sex. Hurried-high-school sex. Drunken-frat-party sex. We-just-met-in-a-bar sex. Friends-with-benefits sex. Even screwing-an-ex-girlfriend's-mother sex. But I've never wanted any woman the way I want Whitney.

I'm in love with her. I think I have been half the summer.

"Princess…"

But what am I saying? I know what I *should* do, should say.

With Whitney, none of that seems to make much difference.

"Please don't say no."

I filter through all my arguments. Vance, her age, what's right and wrong… I've already hit those. They don't matter to her. I'm not even sure how much they really matter to me.

"You're a virgin," I finally say.

"So?" She blinks up at me, looking somewhere between earnest and tearful. "I love you."

"Oh, fuck." I hold her tighter. In all my wildest dreams, I never imagined she was feeling what I was. "I love you, too."

Whitney's smile lights up my world. Then she tosses off her bikini top. "That's all that matters. Make love to me."

"I can't give you anything."

"All I want is you." She clings to me and presses a kiss to my lips. "Please."

"I have to go back to college in a few weeks."

She nods. "I know. But I'll still be waiting here for you next summer. And I get that you're worried about Vance, but—"

"He's my best friend. He'd kill me for touching you."

She presses a finger over my lips. "It will be our secret."

There's a no perched on the tip of my tongue, but she muzzles it by lifting her hips to me and closing her eyes with a moan.

Shit. I've got to stop this.

Soon.

Just one more minute…

Then I lose myself in her kiss again, in the feel of her slender body undulating beneath me, in the way her gaze clings to me with love when I take her nipple in my mouth. She's all cotton-candy sweetness and sweet-sixteen perfection. I want her so badly, every fucking part of my body hurts.

Is going behind everyone's backs and rushing into this good for her?

No. I've got to stop this now.

I sigh. "Whitney—"

Behind me, the door to her bedroom slams open. "You son of a bitch. Get the fuck off my sister!"

Vance.

I jump to my feet and block his view of Whitney with my body. "It's—"

"Not what I think?" he sneers.

No, it's exactly what he thinks.

"Get out!" Whitney screams at her brother.

Neither of us budges. I won't leave her alone to endure her brother's wrath, and he won't leave me alone with temptation.

"I would never hurt her," I promise.

He snorts, silently admonishing me that it's too late. "When did you start fucking her?"

I hold up both hands. "Dude, I didn't—"

Vance silences me with a cross to the jaw.

"What are you doing?" Whitney screeches. "Stop!"

"Don't touch my sister again." He points a finger in my face. "Ever. I fucking trusted you…"

He did. He invited me into his house and let me stay with him so I would have all summer to write code instead of heading back to my hometown in Nowhere, Colorado, to make minimum wage shoveling horse shit or whatever my dad says "builds character." Don't get me wrong; I need the money. But if this app takes off like I think it will, money won't be a problem anymore.

"I can't believe this is how you repay me!" Vance gestures to Whitney, who's got her arms crossed over her bare breasts.

"I'm sorry."

Vance grunts. "You will be, asshole, once I take it out of your hide."

At the time, I thought he was just lashing out. I thought he'd get over his anger and we'd go back to normal. I thought Whitney would believe me when I told her at the end of the summer that none of my feelings for her had changed, to give her brother time, and we'd work things out between the two of us somehow. I believed her when she kissed me one last time and said she'd be waiting.

But I was wrong. So fucking wrong. I learned that weeks later when Vance, with an LLC he created alone, launched our app without me. My idea, everything I'd spent months innovating and coding, my one chance at being someone and crawling out of the blue-collar middle class I've always despised—all stolen from me. My best friend left me with nothing.

And when push came to shove, Whitney backed him up by taking his side in my lawsuit.

She ripped out my heart, too. I've never been the same.

After that humiliation, I launched my own creation the following spring. Over the next half a decade, I amassed a tech empire that far surpasses anything Vance has accomplished. But I've spent eight long, terrible years waiting for the day I could finally have my revenge. I waited for *this* day.

I smile coldly. Now, it's here.

And this time, when she's broken, when I've fucked her out of my system, it will end on *my* terms.

Chapter Two

Present day

Whitney

As I watch the hands of the clock tick away the last of my freedom, I wonder if I've gone insane. That's the only answer that makes sense.

I should have refused Jett's insulting proposition. I should have spit in his face.

I don't have that luxury. While I can criticize my brother for this financial mess, I was away at school when he needed me. Some of the blame rests on my shoulders.

For the next seven days, I have to let Jett Dean use me in whatever way he wants and hope he doesn't destroy me.

Bitterly, I laugh. Every time he touches my life, it explodes into a fiery, horrific inferno, then leaves me standing in a heap of ash.

It took me years to pick myself up after he left the first time. How much harder will it be this time after I share his bed? After I take him into my body?

And what about the secret I'm keeping from him?

A glance at the clock on my mantel tells me it's eight fifty-eight. A pair of headlights slow, turn into my driveway, and stop. The driver doesn't honk. I don't walk out right away. I have two minutes to decide what to do. On the table in front of me is my phone. Beside it sits the burner device.

Which am I going to pick up?

But I already know the answer.

With a trembling hand, I grab my phone and hit the button to reach the person I call most.

"Whit," my brother answers. "What's going on?"

I look at the clock. Eight fifty-nine. I have less than sixty seconds to give Vance an excuse. It's too late to explain the truth.

"I'll be gone for the next week. I'll call you when I get home next Saturday night."

"Where are you going?" He sounds confused.

"I can't say."

"Who are you going with?"

"I can't tell you."

"What the fuck is happening?" Now he sounds alarmed. "I'm coming over there."

"Don't. I won't be here. Just...trust me."

"I do, but this isn't like you."

"I'm doing what's best for both of us. Please try to stay out of trouble while I'm gone. Please. Don't do anything. Don't sign anything. Don't—"

"Yeah, yeah. You don't have to hound me."

Yes, I do, and we both know it.

"I'm sorry," I say finally. "I'll talk to you in a week."

"Can't you call me while you're away?" Now he sounds downright worried.

"No."

Even if I was allowed to bring my phone, I'm sure Jett will keep me too busy under his thumb—and in his bed—to even try.

Outside, the headlights in my driveway flash off and on again. That's my cue.

"I have to go."

"Are you going to be all right? You're not doing anything danger-ous, are you?"

I don't lie to him, at least not any more than I already am. "I'll talk to you next week. I love you." That's something I never say because sentiment annoys him, but I need to get the words out...just in case. "Bye."

Then I hang up. I don't reach out to my fiancé. He won't miss me; he doesn't care. He's probably spending his weekend with strippers and drugs. We both know I'm aware of his coping mechanisms. I'll deal with that mess when I get back.

Resolved, I power down my phone, leaving it on the table. Vance will come over while I'm gone. He'll try to figure out where I went. He'll see my phone right away and realize that attempting to contact me is pointless.

I grab the burner phone Jett foisted on me and rise on shaking legs. Outside, I lock my front door, tuck my house key into the flowerpot on my porch, and make my way to the sleek black Mercedes sedan. It reminds me vaguely of a car my grandmother drove as a kid. But the warm fuzzy ends there.

As I approach, a tall stranger unfolds from the driver's seat and makes his way to me wordlessly, holding the back door open. I nod as I climb into the car. There's a partition between the driver and me. I hear him slide into the idling vehicle, but I can't see where he's taking me. I have no idea what's going on.

I must be crazy.

After a few turns, I lose track of where we're going. North, I think. We're on the highway now. The car is no longer starting and stopping with the traffic. So now this stranger behind the wheel is simply whisking me with no impediments toward my doom.

I swallow and peer out the window, into the night. Nothing. I see nothing but fields. Nothing is familiar. Nothing to use as a landmark to tell people where to find me if I'm in danger. I don't think Jett would hurt me.

But I've been wrong about him before.

I turn the phone he gave me over in my hands. It's not too late. I could still call him and tell him I've changed my mind.

But why? Vance needs his cash, and we have no new prospects.

That's not the only reason, the seditious part of my brain whispers.

If I'm being completely honest, I've waited eight horrible years to set eyes—and anything else I could—on Jett Dean. If this is the only way I can have him, I'm willing to take my chances.

But when I glance down at the device, digital numbers flash the time at me. Nine forty-seven. I'm two minutes late to text him. I don't hurry to rectify my lapse. Instead, I set the device in my lap and wait.

I'm going to surrender to him; that's a given. And despite the fact I'm baiting the bull, I'm not going to make it easy.

Suddenly, the phone in my hand vibrates.

With a bracing breath, I answer. "Yes, Jett."

"You didn't text."

"You made it clear that I would be at your beck and call once I was under your roof and in your bed. Until then, I'm still my own woman. Fuck off."

He doesn't say anything for a long moment. "You know there are consequences for your defiance?"

Of course. I'm looking forward to it. "I'm in your car with your driver, on the way to your location so I can be your sex slave for the week. I'd say you've already won and that you shouldn't bother sweating the small stuff."

"That's not how I operate," he grates out, teeth obviously clenched.

He's on edge. Where I want him.

"It never has been." But learning a little give-and-take would be good for Jett. And it might be fun for me.

Or it would if I wasn't risking everything to be with him.

"Listen, princess—"

"Good-bye." I hang up. A smile curls my mouth because I know I'm playing with fire.

And I hope very much I'm going to enjoy getting burned.

The car exits the highway and veers right, traveling down a winding two-lane road that seemingly leads nowhere. I have to be patient. It's not as if I can ask the driver anything, much less plead for information.

At exactly ten, the sedan rolls to a smooth stop. The engine goes silent. The driver exits and shuts his door. I hear boots crunch the gravel outside. Then my door opens, and the driver holds out a broad hand.

With a nod, I take it. He assists me to my feet, then gestures me toward the house.

But it's not a house, really. It's a massive white French Country estate in the middle of nowhere with a breathtaking fountain, perfectly trimmed evergreens, and ornate wrought-iron front doors.

I turn to the driver. "What is this place?"

"*Ya ne govoryu po-angliyski,*" he says with a shrug of his wide shoulders.

He's speaking Russian, I think. Not that I know the language, but I can only imagine he's telling me he doesn't speak English. Leave it to Jett to think of everything. Even if I'd managed to sucker this guy into talking, we'd run straight into a language barrier.

His ploy should probably scare me more, but he's always paid attention to detail, so I'm hardly surprised.

Just slightly terrified.

"I understand." I lay a soft hand on his forearm.

He nods and pulls away, casting a nervous glance back to the house.

Does he suspect Jett is watching?

He probably is.

I don't bother the driver again. This is between Jett and me.

My journey to the front door seems to last a thousand steps. Not because it's long, but because I take it slow. I want to make him wait. And suffer.

Like I did.

Finally, I push the grand front door open. The white marble floor gleams by the light of an elegant chandelier hanging from the barrel ceiling above. On an exquisite hall table to my right rests a glass of red wine, clearly for me. I pick it up and walk another few steps. I find a white wicker hamper with the lid open. An empty acrylic shoe storage box sits beside it.

He wants me to undress for him. Kneel for him. Suck his cock. Spread my legs. Surrender.

I sip my wine. He can wait.

His stare is all over me. I can feel it. Somewhere, somehow, he's watching. And he's impatient.

Ignoring the receptacles for my clothes, I wander through the house. It's devoid of humanity now, but it has life. I feel the echoes of happiness here. I can almost hear laughter. Once, someone lived a charmed existence under this roof. But not the current occupant. Not at this moment. Jett's brooding seethes through the silence.

He wants me naked—now.

There must be something wrong with me. I'm impatient to give in to him.

"Hi, Jett," I call, my voice echoing across the tile.

No reply.

But I'm not fooled. He's here. He simply won't speak to me until I've stripped myself bare for him. I know that instinctively.

I continue scoping the downstairs, winding past a staircase on the left, then into a beautiful white kitchen with hand-painted tile, a rough-hewn island, and dark rustic beams overhead. Through an arch, I find myself in a cozy family room with a massive stone hearth and simple furnishings, dressed up with colorful accents and an unassuming chandelier. I sink onto a footstool and look out the wall of glass to the backyard beyond.

The swimming pool shimmers. The sound of cicadas singing lulls me. The twinkling summer stars lure me outside.

Not even sure where I'm going or why, I walk out, leaving the door open as a clue for Jett. Not that he needs it; I still feel his eyes on me. But I want this last moment of freedom.

I know he'll snatch it quickly and trap me under him for the next seven days. That's a given. Stalling is both foolish and reckless, but I can't stop. If this is all the rebellion he'll allow me while we're together, I'm taking it. I want him to understand I'm not without my devices.

By the pool, the breeze picks up and whips through my hair. I set my wine aside and pluck the elastic band from around my wrist, using it to wind my long hair on top of my head. Then I tread to the side of the crystal-blue water and start shedding my clothes—shoes, dress, bra, underwear. In a blink, it's all gone, and I'm bare.

I still don't know where Jett is, but his stare has intensified. There's no escape.

I drag in a deep breath and walk into the warm water. It envelops me like a soothing blanket. Shutting my eyes, I sigh.

"Are you incapable of following instructions?"

I start at the sound of Jett's voice. Suddenly, he's standing at the edge of the pool, mere feet away. How did he sneak up on me so quickly?

Never mind that. Will he give me another stitch to wear for the next seven days?

Turning, I cock my head at him to see he's still wearing the same designer suit. "Not at all."

"So you're merely choosing not to."

My smile is nothing short of mocking. "Something like that."

"You understand I'm going to make you regret that?"

Excitement flips in my belly. "I'm sure you'll try."

Jett doesn't merely smile at my snarky reply; he actually laughs like there's a joke—and it's on me. "Out of the water."

"Or?"

"I'll make you suffer."

Thrill rushes through me. It dips low. I feel my sex swell and my womb clench.

He won't actually hurt me. I know him well enough to know that. I've heard the whispers about who and what he is in bed.

"I already am. I'm giving up my work, my life, and my fiancé for a week. And I'm stuck with you."

He rubs his palms together like they burn. "I'm going to count to five. If I have to come in after you, I'll end our arrangement. You can go home. I'll take my forty million and disappear. Your call."

Damn it. I pushed him. I don't think too hard, but he clearly wants some show of obedience. He wants proof I'm still choosing to be here. And he wants to know this week won't be a constant tug-of-war. I can't promise that. But I also can't risk calling his bluff.

With a sigh, I wade back to the steps and slowly ascend. My shoulders break the surface of the pool, then my breasts, my hips, my thighs. Water clings and drips as I meet his gaze and make my way across the deck to him, one swaying step at a time.

Possessive hunger blazes in his dark eyes. He wants me. Just to fuck...or for something more? I can't tell, but it's obvious he craves every inch of skin he sees. He's not even trying to hide it.

Less than two feet from him, I bow my head. Mostly because I can't stand the triumph on his face...but I've also heard the expectations he has of his lovers. I've wondered so many times if the whispers are true.

"There were three parts of my command," he points out.

You will strip. And you will kneel. Then you will wait for me.

I shiver. "I remember."

"Are you cold?"

"No."

I can almost feel his smile. "You're finally naked. Part two now, please."

My head rebels against this, but something far lower flutters with thrill. What does that say about me?

"If I don't?" I ask.

"I won't keep fighting you. And I refuse to spend the next seven days threatening you, Whitney. You agreed to my terms and you got in my car. If you can't comply with these exceedingly simple commands, I'll turn around and leave. I doubt our paths will cross again."

He's right. I haven't seen Jett Dean, except in tabloid rags, since that summer all the promise between us burned away in a fiery blaze of betrayal.

I nibble my bottom lip.

Tick-tock. In my head, I hear time ticking away. I said yes in the bar because my only other choice is far less palatable.

Now I just have to find the courage to surrender to the man I've considered both my first love and my enemy since sixteen.

I swallow, steel myself, then kneel at his feet. The hard concrete beneath my knees presses unforgivingly into my skin. I'm still dripping, and the hot wind blows. Nothing about this is comfortable. But I don't move as Jett scrutinizes me. I feel every second of his stare.

He grabs my left hand. "Take it off."

My engagement ring.

I nod. It's always been a bit tight. At times, I would have sworn the diamond-encrusted band wrapped around my finger was somehow strangling me.

"What will you do with it?"

"Keep it with your clothing for the next seven days. At the end of that time, if you want to return to him, slip it back on." He shrugs. "I won't stop you."

I don't entirely believe he'll let me off that easily. Or is that wishful thinking? "Then why not let me wear it? Wouldn't the reminder that you're temporarily screwing my fiancé out of his bride-to-be give you a thrill?"

"No." His black eyes flash as he snatches my clothes from the table and into his grip. "I said naked. I meant naked. That means *everything* goes."

I've asked myself a hundred times why Jett wants me for the next week. Certainly, if he was going to bail Vance out, the arrangement could have been done through lawyers, brokers, and bankers. Instead, he came to *me* with this indecent proposal. From the moment I read his note, I could only think of two possible reasons why he would contact me directly. First, he could be eager to humiliate me. I've known all along that he'd likely want to repay me for the ignominy he suffered that summer. I'm sure he's even thought a time or two that I'm partially to blame. The second—and much slimmer—possibility is that he's never forgotten me and he now wants all the pleasure stolen from him that summer.

Still, I don't hesitate another moment. I simply slide the rock off my finger. "Does that please you"—I hold it out to him—"Sir?"

In the middle of pocketing the jewelry with a scowl, Jett freezes. "Yes. You've heard the gossip, I take it."

"I have." I want to ask if it's true, but I don't.

He rests his palm on my crown and threads his fingers through my hair before closing them under the elastic band holding my loose bun in place, tugging until I meet his gaze. "Everything goes, Whitney."

"It's just a ponytail holder," I argue.

"It's in my way."

As if his words settle the matter, he plucks the round elastic band from my hair deftly but inexorably. The skeins come tumbling down past my shoulders, clinging to my back, and curling in at my waist.

As he pockets my elastic band, heat flares in his inky eyes. "Wait here. Don't move."

Command rings in his voice. I don't dare cross him, even when he pivots around, turning his back on me utterly, and stalks back inside the house once more.

My knees ache, and the wind grazes my damp nipples again. Still, I don't move, partly because I fear he'll leave if I do…and partly because I'm desperate to know what he'll do if I don't.

So I'm alone with the night and my thoughts. With my regrets and worries.

He's going to realize the truth quickly. Then what will you say? What defense can you possibly muster?

The voice in my head is right, but I don't have any answers except the obvious. Jett Dean will know very quickly that I never got over him.

On the one hand, I want the truth between us because I'm dying to know if the knowledge will make a difference. On the other hand, once he realizes…I'll be so vulnerable it's terrifying.

It only takes him a minute to reappear. My clothes are gone, but he's slung a fluffy white robe over one thick arm.

His eyes are full of approval. "Excellent. I half expected to find you'd disobeyed me and retreated to some other corner of the house."

"No."

He holds out his hand to me. I hate the way I tremble as I take it and he helps me to my feet. "Smart. Hold your arms out at your sides."

I do, and he slides the robe around me, then belts it at my waist. "Until nine o'clock next Saturday night, you will not wear anything I don't provide. Is that clear?"

"Yes."

Jett sends me a quelling stare. "You know what I am. Respond properly."

"Yes, Sir."

He pockets my elastic band, then tucks my hand in his. "Come with me."

I don't say a word as I trail behind him and into the house. He locks the French doors behind us and leads me through the interior, all the way back to the grand foyer. The hamper and the clear shoebox are still sitting, open and waiting. I see he's tossed the garments I came in on the hall table. My engagement ring sparkles in the shadows beside the heap of my clothes. Then he releases my hand, gestures to the receptacles, and steps back.

I have to be the one to tuck my clothes away. It's symbolic. I'm shedding all my outward skin for him and coming to him naked, both literally and figuratively. That's doubly true of my engagement ring.

"I'm waiting," he growls behind me.

I chose to be here. I took a chance.

There's no escape. And once I comply, there's no going back.

Sucking in a steadying breath, I reach for my clothes and toss them into the hamper, then I tuck my shoes into the box, putting the ring inside between them.

"Close them both," he insists.

He's mind-fucking me before he ever fucks me at all. He's making me give up my one barrier between us, to willingly tuck it out of my reach before he commences with debauching me.

It's agonizing. It's awful. It's dirty. And I love the way Jett's mind works.

I do exactly what he says, closing the hamper and settling the lid on the shoebox. Then I turn to him expectantly. "Done."

He gives my effort a cursory glance, then nods and grabs my hand again. "Do you understand?"

The significance of his gesture? Yes. What's to come? Not exactly. We'll have sex, I'm sure. Beyond that…I have no idea what he'll demand for his forty million dollars. But since the price is so steep, I'm sure he won't make anything about this week easy.

"Yes, Sir."

"Very good. Upstairs with you."

He leads me up a slightly curved staircase with an ornate wrought-iron railing. At the top, we reach the landing. His hand at the small of my back guides me to the end of the hall without a word.

My breath catches when I take in the room.

A massive bed dominates the space, topped with soft white cotton and gray velvet. Pillows of all shapes, sizes, and textures are propped against a mirrored headboard and take up half the mattress. Above, a chandelier that's a balance between light-refracting crystals and elemental iron hangs. It's anchored to a ceiling covered in mirrors, too. There are a pair of nightstands flanking the bed and a plush white chair in the corner. A shaggy gray throw rug warms up the milk-washed planks of the floor. There's a cheerful hearth opposite the bed. Open French doors overlook the backyard, blowing gauzy sheers in with the summery breeze.

It's all warm and sensual and so perfect for a romantic seduction.

Except the thick black leather restraints dangling from each corner of the bed.

I can't help it. When I see them, I gasp.

Beside me, Jett smiles and points to an open door tucked into a corner. "Use the restroom."

"I don't need to go." The protest slips out automatically. I'm not trying to be argumentative.

His face tightens as he closes in. "Go now. You won't have another chance to use it for a while."

Because I'll be restrained to his bed. Right.

With a nervous bob of my head, I hustle across the floor and duck inside, turning to shut the door behind me. As I do, I see Jett watching me with an unwavering stare until the second the door clicks shut between us.

Dear God, what am I doing?

I flip on the overhead lights and blink. I look flushed and aroused, pupils dilated, cheeks rosy. What will happen when he actually kisses me? Touches me? Fucks me?

I swallow. I can't come apart yet. I need to hold myself together until I understand what he's *really* after.

Then, I'll have to make another life-altering decision.

After I peek at my lipstick, I take care of business, flushing the toilet and washing my hands. Then I fluff my hair again and sigh. I'm nervous and I'm wasting time. I just need to face Jett. I need to give him whatever he wants and let the chips fall.

Otherwise, I'll be marrying Michael Crawley in three weeks. And I'll never see Jett again.

Bracing myself, I pull the door open and step into the bedroom for what I'm sure will either be the best or the worst night of my life.

Chapter Three

Jett

When Whitney finally pads out of the bathroom and into the room I brightly lit, I clench my fists for two reasons. First, it stops me from tapping my thigh impatiently. Second, if I don't, I fear I'll grab her, kiss her, throw her on the bed…and forget about every plan I have.

Breathe. Stay calm, logical, and measured.

When I see the stare she cuts my way and the uncertainty in her hazel eyes, it's hard not to comfort her. It's almost impossible to feel nothing.

I have to try. Unemotional was the way she treated me last time I saw her—in court. I do nothing except give her my power if I reveal everything in an unguarded moment.

"Are you ready?"

She shrugs. "As I'll ever be."

Maybe, but she looks nervous. That should please me. After all, I need the upper hand if I'm going to win my way. But there's that part of me that remembers the innocent girl I once kissed breathless, who so softly and sweetly offered me her innocence. That girl didn't seem capable of giving me a knife in the back, just her heart. The me then would have punched the me now for my plans.

But the me now is more practical.

"Excellent. Take off your robe and hand it to me." I hold my palm up between us.

She hesitates, seems to gather herself to unknot the belt around her small waist, then slides the robe off her shoulders.

I stop breathing as she exposes her naked body to me again. No, I didn't imagine how sexy she looked by the pool, under the moonlight.

Her breasts, like the rest of her body, have matured. They are definitely more than a handful now, topped with dusky nipples I can't wait to slide my tongue across. She's built like an hourglass with a small waist that's exaggerated by the lingering shadows in the room. Her hips have widened. They're not a girl's now, but a woman's. She's got long, sleek thighs for someone so petite. But it's her pussy I can't stop staring at. Under the sparse dusting of downy, dark hair, it's puffy and pink.

I know where I'm going to expend most of my effort and energy tonight.

Finally, she drops the robe onto my palm. I toss it on the back of the nearby chair, then sit.

"Come here, Whitney." I point to the floor in front of me.

Wordlessly, she does. I'd think she was calm—except for the pulse beating wildly at her neck. When we're sharing breath and space, she stops.

I nod my approval. "Kneel."

She hesitates, then descends gracefully to her knees, looking up at me with big, beseeching eyes that threaten to turn me inside out.

I can't let her.

Instead, I fist a handful of hair at her crown and jerk her head back before inching forward in my seat, leaving her no doubt I mean to kiss her, rob her thoughts, obliterate her resistance.

Make her beg.

God, how many fantasies have I had about that?

"Jett?" Her voice shakes.

She's incredibly brave to put herself completely in the hands of a wealthy, powerful enemy for a week who has an unending hard-on and an ax to grind. I have to give her points for that. The question is, what am I going to do next? Punish her for the choice she made as a girl that ripped out my heart? Or forget revenge for one night and give in to every urge I've ever had to make her scream my name?

"Whitney."

"What am I doing here? What are you hoping to gain?"

She's always been insightful. Then again, she's smart, poised, assured as only someone raised with money and surrounded by a family full of sharks can be.

"I want what you promised me eight years ago. But since I can't have your virginity"—*or your heart*—"I'll settle for my pound of flesh."

Whitney opens her mouth to say something. I don't want to hear it. I'm done talking.

To silence her, I grab her face with one hand, thumb and fingers pressing in just above her jaw with the right pressure to force her to open for me.

Her lips part. Her pink tongue perches on her upper lip as her eyes widen with uncertainty. My heart shudders. My skin is on fire. My cock aches.

God, everything about this woman turns me on.

It's my last thought before I swoop down, seize her mouth, and force her lips even farther apart with my own.

The moment our kiss connects, I jerk. She's like a jolt of pure electricity screaming fire through my body, especially when she stills against me…then suddenly softens with a little cry and throws her arms around my neck.

That's all the green light I need.

I release her jaw, clutch my greedy fingers around her nape, and deepen the kiss by sliding my tongue against hers. Fuck, I can't stop myself from inhaling her. She's every bit as delectable as I remember—but more. She's no longer cotton-candy sweet. Now, she's a complex flavor, like a perfectly balanced dessert, some combination of sugary and salty that lingers and makes me crave more.

I fall into her. I lose myself in her. And even though she's killing my good intentions and self-control, I let myself drown in her.

A groan slips free as I pull her up. She clambers onto my lap. I barely have to encourage her to get closer before she melts against me, angling her head to allow me even deeper into her hot, honeyed mouth.

I drop a palm to her hip and use it to drag her closer. With the corner of my brain still functioning, I realize she doesn't kiss like a woman who's been satisfied well and often by her fiancé. She kisses with the desperate hunger of someone lonely, who's been craving touch. I can use that against her, to make her putty in my hands. But I can also use that to pleasure and sate her, to make her sigh with the kind of bliss she's never known. I'll make it my mission to be her fucking best.

And if she still walks away at the end…well, I really will know what she values hasn't changed.

I'm distracted when her fingers find their way under my tie, to the buttons of my dress shirt beneath. She plucks them open and slides her fingers under the fabric, smoothing the tips over my skin. I start sweating. Then she eats at my lips and makes these seductive little sounds that spark an even hotter desire in my gut. She climbs all over my lap, changing positions, trying to get even closer. It's all I can do not to plaster her against me and forget about everything but the pleasure.

As much as I'm curious to see what Whitney would do and how far she would go if I gave her free rein tonight, I can't forfeit that kind of control. I need her under my hand, under my command, under my body.

When she tosses my necktie over my shoulder and attacks the rest of my shirt buttons, I grab her wrists to stay her. "Don't."

Her breathing is labored, her eyes wide and excited. "Jett…"

I shake my head coolly. But my expression is a lie. Inside, I'm thrilled that she's so unabashed and eager. That she's already begging.

"Who's in control?"

She swallows as a frown settles between her brows. Resignation follows.

Her downshift is a kick to the solar plexus. I hate that I put that expression there.

But I have a plan. I need to see it through.

"You," she finally murmurs.

"That's right. I want you on the bed. Flat. Legs spread."

A wariness I don't precisely understand crosses her face. If she was ready and willing to jump on me mere moments ago, why is she hesitating now? Do the restraints scare her? Or do I?

Finally, she collects herself and nods before crawling off my lap, chin held high. Then she climbs on the bed on all fours and rolls to her back, meeting my stare with challenge in her eyes. She settles her feet a few inches apart.

That won't do.

But damn if she doesn't look absolutely beautiful spread across this sumptuous bed all sleek and rosy-cheeked and ripe for fucking.

Never taking my stare from her, I rise to my feet, standing tall, and slowly tear away my tie. My coat follows, then my half-buttoned shirt. I shrug it off my shoulders and stand over her, naked from the waist up.

She might want me to think she's ambivalent or even reluctant to be here. She might try to act as if she's rebellious, hostile, or indifferent. But the way her hungry stare gnaws at me makes a liar out of her. So does her wet pussy.

"What are you going to do?" she asks.

Her voice still shakes…but I don't think that trembling note is powered by fear now.

"Whatever I want. It's my forty million dollars."

The second the words are out of my mouth, Whitney stiffens. Shit, I fucked up. She might be a lot of things, but she isn't a whore. She'd never do anything purely for money. The question is, did she come with me strictly to help Vance? Or because somewhere deep down she wanted to?

That's what I need to figure out. That will tell me how to proceed for the rest of the week.

Her face closes up. "Don't let the money fool you, Jett. You always did whatever you wanted, regardless of anyone else's feelings."

That bullshit insult is an argument starter. She's baiting me, and I refuse to fall into the trap. "I'm not here to talk, Whitney."

"You're here to fuck me." She spits the words like I ought to be ashamed of myself.

"I am." I have to know what's left between us before I burn this bridge for good. "And I think you're here to fuck me, too. Find out what you missed out on all those years ago."

She doesn't answer right away. "Think what you want. You always do."

"I'm done talking." In fact, I'm over this cat-and-mouse game altogether. She's naked, spread across my bed, and open to me. Why are we even talking before I've stripped away her barriers? Once I've made her beg and plead for orgasm, then we'll see what she really wants.

I cup one of her ankles and reposition her leg toward the corner of the bed, then I bend to retrieve the cuff. She's gasping when I buckle her in, sliding my fingers underneath to ensure she still has adequate blood flow.

When I'm satisfied, I reach for her other foot.

She jerks it out of my grasp, biting her lip, "Jett..."

I shake my head. "You've heard the rumors about me. I've given you plenty of proof they're true. So don't act surprised. I won't hurt you, but I want you completely open to me. You agreed to submit to my every whim this week. I'm waiting."

This is normally where I would give my partner a safe word, but Whitney would only use it to escape her mental discomfort. I won't put her in physical peril enough to need to speak at all except a gasping, screaming plea.

In fact, I look forward to it.

"Do you understand?"

"Yes...Sir."

"That's right. Now give me your foot." I hold out my hand. In the other, I've already gathered the cuff.

Whitney stares at me. I sense her fear. And I smell her desire. She's confused and she doesn't understand her reaction.

I simply smile.

Slowly, she slides her free leg in my direction, then places her dainty instep in my palm.

Without any haste at all, I buckle her in and step back. And I stare at the banquet of female spread out before me. My mouth waters.

Since it's wiser for me to keep my pants on—at least for now—I shuck my shoes, then crawl onto the bed, hovering over her. I study her delicate face.

I remember when I thought I'd be the luckiest bastard in the world if I could just call her mine. It's been eight years, two continents, and too many meaningless fucks later. Goddamn it if I don't still think that having her, even just for the week, will make me a lucky bastard.

Whitney looks nervous. "Are you leaving my hands free?"

"For now." Unless she gives me a reason not to.

When she nods, it takes everything inside me not to give in to my urge to soothe and reassure her. Instead, I dip my head and take her mouth in a demanding kiss. Fuck if I don't have the urge to stay at her soft, bee stung lips and feast. There's something so delectable about them. The top bow tempts. The bottom pout lures. How can I not want her?

But there's more—a lot more—I haven't touched in what seems like forever.

"These breasts. Hmm…" The words slip out. I'm so busy staring at her swells and the dark nipples tipping them that I don't even realize I've spoken.

"I've changed since I was sixteen."

"For the better," I murmur as I open my lips to her neck and taste her skin.

She tips her head back and offers me her vulnerable throat. Absently wondering if she understands the unconscious trust she's giving me, I skim my mouth down her flesh, kissing the pounding pulse point at her neck, tonguing the swells of her breasts, and nipping my way to her hard, tempting crests.

I remember her being sensitive…but it was a long time ago, and I was the first man to touch them. Thankfully, when I catch one of her nipples between my thumb and finger and pull, her body tightens. Her breathing stutters.

Fuck, she's still incredibly responsive to my touch. I shouldn't let that arouse me more, but I gorge on the visual feast of her arching and sucking in a sharp breath as sensation hits her. Need flares through me unchecked.

Again, I pluck at her tender peak, gratified by the way she grips the bedding and stares up at me like she wants to control her body…and she can't.

"Do you want me to suck your nipples?"

I pinch her hard tip again, rolling and thumbing it without mercy.

She swallows and presses her lips together. "Do what you want. You're going to anyway."

"Answer me." When she doesn't, I plant my knees on either side of her hips and take both nipples in my grip, manipulating them simultaneously. "I can do this all night, Whitney, until you're willing to beg me for relief. If you force me to, how much mercy do you think I'll have?"

She tosses her head back and closes her eyes as if she's trying to shove me out of her reality. But we both know I won't let her.

"None," she pants.

"That's right. Last time I'll ask. Do you want me to suck them?"

"No matter what I say, you'll undo me."

The crying catch in her voice flips more than my libido. "Yes, so you're only prolonging the inevitable."

"I hate you."

That hurts, but I hate myself far more for not being able to fall out of love with her.

Whitney is still pushing, testing. What is she after?

"So you've said." I tug and caress the tips. They harden more as she flushes and writhes in unconscious offering. "But that doesn't change anything, so why not take what you want from me?"

I release her and sit back on my heels, watching and waiting.

Seconds later, her eyes flash open. They're even more dilated than before. A little whimper escapes from her throat. Jesus, how long before I get inside her? How long before I feel—at least for a few precious minutes—like she's *mine*?

"Suck my nipples," she finally gasps. "Hard."

"Please?" I taunt.

She nods. "Please."

"Sir?"

She sighs, then jolts when I pinch the sensitive tips again, this time with more bite. "Please suck my nipples hard, Sir."

"I know that wasn't easy for you, so I'm inclined to comply. This time. But next time you want something, the begging will have to be much sweeter."

"You're a bast—Oh!"

Whitney stops berating me when I suck one of her sweet berry nipples past my lips and take it deep. I slide my tongue over the crest, swirl around it, nip gently, then draw it to the roof of my mouth and pull without mercy.

The sounds she makes are both desperate and animal. When I release the tip into the waiting vise of my fingers, I capture the other orally, alternately soothing and torturing it, too.

She squirms and twists, gasping and fisting the sheets. Unconsciously, she parts her knees wider like she burns for me alone. That sends my desire rocketing.

Fuck, she's going to my head.

"Princess..." I murmur against her glistening nipple before switching back to the first and giving it another suckle and jerk. "More?"

"Yes."

"Am I still a bastard?" I scrape the edge of her nipple with my teeth.

Her gasp sharpens. "Yes."

"Do you want me to give you an orgasm?"

Whitney's eyes slide shut as she thrashes under me, her voice and neck straining. "Yes. Please."

"Sir?"

"Yes, Sir." Even through clenched teeth, she sounds breathy. "Please give me an orgasm."

"Better," I praise, but I don't make any move to grant her wish, just keep at her nipples.

I'm enjoying my power over her, I confess. Not simply because I'm tormenting her—though that's part of it—but because she's so close to admitting she wants me, too.

I've fucking fantasized about this more times than I can count.

"Will you?" she pants.

"Probably. Eventually." I shrug. "We'll see."

Her keening cry of demand is music to my ears. As I curl my tongue around her nipples again, one after the other, I let the agonized sound crawl into my brain and fill the space between my ears so I can replay it over and over.

"Jett…" she whines. "Don't do this."

"Do what?"

"Deny me." She lifts herself enough to stare at me, eyes soft and pleading. "Deny us."

Her reply makes my heart stop. I feel my resolve wavering.

I'm so close to stripping her bare. Not physically. Getting her naked was easy. But emotionally, in the way I need her most? Yes.

God knows I'm ridiculously hard for her. But it's more—far more. I'm fast coming to a fork in the road. What I choose next may dictate my entire future.

Revenge or Whitney?

She reaches for me, pressing her palm between my legs. I have to bite back a groan. But it gets ten times worse when she curls her fingers over my aching ridge.

Why the hell didn't I take my pants off?

"Don't play games," she implores.

"We're already playing, princess." Brow raised, I grab her wrist and tug it away. "Right now, I have the power. The more you insist, the less likely I am to give in to you."

"Because you're vindictive?"

If I'm being honest? Because I'm susceptible. Because the minute I hear her scream for me, I'll probably rush to get inside her—heedless of the consequences—and meld myself with her. Because when she's near me, I have to fight for every ounce of my control.

Because I know if I don't have my head screwed on straight, my brain won't be the organ making my decisions.

"Think what you want. I only care what you do. Put your hands on the mattress, palms flat. Now."

She scowls. "Who are you? Not the Jett I used to know."

It's a valid question I'd rather avoid answering. "Ah, guilt. Sadly for you, it's a trite, ineffective response. Surrender, Whitney."

"No."

"Then we're both wasting our time. I'll call Valentin. He'll drive you home. Our deal will be null and void." It takes Herculean effort to back off the bed and stare at her, naked, restrained, and aroused, knowing our lust—and probably more—is mutual.

I can't force her to give herself to me; I know that. Just like I know I'm probably wasting my time. But Whitney is the single biggest regret of my life. Giving up now is the last thing I want. She's leaving me little choice.

Because she's moved on.

Biting back a sigh of defeat, I turn away.

"Wait." She grapples to her knees and grabs my arms. "Don't go."

As much as I'd like to sprawl her across the bed once more, urge her flat on her back, and tunnel inside her, I can't—at least not yet. "Your pride has no place in our bed."

"And yours does?"

"No." If I want to keep her, I not only have to meet her halfway, I have to give her the kind of reassurance she needs. "If you haven't figured it out, you're here because I want you more than forty million dollars. You're here because you haunt me. Because there hasn't been a day gone by that I haven't ached for you. Did you need to hear that?"

She blinks as if my blunt honesty startles her. "Oh."

"And unless you've completely changed, I know you too well to believe you came here simply for the money."

"I didn't." Her whisper is so soft I can barely hear it.

"Did you come to fight me?"

She shakes her head. "I fight you because you terrify me."

That deflates what's left of my righteous anger. "I said I'd never hurt you and I meant it."

"That's not what I'm afraid of." She lets out a trembling breath.

Now I understand. Whether she likes it or not, she never purged me from her heart. "Be honest. Why did you come?"

Whitney softly blushes. "I think you know."

I finally do. And I'm so fucking relieved.

Fighting a smile, I climb on the bed again, forcing her to her back and hovering over her as she lies bare and vulnerable. "I won't lie to you. I plan to exploit your feelings."

"I know."

And *that's* why she's terrified. But it's a two-way street. Maybe she hasn't figured that out yet, but I doubt it will take her long to realize that no matter how many years have passed, how far I've traveled, or how many hookups I've used to forget her—it was all futile.

"I understand."

"And?"

"Let's try this again. Do you want me to kiss you?"

"Yes."

"Do you want me to touch you?"

"Yes."

"Do you want me to give you an orgasm?"

An emphatic nod accompanies her response. "Yes."

"Are you going to surrender your body and will to me?" When she hesitates, I press. "Lie to me if you want. But don't lie to yourself. If you don't give in now, won't you spend the rest of your life wondering what if?"

Her eyes slide shut, as if she can't quite face the answer. She looks like she's fighting tears. "Yes."

Finally, she's being really, truly honest.

"Then offer me your mouth."

She closes her eyes, curls her arms around my neck, and lifts her face to me.

I've waited nearly three thousand empty days—and nights—for this. If my life depended on resisting her invitation, I'd be utterly doomed.

With a rush of breath, I bend and slant my mouth over hers, losing myself in the sweet spice of her kiss, in the whispered promise of what might be between us.

When I finally back away long moments later, my heart pounds. My breaths are unsteady. "Good. Offer me your nipples."

It takes her a minute to puzzle out my meaning. Impatience nearly rubs me raw before she finally cups her breasts and lifts them to me.

"That's it. Who do those belong to?"

"You."

"Yes." I fall to my elbows like a man kneeling at the altar of her nipples and take a stiff one in my mouth again, sucking, laving, tasting, tonguing, and tugging until Whitney claws at me, urgent for more.

With a final lingering lick, I back away from the hard, glossy crests. "Now offer me your pussy."

Her breath catches. She bites her lip as she meets my desperate stare—then flares her knees wider and raises her hips to me.

Oh, thank god, yes.

I can't even pretend to be removed or restrained. I drag my lips down her body without any teasing or finesse, with one imperative in mind.

To get her on my tongue.

Quickly, I wriggle down until I wedge my shoulders between her spread legs and lie on my belly, inches away from the succulent nirvana. She's swollen and rosy and pouting. When I part her with my thumbs and my gaze devours her most secret flesh, it's as if I've opened a whole new world. Yes, I've seen a woman's pussy before—lots of them. But *this* is the one I've craved for too many years.

My nostrils flare. I bite back a groan of need at her hard red clit silently begging me.

"Jett?"

"Do you tingle?"

"Yes."

"Do you ache?"

"Yes. I want you so much I'm cramping and throbbing. Please..."

If she's switched tactics and decided to use my own weakness against me, she couldn't have played her hand any better.

"Fuck." I grip her thighs and lift her to my hungry mouth, needing to worship her.

It seems like I've waited millions of barren minutes, but I'm finally pressing my greedy mouth against her pussy and dragging my tongue through her folds. Then I suck in her clit, drawing on her, pulling and working her stiff bud until she moans.

The second her spicy-sweet flavor coats my relentless tongue and registers in my brain, all my grand plans to toy with her half the night, then make her pant and scratch her way through a savage blow job before I ramp her up again—only to refuse her relief until she begs me to fuck her however I like—all fall away.

Now I only want her to surrender to the pleasure I give her…and the possibilities of our future.

"Come for me, princess." I swipe my way through her furrow again, drowning in her taste, desperate for her. "Come."

Under me, she grips my hair until my scalp tingles, gyrating and mewling, thighs parting more, cunt turning sweeter. "Jett…"

"Do it." I suck on her clit, tongue working the stone-hard tip. "Give in."

"Jett," she gasps, the sound rising another octave as her spine twists and her head falls back.

I glance up at the mirror above. The beautiful agony on her face undoes me. "Goddamn it, you're mine."

Relentlessly, methodically, I dismantle her with my touch. I'm never going to get enough of her. Ever. Hell, I'm still half-dressed, and I feel dangerously close to coming undone.

Digging my fingers into her, I press her even more tightly against my mouth and work a pair of fingers into her fist-tight sheath, already tightening and clamping around my digits.

"Jett!"

I barely have a moment to relish the heady broken cry of her surrender before her entire body jolts and shudders. Then she's clutching, clasping, and breaking around me. Her nipples peak. Hips to cheeks, her body flushes a splashing rosy red. Her lips part, and her eyes flash open.

Our gazes meet in the overhead mirror.

I've got her. We both know it.

I ride her to the end of her orgasm, until she's struggling to recover her breath and her body turns limp, until she sighs sweetly and reaches for me.

I can't wait another second to claim her.

Goddamn it, I hope she's the last woman I have sex with for the rest of my life.

I crawl up her sated body, taking advantage of her spread legs to fit my hips between them. With one hand, I cup her nape and fit our mouths together, reveling in the fact that her kiss no longer holds fight, just sweet, open acceptance. I work my free hand between us, make quick work of my zipper, then get my cock free just enough to align my crest to her still-pulsing opening.

Her eyes flutter open. Worry crosses her face. "Jett."

I grit my teeth. I've waited eight years to be inside her, but I can tell she needs to say something. "What, princess?"

"Gently." She swallows. "Please."

Everything—both the anger and the passion—is so hot between us. And all this time, she's fought back. Now she's asking me for mercy. Why? If I wasn't so rabid to be inside her, I might be able to apply two brain cells toward finding the answer. But I can't.

"All right, I will. For you."

"Thank you." She smooths her hands up my arms, then cups my shoulders as she spreads her legs wider in silent invitation.

Jesus, how am I supposed to maintain any self-control?

I'm still trying to figure that out when I sink the head of my cock inside her.

And I run into resistance.

Whitney isn't merely tight, she's... I freeze. No. That's not possible. There's no way.

"Jett?"

"You're not..." But she seemingly is. "Still a...virgin?"

Slowly, she bites her lips. Then she nods.

Holy shit.

And yet, she came here to spend a week with me, knowing full well I intended to fuck her?

That small, problem-solving corner of my brain is working over-time to figure out if that means what I desperately want it to. The rest of me has shoved off all mental protective gear.

I'm dying to be her first.

If I play this right, will I be her only?

At that notion, my heart thuds and thumps. Waiting doesn't feel like an option. Sure, we could talk, but I don't want to give her any reason—or opportunity—to get away.

"Oh, princess." I nudge inside her, incrementally working my way through her slick clasp until I lunge deep into her with one softly insistent thrust. Then I rock my hips forward, pressing as far into her as I can. "Now you're mine."

Finally.

If she has any objection, I don't want to hear it in this moment. At least this once, I want the fuck of my fantasies, where I'm deep inside her, bareback, for the first time, and she's with me, thrust for thrust, cry for cry, all the way to the scratching, hoarse-throated, cataclysmic end.

She lets out a soft, shuddering breath, her eyes sliding half shut.

"Right?" I prompt as I withdraw from her so slowly I groan the question.

"Yes," she breathes.

"Tell me who you belong to."

She doesn't hesitate. "You, Jett."

"That's right." I glide back in and set up a rhythm I suspect will unravel her restraint. "How long have you belonged to me?"

Her lashes flutter open. I see tears swimming there. "Always."

That's it. With one trembling admission, there's no denying she still owns my heart, too.

I dreamed up this scheme to indulge my every desperate desire, to show her what she was missing, to purge her from my system once and for all.

She's felled me instead. Now, my only hope is to fight to keep her.

"And I'm yours." I press inside her again, deeper, deeper, where she's so fucking sweet. Where I want to live. Where no man has been.

"Jett..."

I hear the pleading in her voice. My thrusts pick up speed, and she rewards me with a gasp. Her fingers curl around my shoulders. Her thighs do the same to my hips, as if she can hold me against her and keep me here forever.

I sink deeper into Whitney. Not literally, since I'm already as deep into her as I can be. But figuratively, viscerally, emotionally. And I drown. If she's how I'm going to die, I'll go gratefully and willingly, ending my time on earth a happy man.

I grip her hip with one hand and grab a fistful of her hair with the other, forcing her to look right into my eyes. "I never stopped loving you."

The tears spill over. "I never stopped, either."

Oh, fuck. That sends my heart careening.

I bang into her again, each stroke faster and more insistent than the last. "You really love me?"

Whitney hesitates, then she nods and lets out a low moan full of need and pain.

"Answer me," I bark. "Say it."

"I love you," she cries out, holding me tighter, pressing kisses across my shoulder and into my neck.

That's all I needed to hear. "I love you, too."

And I'm never letting her go. I don't give two fucks who she's engaged to, she's marrying me. And I hope like hell she's not on birth control because I'm going to do my level best to get a ring on her finger and a baby in her belly this week.

She's never getting away again.

"Oh, princess." I shuttle into her faster, faster. My lungs work like a bellows.

"Jett!" she screams seconds before her pussy grips me like a vise, her body jerks, and a low groan tears from her throat.

I keep pace, doing my best to prolong her pleasure, but I can't hold out anymore, not physically. Orgasm is going to run me over, ruin me, and it will be the most delicious end ever.

But I can't resist emotionally, either. Whitney has my heart; she always has. I've been lying to myself about that for far too long.

As she grips me tighter, the wave crests over me, too. I'm suspended in a pleasure unlike anything I've ever felt. Lights flash behind my eyes. There's a buzzing in my brain. Every part of me from top to toe pings electric. I clutch Whitney and let go, pouring every bit of myself into her.

There's no denying it now; I'm hers forever.

And there's no going back.

Clinging and kissing, we come down together, hearts racing, breaths harsh. As if by some unspoken understanding, our gazes connect.

We both know everything has changed.

"Did that really just happen?" she whispers. "Did you tell me you love me?"

A little grin flits at my mouth. Honestly, I haven't smiled much in years, and it feels good. "Yeah. As we were having sex."

"And it's true?"

"One-hundred percent."

Her lips curl up, brightening her expression. "Wow."

"Wow."

"So that's what all the fuss is about?"

"You could say that." Honestly, what we shared was so extra, it was news to me, too. "You waited for me?"

"To have sex?" She nods. "I had opportunities. There was always someone I tried to date or some flirty dude at a party. But I never wanted any of them. No one made me feel like you."

"No one has ever made me feel like you, either." When I'm with Whitney, I'm centered. I'm myself. I'm whole. I never got married or serious with another woman because I couldn't replicate the feeling I had when I was with her. "How were you going to marry some guy you'd never slept with? And didn't love?"

She grimaces. "It was a business deal. You know Vance needs money. My fiancé needs plausible cover because he's in love with someone he can't have. He doesn't have any more interest in me than I have in him."

As far as I'm concerned, he's her former fiancé, but I'll get to that. "So he never touched you?"

"Except to give me a peck for some engagement photos, no."

Then I won't have to kill him. Good.

Reluctantly, I pull free of Whitney's body. When she winces and shifts, I'm instantly concerned. "You okay, princess? Sore?"

"A little, but I'm fine."

That's a relief because I'm going to want her again soon.

For now, I lie back and nestle her body against mine. She rests her head on my chest as if curling up against me is the most natural thing in the world. I caress my way down her back with a light stroke.

I sigh. We may be in love, but that doesn't make the road in front of us easy. Eventually, I'll have to be unflinchingly honest.

But first, it's time to talk about the elephant in the room. "What about your brother?"

We can't let him stand between us.

She nibbles on her bottom lip for a long minute. "Being here with you has made me realize I can't sacrifice my future for him. He has to stop being impulsive and getting himself into stupid situations. And if he doesn't, I have to stop bailing him out. He regrets everything eventually, but by then…it's usually too late. I think that's especially true of you."

I have mixed feelings about that. I'll deal with those later. "Tell me how he got in his current financial situation."

How much does she know?

"A few months ago in Vegas, he was drunk, and some asshole—he won't tell me who—dared him to bet a stupid amount of money on a hand of poker. It just happened to coincide with the value of his company. I think it was a setup. But like an idiot, Vance did it. And he lost. I was crushed because I went to school to help save and grow this company. Now it's…gone." She looks so distressed that I soothe her with a caress.

"Has he signed it over to this guy yet?"

"He refused to. I told him that's not the way the world works, that he needs to grow up and face his consequences. His answer was to call Michael, someone we've known personally and professionally for a few years. Vance begged him for a bailout. Michael agreed if I would marry him. Not that anyone asked me." She shakes her head. "I've had cold feet from day one. I've wracked my brain to figure out how I can help my brother without sacrificing my future. Then the courier knocked on my door with your note."

"And you met me in the bar."

Her face softens as she nods. "Not for the money. I couldn't not see you. I had to know…"

"If there was anything left between us? I needed to know, too." And it's time to come clean. "That's why I created a fail-safe plan…or so I thought."

She props her chin on my chest with a frown. "What plan?"

"I'm the, um…asshole who got Vance drunk in Vegas and encouraged him to bet the value of his business. I knew he'd lose. For me, it was a win-win. Either I'd get back the company I lost or—more importantly—I could use the debt as leverage to see you again. So I'd finally know if I was still as much in love with you as I suspected. If so, I planned to forgive Vance's debt if you'd marry me."

Whitney gapes. "Why go to all that trouble? Why not just reach out and talk to me?"

"And risk rejection? My fragile male ego…" I roll my eyes at my foolishness. I'm usually so fearless, especially in business, but knowing Whitney would likely rebuff me terrified me. "I thought you'd tell me to go fuck myself. My negotiations with Vance seemed to be going great—until he suddenly stopped responding to my calls. Then I heard whispers that he'd arranged your marriage to someone else for money. So I came straight to you."

"And you sent me the note?"

I nod. "One way or another, I was going to get my hands on you, princess."

She giggles. "I'd say you got a lot more on me than your hands."

"Thank god. My sanity couldn't stand not touching you anymore." I tuck a strand of dark hair behind her ear. "I think I've always known you were it for me."

"You always have been for me." She caresses my chest. "I'm sorry I took my brother's side after that summer. He told me you gave him a few pointers on the app but that he'd actually written it. According to him, you only said you'd created it to impress me. I didn't believe him, but my dad pressured me to support Vance. If I didn't, he threatened to have you arrested for touching me. I had no reason to doubt him."

As she should have. Vance no doubt spilled my "transgression" to their father to use as leverage. The old man never liked me much and probably saw my lust as leverage to use against me.

"I get it. You were so young, and they didn't leave you much choice."

"I've spent a lot of time hoping I didn't hurt you too much." She bit her lip. "But I did."

There's no point in lying. Whitney crushed me. "You didn't mean to."

I see that now.

"I didn't," she rushes to agree. "Even the thought of it killed me. I suspected you hated me for my decision."

"I'll be honest. I tried."

"I know. After that summer, you flaunted all your hookups like you were trying to throw them in my face."

When I think back on the way I acted out after the rift between Vance and me, I'm ashamed. "I kept hoping like hell you would say or do something because I mattered to you."

"You did, and I was hurt."

Her quiet admission makes me feel like an ass. "I'm sorry. I wish I could take all that back. The whole rift seems stupid in hindsight. But I was young and dumb, too."

"What happens next, Jett?"

"What do you want?"

Whitney stretches up and plants a soft kiss on my lips. "I think you know. I want you. I want everything we should have had all along."

"I do, too." My heart starts pounding again for a totally different reason as I reach across the mattress and manage to fumble my way into the top drawer of the nightstand. I pull out an oblong box. "This is yours, no matter what happens between us."

She scrambles to sit up as she takes the box in hand. I'd protest the loss of her warm skin against mine, but the view of her breasts is spectacular. And I want to see her face.

She lifts the lid and plucks up the letter inside. As she scans it, her lips slowly part until she's gaping. "You're giving me forty-nine percent of Vance's company? I don't understand."

"You've more than earned it. I know you've been trying to advise him for years. I know you're the reason the business has survived at all. He hasn't been a good financial steward, but he's occasionally listened to you. Now I'm giving you real power."

"How is this possible? You don't own—"

"I do. While Valentin drove you here, I called your brother again. It took some doing, but we finally hashed out a deal. So I own the company. Well, fifty-one percent as of now."

"What are you going to do with your part? And with Vance out of the organization, who will run it?"

"That depends on you. If you want the job, it's yours."

"Really?" Her hazel eyes widen. "You'd let me?"

"I can't think of anyone I'd trust more." I kiss her.

"Oh, my god. This is like a dream come true," she squeals. "I went to school for a position like this, so I could handle the responsibility and grow the organization. I mean, it's still relatively small, but it has so much potential and—"

"It absolutely does." Her enthusiasm makes me smile. "You've got some amazing tech developers on staff, too."

She nods. "I'm so excited about new products and updates we have in the works."

"So you're saying yes to the job?"

"Yes!"

"Excellent. I know you'll be great. And I'll be your supportive but silent partner."

Suddenly, her expression falls. "Is that all?"

I smile. "What do you think?"

Whitney looks nervous to jinx herself, but she draws up her courage. "You want to marry me."

"I do." Again, I reach into the drawer at my side and pluck out a smaller, plush square box. "And you want to marry me."

"You intend to ask me?"

Her hint of mischief makes me laugh as I sit up and pull her into my lap with a long, sweet kiss. Then I open the box to reveal a simple, elegant engagement ring that looked like it belonged on her finger the moment I saw it earlier this evening.

"I love you, Whitney. We've both made mistakes and wish we could take back some things we said and did, but all roads led us back to each other. I can't imagine the journey ahead with anyone but you. Will you do me the honor of marrying me?"

"Yes!" As I slip the ring on her finger, she cuddles closer and kisses my face. "I love you, too. Oh, my god, now we're official!"

Her excitement makes me laugh. I haven't felt this light in years. "We are."

"Why do I get the feeling this may be one of the last times you ask rather than demand anything of me?" She grins.

"You know me well."

"Yes, Sir." She presses her lips to mine once more.

From there, I take over, already hard for her again. I'm so aroused by the idea of making love to Whitney when she's wearing nothing but my engagement ring, I can't wait to get inside her.

Rolling her onto her back, I follow her to the mattress, fasten my mouth over hers, then ease inside her swollen, sweltering pussy with a groan.

Beneath me, she gasps and digs her nails into my shoulders. "Jett!"

"Yes, princess. Want more?"

"Yes. God, yes…" She wraps her legs around me. "But fair warning… I might need help with my job."

She wants to talk about work now? "If you need sex to do it right, I'm your man."

Whitney curls her arms around my neck and rocks with me. "I just might. But then I'll need time off. Unless we start being safer, we're going to have some babies."

Ah, she's figured out the other part of my plan—and she seems blessedly happy with it. "I sure hope so. I want you pregnant now."

"Me, too."

After we share bodies, passion, and our love, we fall into a heap, arms around each other. I cup Whitney's still-rosy cheek. "You happy?"

"Since you've made my every dream come true? Yes, Sir."

Epilogue

Sunshine Coast Bed-and-Breakfast, Maui
A month later…

Whitney

*D*reams really do come true! Jett has found nearly every moment of every day to prove that to me. He's worshipped me. He's kept every promise. And he's made me fall even more in love with him.

Finally—after a lot of rushed planning and tricky arrangements— we're standing on the beach at the most beautiful bed-and-breakfast in Maui, just about to say "I do."

"Are you ready?" my brother asks, looking surprisingly dapper in a pale blue suit.

"Beyond. Thanks for being here and walking me down the aisle."

"I wouldn't have missed this for the world. I just want you to be happy." He kisses my temple and offers me his arm, then he escorts me toward the palms swaying gently in the sunset and my waiting groom.

I'm about to burst with joy.

For the last month, my brother has been a lot different—quiet and contemplative. He started seeing a therapist. He admitted he's had a drinking problem since college. He started apologizing to me a lot for things he's done over the years. And he's doing his best to mend fences with Jett. My husband-to-be, bless him, has been receptive. Guarded, yes. That's Jett, and Vance burned him horribly once. But they're working it out. Jett reached out with an olive branch—and offered to let Vance stay on as head of development. My brother recip- rocated by inviting Jett to join an upcoming fantasy football league. It's progress. That's all I can ask for now.

The inn's owner, Keeley Reed, sings me down the aisle with her lilting, melodic voice. The gentle music carries on the breeze as my bare feet pad over the white runner, flanked by tiki torches leading me under a trio of arches seemingly braided out of twigs and bright pink flowers. At the end, we stop under a tall white awning framed by soft, draped swaths of white gauze. In front of an altar adorned by a floral garland stands the officiant.

And Jett, waiting for me.

He looks so handsome in tan pants, a billowy white shirt, and a navy jacket. As I approach, his smile turns brilliant. He has eyes only for me. Which is perfect because my heart is only for him.

Vance gives me away. Jett sticks out his hand. My heart threatens to turn over with love.

My brother shakes it, then pulls my fiancé in for a bro hug. "There's no one I trust more than you to make my sister happy."

There are a hundred caustic things Jett could say, but he doesn't. "I love Whitney. I always have. Thank you for your blessing."

With a final nod, Vance makes his way to my side of the small crowd, consisting mostly of friends and a few cousins, and sits next to my mom. Jett's side of the aisle is filled with his father and new step-mom, Iris. The woman's daughter, Calla, recently married Jett's older brother, Quint. They announced last night that they're expecting a baby in the spring. His sister Ivy came with her husband Derrick. The younger sister, Lacey, is a wild child. I don't know if she'll ever settle down. It will take quite a man to tame her.

"Dearly beloved…" the officiant begins the ceremony.

My heart takes flight while Jett and I look into each other's eyes. The sun dips down the vivid, cloudless sky toward the horizon as we commit our lives together. Then Jett slips a wedding band on my finger, and I slide one on his. We seal our bond with a lingering kiss.

Finally, we're man and wife.

"Are you happy, Mrs. Dean?" my husband asks as we make our way down the aisle, toward our reception. He's all smiles.

If he's happy now, just wait. I'm going to give him the best wedding present ever.

I send him a glance so full of love and joy. I never imagined my life could be so sweet. "I am. How about you...Daddy?"

As we reach the threshold to the inn, he stops in his tracks and searches my face. "Are you saying..."

"I'm pregnant. I found out this morning."

He embraces me with a hearty laugh. "Well, that's one thing I can cross off my honeymoon honey-do list."

"You were making it your mission to knock me up?"

"Hell yeah." He kisses me. "I've missed out on eight years of being with you. I need to accelerate the timetable to start this family. Besides, you're going to be hot all round and pregnant."

I beam a smile at him. "You always seem to think I'm hot."

"Because you are. But it's more. You're smart. You're funny and understanding. And you're my other half. I love you, princess."

"If you had told me that afternoon you summoned me to the hotel bar that we'd wind up deliriously in love, married, and pregnant within a month, I would have called you crazy."

"I'm sure. But I arranged everything because I hoped all those things would happen." He swallows. "I would have done anything to be with you."

"I know." I cup his beloved face. "So instead of calling you my enemy that day, I guess I should have called you a genius."

"Oh, I like that," he kids. "A visionary genius, even. Maybe add brilliant to that, too."

I laugh. "Now you're laying it on thick. I don't need to inflate your ego any more."

He leans in for a long, slow kiss. "It's not my ego you're inflating, wife."

When he rocks into me, I giggle. "I can tell."

My husband takes my hand and leads me inside, facing me in all sincerity. "Can I do anything to make you happier? Nothing is more important to me."

When Jett looks at me like he could blissfully stare at me forever as he brushes a gentle thumb over my lower lip, I melt. "Why?"

"You've made me ecstatic every day since you came back into my life. I'm going to make you happy for the next seventy years."

"That's a deal I can get behind. I love you, too."
Then we seal our forever with a kiss.

Hungry for another sexy, tempting *Forbidden Confession*?

Meet brash, dangerous Rand Garrison, personal protection specialist. He should never fall for his off-limits client. But when the bullets go flying, he can't stop himself from falling for sweetly sexy pop-star princess, Sophie.

SEDUCED BY THE BODYGUARD
Forbidden Confessions: Protectors, Book 1
by Shayla Black
(available in eBook, print, and audio)

What will he demand in exchange for keeping her safe?

I'm Sophie, pop-star princess.
My career is on a superstar trajectory.
Until the bullets start flying.
The bodyguard I hired to protect me drags me to safety.
But now I'm trapped alone with a man I barely know.
One who lights my body on fire.
But someone wants me dead.
Rand can save me from evil.
But his protection comes at a price…

EXCERPT

"Run!" I pick up speed and yank on her wrist.

She stumbles in those ridiculous shoes. "Wait!"

No time for that. I wrap my arm around her waist, lift her against my side, and haul ass for safety. Another bullet whizzes by, where Sophie stood just moments ago.

Then we're around the corner. We're safe—for now. We can't stay long, but we can regroup and strategize for a minute or two. Hopefully, it's enough.

I press my back to the wall, panting, and lower her to her feet in front of me before flipping our positions and blocking her from any other possible threat.

"You okay?"

More screaming fills the streets. Sirens roar close to the scene. She presses a hand to her chest, struggling to catch her breath. "I-I'm not hurt."

She doesn't try to claim that she isn't terrified out of her mind. I know she is.

"Are you familiar with this area?"

"Not really. I'm from DFW, but never spent much time in Arlington."

Damn. I'm not familiar with this chunk of the city, either.

We've got to get out of this alley—and this fucking vicinity—fast. Then we need a safe location without anyone knowing where Sophie is hiding. Only then can I figure out who wants her dead and why.

I scan our surroundings and come up with an idea. "Take off your dress."

"What?" There's a whole lot of *hell no* crossing her face.

She probably thinks I'm propositioning her. To be honest, in a less dangerous situation, if she was willing, I'd be more than game. Sophie may have been a pretty girl who burst on the music scene when she was still in pigtails, but she's a hella beautiful woman now. I certainly wouldn't turn her down. But that's not why I'm asking her to disrobe.

"Your red spangly dress is a bright, shiny target to this shooter."

"Oh." She frowns. "But I can't run around naked."

As much as I might like the view, she's right. Everyone has a camera on their cell phones these days, and she doesn't need that kind of exposure. Hell, we're lucky that everyone is too busy running for their lives to notice us tucked into this narrow alley.

I yank my T-shirt from my waistband and tug it over my head, leaving my torso covered in a thin wifebeater. The T-shirt is damp with my sweat and it smells like me, but that's all I've got to give her. "Put this on."

Sophie takes the shirt from my hand, her gaze glued to mine. "Where am I supposed to change?"

But she knows the answer; I see it on her face.

"I'll block you." After all, she's tiny. I'm pretty big. We'll make it work. "But we don't have time for modesty."

She hesitates an instant, then drops one strap of her low, scoop-necked dress down her arm, followed by the other. As she does, one thing becomes obvious: Sophie Larsen isn't wearing a bra.

I start to sweat again, and this time it has nothing to do with heat or danger.

Holy shit.

WATCH *Me*

SHAYLA BLACK

Steamy. Emotional. Forever.

ABOUT *WATCH ME*

To achieve her dreams, all she has to do is seduce the enemy...

Shanna York was set to achieve her glittering ballroom dreams and become a dance champion—until her dance partner gets tangled up in scandal and blackmail. With the clock ticking and all her ambitions at stake, the last thing she needs is the gorgeous owner of a sex club tempting her with the forbidden. Or maybe that's the very thing she needs...

Alejandro Diaz has sizzled for Shanna since he set eyes on her months ago. Her repeated rebuffs will make her surrender that much sweeter. She's ambitious and driven...but so is he. When she asks for his assistance to ensnare a voyeuristic blackmailer with a video fetish, he doesn't hesitate to help her stage a bedroom trap. But neither is prepared to face scorching, endless passion, the blackmailer's real identity—or the undeniable love that grows between them.

1

*W*ho'd known it would only take two minutes, seventeen seconds to ruin her life?

Shanna York ejected the flash drive from her laptop, resisting the pointless urge to fling it across the room. Instead, she set it gently on the table beside her and stood.

Damn Kristoff! What *had* he been thinking?

Besides looking for inventive ways to get off, absolutely nothing. That was obvious.

Any hope of the life she'd worked and sweated for was over. Good-bye, California Dance Star competition, which she and Kristoff were favored to win in eight days. *Adios*, any chance of making World Cup Latin finals—something she'd been striving for her entire dance career.

Kristoff knew how important this season was to her. *Knew* it. She was twenty-eight—old by ballroom standards. He was the best partner she'd ever had, which was saying something. This year was their year; everyone said so.

All it had taken was one piece of footage recorded just last week—according to the date in the lower right corner of the screen—and a note with a scrawled *Watch Me* to shatter her dreams.

Sighing, Shanna closed her eyes and tried to think. But that only focused the drive's every image into full Technicolor in her memory. Kristoff, tall and ungodly handsome, standing above two figures, one male, the other female. He cradled each of their heads in his hands as they knelt before him. Their tongues slid up and down his erection, licked over his balls, and occasionally met at the head of his cock for a juicy kiss.

"You like that big dick?" he asked. They both moaned. The camera zoomed in as the woman, a stunning blonde with a starburst tattoo on her breast, deep-throated Kristoff.

The other male, a buff guy with military short hair and his own raging hard-on, stood and licked at Kristoff's nipples. Kristoff groaned, the sound soon drowned out by the man capturing his lips and devouring them in a harsh kiss.

That was the first thirty seconds—plenty depraved by the deeply traditional standards many ballroom judges held. Then came the middle of the clip...

Kristoff, intent and focused as he penetrated the woman's sex, plunging in for slow, agonizing strokes. A surprise, given the fact Shanna had always believed he was strictly gay. But thrusting into the woman, he appeared like any other hetero man...until the camera panned back and showed the other man penetrating Kristoff's ass, the forward momentum of that stroke pushing Kristoff's erection into the panting female.

The end of the video, however, was what Shanna feared could really kill her dreams of being a ballroom champion. The other man, apparently at the end of his restraint, tore off his condom and stood near the woman's sex as Kristoff so diligently pounded it. The man with dark hair watched them, yanking on his cock until semen shot out, coating the woman's clit and wet folds. They all groaned.

Kristoff quickly pulled out of her, tugged on his erection, and came on the woman's swollen sex, too. She dripped semen, oozed with the fluids of the men's satisfaction. Was that enough for Kristoff? Of course not.

He grabbed the other man's shoulders and forced him to kneel before the woman's dripping sex beside him. Together, they licked her. Clean. Deep. Until she orgasmed against their dueling tongues. During the clip's final moments, the camera panned back again to reveal that the trio had performed the entire scene for a rapt audience.

Shanna put her head in her hands and groaned. She was so screwed. If the conservative judges of ever-elegant ballroom dance got hold of this footage… The thought of what they could—and would—do to hers and Kristoff's scores at the California Dance Star made her shudder. Nothing like going from first to worst in the standings.

Equally unnerving, watching the scene had more than vaguely aroused Shanna. Not that she was attracted to Kristoff—and definitely not after the position he'd put her in with this stunt. But the freedom to just let loose and fulfill her fantasies, particularly with people watching, flipped her switch way more than it should.

That had to stop. She must deal with the situation, somehow ensure this video didn't fall into the judges' hands. She must not think about her neglected libido.

Where was Kristoff, damn it? He had to have known that his recent jaunts to that damn sex club, *Sneak Peek*, would eventually come back to haunt them. She'd warned him. Clearly, he hadn't heeded a word.

The door of her small dressing room burst open. Kristoff glided in. The graceful bastard moved like glass, especially on the dance floor, which was a treat after living with her father and three brothers: an Olympic sprinter, a world-class decathlete, a former champion weightlifter, and a pro football player, respectively.

They all considered her a failure because she'd never been a champion. By their definition, ballroom dancing wasn't even a sport. Which made her a double loser.

This year, she'd intended to show them different.

With Kristoff's night at that crazy sex club for exhibitionists and voyeurs, her dreams were gone.

"Three minutes, Shan. Are you ready?" Kristoff held out his hand to her.

Normally, that was Shanna's cue to take it and follow his lead. Not tonight.

"To kill you, yes!" She held up the flash drive. "Obviously, your brain sunk into your pants. Could you not have waited to get your jollies for another few weeks?"

He frowned, looking totally unamused. "What do you talk of?"

"Your recent threesome at that club."

Kristoff's polished smile faded. "I was just, um, how do you say, blowing off a little steam. How did you know?"

"Someone filmed you and sent me the footage. Full color, high quality, great sound. No question it's you, near a sign that said *Sneak Peek*."

"Filmed me… I had no idea. And someone sent it to you?" he croaked. "You saw it?"

"Yes, along with a little note informing me that if we show up to the California Star, they'll distribute the clip to all the judges. And you know what will happen then. We'll have no chance in hell of winning."

He cursed, a popular Angelo-Saxon syllable that started with an F. Shanna shook her head. He'd already done that, thanks so much.

"I agreed to take you as my partner for two reasons: You're an amazing dancer, and I thought you were discreetly gay. Gay, the judges can handle. Discreetly gay, even better. Clearly, I was wrong about your orientation. And if the judges see this, your talent will no longer matter to them."

Kristoff flushed. "I am, um…equal opportunity when it comes to sex."

"I gathered that." She gritted her teeth. "And it's fine. I don't care what you do in your private life as long as it's *private*."

"One minute!" someone shouted from the hall.

Squatting, Shanna peered into the mirror at her dressing table, secured a pin holding back a lock of her pale blond hair, then smoothed a hand down the silver sequins of her tiny costume. God, she felt sick to her stomach. All the years of sacrifice and work… If she wanted to win—and she did—she was probably going to have to start over. New season…new partner. Even the thought made her sick. She hoped her tumult didn't show on her face.

"We have to go," she said. "Or we'll be late."

"Stop! We must talk about this. Winning is important to me, too, and—"

"Champions aren't late."

"It does not matter. This a charity event, not a competition. And your dance card is empty, no?"

Ouch! Still, she lifted her chin, despite his low blow. "Not the point. People are still watching."

"Not everything is work, Shan. Must you be so driven? Enjoy life a little."

"I enjoy winning." Her teeth hurt from grinding them together.

"Except for dance, you have no life. When did you last go on a date?"

"Are you keeping track?"

"I grow tired of your so-serious attitude. Maybe you need to go to *Sneak Peek* and um, how do you say, let loose like me."

"We have the biggest competition of our careers in eight days, and you think I need to get laid?"

"Yes."

Shanna tried not to see red—along with violet, crimson, and magenta.

Kristoff met her angry gaze squarely. "Until you smile and be nice, you are not fun to dance with. You will certainly make no money for the cause tonight in this mood."

It might be uncharitable of her, but it was hard to think about someone else's cause when her own was falling apart. And the fact that he took no responsibility for putting her in this mood really annoyed her.

"Go to hell, Mr. Palavin!" She made to stalk past him.

He grabbed her arm. "You are angry. I fucked up, yes. I am sorry. I know what this means to you. But no matter how much I apologize, no matter that we have become friends in the past year, will you forgive me? Stand by me? By tomorrow, I believe you will be holding auditions because everyone knows any partner who is a liability to your ambition is quickly replaced." He grabbed the flash drive off the table. "There is a reason your dance card is empty tonight and everyone calls you the Bitch of the Ballroom. In the past, I have defended you, but now… Have a lovely time alone."

"Are you staring at that *ramera* again?"

Alejandro Diaz ripped his gaze away from Shanna York and sent a rebuking stare to his dance partner. "*Mamá*, you've been listening to gossip. We do not know her well enough to know if she's a bitch."

But he'd looked at her enough to know he wanted her bad. Her soft blond hair shone under the lights like a halo around her face. Those blue, blue eyes projected a little-girl-lost quality that made him want to hold her close and whisper reassurances. But the fiery way she moved her killer body when she danced, like she performed sex to music, made him hard as hell.

Oh, he had fantasies about her—about taking her to *Sneak Peek* and melting away all that icy reserve by stripping her down, tying her up, filling her full of his cock...while she wondered if they were being watched. Would she get off knowing that others could see the rise of her pleasure and hear the gasps of her orgasms as he gave them to her, one after the other? The way Shanna danced lured men in, as if she loved having their eyes on her, as if she craved hot stares and knowing they had even hotter fantasies with her at the center.

How would she feel if she knew *he* harbored lots of fantasies about her?

His mother shook her head. "Hmm. You met her once. She was not polite."

Not true. She'd been very polite, in an icy, reserved way. In retrospect, he'd come on too strong, been too direct. Clearly not the way to approach an independent woman who valued being in control.

"Tonight is another night." He turned his mother around the dance floor in a gentle waltz. And he watched Shanna.

Her appearance lived up to her ice princess reputation in a short, silvery, barely-there costume of sequins and crystals. She was unsmiling and a bit aloof. He'd love to melt her.

"There are other single women here. Girls who are good. And Catholic. And yet you focus on the *ramera rubia*."

"*Mamá*," Alejandro warned. "You don't know her personally. Just because she's blond does not mean she's a bitch."

He sighed. He loved his mother and owed her much. As a single woman, she'd raised him with loving arms and a firm hand, since his father had left them just before Alejandro became a teenager. She hadn't given him much in the way of luxuries as a kid, but she'd made up for it by providing all the affection and guidance he'd needed. As an adult, however, he realized she was incredibly old-fashioned.

"Spending too much time at that club of yours has confused your thinking, *mijo*. Nothing but *putas* there."

Ali laughed. His mother didn't disapprove of the club...but she only knew about the bar and pool tables, the dart boards and the dance floor. She had no idea what went on upstairs.... Better to keep it that way.

He made damn good money as *Sneak Peek's* co-owner. Between that, his savings, and his other investments, he'd been able to buy his mother a condo and a new car, set up a trust for her, and give her a bit of luxury in the last two years. She just wanted him to settle down, marry, have babies. *Mamá* had made that *very* clear.

He would...in his own good time.

"Let's not argue." He twirled her toward the punch table, not far from where Shanna sat alone. As he looked at the gorgeous dancer again, he had to fight the rise of his erection. *Not here, not now...but soon.*

His mother followed the line of his sight. "*Dios mío*, can you not look at one other woman tonight?"

No. He'd come tonight specifically to cozy up to Shanna York. What a happy coincidence that making his mother's night would help him to make his own.

"*Mamá*, did you sign up to dance with your favorites tonight?"

She shook her head. "No."

"Why not?"

"Alejandro, it is too much money. You paid for me to be here, and that is enough. I will watch."

And send a disapproving stare every time he rumbaed Shanna into a dark corner? Not truly enjoy herself? No.

"You will dance."

He stopped her before the punch table and handed her a drink. While she sipped, he eased over to the table that held the dancers' cards. There were still a few empty slots available to foxtrot or tango with some of her favorites. And Shanna's card was completely empty. He wrote his mother's name onto the empty spaces of the male dancers' cards, then he wrote his own on Shanna's in every space. With a smile, he called the attendant over.

After settling dances for his mother, he handed the volunteer, a perky brunette, Shanna's card. "I would like to purchase all these dances, as well."

The brunette looked at it and frowned. "Hers? All of them?"

"*Sí.*"

"That's three thousand dollars." She pointed out with a hint of incredulity.

He handed her his credit card. "Then I will have the pleasure of knowing more children will have full bellies and be attending school, while I dance with a beautiful woman."

The woman sent him a look that plainly said she thought he was unhinged. "She isn't known for keeping her partners long. You may not last the whole night."

For what he had in mind, a night was all he needed.

With a smile, he finished paying, then found his mother.

"The charity dances start in five minutes, and you will be busy." He handed her a schedule of her partners.

"Alejandro! You spend too much money on an old woman. I cannot dance so much."

"*Mamá*, you are barely fifty. It's only money, and I can afford it. Enjoy yourself."

He certainly planned to.

2

*T*he event's emcee announced the beginning of the charity dances, and Shanna poised herself in a chair, plastic smile in place, at the edge of the ballroom floor.

People around her were beginning to pair up for the first of the dances, names and smiles being exchanged. She tossed her hair off her shoulders. That twisting of her stomach was not a pang of hurt. She didn't care if no one bid on her dances. Sitting back would give her an opportunity to observe her competition, since most of the other dancers were here…just in case she and Kristoff still had a chance to win, in spite of his indiscreet sex life.

Tomorrow, she'd get to the bottom of that shocking video. She wasn't giving up on years of hard work and her dreams of being a champion without a fight.

"I believe this dance is mine."

Shanna followed the deep voice and looked up into an incredibly handsome face. Strong features, burning hazel eyes, heavy five-o'clock shadow, perfectly tailored gray suit with a vavoom red tie. Her heart lurched; this one had sin written all over him.

He also looked familiar. She stared, hesitating, but the more she thought about it, the more certain she became. Somewhere, somehow, they'd crossed paths before.

"Have we met?"

He smiled, all dazzling charm, oozing Latin charisma and hot sex. "Yes. Three months ago. The Bartolino Foundation thing."

That night rushed back to her with overwhelming clarity. This sexy man with his killer smile, flirting outrageously and whispering shocking, hot suggestions as he tangoed her around the dance floor. At the end of the night, he'd asked her out...while trying to kiss her. She'd refused every would-be swain for the past two years without a single regret. But he sorely tempted her. The man might as well have the word *Distraction* tattooed on his forehead. Dating him was impossible. That night, she'd refused him and disappeared into the crowd. She assumed she'd seen the last of him.

Now she suspected she'd underestimated his resolve.

"Ah, I think you recall that night." A smile lifted the edges of his lips.

"Alejandro, isn't it?"

"Alejandro Diaz, yes."

Shanna drew in a deep breath. Just like their first meeting, he caused an unwelcome dizzying effect, complete with revving heartbeat. *Warning!* When she had to bring a date to a social occasion—the only time she went out—she chose safe men who were too busy with their own work to be demanding and too dull to keep her interest for more than an evening. She just didn't have time for a relationship when she had a dance career that needed all her attention.

This one might as well shout that he'd be both fascinating and determined. He meant to get his way—and have his way with her.

Not if she could help it.

Steeling herself against the impact of his touch, Shanna put her hand in his. No matter how prepared she thought she'd been for the skin-on-skin contact, she'd been wrong. A wild gong of want beat through her the second her palm brushed his. She braced for the rush of heat as she stood.

"The music is starting. Shall we?" He gestured to the dance floor, then eased her forward with a hand at the small of her back.

"Sure." What else could she say? This was his three minutes; he'd paid for them, so she owed him that. But no more.

God, not a second more.

A soft Latin rhythm began to wash the room from the overhead speakers. Sensual, hypnotic, the music spoke of a humid summer night shared by lovers. Shanna nearly groaned. Great, a rumba, the dance of love. The one that most emulated passion and sex. Why now?

On a strong beat, Alejandro grabbed her wrist and pulled her against him. Shanna tried to stop herself from crashing into him by planting a hand on his chest. But her fingers only encountered hard muscle. He was like a rock under that shirt, and given his mile-wide shoulders, she was suddenly sure that seeing him naked would be ten times better than a slice of her favorite sinful chocolate cake.

He hooked a finger under her chin. Reluctantly, she lifted her gaze to his. The heat in those hazel eyes could melt steel. *Look away. Get away!* But she couldn't. Once her gaze connected with his, she was locked in, fused to him in a way she didn't understand.

That stare sizzled all through her...and settled right between her legs. She felt unable to break his gaze.

Sex had always been something she could take or leave. At the moment, she wanted to take anything he was willing to dish out.

How could he do that to her with just a glance?

As she drew in a deep breath and tried to find her wits, he curled a thick arm around her waist, drawing her even closer. His whole body was hard...every inch of it. From the feel of him, many inches. Shanna trembled to realize he was every bit as interested as she was. Thank god these dances were short.

Then he held out his left hand, palm up. Slowly, she placed her hand in his.

They began to dance. He was incredibly smooth, never dancing on his heels, never losing the beat of the music. Wow, could he move his hips. Perfect figure eights with them. No doubt, he'd learned how to dance very well somewhere along the way.

Basic boxes quickly gave way to an open position, then a cross, which he used as an opportunity to brush his body against hers and caress her hip. An underarm turn led her right back to a basic.

He was good for an amateur. She had an inkling that he might be good at other things, too.

"So, what brings you here tonight?" she asked, grasping at conversational straws. Maybe if she was talking, she wouldn't be thinking about how much this guy turned her on.

"Helping orphans is not a worthwhile cause?"

"It is. Most men would rather simply write a check than ballroom dance."

"I brought my mother. She enjoys these things, and it is a very small thing to do in order to see her smile."

Sexy, a good dancer, family-oriented, crazy handsome—Alejandro seemed like every woman's fantasy and way too good to be true. He must have some terrible flaw she just couldn't see at the moment. If not…she was in a heap of trouble.

Her body temperature was rising with every suggestive look, every sweep of his hand over her waist and low dive on her hip, each brush of his palm that inched toward her ass.

Damn! Why hadn't she found some man to scratch her itch in the last two years? Or even invested in a good vibrator? Maybe if she had, she wouldn't feel wound so tightly right now, so ready to jump on Alejandro and every protruding part of his body.

"That's nice of you," she managed to say.

"Not really. I knew you would be here."

"M-me?"

"Hmm." He led her into another open position, then curled her against his body, hips crushed against hips. She felt way more than his pelvis.

"Certainly you can feel my…enthusiasm to see you again." He laughed, seemingly at himself.

Yeah. His enthusiasm was sizeable and very hard to miss.

Then he leaned her back over his arm in an exaggerated dip and followed her down. Until his face was an inch from her breasts. Shanna felt him exhale, his warm breath caressed her cleavage. Her nipples beaded instantly.

Slowly, he lifted her upright again, then spun her around until her back rested against his chest. He nestled his erection in the small of her back. The flat of his palm covered her abdomen, and he took her other hand in his. The gesture probably looked possessive. It certainly felt that way.

Straight ahead, she saw Kristoff dancing with a thin, middle-aged woman with hair a dubious shade of red. He peered at her with a questioning brow raised.

Alejandro led her to swivel her hips against his, in time with the music. Kristoff didn't miss a second of it. In fact, as Shanna looked around, she realized they'd gathered quite a bit of attention.

A blast of moisture flooded her sex.

"Everyone is watching," he whispered.

"I see that." Her voice shook.

He bent and lifted her leg, wrapping her calf around his thigh and urging her head to fall back to his shoulder. Their eyes met, their mouths inches apart.

Shanna felt stripped down, as if she was naked under Alejandro's knowing gaze. God, if he didn't stop that, she'd melt against him right here, right now.

"Men are watching you, wanting you."

He grabbed her thigh, spun her around to face him, then placed that thigh over his hip. They rested nearly hip to hip again. As he leaned back slightly, he forced her chest against his. Still, she couldn't break his stare.

"And you like it," he whispered.

She opened her mouth to deny it, but Alejandro's gaze stopped her, warning her before she could do anything foolish, like lie.

"I can tell you do."

The intensity of his stare, the way in which he'd dug past her icy defenses, seemed to see the real her, and guessed her dirty secret... He was a walking wet dream. He was her worst nightmare.

How had he known she loved being watched?

Alejandro swayed with the music in the opposite direction, bringing her body with him. With a gentle caress of her cheek, he directed her gaze back to his—all while making it look like a part of the dance.

"You know you do," he murmured. "You love that most every man in the room would kill to have your body against his and an up-close view of that smoldering sensuality melting the ice you wrap yourself in."

His words made her shake because they were so true. "Stop."

He performed an open step, then brought her back for a box. "Their stares cling to you as you lure them in with the sway of your hips to the beat of the music. They are drawn to your femininity. Their gazes caress your breasts as your chest lifts with every move and breath. They watch the movements of your sleek thighs and wish they could lie between them."

A glance around proved he was totally right. Easily a dozen men were openly watching she and Alejandro dance, their gazes ranging from more than mildly interested to sizzling with heat. Desire vibrated deep inside her, pulsing under her clit. How wet could she get before she stained the front of her thin costume?

And how had Alejandro known exactly what turned her on?

Most people had only seen the driven dancer who yearned to win and find some way to make her family proud. No one else had seen the woman inside who used dance to express the sexuality she otherwise repressed. No one.

This man had known her secret in the blink of an eye. He'd all but mocked her chilly reserve. He looked at her as if he could see beyond her façade, to the fear and emptiness that fed her ambition.

Thankfully, the music ended.

"Thank you for an interesting evening, Mr. Diaz. Perhaps our paths will cross again." But not if she could help it.

Still, he didn't let go. Instead, he continued to stare with that sultry hint of a smile. "The evening is not over. I bought all of your dances tonight. Every last one."

Shanna stared at him, wide eyed and stunned. Panicked. That was bad. Very bad. Just being in his arms and hearing his words made her feel vulnerable in a way she didn't like and would not tolerate.

And she was stuck with him for the next three hours? Lord, she was in so much trouble.

"Why?"

"I enjoy watching you being watched and the way it arouses you. I love knowing that so many men in the room are fantasizing about slaking their lust with you—"

"You don't know what other men are thinking," she protested.

"Yes, I do. It is exactly what I'm thinking. It is even more delicious because I alone am holding you in my arms."

Oh, god. "This conversation is inappropriate."

"Honesty disturbs you?"

"I'm not...I—I don't get aroused by knowing that men are watching me."

"Really?"

He urged her into a cross again. No sooner than she turned to step into the next box, he pushed against her hand, sending her spinning to face the wall. Then he was behind her, cradling her swaying hips, his mouth hovering just over her sensitive nape in a darkened corner of the ballroom.

Shanna shivered as he exhaled on her sensitive flesh and gripped her hips.

Then he reached around to place his hand flat on her stomach again...but he aimed high, flattening his palm on the upper swells of her chest and smoothing his way down.

"Hard nipples," he commented. "Such pretty, edible, want-to-suck-them-in-my-mouth buds."

She opened her mouth to stop him with a hiss, but he kept tantalizing her as he caressed his way south, down her ribs, over her stomach, until his fingers brushed the front of her costume right over her very wet sex. He lingered. Shame and arousal crashed inside her. She closed her eyes.

"You're always wet when you dance in public...like now, aren't you?"

At his touch, his words, pleasure spiked, hitting her full force, like a blast from a raging fire. She sucked in a breath. Damn it, why did he have to be right?

If he could read her that well after a few minutes with her, Shanna knew he'd quickly dig deeper into her soul unless she put distance between them now.

"Stop," she demanded in her best ice-queen voice.

"Answer me, *querida*."

"No."

He danced her to face him again as one song segued into the next, this one a waltz.

"Do not be embarrassed. Your arousal turns me on. It's one of the reasons I chose not to give up when you rebuffed me at the Bartolino event. I want that arousal," he whispered in her ear. "I want it in my hands, my mouth, all around my cock when I fuck you. Will you wonder then exactly who is watching us?"

His words hit her like lava, sizzling her skin, charring her resistance and sanity. No one had ever talked to her like that. Between her brothers and the bitchiness she wore like armor, no one had dared.

God, even without uttering a word, Alejandro was stunning. When he murmured that sort of sin, he didn't just turn her on; he turned her inside out.

He was dangerous. She could see getting lost in such a man and his smoldering promise of spectacular sex—the kind she'd never experienced.

"That's enough," she forced herself to say.

"We haven't started. I think about undressing you under soft lights, your back to my front and letting my hand smooth your dress from your lush curves. I ache to brush my palms over your hard nipples before I roll them between my fingers. I fantasize about feeling my way lower, down to that soft, wet pussy, then grazing your hard clit. And stroking you until you come. I obsess about bending you over and filling you with my cock—all while you suspect the hot stares of strangers rake you. Want you."

Desire pulsed, flared with every mental image he created. She could *see* herself naked, flushed, writhing under his hands or as he impaled her. She could feel herself dissolving at the thought of orgasming for him—and a roomful of aroused men.

This was dangerous. Bad. Wrong. *No, no, no.*

"I said that's enough!" Her voice shook as hard as the rest of her.

He kept on, as if she'd never uttered a protest. "I am part owner of a club where you could express yourself in any way you like. In every way that gets you off. *Sneak Peek* was made for women like you."

Sneak Peek? The club where Kristoff's video had been filmed in his soon-to-be-infamous threesome? That jolted her.

"I know what goes on there."

A smiled toyed with those sensual lips of his. "Good. If we weren't waltzing now, I would reach between those sleek thighs of yours, and I bet I would find out you're even wetter now than the last time I touched you."

Shanna wanted to lie, but she didn't trust him not to waltz her in a corner and test his theory.

"I need to use the ladies' room."

He hesitated, then released her. "By all means."

She turned away, resisting the urge to run to the sanctuary of her dressing room. No, she would walk. Calmly. *Breathe in, breathe out.*

And screw charity. Yes, Alejandro had paid his money. He'd gotten his dance and his cheap feel, too. He could pat himself on the back, knowing that he'd dug up her naughty secret and rubbed it in her face. She wasn't coming back. If she ever saw him at one of these charity events again, she'd run in the other direction. Fast.

Before she could take the first step, he grabbed her wrist and whirled her around. Suddenly off balance, she collided against his chest. Her head snapped back…her mouth right under his.

"Come to *Sneak Peek*. There, I will fulfill your every fantasy."

Of that, she had no doubt. But no way could she give him that chance.

3

"*S*o I've got two choices, both really lousy." Shanna sighed as she stirred her hot tea at the outdoor café's wrought iron table the next morning. "Either I stick it out and hope this threat is just a sick joke or I dump Kristoff, try to find yet another new partner, and wait a season or two before we mesh well enough to win anything."

Jonathan winced. "Don't you think it's time you stop dropping partners, love? Your reputation in that area isn't exactly sparkling."

She regarded her former dance partner with a frosty stare. "Ending our partnership was a mutual decision."

The handsome Aussie reached for her hand across the table. "The handwriting was on the wall. We weren't going to make it. I didn't want to win as badly as you did. And sleeping together was a terrible mistake."

Shanna wanted to deny his assertion, but couldn't. Jonathan simply hadn't possessed her drive to win. They'd both known it. Their one night of impulsive sex had merely brought their problems to the fore.

Admittedly, sex between them had been stupid. But a late-night practice, Jonathan suffering a recent break-up with his fiancée, Shanna fearing their days of competing together were numbered, hours upon hours of nothing but sexually-charged dances, with the tension between them so thick... The dam holding their restraint had burst.

Afterward, their partnership had gone from strained to doomed. Her ambition on the dance floor hadn't meshed well with his need to check out to deal with his recent turmoil. Belatedly, Shanna had realized he needed more emotional support from a partner than she'd given. Their fights had become hellacious. They'd said terrible things, and he'd walked out.

In retrospect, the end of their dance partnership had been best for both of them. Jonathan's fiancée had returned, and he'd retired to married life and modeling. After a few months of silence between them, he'd reached out to her. Over the last eighteen months, they'd repaired their friendship. During that time, Shanna had been happily paired with Kristoff...until she'd seen his porn-inspired deeds.

"Let's not rehash ancient history," Jonathan said. "You came to me with a problem. Are you sleeping with Kristoff?"

Shanna shook her head. "Of course not. Until I saw the video, I thought he was firmly in the gay column."

"At least that's one less complication."

The early-morning breeze whipped through her hair. Shanna looked down into her steaming mug. "I have to decide what to do. I don't want to lose Kristoff as a partner. Training a new one would take so much time. But if the judges get their hands on that footage..."

"That would be devastating. The old crones would crucify you. The men...they'd either try to bury or debauch you."

"Exactly. I want to strangle Kristoff every time the realization that he's jeopardized everything hits me."

"In the dance department, you're well-matched. Kristoff is a fabulous athlete who wants to win every bit as badly as you. Admit that much."

She rolled her eyes. "I suppose."

"Stop," he demanded. "I know you too well. Everyone else may buy that puffed-up bitch act, but we both know better. It took me years to realize you're not half as pissed as you are afraid. You're trembling at the thought of being vulnerable and of not holding that trophy so you can finally prove to your family that you're a champion. Is

Daddy's opinion really more important than friendship? It's okay to stand by your friends, even if your family will disapprove."

God, he had her number.

"Have you taken up psychotherapy on the side, Freud?"

"Just calling your bluff."

"I came to you for help, and you're giving me hell." She stood and grabbed her paper mug.

"Sorry," Jonathan murmured, looking like he wanted to say more on the subject. Mercifully, he didn't. "Do you have any other information about the video or its delivery that might help you track down the blackmailer? Or did Kristoff know anything about how it was made?"

"No, I don't think Kristoff has a clue. But last night, the owner of the sex club in which the footage was filmed tried to seduce me out of my panties. If the event hadn't been for charity—"

"You know where this tape was made?"

She nodded. "A place called *Sneak Peek*."

"The club for voyeurs and exhibitionists?"

Jonathan knew about that place? "Yes."

He sat back in his chair, a taunting smile curling up his mouth. Shanna felt her heart seize. He looked at her as if he knew being watched made her wet. Did he? Did every man who watched her dance?

Thankfully, he didn't go there. "So when you danced with this mate, did you talk to him, see what he knows about the video and its creation?"

"No." She'd been too busy resisting his seduction, trying to fend off his unnerving ability to see past her defenses.

"There you go." He shrugged. "Maybe he can help you track down who's blackmailing Kristoff."

Shanna gripped her tea. Jonathan was right. The answer had been staring her in the face. Alejandro could find out exactly who had filmed Kristoff.

All she had to do was put herself in his path again and pray she could resist him.

"I need your help."

Alejandro Diaz looked up at the female with the trembling voice hovering in the door of his office. Platinum hair pulled tightly away from her unusually pale face. Blue eyes smudged with the bruises of sleeplessness. Shanna York. Here, in his office.

Well, didn't this make his morning interesting?

"Long trip to the ladies' room," he drawled.

She lifted her chin—her silent way of telling him she would not bend her pride to apologize for having deserted him last night. Alejandro frowned…though he was silently amused.

"You came on too strong. Again. I needed to put space between us."

"And now you do not? Today, I'm supposed to forget that I enjoyed a dance and a half, rather than the eight I paid for."

"You gave that money to charity."

"To be with you. The charity was the cherry on top."

"You paid for the opportunity to dance with me, not seduce me."

Why not both? he wanted to ask, but tactically retreated from that line of questioning. Starting a fight with Shanna wasn't the way to entice her to stay. Raising her hackles would not get him the up close and very personal time he wanted with her.

"Perhaps I succeeded, since you have come to *Sneak Peek* because… What was that you said? Ah, yes. You need me."

"I'd still be avoiding you if I didn't need your help," she shot back. "Which I happen to need now. Please."

Hmm. She'd likely choked on that word. Shanna was stubborn and tough and wore her ice like armor. No doubt it warded off most men.

He was made of stronger stuff.

Alejandro stood and faced her. "What can I do for you? Take you on a tour? We have great facilities."

Her expression softened. "It's a beautiful place. I was expecting something…"

"Dark? Sleazy? Dirty?"

She hesitated. "Glass-and-chrome seedy, yes. This is really…warm."

That's what had attracted him to the house in the beginning. Ali

thanked God every time he set foot in the place that his business partner, Del, had agreed with his choice of locations. Its shimmering white
plaster walls glowed Hollywood golden when the sun set over the hills
of Los Angeles. The expansive gardens had a charming Spanish
Revival feel, complete with decorative tile that rimmed the pool and
outlined the patio steps leading to the second floor. The bars, both
indoors and outdoors, welcomed guests. Converting the house into a
club had given it the feel of an intimate party, rather than a bunch of
strangers getting naked together. That instant comfort level was one of
the reasons he and Del had been so successful since opening *Sneak
Peek*. That and good business sense.

Alejandro shrugged. "I took one look at the house and fell in love.
Cary Grant built it in the 1920's. The previous owners started restoring
it about ten years ago…and ran out of money. Del and I spent a small
fortune to buy the place and finish renovating. I have not regretted it."

"It's gorgeous."

"As are you. Since it's clear you are not here for me to seduce, what
can I do for you?"

Her charmed smile disappeared. The tense hand-clasping returned.
"My dance partner and I have a…situation. A delicate one. Kristoff has
been here, as a customer, right?"

"I'm not at liberty to answer that. Privacy is something we protect
fiercely here at *Sneak Peek*. I hope you understand."

"But that's just it. Someone invaded his privacy. They filmed
him…" She shook her head. "It would be better if I showed you."

Alejandro frowned as Shanna reached into an oversized bag
hanging from her shoulder and extracted a flash drive in a clear plastic
case. She handed it to him, her expression tense. He popped it into his
laptop.

Two and a half minutes later, anger boiled his blood.

"Where did you get this?"

"Someone left it in my dressing room last night just before the
benefit began, along with a note telling me that if we competed in the
upcoming California Dance Star, this footage will be sent to all the
judges."

"And neither you nor Kristoff have any idea who sent it?"

She shook her head. "That's why I'm here. I was hoping you could help me. That competition means…everything to me. I've worked *years* to win this."

As driven as she was, as ambitious as rumor painted her, Ali believed it. She had dumped three partners in the last five years. One after breaking his leg badly skiing just before dance season began. The next partner had been history when he dropped her during a lift—in the middle of a competition. The third…he was a mystery. There one day, gone the next. Alejandro's mother had the pulse on all her favorite and not-so-favorite dancers. *Mamá* said there had been rumors of a torrid—but brief—affair between she and Jonathan Smythe.

Alejandro extracted the flash drive, slotted it back in its case, and handed it to her. "There are absolutely no still or video cameras allowed in the club. Period. That is part of our strict privacy policy."

"Which someone clearly violated."

"Yes, because that isn't security footage. If it was, it would be black and white and from an aerial view. It certainly wouldn't be in full color and focused in tight on the action." Alejandro rose, paced.

This was very bad news. People paid a lot of money to enjoy themselves at the club anonymously. Often high profile people. Stars, senators, diplomats. If that privacy was compromised and people found out… He didn't want to think about what it might do to their business.

"Would you excuse me for a moment?" he asked.

"Yes."

Alejandro pulled his cell phone from his pocket and hit the speed dial button to reach his partner.

"Del?" he asked after hearing a familiar voice rumble at the other end. "We have a situation you ought to know about."

"I'll be there in five."

It was more like ten minutes later when Del sauntered in, buttoning his shirt and wearing a smile. His mussed hair explained why. Damn, it was barely past ten in the morning, but his buddy had already been getting busy. A glance at Shanna reminded him that he hadn't been busy like that in longer than he cared to admit…and he knew exactly who he would like to change that fact with.

"What's up?"

"Del, this is Shanna York. She is a professional ballroom dancer. Shanna, my business partner, Del."

Shanna held out a prim little hand for a professional shake. Del, being the Frenchman he was, enveloped her hand and brought it to his mouth for a soft kiss. "*Enchanté.*"

No doubt he was enchanted, but this wasn't a free-for-all.

"Back off," Alejandro growled in Del's ear.

His friend sent him a dark-eyed glance full of curiosity. Ali wasn't saying a word. Del wasn't stupid. He understood.

When Shanna snatched her hand away, Ali had to repress a gratified smile. When had any woman ever pulled away from Del? Never. Usually, they threw themselves at his dark stubble, wealth, and bad attitude.

"This is Shanna's situation…"

Ali clued Del in, and Shanna provided the flash drive for viewing again. After the clip ended, Del was gnashing his teeth and looking none too happy.

"I wish I knew who to beat the shit out of for violating the rules."

"Me, too," Alejandro agreed.

"Okay, so you don't know off the top of your heads who might have done it," Shanna said. "I'm assuming you know in which room this…event took place?"

"Yes," the men answered together.

"Maybe by figuring out who might have used the room in the last week, you can get a list of likely suspects. Do you keep records?"

"For payment purposes, yes," Del confirmed. "But that room, it's likely been used at least fifty times since that recording was made."

Shanna did the math. "Ten…events in there a *day*?"

With a shrug, Alejandro smiled. "We go through a lot of sheets."

Del laughed, the sound hearty and male.

"Aren't you two cute? Freshman Frat Boy and his sidekick, Horny." She rolled her eyes. "I'm assuming you don't want it known that someone is sneaking into your club and recording your guests' most private actions without their consent or knowledge."

He and Del sobered up quickly. She was right. Business now. Pleasure…soon.

Still, his mind took a little detour. Her shock about the room's constant use was amusing, and it pleased him that she did not understand how addicting watching—and being watched—could be. Yet. He intended to introduce her to that delight.

"Of course we don't want our guests compromised," Del cut in smoothly. "We could make a list of all the guests who have used this room in the last week, but I doubt it would help. In all honesty, I would never have believed any of our members would violate such a cardinal rule. The fee to join is steep enough to attract only the most serious. Our rules are absolute; there is no room for gray. We also have ways of ensuring that anyone who violates our rules finds themselves unwelcome at similar clubs elsewhere."

"This feels to me as if you were targeted specifically," Alejandro said. "The note was delivered to your dressing room, so close to a major competition…"

"That's it! Do any of my competitors belong to your club?"

Ali looked at Del, who looked back at him. That was the great thing about having been friends for nearly a decade. They could almost read each other's minds. Answering the question wasn't really giving away information…

"No. Kristoff is the only ballroom dancer and he's recent. He came highly recommended and has been very active since he joined."

"I'll bet." She snorted. "And here I thought he was your average, garden-variety gay man…"

Del choked. Alejandro resisted the urge to laugh himself.

Shanna swatted his shoulder. "Okay, clearly that's untrue. You two can stop snickering now."

Alejandro couldn't resist her ruffled feathers for another second. He was dying to soothe them…right before he melted her.

"What about any of my former dance partners?" She directed the question to Alejandro. Not that she suspected Jonathan, but the first two hated her. "Do you know who they are?"

"No and yes. None of your former partners are members."

"Hmm." Shanna bit a pink, bee-stung lip as she thought. "Have any of your other members indicated this breach of privacy has been a problem for them?"

"Hell no! Whoever took the footage isn't one of your competitors, but it is someone who knows about your world of ballroom. About you and what you value."

"Yes," Del agreed. "Someone who knew that competition was coming up and that the judges would punish you if such footage became public."

"Any ideas who among your members that could be?" Shanna prompted.

Again, Ali looked at Del, who shook his head. "Not a clue. I could ask you the same question. Who are your enemies?"

Shanna's blue eyes darted around as if scanning her memories. "No one else I can think of. If it's not a former partner or a competitor, I know of no one who hates me enough to want to destroy me."

"Well, if any guest was a friend of one of your former partners or competitors, we have no way of knowing."

"True…" Shanna nibbled nervously on a hangnail, then, as if realizing she'd done something less than perfect, she stopped. "What about your employees? Do any of them have access to video cameras and those rooms?"

Del shook his head. "We have four types of employees: security, housekeeping, waitstaff, and bar crew. That's it. They are paid to be invisible unless they're needed. None of those employees should be anywhere near a room when it's in use. All the watching and exhibiting is done for and with fellow members."

"So, another dead end…"

"It appears," Del agreed, then looked his way. His buddy had the glint of the devil in his eyes. "That we should draw this blackmailer out."

"Have Kristoff come back and do it again and hope someone makes another recording?" She sounded confused.

"No," Ali said, catching on to the idea. "Kristoff has been recorded. He has served his purpose. It is interesting that whomever recorded him chose to give the video not to him, but to *you*."

"Exactly," Del chimed in. "The blackmailer is trying to get to you. He or she wants *you* to suffer. Kristoff is just one avenue."

"So what are you suggesting I do?"

One more time, Alejandro and Del exchanged a meaningful glance.

"I think, *querida*, he's suggesting that I arrange a scene for you here and see if we can catch him red-handed in the act of filming you."

Shanna's jaw dropped. "Are you insane!! You think I should come here and get naked and…"

"Spend a little time showing our members what you enjoy," Alejandro supplied.

"I can't give this creep any more ammunition to ruin me."

"He already has everything he needs to discredit you with the judges. But I do not think he's actually trying to prevent you from competing, as much as he's attacking you. This feels personal, not business related. If you want to find out who is behind this, you must…expose yourself."

"I'm not into that!"

After last night, Alejandro knew better, but now wasn't the time to remind her. "Pretend, if you must. But I believe the plan will work."

Shanna hesitated, as if she was pondering his words. "*If* I agree to this crazy scheme, can I do…whatever it is alone?"

Alejandro couldn't resist the grin spreading across his face. "Plenty of our members would jump through rings of fire to see you touch yourself."

"Wait. You mean masturbate for an audience?" She turned terribly white under her usual golden glow.

"Even the thought of it makes me hard," he whispered for her ears alone.

"Absolutely not!"

"No? Then I will be more than happy to assist you," Alejandro volunteered.

"I'll bet."

"It would be more believable…and more blackmail-worthy," Del chimed in. "I will hide in the room and watch all doors, windows, and passersby—see if I can identify our camera-wielding asshole."

Her jaw dropped. "It's bad enough to contemplate getting naked with the Latin Lover, here. But having you watch? No."

That horror on her face was nothing but a lie. Her suddenly hard nipples told him that. She was scared—of herself, of him, of whatever was fueling her ambition. Suddenly, he wanted to get to the bottom of it all. He wanted to learn her.

"What troubles you? Is the idea too arousing?"

Shanna sent Ali a hard glare. "It's too weird. And it won't work."

"What are your better ideas?"

Pausing, Shanna bit her lip. Oh, yes, she was thinking her options through.

A few moments later, she gritted her teeth. "I don't have a better idea. But there's got to be one."

"This guy will return to the scene of the crime if we dangle the right bait in front of him. Catching him in the act of creating or delivering a video is the only way to be certain he's the guilty party."

Shanna's firm ass outlined in white capri pants that made Ali's tongue melt as she paced the floor and contemplated in a silence broken only by her high-heels.

"God, I can't believe I'm actually considering this. I must be out of my mind."

"It may be the only way to figure out who's trying to screw up your career," Del supplied.

"Which is the only reason I haven't already said no."

"Would you feel more comfortable if I showed you the room and all the places Del can hide in order to catch this bastard?"

Del sent him a knowing smile.

She nodded. "I'm not sure this will work, but maybe if I see the room, something will occur to me."

"You two come up with the plan and let me know. I need to get back to my…company." Del clapped him on the back, kissed Shanna's hand again, and disappeared upstairs.

In charged silence, Alejandro led Shanna down a hall and up another set of stairs, to the play rooms. At the second door on the left, he paused and eased it open into a dark, enclosed space.

Beyond the handful of comfortable chairs and a long, cushy sofa lay the far corner of the room, which comprised the stage, currently devoid of guests. The muted lights in that corner shined down on a sleek bed with four chrome posts and matching restraints.

"Oh." Her voice fluttered beside him.

Alejandro would bet this week's take that Shanna was envisioning herself on that stage, her pussy shoved full of his cock—and a rapt audience watching. He'd bet next week's take that she was uncomfortably aroused.

"Other members sit here or look through the windows at the far end of the room and watch the scene. From the clip you showed me, I suspect your blackmailer sat in the room, here." Alejandro pointed to a small chair in the shadows, a mere three feet from the end of the bed. "He either used a zoom lens or moved the chair closer to the bed to get the tight penetration shots. But we won't know for sure until we catch him."

"I understand." Her voice trembled even more.

Alejandro smiled to himself as he turned and pointed to a bare wall. "Through here is a doorway, accessible only from the security area. See, no knob on this side. We can position the cameras to watch this chair. Del can either monitor the room from the bank of cameras or from the chairs in the far corner."

"I see." She cleared her throat. "If you have security cameras viewing this room, can't you review the footage and see if anyone holding a video camera is in the shot?"

He shook his head. "They point only at the stage areas. Our primary concern here is for the safety of the players. We make sure everything that happens on stage is consensual. If there's a hint that something is not, we bust in. But we do not regularly monitor the audience. For this scene only, we will change the camera positioning."

"Wouldn't the blackmailer be able to spot Del if he was watching from one of those chairs?" She gestured across the room.

"Come with me." Alejandro held out his hand to her.

Shanna looked at it, then looked at him, before reluctantly placing her hand in his. Immediately, sparks danced in his palm, down his fingers. God, he could hardly wait to get his hands on this woman.

For the moment, he led her across the room instead to a dark pair of padded armchairs. He gestured for Shanna to sit in one. He plunked down in the other.

"In this corner, the light is too dim for anyone in the audience to discern more than a shadow. Players cannot see back in this corner. It's a good place for Del to hide, if you want him nearby."

"It's dark."

A click and a whoosh alerted Alejandro to the fact the players' stage door had opened. He glanced at his watch. Noon. Right on time.

In walked a broad man dressed in leather pants, a half mask—and nothing else. Colorful tattoos covered his left arm. In his right hand, he clutched a woman's fingers.

As small as he was big, as delicate as he was strong, the petite redhead followed him to the bed. She wore a flowing, floral skirt that ended at mid-thigh, a button-down blouse in a soft ivory, and a pair of pink high-heeled sandals.

"Are you wearing a bra, slut?" he asked.

"No, Master."

"Show me."

Without pause, she unbuttoned her blouse to reveal a flat stomach, fair skin, and pink nipples that stood straight out and begged for attention.

Shanna gasped. "We shouldn't be watching this."

"They come here knowing that being watched is not only possible, but probable. It turns them on," he whispered. "Shh."

"Good," the Master in leather praised, petting one of her breasts in reward. "Are you wearing panties?"

"No, Master."

"Show me."

The small woman lifted her skirt to reveal slender thighs and a pussy devoid of all hair. Beside Alejandro, Shanna tensed.

"Excellent." The Master cupped her mound and fondled her. "Who do you belong to?"

"You, Master."

"Who decides what's right for your body?"

"You, Master."

"Take off your skirt, lie back, and spread your legs."

The woman complied without hesitation. Even at this distance, once her thighs parted, Alejandro could see a little silver bar passing through the hood of her clit.

"She's...pierced." Shanna sounded shocked.

"Yes," Ali answered. "He marked her. Shh."

"Pretty," said the man in leather as he stared. "Has it healed?"

"Yes, Master."

"Does it arouse you when you walk?"

"Yes, Master."

"Do you rub yourself and make yourself come?"

"No, Master. You did not give me permission."

"That's right. I didn't. You're wet."

"Yes, Master."

"Do you need to be fucked?"

"Yes, Master. Please," the redhead pleaded.

The large man said nothing. He merely walked to all four corners of the bed, restraining his submissive into the built-in cuffs.

"As a reward for your obedience, you will be well fucked." The Master snapped his fingers.

In walked another man, completely naked. Young, blond, somewhat thin—but very well hung.

"This is Micah. He will fuck you now. If you please him and obey me, you may suck my cock as a reward. Do you understand?"

"Yes, Master." Her smile said the idea excited her.

Shanna gripped the arms of her chair and stared at the trio with wide eyes. "She's going to let a complete stranger have sex with her just because he said so?"

"He wants to watch her be fucked, and she has given him domain over her body. She obeys his commands. That is their relationship. Shh."

By now, the blond man had a condom on his thick cock and was easing onto the bed.

"Micah," the man barked. "Test that piercing first. With your tongue."

The younger man smiled. "With pleasure."

"I will tell you when you have permission to come, slut."

"Yes, Master," she panted as Micah took his first swipe across her clit with his tongue and groaned.

The woman lifted her hips to Micah, who used the opportunity to fit his arms under her thighs and grip her, holding her wet folds against his mouth. He licked her unmercifully, insistent lashes with his tongue, and toyed with the little bar piercing the hood of her clit.

Master shucked off his pants, pulled out a wide cock with a pierced head, and stroked slowly as he watched.

Soon, the redhead was flushed and panting, mewling and pleading for release.

"Stop," said the Master.

Micah lifted his head slowly, his lips wet and glossy.

The woman whimpered.

"Are you ready for Micah to fuck you?"

"Yes, Master. Please, yes!"

"Good girl. When I give you permission, you may show me how pretty you are when you come as Micah fucks you."

The woman opened her mouth to answer, but Micah thrust ruthlessly inside her sex first, cutting off all speech. Instead, she gasped, then groaned. Before she recovered, Micah plowed into her again. And again. Once more…

"Come," her master commanded.

She gasped as she orgasmed in a spectacular tensing of limbs and jolting of muscles. Micah gritted his teeth, looking like a man hanging by a thread.

"Beautiful. Micah will continue to fuck you while you suck my cock. You do not come again until I do."

"Yes…Master," she said in a breathy, high gasp just before she turned her head and took Master deep in her mouth.

Beside him, Alejandro noticed Shanna squirming in her seat. Around him, the scent of her arousal wafted. She might pretend to be scandalized, but her body told him exactly how much she loved what was happening before her eyes. How much she liked watching it. He knew from dancing with her that she ached to be watched herself. No doubt in his mind, fucking her in front of a faceless audience would completely arouse Shanna. She couldn't possibly hang onto her ice-bitch persona then.

It didn't take long before Master's buttocks were clenching. He shoved his hand into his slut's red hair and thrust deep in her mouth.

Micah had apparently gotten his urge to come under control and now pounded her like a man possessed, beads of sweat dripping down his face, his sides. The woman's skin was a gorgeous shade of aroused rose as she writhed between the two men, giving and receiving pleasure.

Soon, Master tensed, shouted, then erupted into the woman's mouth.

"Come," he told them through clenched teeth.

They did. Loudly, bucking and rocking and clearly enjoying the hell out of themselves.

Moments later, Micah withdrew from the woman's body and disposed of his condom. Master reached out and gave him a brotherly handshake.

"She's one hell of a fuck," Micah commented. "You're lucky, man."

Master nodded and smiled, then Micah disappeared through the door from which he'd emerged. When Master turned his profile to the audience, Ali had no trouble spotting the fact he was hard again. Shanna's gasp told him she'd seen it, too.

Without a word to his woman, Master released her ankles and flipped her onto her belly. As her arms crossed above her head, he urged her to curl her knees under her body, then smacked her ass a half dozen times in harsh, regulated swats. The woman tensed, moaned, bucked.

Then Master reached for the table on the far side of the bed. Moments later, he had lube on his erection and was sliding it inside his woman's rosy ass.

She moaned and writhed when he penetrated her, and he reached around to toy with her clit.

"You're a good girl. Watching you get fucked turns me on, but fucking you myself is heaven. You accept my cock wherever I put it, don't you?"

"Yes! Master, yes!"

Shanna crossed her legs and squirmed again. "Is he...having anal sex with her?"

Alejandro nodded. "It is another show of her submission to him."

She drew in a sharp breath. Even in this light, he could see her hard nipples go even harder. Oh, another something on his long list of things to do to her body once he got the chance. Alejandro managed to keep his smile to himself—barely.

"Seen enough?"

"What?" Shanna tore her eyes away from the couple reluctantly. "O-oh, yes."

He rose and helped her to her feet, then guided her out the door, back into the well-lit hallway. Flushed cheeks, very hard nipples, rapid breaths, pulse beating at her neck. If she owned a vibrator, he'd bet it would get a strenuous workout this afternoon. First time he could ever remember being jealous of plastic and batteries. He'd offer his own flesh, but if he pushed her too hard, too fast, she would run in the other direction.

"So, the scene... How does tomorrow night sound for catching a blackmailer? I will make sure the room is free then."

Shanna took a deep breath. "I haven't made up my mind."

"Whatever you wish. You are the one with a competition in a few days and a blackmailer with an ax to grind."

She sighed in annoyance, clearly not appreciating his reminder that her options were limited. "All right. Tomorrow night."

"Be here by nine." Ali tamped down his smile of triumph with effort. "What sort of scene should I set up? Something for you to do alone?"

Shanna paled a bit more, then mustered her bravado and lifted her chin. "Maybe...you should participate, too. But don't get the wrong idea."

"Wrong idea?"

She sent him a suspicious glare. "I'm serious. This is business. I need to find out who's trying to sabotage me. You need to know who's jeopardizing your club. I'm not interested in you personally."

"Of course not."

"And I'm not sleeping with you."

Who said anything about sleeping? Ali thought.

"Whatever you want, that is what we'll do. Nothing more." *And absolutely nothing less.*

4

"*Y*ou sure about this, man?" Del asked him at eight-thirty the following night as they headed downstairs.

"Yes." Alejandro led the way down the hall, to the second door on the left and pushed it open.

Del closed it behind him. "You want guests in here? They will flip. You're the brains of this place. You almost never play in public. You know the curiosity. There *will* be a crowd."

Ali shrugged. Generally, he watched rather than put on a show, but this was about Shanna tonight, about making her hot. And she adored being watched. He knew that all the way down to the soles of his feet. Now he just needed to let her feel it firsthand and prove it to her.

"Good. I want anyone who attended in the last week, especially if they watched in this room, here tonight. I sent you a list of members who fit that description."

"I got that."

Ali nodded. "Security is looking the names over as well. If Shanna is videoed, we should be able to narrow our list of suspects. I've e-mailed the members who watched last week and hinted at something tantalizing happening in this room tonight. That way, our friend with the video camera is more likely to show up. But wait until nine-fifteen to unlock the door. I want Shanna comfortable. It will be easier for her to let go the first time if the only one watching when we get started is you."

"Even if we only allow the people who've observed in this room recently, others will follow. There will still be a crowd."

Alejandro shrugged. Likely so, but he would deal with it. And with Shanna...

She would be very nervous when she first arrived, but Ali didn't think that would last, especially when she didn't see a gathering crowd right away. And God, he couldn't wait to feel her melt against him, her body opening to accept him deep, her pussy clasping him hard as she came. By then, she'd be desperate for the crowd to see her come undone.

"I need to finish readying the room." Alejandro turned away, eager for the night to begin.

"Wait." When Ali turned back, Del went on, "You're going pretty far to catch this blackmailer."

"The club is important. We both have over a million dollars tied up in it. We cannot afford to allow anyone who would film players without their knowledge to continue as a member here."

"Yeah. Absolutely. It's just...normally you would let security handle it. Or bring in help, if you needed it. This time, you seem to be taking a very personal interest."

"Stop sidestepping your point. What are you saying?"

Del crossed his arms over his wide chest, looking way too pleased. "You like this girl."

"She is very sexy. Why should I not like her?"

Disbelief peppered Del's expression. "There are sexy women here every night more than willing to fuck you. You haven't played with or for the membership in over a year. So there's more to your decision to get on that stage with Shanna than her sexiness."

Mierda. Why couldn't Del leave it alone?

Alejandro sighed. "Yes. I confess, even I am not entirely sure why I am pursuing Shanna so hard. She has rebuffed, left, and insulted me."

"But...?"

Shifting his weight from one foot to the other, Ali sorted through the tangle of his thoughts and feelings. It was damn uncomfortable. He was a gut-instinct sort of guy. If it felt right, he did it. That philosophy had never served him wrong. But even he had to admit that his logic where Shanna was concerned...

There wasn't any.

"Under her brittle façade, she has this lost quality. I don't want to save her, exactly. Or change her. But I cannot resist wanting to hold her. Touch her. And, of course, pleasure her. She looks at me and her expression is like a siren's song. A glance, and I'm hard as hell. A snap from that icy voice I know is hiding a wealth of heat and I'm dying to lay her out, get deep, and melt her into a puddle."

Del laughed. "You're screwed."

"How so?"

"You're falling for this girl."

Was it that obvious?

"And you haven't really touched her yet." Del laughed. "This is going to be fun to watch for more than one reason."

"I'm so happy you're amused. You may fuck off now."

"Ten-four." Del clapped him on the back. "I'll finish making the arrangements with the other employees. The room should be ready. All you need to do is meet Shanna at the door."

No, what he needed to do was please her, not just by lighting her senses and firing her fantasies, but endearing himself to her. Great, but how to do that? Because his gut was telling him that he should not let Shanna out of his life.

With a shaking hand, Shanna shoved the door open and entered the cool, air-conditioned space of *Sneak Peek*. At night, the club still had that golden shimmer. But instead of the homey warmth it conveyed during the day, a shimmering glow now illuminated the club. It sparkled and glittered like old Hollywood, except this classic glamour provided the backdrop for today's beautiful people to have dazzling sex.

Del and Alejandro had created a perfect ambiance.

Just past the club's front door, wall-to-wall bodies gyrated to a suggestive techno beat. Couples grinded, intimating sex vertically. In fact, one couple against the wall, shielded by the man's long leather duster, probably *was* having sex. No one seemed to notice or care.

The bar beyond was crowded with people drinking their liquid fortification. Several men crowded around a woman downing shots as if they were waiting for her to give one—or several—of them a sign that she was ready for more personal action.

The whole place oozed sex.

She *so* didn't belong here. Sex had never been her thing. She'd had it, of course. A college boyfriend had been her first, but he hadn't had much experience. Nor had he understood her dancing. They'd spent the relationship fighting because he assumed she was sleeping with her partner at the time, which she hadn't been.

A few years later, she'd had a one-night stand after a wedding. Stupid—and awful. Downright bad sex.

Jonathan…utter disaster—right on the dance floor they'd practiced on for years. She'd clung to him out of desperation. He'd taken her body as if exorcising some demon. The whole episode had lasted less than ten minutes. And created twelve months of pure havoc.

By tonight's end, if she wasn't careful, she would be adding Alejandro to her short list. She'd said she wouldn't have sex with him. But she wondered… Would failing to let loose in a club like this rouse her blackmailer's suspicion? Shanna couldn't let this opportunity slip past her without making the most of it. She had to ferret out this jerk before the California Dance Star.

But that wasn't the only reason she contemplated surrendering to Alejandro. He tripped her trigger in a way she'd never experienced. Maybe she could enjoy herself—just this once.

Then again, did she really have the strength to resist such a sinfully sexy man, especially when he lured her with an offer to fulfill her secret exhibitionism fantasy? He made her feel sexual, made her believe that he understood her. Admitting that fact was uncomfortable, but even when Ali annoyed her, he turned her on. Maybe the chemistry between them was worth exploring.

And maybe she was out of her mind.

Crossing the room, Shanna was conscious of male eyes following her. God, why had Alejandro sent her this sheer halter top, held in place by nothing more than two little bows, along with a matching wrap-around skirt? Why had he insisted she wear a skimpy outfit in shades of soft creamy-gold that blended in with her skin?

"Hi," a voice whispered in her ear. She turned to find a guy with dimples and incredible blue eyes visually eating her up. "Dance?"

Okay, he was attractive. Who was she kidding? He was gorgeous. The way he looked at her made her burn. But to dance with him? Touch him? Hmm. The thought of getting physical with this guy—with most any guy—wasn't quite as tempting. For her, it was always that way.

Except with Alejandro.

"I—I..."

"She's spoken for tonight."

Alejandro. She recognized that deep, slightly accented voice caressing the back of her neck. And the tingle that shimmied up her spine when he wrapped his arm around her bare midriff in a gesture designed to lay his claim.

Dimples shot her a brief look of regret. "Sure, Mr. Diaz."

"She'll be around later, in the chrome room."

That information perked Dimples up. He raked her with a lingering glance. "Sweet. I'll definitely be watching."

Before Shanna could protest, Alejandro urged her forward, to an employees-only entrance, and shut the door behind them. The decibel level went down about a thousand percent.

She whirled to face him "You *invited* him to watch us?"

Shanna was glad she'd managed to parlay her shock into actual words quickly. Because once she saw his casual black shirt unbuttoned all the way down the front, exposing a healthy glimpse of hard-steel pecs and smooth bronze skin, she lost her train of thought.

"Yes, I did. He is one of the newer regulars and he was here last week. Think of him as a potential suspect."

His voice brought her gaze back up to his face, where a hint of a smile played. The bastard knew she'd been staring at his chest.

She needed dispassion, not lust. *Focus.* "He had no idea who I was. No concept that I'm Kristoff's partner."

"Not that he let on. But if he was guilty, why would he tip his hand?"

Good question. One for which she had no answer.

"You are not required to play this scene. Do you want to change your mind?"

He was wrong; she was absolutely required to play this scene, at least if she wanted to win the competition and hold that trophy in her hand after sixteen years of hard work. But that wasn't the only reason. If she wanted to find out if Alejandro had been right about her desire to exhibit, she had to go through with this. And if she wanted to know if she could actually feel pleasure in this man's arms… Well, then she couldn't chicken out.

"Just lead the way."

With a slow nod, Ali grabbed her hand and gave it a reassuring squeeze, then led her down the hall. Despite her nerves, Shanna had a hard time ripping her gaze from his tight ass, displayed so mouth-wateringly in black slacks. The view alone made her want to jump him. That had to stop. This sexual hunger wasn't like her. Being too into him wasn't a good idea, either. She wasn't into flings, and a guy who co-owned a club like *Sneak Peek* probably wasn't into relationships.

Tearing her gaze away and focusing on her surroundings, she noticed they filed past some open doors containing offices brimming with computers manned by staff members. A wall clock said it was ten `til nine.

The butterflies in her stomach were head-banging and had set up a rave. She wondered if she was going to throw up before she and Alejandro got started.

He stopped in front of a door. "Relax. You will be fine. We're going to handle this together."

"Why are you being nice about this?"

He cocked a brow, the strong angles of his face dusted by shadow and stubble. The frankly sexual stare he sent her made Shanna suck in her breath.

"Certainly, it has not escaped your notice that I want you."

How could it when the thought thrilled her so much? She shook her head.

"Good. I also want to catch the scum taking advantage of our members. You want to catch him, too, so Kristoff's video doesn't fall into the judges' hands. It is a win-win for us both."

"Is that the only reason?"

He shook his head. "I suspect you're not the untouchable bitch you wish me—and everyone else—to believe you are." He shot her a wolfish grin. "But I intend to find out tonight for sure. Personally, I think we will be very hot together."

Before she could protest and slap up the armor he'd verbally stripped away, he thrust the door open and walked through.

They entered the room she had observed the Master and Slut use yesterday. Only things had changed. The chrome bed had been pushed to one corner, at the edge of the stage. The rest of the furniture had been moved out, leaving a large amount of the painted concrete floor well lit and totally empty. The bedding had changed as well. Luxurious white and silvery linens with fluffy pillows dotted with beads and tassels decorated the bed, looking sumptuous on top of the downy blanket. A far cry from yesterday's stark black sheets.

"What's this?"

"I thought you would be more comfortable if we changed the room up to something softer. Something more…you."

Normally, she would protest his judgment that she was soft. But he was right; the look of the room did reflect her more. She wondered how much of her he already saw.

Against her better judgment, she was touched. "Thank you."

"You are very welcome. Come with me." Alejandro tugged her to the edge of the stage. Deep in gray shadows, she saw a lone, imposing figure.

"Hi, Shanna."

"Del?"

"Yes. We're ready to go. How are you doing?"

She resisted the urge to press a hand against her fluttering belly. It would reveal too much, make her look vulnerable. She already felt too much that way for comfort. "Fine."

"Good. The security cameras have been positioned to watch the audience, specifically the corner in which we think the last video was made. The lighting in the audience is a bit brighter, so the cameras can capture whatever is going on. None of the cameras will be pointed at the stage, and Alejandro will take care of you if something unexpected happens. Security is through that door." He pointed to the door without a handle. "Just knock, and they'll let you in immediately."

Wow, they'd thought of everything. "Thank you."

"We will start slow," Alejandro assured her. "Right now, just you and me. Del will watch. As you get comfortable, he'll open the door. Hopefully, your blackmailer will be waiting to get in."

Del watching them. Other strangers staring. Now came the hard part. And the arousing part. She wished the thought of Alejandro touching her didn't turn her on…almost as much as she wished the thought of a crowd seeing their every move didn't make her blood race.

But it all did. Unbearably. And Ali knew it.

Shanna bit her lip. "O-okay."

"Good." Alejandro smiled, something that both set her at ease and made her heart trip. In one look, he managed to both calm her fears and rouse her body.

Shanna couldn't shake the feeling this night would be unlike anything she could possibly have imagined.

She glanced at Del. He was a big shape sitting in the dark corner, his head cocked, his arms crossed over his chest.

"Focus on me, *querida*," Alejandro murmured. "Only me."

She gave him a shaky nod, and he tugged on the hand he was holding, pulling her body into his.

"Dance with me."

"D-dance?"

He nodded. "Just dance."

After a quick snap of his fingers, music filtered through the room, a soft but spicy Latin tune, perfect for a rumba. In fact, it was the music they had danced to just a few nights before.

As Alejandro led her into a basic, her body brushing his with every step, her feet moved automatically to the beat. His unbuttoned shirt fluttered as he moved, offering tantalizing glimpses of hard pectorals, flat, brown nipples, hints of dark hair. Her mind whirled with possibilities.

"You recall the exact music we danced to the other night?"

"I never forget a thing about you."

She melted—on the spot. No man had ever taken such an interest in just her, been so keenly attentive.

Shanna relaxed against him and drifted into the dance. He sensed it and spiced up their steps. After a sharp turn in his arms, her nearly bare back rested against his half-covered chest, his hot breath on her neck, her hips gyrating against his erection. His palm flattened against her naked belly, which flared hot with arousal at his hot touch.

She turned her head, glancing over her shoulder at him. His fiery gaze was full of challenge as he slowly caressed her until both of his hands came rested on her hips. Then he guided them in a movement that was pure, raw sex.

"Del is watching us. Watching you. Getting hard for you," he whispered.

"No," she protested automatically.

But her blood flashed hot at the thought.

Alejandro turned her out in a sharp spin and brought her crashing into his body again, then into a deep dip.

Her gaze snapped up to his. His face loomed dominant, masterful. "Yes."

Her nipples went hard.

As he brought her up slowly, he curled one hand around her nape. The other he flattened between her breasts...before slowly shifting to press over one soft mound. He teased her nipple with a soft touch.

Shanna sucked in a breath. Desire dropped like a bomb into the pit of her stomach. That strong face of his—all hint of teasing, of reassuring, of politeness—gone. In his place stood a man who meant to have her.

While he fitted his hips against hers and rocked, his lips collided with hers. A brush, a slide, a taste. Shanna followed his lead, shocked at the way her heart accelerated like a race car's, zooming to hyper-speed in seconds until it pounded in her ears. He tasted of coffee and man and aggression. She opened to him, aching for him to sink deeper.

Instead, he spun her out. She whirled away from him on instinct.

The rumba was the dance of love...but there was teasing involved. The woman hesitating, the man pursuing. Somehow she knew Alejandro loved to pursue.

The last thing she should do was make her surrender too easy for him.

She walked away, hips swaying, head held high. For a moment, she focused on Del. He leaned forward in his chair, his posture tense. His fingers clutched the chair in front of him. She smiled, writhed, and caressed her way between her breasts, down her belly, skirting her aching sex to caress the tops of her thighs. She heard Del's indrawn breath when the music paused.

Feminine power, heady and amazing, crashed into her. This was why she loved dancing, knowing she could make men want, people feel, just by watching her body.

Then she glanced over her shoulder as Alejandro prowled closer, shedding his black shirt, leaving it forgotten on the floor, as he neared. Powerful bronze shoulders snagged her gaze. His hard-muscled chest narrowed into six-pack abs dusted with a treasure trail that disap-peared into the waistband of his pants. The enticing view made her mouth water. But the look on his face...hungry, unrepentant, demand-ing, made her shudder with want.

Damn, she was staring—and loving it.

Alejandro stopped directly behind her, so close she could feel the heat of his body. Even though he didn't touch her, he sucked her deeper into his sexual web just by being near and sharing the rhythm of the dance.

Suddenly...a tug, a brush of his fingers. The little halter top fell to the floor at her feet.

Leaving her naked from the waist up.

Instinctively, she reached up to cover her breasts with her hands. Alejandro slid his palms down her arms, skin to skin, until his hands covered hers. He rocked against her ass, his erection insistent at her lower back. He planted teasing kisses down her neck, across her shoulder.

Tension tightened in her belly. Resistance melted.

Then he forced her hands down, over her ribs, down her belly, right over her swollen, aching folds. His hips swiveled to the music, moving hers in time—grinding her clit into her fingertips.

"Jesus," Del muttered from the audience.

His voice slammed through Shanna's head. Sensation exploded. She gasped as a riot of feelings tore through her, leaving fire in its wake. Her knees melted. Her head fell back to Alejandro's bare shoulder. Her eyes closed as she moaned.

One of his hands swept across her abdomen again, soft, slow... inching up, up... Until Alejandro claimed her bare breast, his palm burning her sensitive flesh.

Del watched their every move, his gaze riveted to Alejandro's hand moving over her skin. Shanna knew Del saw her arousal, knew he wasn't missing the fact she was spiked up on need and desire. Aching. And it only climbed higher, knowing that Del couldn't peel his eyes away.

Her nipple poked Alejandro's palm. She arched into his hand as his thumb teased the hard tip.

"Touch me," she whispered.

"Every last inch of you." Alejandro's mouth strung a fresh line of shiver-inducing kisses up her neck.

Suddenly, he grabbed one of her hands, twirled her out, then reeled her back in, her chest crushed to his. Slowly, he eased her away in a rumba rhythm.

His hazel eyes flared as he drank in his first clear glimpse of her bare breasts.

"Such hard, pink nipples. I'm going to enjoy making them red."

Her heart all but stopped before pounding again. "H-how? By pinching them?"

He reached between their bodies and slid blistering palms over her breasts. His thumbs cradled their aching tips as his fingers closed in and pressed, jolting her with a flash of pain, followed by a haze of pleasure.

"That is one way."

"And b-by sucking them?"

His gaze was like an inferno burning her up as he dipped her back over his arm, arching her breasts toward his mouth, fusing their hips together. God, she could feel every inch of his thick erection pressing right against her sex. She ached in a way she never had before and never believed she could.

Then he lowered his head and sucked her nipple into his mouth.

Hot. Wet. Wild. Thrilling. Sensations screamed through her body as he suckled her, his mouth pulling, tugging, creating friction that zipped right from her breast to her clit until pleasure tightened, converged, pounded at her body.

Shanna clutched his shoulders, praying the sensation would never end.

After a long, lingering lick, Alejandro eased away from her breast and stood her upright again. "That is another possibility."

"Do you... W-would you bite them?"

He didn't even answer, just bent to capture her breast in his mouth again, the hot silk of his tongue over the sensitive bud giving way to the tug of teeth—and a bolt of pure fire straight down to her sex.

Oh god.

"Yes!" The word slipped out of her mouth. Surrender in one sylla-ble. She knew it. So did he.

She was going to give him anything—everything—he wanted tonight.

Alejandro straightened and smiled down at her. That expression captured her, but he enthralled her when he slid his fingers into her hair, scattering the pins holding her French twist everywhere, and ravaged her mouth.

Need, impatience, aggression, the promise of unbelievable sex—it was all there in his kiss. His tongue stroked hers and stoked the fires licking inside her, sending her higher and higher.

Alejandro had barely touched anything below her waist and already she felt screamingly close to orgasm. He'd already brought her closer to the pinnacle than any of her other previous lovers. Damn, what would happen if—when?—he laid her down on that sumptuous bed and covered her body with his? When he filled her up with every inch he taunted her with even now as he rocked against her?

Panting, mewling, Shanna grabbed his face with clutching fingers and pressed her lips harder against his. God, it was stupid and danger-ous...and she ached to find out just how good he really was.

5

Shanna panted, clinging to Alejandro when he lodged his thigh between hers and urged her to swivel her hips against him.

Thick bolts of need speared her belly, slicing down her legs. Her blood turned thick. The wanton within her demanded more.

She wasn't the Bitch of the Ballroom tonight. She was just a female surrendering to the hot sensations her lover's touch roused. How it happened, she didn't know. Why now and with this man, in this situation, was a mystery, too. But for once, she felt like a woman. Not just an athlete, a dancer, or a competitor. Just a woman in touch with her sexuality.

Orgasm approached hard and fast. Tension built between her legs. Heat fractured her thoughts. She moaned, feeling Alejandro's hands at her hips, urging her on, and Del's hot stare burning her back.

As she climbed up, up, Alejandro lifted his mouth from hers and sent her a deliciously wicked smile. God, the man could melt steel with that look. And she was nowhere near that solid.

"You ache." He didn't ask; he stated.

"Yes."

"You are wet."

No doubt, he felt her wet folds through the thin fabric of his slacks, and the friction it provided was driving her out of her mind.

"Yes."

Then he reached around her, lifted her skirt to her waist , and gliding rough palms over her bare ass. Shanna knew Del could see her cheeks and the delicate white thong bisecting them. She swore she could feel his stare burning her backside. And she knew it affected him because he groaned.

That sound reached between her legs and jolted her. Why it turned her on so much to turn Del on she couldn't explain. And she didn't want to know. Tomorrow, she'd likely be mortified. Tonight, she just didn't care.

"Do you like knowing that Del is eating up your ass with his hungry gaze?" Ali rasped in her ear. "That he's so hard for you and would kill to be in my place right now?"

Shanna couldn't help it; she whimpered.

"That's right. But he will not touch you. He will watch and he will want, but *I* will take every sinful pleasure your body has to offer."

The man knew how to talk to her. With a few choice words, he utterly unwound her.

Then he tugged on the tie securing the skirt around her waist and, slipped the last button free. Her skirt fluttered to the stage. Now she wore nothing but her very damp thong.

He lowered his hands to her hips again, forcing her sex down on his thigh once more. To the music, they swayed, his impressive erection brushing her belly, inciting more hunger. Her need to come grew, expanded until she was moaning, muttering words of nonsense and need.

"Please. Please!"

"I will give you all you can take. Then, *querida*, I will give you more."

He barely finished whispering the promise when he bent her back over his arm, arching her breasts up so he could feast on them again. Her nipples were so hard under his tongue, and no matter how he licked, suckled, bit, she only wanted more.

To be so lost in the moment, in the sensation, stunned and amazed

Shanna. For all the times she'd wondered if she was "normal" because she didn't respond to a man's touch, she now had her answer. She responded to Alejandro. To Del standing now, his eyes on her. To the forbidden burn of everything they night transpire tonight.

Still bent over Alejandro's arm, Shanna locked her stare with Del's, to entice him with what he couldn't have. And though the room was upside down from this vantage, she could not miss the small crowd filing in. Men. More than five, less than a dozen, they all had tense bodies, hot eyes.

"Fuck, she's hot," murmured a total stranger.

Del stood in the middle of them, fists clenched at his sides. "She is that."

"They want you," Alejandro murmured against her neck. "And I want to show them what they're missing."

Before she could even process what he meant, Alejandro spun her around to face the audience. Oh, God, they stood a mere three feet away. So close she swore she could feel their hot breaths on her skin. She recognized Dimples there. His smile was gone, replaced by seething want and an erection a blind woman couldn't miss.

He and the rest of the crowd were focused on her bare breasts, loose and heavy as Ali forced her hips to maintain the rhythm of the music.

Collective groans resounded, sending a rush of desire inside her. Could she actually come simply from being watched?

Since she frequently had trouble orgasming during masturbation, simply letting loose here, now, was a heady, wonderful thought.

Then Alejandro slid his palms down her arms, still behind her, rocking to the beat of the music. Then he grasped her wrists and lifted her hands above her head until they encircled his neck.

Another chorus of groans erupted from the audience. A quick glance down proved the new pose raised her breasts, made her nipples stand straight out like an invitation.

"Don't move," Alejandro commanded. "Just feel...and let go."

She gave him a shaky nod, wondering, eager—aching—for whatever he planned next.

Shanna didn't have to wait long. A moment later, his fingertips trailed down the side of her breast, across the flat of her abdomen, and disappeared right into her tiny wet thong.

He gave her no time to absorb the fact he was fondling her in public—and that she loved it—before his fingers zeroed in on her clit. A brush, a rub. An electric spark. Tingles danced through her sex, in her belly, down her thighs. The tension ratcheted up until she could barely breathe.

"You going to come for them?" Ali whispered in her ear.

She nodded erratically.

"You going to come for me?"

"Yes!" She bit her lip to keep from screaming as the ache deepened into something nearly unbearable.

With the music throbbing in her ears, Alejandro's fingers shoving her past the breaking point, with nearly a dozen sets of hot male eyes and thoughts enveloped in only her, Shanna came apart.

Her hoarse cry erupted above the music. Her eyes closed, and pleasure washed over her, sharp, golden, unbelievable.

Nothing had ever been like that. Nothing had ever prepared her for the addicting rush of pure sensation lighting up her body. *Oh. My. God.*

Alejandro took her down slowly before extracting his hand from her panties. When he did, she looked down to find his fingers saturated with her cream.

He gave a satisfied chuckle in her ear. "This is how I want you, soaked for me."

She gasped as he anointed her nipples with her juice, then whirled her to face him. With long, languid swipes of his tongue, he licked her taste away with a moan that reverberated deep inside her, stirring the ache back to life.

Shanna was shocked when he stepped away and took her hand in his. Suddenly, she was aware of being almost totally bare, while everyone around her was half clothed or more. She *felt* naked. Vulnerable. Yet oddly strong. She glanced between Alejandro and the tense, shuffling audience.

"That's it?"

He leaned in, looking to the world like a lover planting soft kisses just below her ear. "If you want it to be. We certainly gave the black-mailer something to film."

Yes, but was it enough? And was that really the reason she was contemplating the words about to come out of her mouth?

"I want more."

Alejandro glanced down into her face, his stare delving deep into hers. "Are you sure?"

All she knew was that she wasn't ready for tonight to end. She nodded.

Gently, he grabbed her wrist and placed her hand over his erection. Damn, he was hard. And very large. *Oh, wow…*

"I'm dying to feel you around me," he whispered. "Your mouth, your pussy… Tell me what you want. How much of you will you give me?"

The real question was, could she actually hold anything back?

Shanna felt her way up his cock, to the catch of his slacks. She flipped it open, and he sucked in a harsh breath. Another groan from the audience spurred her on. With slow torture in mind, she eased down his zipper, taking her sweet time.

"If you have a 'no' on the tip of your tongue, say it now."

Shanna leaned closer to his primal male heat, her mouth hovering above the hard nub of his brown nipple. She flicked a sultry gaze up to his face, latching onto his burning stare. "Never heard the word."

When had she ever been brazen? Or assertive or hungry or dying to feel a man's animal heat burning her up? Never. For years, she'd poured her passion into dance. When she performed, she could express all her pent-up feelings through the movements of her body and the interaction with her partner. In real life…she'd never put a tenth of her passion into sex. Tonight—now—she wanted to change all that.

Alejandro had compelled her to.

She closed her mouth around his nipple and nibbled him with her teeth. He groaned long and loud. Holding in her satisfied smile, she pushed his pants over his hips, sliding them down his thighs.

His sex sprang free, so hard it nearly lay against his belly. So long, it reached toward his navel. So thick, she could barely get her hand all the way around it. So perfect, she knew that once he sank deep into her, she'd feel not only more pleasure she'd ever experienced, but ecstasy beyond her wildest fantasies.

Panting, Shanna fell to her knees. She could hardly wait.

When his slacks reached his ankles, Alejandro was very glad he hadn't bothered with anything underneath.

He was even more glad to see Shanna on her knees, eyeing his cock.

Alejandro took himself in hand and guided the weeping head closer to the red haven of her lush mouth.

He barely anchored his palm around the crown of her head when she opened wide to take inch after inch inside the stunning, wet heat as she cradled him on her tongue. *Dios mío!*

She sucked hard, and he felt her all over his cock. His head nudged the back of her throat. Her tongue swiped the sensitive underside of his erection, swirled around the purple crest.

Heaven—Shanna had to be it. She was definitely sleek and built for long, sweaty, intense fucks—and to show off for the audience that would masturbate to the sight and sounds of her.

About that, he had no doubt.

To his left, the audience watched. Moaned. A few guys were adjusting themselves. Others had given up and were already stroking their own cocks. A few women had wandered into the room, and he hoped they understood there would likely be a long line to fuck them if they stayed.

Then Shanna drew back, her tongue laving the head of his cock, igniting a maelstrom of icy-hot tingles in his balls, down his spine. He stopped thinking completely. Too full of sensation now, he fucked her mouth slowly as she whimpered around him, her fingers locked on his thighs…slowly inching up to his ass.

She took him to the back of her throat again. Her nails dug into his skin, and the hint of pain pushed him closer to the edge of pleasure. Damn, he was going to come if she kept that up.

A part of him wanted to rush into the ache and explode on her tongue, down her throat, just for the joy of watching her take and swallow him.

But he wanted to fuck her more. Way more.

Gritting his teeth, Ali pulled out of her mouth. She protested with an unintelligible groan, but he bent and grabbed her waist, lifting her until she stood. Then he whirled her away from him, to face the tall, chrome bed poster. He forced her to bend toward it, then with his fingers over hers, he clasped her hands around the pole.

"Hold on. You will need to," he growled in her ear.

Bending quickly, he found the condom in his pocket and rolled it on, counting the torturous heartbeats until he could be balls deep in the sweet heat of her pussy. Seven seconds. That's all it took until he gripped her hips and thrust inside her.

Scalding hot. Fist tight. *Madre de Dios*, he wasn't going to last. But by damn, she was going over the edge first.

Bracketing harsh fingers on her hips, he pushed his way inside. Shoved hard. It seemed to take forever. Her pussy was so swollen, and if he had to guess, she had not had sex in months, maybe longer.

That was going to change. No way would tonight be the last time he fucked her. No way would he wait weeks, or even days, to feel her again. Even waiting hours sounded doubtful in that moment.

Jacked up on an overload of sensation and a burning need to come brewing at the base of his spine, Ali took a deep breath and plunged into her slowly. Hell, it wasn't helping his concentration to see people masturbating to the sight of Shanna's naked body. Or one of the women in the room with her skirt around her waist and a man's cock buried inside her as she straddled his lap.

Tearing his gaze away, he focused on the long line of Shanna's graceful spine, her mussed golden tresses spilling across her narrow back. He couldn't *not* touch her.

Lifting one hand off her hip, he reached around her body and toyed with her breasts, pinching one of her responsive nipples. She gasped, and Alejandro felt his primitive side take over. He sank his teeth into her neck. He squeezed her other nipple. Her body responded instinctively, tightening on his cock. She was close.

Thank god. So was he.

Gliding his palm down her belly, he buried his fingers into the sparse curls between her legs. *There.* Her clit stood up, hard and swollen, pleading for attention. He wasn't about to say no.

He swiped his fingers across her bundle of nerves. She moaned, tightened again. The friction of moving inside her was about to blow the top off his head. But he kept moving.

"Do you see them watching you?" he snarled, on the edge. "Do you see them wanting you?"

"Yes," she cried. "Yes."

"I want you more."

"Oh, god," she gasped. "Alejandro!"

He strummed her clit once more. "You are going to come."

Damn, he was trying so hard to hold it together, he was cross-eyed and slurring his words. But she understood.

"Yes!"

And then she did, crying out as she clamped down on him, massaging his cock with the pulsing walls of her sex. His self-control didn't stand a chance.

The sensation started deep in his gut and dropped with heavy need right into his balls. Pleasure climbed up, up, up his cock until he found himself shouting his throat raw in release.

He clutched her tight, pumping his way through utopia, with just one thought rattling through his fevered brain:

Mine.

6

*L*atin music throbbed—kind of like Shanna's head. The insistent beat of the dramatic notes echoed off the hardwood floors and bounced off the mirrored walls of the studio. Her feet ached. She was hot and sweaty after three hours. And really annoyed. She and Kristoff were *not* having a productive practice.

And as much as she hated to admit it, Alejandro kept invading her thoughts every three seconds. How could she miss him so much after a mere two days? Why couldn't she stop thinking about the way his hands felt on her, of his unique scent like midnight and man all wrapped in pure sex. Why hadn't she stopped remembering the way he'd looked at her—as if she meant something—before she thrust her clothes on and darted out of his embrace? It would be far more practical if she could focus on the fact that the security cameras hadn't picked up on anything suspicious that night at *Sneak Peek,* so she was no closer to finding—and stopping—the blackmailer.

"I have never had to say this to you," Kristoff broke into her thoughts, "but if we are going to win, you must concentrate. You know this, yes? The cha-cha-cha, it is strong and passionate, not lethargic and distracted."

Damn Kristoff for stepping on her last nerve.

Shanna thrust her hands on her hips. "If I'm distracted, it's because I'm still trying to figure out how we're going to keep that porn-worthy footage of yours out of the judges' hands. And guess what? The fact that's even a problem is not my fault."

"I made a mistake. I have apologized. Either forgive me or find a new partner. Or have you already been having auditions behind my back?"

In the past, that comment alone would have been enough to push her over the edge. She would have told Kristoff to spend his time at *Sneak Peek* and stop wasting hers. Then she would have begun auditioning partners the very same day.

So why wasn't she walking away now?

Kristoff was, in a word, amazing. A powerful dancer, determined, dedicated. He brought a glamour to their dancing that had been lacking with Jonathan. The ladies loved him. He oozed charm even when making his matador face during the paso doble. He was spirited, and normally, he made practice fun. And yes, she wanted to find a partner with whom she could finish her career.

That wasn't why she didn't want to lose Kristoff, though. During their time together, he'd become…almost a friend. She tried very hard not to bring her emotions into her dance partnerships, but Shanna knew he hadn't intended to make a mess of things. She hated the thought of turning her back on him and proving his suspicions about her right.

In the past, it had never bothered her to be known as the Bitch of the Ballroom. Now, for some reason…it bothered her. A lot.

"Shut up and dance," she snapped.

"We can still win."

They could, if they didn't have that footage hanging over their heads. But why bring it up again? It wouldn't change their situation. Still, she usually would have added the dig just to remind him exactly how he'd screwed up. Today, she didn't have petty in her, not when there was a bit of kicked puppy in his expression.

Damn it, had the handful of orgasms Alejandro had given her softened her that much? Shanna stiffened her spine. She couldn't afford to think with her heart if she wanted to win. And winning was all she had, even if it sounded…empty.

No, she was just tired or something. She'd worked too hard to lose focus now. If she couldn't figure out who was behind this blackmail before the competition, she would likely have to cut Kristoff loose.

"We can win if we keep that video out of circulation. I'm working on that."

"Is that why you went to *Sneak Peek* and performed a public scene with Alejandro Diaz?"

Shanna nearly choked. It hadn't occurred to her that Kristoff would find out. In retrospect, she should have known. He was a member. She hadn't seen him there, but clearly someone had told him.

He laughed. "I heard it was very hot and that you had a rapt audience."

"I did what needed to be done to lure our blackmailer."

Or had she really done whatever she had to in order to achieve those stunning pair of orgasms. She'd barely resisted Alejandro's offer of a third, which he'd promised to give her in his bed, just the two of them on soft satin sheets.

"And you did it very well, I hear."

Shanna rolled her eyes and turned away so he wouldn't see her cheeks turning pink.

But she wasn't fast enough.

"You're blushing. You?" Astonishment laced Kristoff's voice. "I have never seen you do such a thing."

It was rare, and all because Alejandro had blown her away, and she hadn't recovered yet. She had never craved sex or ached for any man. Until him. Last night, before she'd lost herself in the sensations of self-pleasure while thinking of Ali, she'd wondered exactly what he had done to her and why she was so fascinated by him.

How had he gotten under her skin so quickly?

Pretending to walk across the studio nonchalantly, Shanna sought her bottle of water and drank deep, then turned back to Kristoff. "Apparently, our plan wasn't good enough. We didn't catch anyone in the act of filming us, as we'd hoped. No one has sent me another blackmail video or threatened me as a result of the whole thing." She shrugged. "I guess it was a waste of time."

But it didn't feel like a waste, given what he'd done next…

After the scene had ended, Alejandro had pressed a button to drop a partition between them and the audience. Shanna heard the watchers filing out, which filled her with a sense of both loss and relief. Then he had turned her to face him and taken her into his arms. For a simple hug. He'd said not a word, asked for nothing else for long moments. He just held her, stroked her hair. She hadn't had that in a long time. Years. Her father and brothers certainly never gave affection. And she had needed it even more than she'd realized.

Shanna had clenched her eyes shut tightly, resisting an urge to crawl deeper into his embrace and cry for all the fear—and conversely, the bliss—soaking her body. In the aftermath of their sex, her emotions had tumbled, jumbled, whirled all around. Up was down, backward was forward; nothing made sense except holding onto him.

Somehow, she'd managed to restrain her tears, tear herself from his arms, and reach for her clothes.

Within minutes, Del emerged into the room with the unhappy news that security had been scouring the footage of the event and found no one in the audience with a camera of any kind.

After Del left, Shanna had lost it. Tears had fallen hard and fast. But silently. She'd hoped Alejandro had noticed.

Wishful thinking.

"Don't cry," he'd whispered as he swooped her up into his arms.

She'd been too weak to fight Alejandro, especially when he'd felt so strong while he'd settled her against his solid body and in the shelter of his arms. As he'd kissed his way down her face, he'd been so tender, as if he'd known exactly what she needed. He'd ripped right through her fragile barriers. She'd opened up to his whispered words and tender mouth…

Then he'd taken her hand and led her out of the main house, down a pathway hidden by tropical plants and climbing ivy, softly lit by the full moon, then pushed his way toward a luxurious cottage.

His private quarters.

Being alone with him when she was so emotionally raw…not

smart. Downright scary, in fact. Even the idea had made her heart skid, her palms go clammy.

Clutching her keys, Shanna had mumbled something about a fictitious early-morning practice and fled.

So, it was done. They were done. Now, she needed to get her mind off of the repeated messages he'd left since and focus on dancing. She had the biggest competition of her career to prepare for. He had a business to run. Why he continued to pursue her, she had no idea. They had nothing in common.

Except great sex.

"Earth to Shanna," Kristoff joked. "Are you with me?"

"Yes. Sorry. I have a headache." That wasn't a lie actually...just not the whole truth.

"Sorry. What should we do next about...the problem? Perhaps you should seek out a new partner."

He looked so sad at the prospect. Something in her chest twinged, and she tried to shove it aside, but that wasn't working.

"We don't have time to talk about this now. You have to be at work in two hours, and I have to meet with the costumer shortly. Let's focus on today."

"It would not hurt you to talk to me. Do you want to talk about what happened at *Sneak Peek*?"

As her brothers would say, *oh, hell no*. "Talking won't win us any trophies. From the top."

Using the remote control, she started the music again and got into position. Sighing, Kristoff assumed his pose and they danced for another grueling half hour.

Until the door to the studio swung open unexpectedly.

Alejandro strolled in looking dark and yummy and like a man with an agenda—one that started with getting her out of her clothes.

Shanna sucked in a breath. "What are you doing here?"

"I assume your phone is broken, since you have not returned my calls." He arched a brow. "So I decided to find you."

"We're practicing."

The protest was automatic. His presence here, so unexpected, raised her defenses. Thank god. She needed those barriers against him.

If she spent another hour with the man, feeling as weak as she had while he touched her, she'd collapse against him and… Shanna shivered. She'd be vulnerable to him, probably admit that she cared.

Not acceptable.

"You will win because we will uncover who has been blackmailing you," Alejandro vowed.

"The security tapes turned up nothing, you said."

"That is true. And I assume the blackmailer has not contacted you, or you would have let me know."

"Yes, I would have." And she would, no matter how much talking to him would have tempted her to do more—the way she wanted to right now. "But I haven't received anything so far. So we have nothing else to say."

Alejandro's expression told he her could see right through her bluster and wasn't put off in the least. Damn him! Why couldn't he cringe, like most people?

"How did you find out when and where we were practicing?" she demanded.

With a sweep of his hand, Alejandro outted Kristoff as the culprit.

She whirled on her partner angrily. "This is practice time, not social hour. What the hell were you thinking?"

"That if I did not tell him how to find you, he would end my privileges at *Sneak Peek*."

Shanna gritted her teeth. Fabulous. Yet another example of a man thinking with his penis. Apparently, it had never occurred to him—or he didn't care—that she hadn't wanted Alejandro to find her.

"I have been thinking," Kristoff said. "Since your first effort to draw the blackmailer did not solve the problem that you should try again."

"Are you serious?" Her jaw dropped.

Kristoff nodded. "Stage another public scene. The word about it is out now. People in the community are buzzing about you two. If you give advance warning, I believe the person responsible will come."

Shanna considered Kristoff's words with dread—and excitement. More of Alejandro's touches, his wild sort of lovemaking… So very tempting. She hadn't just liked what they'd done together; she had basked in it. And had been aching for more since.

Not a good idea. More Alejandro would only addict her further to the man. And while she didn't know him well, she doubted he would settle for a woman whose schedule was as demanding as hers, especially since she spent nearly every day dancing in very suggestive ways with another man. Besides, she'd bet Alejandro would expect a great deal emotionally from the woman he called his—certainly more than she was comfortable giving. He had to see her limitations.

So why was he still pursuing her?

As much as she'd like to give into her fears and dismiss Alejandro, what Kristoff said made sense. Maybe the blackmailer had not acted last time because he hadn't known about the scene. Or been able to be there that night. She and Alejandro had done little to spread the word beforehand. The audience who had witnessed her coming apart in Ali's arms had largely been there by chance.

"I agree," Alejandro said. "I want to catch this bastard. But the choice is Shanna's."

She bit her lip. With the competition in three days, her options were running thin. Throwing away almost twenty years of training, sweating, and suffering to avoid having sex with Alejandro seemed beyond stupid, even if fear screamed that she should run like hell.

Reluctantly, Shanna nodded. "I'll be there tonight."

Alejandro shook his head. "Tomorrow night. Give me time to suggest that there may be a repeat performance, just in case the scum does not have his ear to the ground, so to speak."

Shanna released the breath she didn't realize she'd been holding. She wanted desperately to be with him. At the same time, she didn't. It was so unlike her to be indecisive and conflicted. She had to regain balance, get a grip on her control.

"Fine," she announced. "I will be there at eight. We'll commence at eight-thirty. I need to be home by ten."

Turning away with a dismissive whirl, she reached for the remote control, intent on starting the music, resuming practice…and ignoring Alejandro before he noticed her trembling and made her completely insane with those hungry stares of his.

Instead, he grabbed her arm and turned her back to face him. "You will be there at eight-thirty. We will commence at nine. If it takes a whole night of public performances, you will stay until we know who and what we are dealing with."

She jerked from his grasp. "Don't presume to tell me what to do."

"Shanna, can you really afford to be impractical and put on your bitch armor with me?"

No.

"I know that is not you," he murmured. "I seek only to help you."

Still, she raised her chin, refusing to back down. "Whatever. If it amuses you to play the caveman—"

"It does not." He leaned close and whispered for her ears only, "But it intrigues me to see you hide from me and the pleasure you know I am going to give you when I have you naked and under me again."

Hours later, Shanna had showered, changed, and run errands. Life was normal…and yet she was still both seething and overheated by Alejandro's arrogant comments. How could the man manage to irritate and arouse her in a single sentence? For that matter, why did he always incite conflict inside her?

Argh! She needed to forget him.

Her doorbell rang. She wasn't expecting anyone. Probably someone trying to sell her something, maybe Girl Scout cookies. One of the neighbor kids had been selling them yesterday, and the thought of indulging in mindless sugar perked her up.

Shanna opened the door.

Someone stood on the other side, all right. It sure wasn't a Girl Scout.

"Alejandro." His name slipped out as a whisper.

"Good evening, *querida.*"

When he murmured that endearment, she melted. Every time. "Don't call me that."

"It bothers you when I call you darling? Why?"

"I am not your darling. We are working together to solve a common problem."

"We are. But I fail to see how that must be the end of it."

Shanna opened her mouth to set him straight, but Alejandro cut her off. "Though I am sure you will invent some reason, but for now, let's not argue. I came to talk."

With narrowed eyes, she tried to gauge his sincerity. "Just talk?"

"Nothing more."

She didn't quite believe him, but he'd roused her curiosity. What could he possibly have to say to her?

"All right. Come in." She stepped back to admit him.

Alejandro shook his head and held out his hand. "Come with me."

"Where?"

"It's a surprise."

"Not the club," she warned him.

He shook his head. "Not the club."

Now she was *really* curious.

Sliding into the sandals she kept by the door, she grabbed her purse and keys off the nearby table. "Will it take long?"

"Hot date tonight?"

His words mocked her. As if he knew that she could hardly wrap her mind around her interest in him, much less imagine being attracted to anyone else right now.

"With dreamland, yes. I'm tired."

"And I am here to cheer you up." He held out his hand to her again.

This time she took it and let herself out the door. "Where are we going?"

"The nature of a surprise is that you should be surprised."

"So you won't tell me?"

He shook his head, sending her a dazzling, unrepentant smile as they walked toward the condo complex's parking lot. "That would spoil it."

"You know that annoys me."

"I know you are used to being in control and making all the deci-sions. A little relaxation will be good for you."

People had been saying that to her for years. Generally, she ignored them.

"That's your opinion."

"And you cannot change it."

"Okay, but you're wrong."

"How about humoring me, then? Pretend."

She rolled her eyes, holding in a smile. He was persistent, if nothing else. "Whatever."

Alejandro sliced her a victorious grin but wisely said nothing more.

When they reached the parking lot, he lifted his key fob and pressed a button. A sleek, black Mercedes convertible, so new it still bore the temporary plates, beeped and flashed its lights a few feet away.

Business at the club must be *very* good to afford the old place that housed their business and four-wheeled trinkets like this.

He assisted her into the car, then rounded the car to the driver's side, and eased in. "My father was a wealthy man."

"What?"

"I saw the way you looked at my car. I believe you had similar thoughts about the club. I am answering your unspoken question. My father was a wealthy man, and he left me his fortune."

"Not your mother?"

He shrugged and started the car. "I am the only part of him my mother will have anything to do with."

"They divorced?"

"In the Catholic church, no. They separated when I was twelve." He backed out of the parking space and steered into the gorgeous summer night.

"Why are you telling me this?"

"You cannot like someone you do not know."

He wanted her to like him?

"My father was a philandering bastard, if you wished to know why they split up. I remember my mother's tears many nights when my father did not come home. They became my tears, too. He acted as if his affairs were both common and acceptable. Perhaps that was so in their generation… Perhaps it was accepted in his native Argentina…"

Alejandro was sharing something so shockingly private with her. Why?

"I do not agree," he stated. "If you speak vows and make a commitment, it should be solid. You should mean those words."

"True." Was he trying to tell her he'd be faithful? Why did he think it mattered to her?

The fact he felt compelled to give her his opinion known unnerved her. But, being honest, it also thrilled her treacherous soft side. Having a man like Ali in her life full time would be wonderful…but distracting. Indulging was *not* an option. Their search for this blackmailing bastard and her need to win the California Dance Star consumed her every thought and waking moment. Her commitment was to winning. Romance would only interfere.

"Take my friendship with Del," he went on. "Del and I met in college. We quickly became friends—both outcasts to some degree, being foreign-exchange students with somewhat poor English here in Los Angeles. We discovered we shared a lot of similar interests and passions.

"So after graduation, we decided to put our degrees to work on something mutually satisfying. Del used his marketing degree and social media skills to spread word of the club and promote it all around. I used my finance degree to secure the funding, run the back end, and invest our profits. We operate in the black, and each year is more profitable than the last. But two years ago, I had the opportunity to sell out my half for triple the amount I paid to get in." He shrugged. "Long ago, I promised Del I would stay in until we were both ready for a change. I declined the opportunity."

"That cost you a lot of money, I'm sure."

"Losing the friendship would have cost me more."

"You can afford to say that; you have your father's money."

"Not so much anymore. I put a fat chunk of it in a trust for my mother. She thinks I set it up with my money. But the bastard owed her more than he could ever repay. I thought this was fitting."

Shanna stared at Alejandro as if seeing him for the first time. In a way, she was. It was hard not to like him when he was protecting his mother and defending his friendships.

A moment later, they stopped in front of a local ice cream shop, quaint and somewhat old-fashioned. In a few hours, after dinner, this place would be crawling with families. But during the dinner hour, it was nearly empty.

"Ice cream?"

"I assume you like it."

"I haven't eaten dinner yet. I was planning to cook before you came over…"

He climbed out of the car and helped her out. "Who needs dinner when there is ice cream?"

"Who doesn't need protein and nutrients? Ice cream isn't a dinner food."

Alejandro slipped an arm around her, and Shanna tried not to melt against the tempting heat of his body. Why did he have to be so damn sexy?

"I will not tell your mother if you won't," he teased.

"My mother died when I was four."

She found herself choking out the words. She shouldn't have opened her mouth; the truth only made her more vulnerable to him. But withholding that fact after he'd confessed all about his past seemed petty.

"I am sorry."

She hung her head. "I don't remember her. I have this…impression of what her laugh was like. I don't even know if it's accurate."

He squeezed her against his side as they approached the counter. "So your father raised you?"

"Along with my brothers. They're all athletes."

"Which is why you are so driven to win." It was a statement, not a question.

"Second place is nothing more than first loser. It's the family motto."

"Ah, this explains so much about you." He turned to the teenager behind the counter. "A scoop of chocolate peanut butter and…raspberry amaretto. Shanna?"

"None for me. I have to fit into my costume—"

"She will have the same."

"I will not!"

"Then pick your favorite flavors."

"You're going to force me to eat ice cream?"

"I am going to help you take a moment away from ambition and enjoy life."

When was the last time she'd done that? Shanna thought back through the weeks, which became months…and quickly turned into years. The realization stunned her.

She hesitated, then caved in. It was ice cream, not a commitment. Tomorrow, she had a grueling practice. She'd work the calories off.

"Chocolate chip cookie dough and French vanilla."

Alejandro paid as other teenagers behind the counter assembled their cones. In moments, they wandered to a little table outside and began licking on ice cream as the sun dropped closer to the horizon, with the California breeze stirring all around them.

After the first taste, Shanna moaned. "This is amazing."

He smiled. "I discovered this place a few years ago. It's part of my weekly ritual."

"Where do you put it?" She eyed his hard body, absolutely no stranger to his rippled abs.

"I make up for it with plenty of cardio and carrots the rest of the week. But life is meant to be lived, no?"

Had she ever really thought about it in that context? "I suppose so."

"You have been a very single-minded woman for many years. Dance has been your focus, your ambition."

"And my passion."

"No one watching you dance would deny that. You are very talented. You know this, right?"

She supposed. Yes, she could dance. When she watched footage of competitions, she knew she held her own in a room full of talented dancers. For the past few years, she even believed she began to shine a bit brighter than them because she practiced harder and wanted it more.

"I'm pleased with my performances."

"This ambition, does it make you happy?"

Happy? An odd question. She didn't enjoy being frustrated by the champion status she had not achieved yet. But she *would* be a champion. Once the trophy was in her hands, life would be very sweet, and the sacrifices she'd made along the way would have been worth it.

All she had to do was get dangerously close to the most tempting man she'd ever met in order to catch her blackmailer.

His question unsettled her. She'd never thought of her life in a happy/unhappy context. It just was. Of course, questioning her life was too easy to do when she had a man like Alejandro in front of her, reminding her of everything she'd been missing.

"Why shouldn't it?" she asked.

"The way that ice cream cone is dripping and the fact I've rarely seen you smile, I suspect you have spent so much time dancing, you are out of practice when it comes to living."

Dancing was life for her. So what if she didn't eat a lot of ice cream? "Why do you care?"

"Because I am a man who would like to see you happy." He brushed tender fingertips across her cheek. "What is the worst thing that could happen if you do not win Saturday night? Or ever?"

Immediately, she rejected the thought. But it was a fair question, one she'd asked herself during long nights when aching muscles, nagging injuries, and loneliness had kept her awake.

"I don't know." She shook her head. "I can't let that happen. Failure is not an option."

"You cannot control what will happen."

Yeah, that's what worried her.

"So what happens if you never win?"

She hated to even think the answer. But to speak it seemed unbearably personal. Yet Alejandro had poured out a part of his soul to her. He had not mocked her when she'd spoken of her mother, the rest of the family, or the origins of her ambitions. She had no reason to hide from him...except that he kept slipping behind her emotional barriers, which scared the hell out of her.

Why couldn't she put distance between them? Why did she even care about his feelings? Normally, she had no problem with pushing people away, but Ali was...different.

"I would feel like a failure," she whispered.

"You would consider yourself a failure, even after everything you have achieved?"

"Probably. My family would think I'm a failure. I have one brother who has been the top decathlete in the world. One has played in the Super Bowl. My father has two gold medals. I can't compete."

"Who asked you to?"

"You'd have to understand my family. For years, my brothers have endlessly tormented me."

He shrugged. "The nature of men and their sisters. Their way of showing affection is to harass you. More manly that way."

It wasn't that simple, and she didn't know how to explain it. "Family aside, I couldn't give up dancing. I *want* to win, more than anything."

"I would not suggest you give up dance. I merely think you should take the floor to indulge your joy of dance, not to pursue a trophy. The journey is the treasure, not the prize at the end."

"Now you're a philosopher?"

Alejandro shook his head and placed a soft kiss against her ice-cream cold lips. "Just a man who wants to see you smile. Will you?"

Shanna looked at Alejandro. He was so comfortable with himself. Somehow wiser than a man who ran a club for sexual indulgences should be. He made everything seem so easy. Even personal discussions, which she usually downright loathed, felt freakishly natural. No pressure. No scolding or telling her how to do things. No taunting her about her failures. Just a steady voice, a tender touch, with lots of insight.

Lovely…but none of that would put a trophy in her hand.

Shanna wrapped her fingers around his and smiled. "There. Are you happy?"

"I have seen more genuine smiles at a beauty pageant."

Sighing, Shanna sat back and licked at her cone. "Really, why does it matter to you if I'm happy?"

Ali paused, seeming to weigh his words. "You matter. I would hate to see you sacrifice everything for something that may never happen.

You have given up high school frivolities, friendships, romances…for a hunk of metal and a title."

He was right…and wrong. Being a champion was everything to her.

"This is why I don't date." She stood and glared down at him. "I don't expect you to understand. No one does."

He stood and met her glare. "You have ended more than one dance partnership to pursue winning over friendship. What has that gotten you except a bad reputation? Those partners invested in you, cared about you. You cast them aside."

"I had to! One was so injured, it was clear he was never coming back."

"Might he have tried harder to recover if you had given him both a reason and a partner to return to?"

Guilt sliced through her. Maybe. Likely not…but maybe. Curt had been a hard worker and possessed a drive to win. Last she heard, he was selling insurance.

"Martin dropped me in competition. I could not risk it happening again. I'd lost faith in his ability, and a couple without trust does not function well."

"The drop must have been painful, and I understand why you would not want to partner with someone ill equipped for the job. But as you say, trust is essential. After nearly two years together, you never gave him a chance to rebuild it between you."

She rolled her eyes. "What are you, my dance pimp? And before you start in on Jonathan, that decision was mutual. He wanted to get married more than he wanted to dance."

Surprise flashed across his dark face. "Really? My mother will be happy to hear that. She hates you because you ran off her favorite."

Shanna sat again. "Ugh! Everyone thinks that. We…just knew it was time to move on, both of us."

Speculation crossed Ali's face, but he didn't ask if she'd slept with Jonathan. For that, she was eternally grateful. "And now, you have issues with Kristoff. What will you do if we cannot find our black-mailer in time?"

Good question. She'd been putting that decision off. This was her year to win; she couldn't imagine forfeiting. But... "If we don't succeed in fishing this blackmailer out, I won't have a choice. I like Kristoff. He's so talented. He's got great work ethic—"

"But you have no problem leaving him behind?"

"It's business."

"And you will not let anything or anyone stand in your way, will you?"

His soft question nearly crushed her with guilt. She shoved the feeling aside. Giving up over half her life and the chance to finally reach her dreams? "I can't.

*A*lejandro paced in the security room, watching the cameras positioned over *Sneak Peek's* front door. He checked his watch. Eight-forty five. People were beginning to stream in, in greater numbers than usual for this time of night on a Thursday.

The word about his scene with Shanna was out. He and Del had seen to it personally, not using names, of course…but socializing everywhere that it would be special.

The stage was set—if Shanna showed up. Now he worried she wouldn't. After all, the woman who prided herself on punctuality was fifteen minutes late. Was she trying to make a statement or yank his chain? Or was there some other reason she refused to come here tonight? What could possibly be more important to her than losing? Not embarrassment or modesty. She'd already survived her first public scene, which was always the most nerve-wracking. But one thing he had noticed? Every time he tried to get close to Shanna, she seemed increasingly anxious and tense.

Was it possible she feared being close to him more than she feared losing?

"You're wearing out the carpet," Del teased.

Ali shot him a dark glare. "She's not coming."

"She'll be here. You said yourself the woman is prickly and contrary for the purpose of being such. You admitted that she likes to control her situation, so it can't have been easy on her when you told her when to show up, what to wear…and nothing about what she could expect."

All of that was true, yet he'd had a larger purpose than being a controlling jackass. "I want Shanna to lean on me. I want her to know that she can trust me."

He wanted her to see what it felt like for someone to stand by her, even if she wasn't winning.

"You can't force her to figure that out."

"Normally, I would not try, but with Shanna…" He sighed and stared at the video cameras that showed no sign of her arrival. "If I cannot find some way now to encourage her to latch on to me, she will slip through my fingers."

Del shrugged. "Why does it matter? I mean, I agree she will be helpful in finding whoever has violated the club's rules, but we can flush out the asshole with or without her."

"She is not business to me; she's personal."

"How personal?"

Interpretation: how deep were his feelings? That question had been plaguing him all day. Shanna was more to him than catching a scumbag blackmailer, more than an amazing lay, more than an intriguing woman. Analyzing how it had happened and why was pointless. It was what it was, and Alejandro always trusted his gut.

"I think I am in love."

"That was fast. Less than a week." Del arched a dark brow.

"More time will not change what I feel, except to make it deeper. She is strong and vulnerable, smart, adorably stubborn, and in utter need of someone to love. How can I resist?" He flashed Del a self-deprecating smile.

"How, indeed? If you intend to resist, figure it out fast. She's here."

Ali whipped his gaze up to the bank of cameras and smiled.

"Aww. She's wearing a damn trench coat," Del groused.

Laughter bubbled up inside Alejandro. "Of course she is." Her little rebellion. "But I will bet she wore what I sent her underneath."

"I can't wait for this." Del rubbed his hands together.

With blood burning a path through his veins, Ali burst out of the security office and stalked toward the front door. Del followed close behind.

Alejandro intercepted Shanna two seconds after she walked in. "*Querida*, are you all right?"

As Shanna strode in, she lifted her lashes in a skittish glance. "Fine. Why wouldn't I be?"

Her guarded tone sent off alarm bells. So she was trying to push her armor back in place, put distance between them. He frowned. Perhaps he had pushed her too hard last night…or made her feel too guilty.

"When you did not arrive at eight-thirty, I grew concerned."

"No need."

He reached up to help her with her coat. She jerked away. "Don't. Just wait until…"

"We are on stage and I'm supposed to perform by fucking you?"

She swallowed and sent him a shaky nod that seared his guts with panic. After tonight, she was going to turn around and walk out of his life if he didn't think fast.

"Is something wrong?" He gentled his expression.

She looked away. "This is business. You're doing what you need to do. So am I."

"Shanna, this is not a business dealing or mere sex to me. I want it to be more than that for you, too."

She shot him a wary stare. "Until Saturday, I have to focus on fixing my problem. You want me to dance for the joy of it, not for the trophy. I can't be joyful if I already know before I dance a step that I can't win."

Alejandro sighed. He'd hoped he'd gotten through to her during their ice cream date, at least in some small way. But he'd been deluding himself. She was determined to shut him out and focus on nothing but the prize.

"Not to interrupt, kids," Del said, "but you need to make your way back to the room so you can get started. Showtime is in eight minutes."

Resisting the urge to rake a hand through his hair, Ali gnashed his teeth. He needed a minute to collect a few props and his thoughts.

"Can you show her to the room?" he asked his business partner. "I'll be there in five."

Ali didn't wait for the answer. He brushed past them, into the security corridor, and let the door slam behind him. Dread and anger crashed to the bottom of his stomach. Unless he acted fast, this could well be his last chance with Shanna. He had three minutes to figure out how to turn her head in his direction, convince her he wasn't simply out to save his business or get laid, and persuade her they could be more permanent partners beyond tonight.

Miracle, anyone?

Del escorted Shanna through the club. She was aware of people all around her swaying and writhing to the techno music. But her thoughts... Alejandro had the lock on those.

Last night and today, he'd acted like he cared. Why? She'd told him over and over this was business.

Yeah, did it feel like business when he was deep inside you, making you scream? Or when he fed you ice cream and did his best to be there for you?

The man had her so confused. What should have been nothing more than a temporary arrangement for the sake of ferreting out a mutual enemy—and okay, maybe a little mutual pleasure—had suddenly become very tangled. In the space of a few days, she'd come to think of Ali as a fixture in her life. The thought of that fixture being removed hurt.

So dangerous. How could she focus on the competition with everything hanging over her head if she had to add new and scary emotions for Alejandro to the mix?

"Follow me," Del said.

They crossed the dance floor and pushed aside a couple panting heatedly and letting their fingers do the walking. He escorted Shanna into a long hallway. At the end, he held a door open.

One peek inside, and she sucked in a surprised gasp. This was out of a fantasy! Plush, like a Pasha's palace. Rust, gold, bronze, with accents of black and cream. An enormous bed. Pillows everywhere.

The audience would be bigger in this room. And closer. The odds of someone to bringing in a camera was definitely greater.

"We've got the security angles covered," Del assured her before she even opened her mouth. "There are cameras all over this place. We've spent all day rigging it up. If someone tries to film you here, we'll nail him."

He wandered closer. Shanna tensed. Truth be told, the man made her nervous. He was dark like Alejandro. Both men had a wide streak of bad boy. Ali was like a fire, hot and sometimes unpredictable, never quite tamed. But Del...he could be a very cool customer. He'd do everything on his terms, in his time, his way. And show zero emotion doing it.

Now, he gave off the vibe of a predator. Shanna swallowed and raised her chin as he sauntered closer.

"Can I take your coat?"

Feeling too vulnerable for her comfort, she unbelted the garment and stripped it off. The red corset underneath and the matching black thong, garters, and stockings went way beyond suggestive. Being naked would make her feel more clothed.

Del whistled, looking her up and down, lingering on her breasts. "You look hot. Damn hot."

She cleared her throat. His hungry gaze eating her up when she'd last been on stage with Alejandro had turned her on. Being alone with him, having him this close, while he wore that ravenous expression? Disturbing.

She shrugged off his comment casually. "A costume like any other."

"You and Ali got a real thing going?"

Shanna frowned. When this was over, it was unlikely she and Alejandro continue to see each other. They were from different worlds. Whatever they might have had would be another casualty to her ambition. It didn't bother her. Well...it shouldn't.

But something wretched and heavy that felt an awful lot like regret smothered her. Pain followed. It wouldn't do anything but distract her, so she shoved it down.

"No."

Flashing her a hot smile, Del leaned in until he was invading her personal space. "That's good news. Very good, in fact."

The rapacious way he watched her gave her major pause.

"When you and Ali are done here...maybe you and I could hook up?" he dragged a fingertip down her arm, leaving a prickle of unease in his wake.

Did Del really imagine that after having sex with his friend and business partner, she was just going to throw Ali over and hop in his bed?

She put space between them. "I don't think so. Get your hand off me."

He complied slowly. "If you and Ali don't have a thing going, why not? You're a gorgeous woman. I've seen you in action, and you make me hard. I'll treat you right, make you scream. I hear you're good at switching partners. C'mon. What do you say?"

He reached around her and slung his hand low on her hip, almost on her ass.

Fury erupted in Shanna's gut. She grabbed his wrist, squeezed his pressure point until he winced, then shoved his hand away from her backside.

"What the hell are you thinking? No, the better question is, which part of your body is doing the thinking for you? I'm pretty sure I know the answer." She cut a derisive glare in the vicinity of his crotch, then shot a quick glance to the door. Where was Ali?

"What's the problem, baby?" He moved in closer again.

Her temper flared. *Douche bag!*

She lifted her foot and dug her stiletto into his toes. He swore, and she smiled. "The problem is, I'm supposed to have sex with your friend in less than five minutes. Let's focus, shall we?"

His voice was strained as he reached down to cradle his injured toe. "You don't get sentimental about your partners. And you said you weren't involved with Ali. So why shouldn't I ask a gorgeous woman if she wants to hook up?"

Why, indeed? Del was attractive physically. She doubted he would be demanding of her time or try to delve into her psyche. Del would never take her to his bed after a wild night on stage, love her privately, and rip past the barriers around her heart. He would probably never press her for more than sex.

But if she disliked Alejandro for all those things, why wasn't she eager to spend alone time with his sinfully good-looking friend?

"Alejandro is your business partner and best friend."

"Yeah, but if you're not into him, that makes you fair game."

Shanna was still processing Del's words when he grabbed her and crushed her body against his. His mouth swooped down, and he captured her lips. At the first swipe of his tongue against hers, she knew nothing but panic.

And pure rage.

She twisted in his grasp until she delivered a hard knee to his balls. He backed away instantly, doubled over and clutching himself.

"What the hell is your problem?"

"I'll tell you exactly what I've told Alejandro: I have the most important competition of my career to focus on. I intend to win, and anything else is just a distraction I don't need."

"And that's your only reason for turning me down?"

Alejandro shoved the stage door open. It collided with the wall, echoing across the stage as he strode inside. He had the distinct impression he'd interrupted something.

In the middle, Shanna stood wearing the corset, garters, and thong he'd sent her—and looking every bit as drop-dead sexy as he'd known she would. Though his dick was already hard at the thought of being inside her, this outfit added to the red blood cell count below his waist.

But the righteous anger on her face made him pause. Especially when he saw Del two feet away, hunched over, clutching his balls and glaring at her.

What the hell?

"She's got a mean knee, man."

"He's got the disposition of a manwhore."

Anger crashed into Alejandro with the same impact as driving a hundred miles an hour straight into a brick wall. "You made a move on her?"

"Yes!" Shanna shouted.

Del tried to stand up straight and shrug. "You said she had a habit of switching dance partners. I wondered if that extended to sex. She swore you two had nothing going. If that's true, why would she kick me?"

Then his friend did something bizarre. He winked.

Ali frowned…until everything started falling into place. Del had been testing her. If Shanna didn't care a thing about him, Alejandro knew she would have gone for Del. Women did—in droves. Shanna had been turned on by him watching her just days ago. Why not follow through?

Ali suspected that the only reason Shanna had kneed his pal was because whatever feelings she had developed between them since their last scene together were stronger than she wanted to admit. And Del had pissed her off.

Suddenly, Ali resisted the urge to smile. Hope curled in his belly, warmed his heart, made his dick even stiffer. He'd test his theory tonight.

"We have no time to argue. Let us start this party. Del, show the crowd in. Security tells me they are lined up down the hallway. Shanna, turn around and put your hands behind your back."

With a nod, Del turned and headed for the door.

No surprise, Shanna hesitated at his command. She'd assumed he would be angry that Del made a pass at her. She'd assumed Ali would behave possessively. If he hadn't known Del for years and hadn't known quite well how his friend's mind worked, Ali would have been.

Instead, he intended to enjoy the fireworks between he and Shanna before he got to the bottom of whatever was in her heart. Del was just helping him along.

"Is there a problem?" he asked. "People will begin filing in soon. We should be in position."

"Fine." She presented him with her back.

What a luscious view! Feminine shoulders tapered down to a narrow, red-corseted back. The black thong bisected a firm, feminine ass he'd fantasized about fucking. Those garters and black thigh-high stockings hugging the toned curves of her legs damn near had him on his knees.

And if he played his cards right, she would be all his.

Forcing his stare back to her wrists crossed at the small of her back, Ali grabbed them. With a flick and two quick clicks, he secured her in handcuffs.

She whirled on him, murder in her eyes. "What the hell are you doing? Unlatch these! I didn't sign up for this. We didn't discuss—"

Ali cut off her tirade by cupping her nape and covering her mouth with his. She struggled...for a moment. Then he swept inside her mouth, tunneled his hands in her hair, and kissed her as if his very life depended on it.

She melted.

With a gentle nip and a soothing kiss to cover the sting, he pulled back and whispered, "We have an audience."

Releasing her, Ali walked a half circle around her and cozied up to her back, letting her feel the heat of his body and his erection. She gasped.

The curve of her neck beckoned, and he trailed his lips up the graceful line and soft skin.

Briefly, he opened his eyes and discovered at least twenty-five people in the room—and more filing in. Perfect. Maybe they would catch the asshole tonight.

Then he put everything out of his mind—except Shanna.

He started at her shoulders, but his hands seemed to develop a mind of their own. Down they plunged, right over the curves of her breasts, pushed up by the tight corset. But having those nipples covered wasn't going to do.

In a few seconds, Alejandro brushed through the little fastenings holding the garment together. It fell to the stage in a boned rustle of fabric.

Men groaned in the audience as he bared her breasts to them. Shanna tensed. Ali could feel her shivering. Cold? He didn't think so. Nerves? Maybe. Excitement. Definitely. He could smell a hint of her arousal.

Eagerly, he reached around and cupped her breasts in his hands, squeezing her nipples between his thumbs and fingers. She writhed, wriggling her ass against his cock.

He was about to lose his mind.

With a yank, he tugged the sheer thong from her body. Another collective groan rang from the audience. Guys shifted weight from one foot to another, adjusted themselves in their pants, sat forward in their chairs. Shanna began to pant.

Ali dragged his palms down her abdomen. He itched to feel the silk of her pussy, see just how wet she was.

Moments later, he had his answer. She was wet, welcoming, lush. Shanna might lie about her feelings for him, but her body couldn't.

Now was the perfect time to start testing his theory…

A quick point at Del brought his friend up on the stage. Shanna tensed again. This time, he didn't think it was due to excitement.

Before she could say a word, he whispered, "I want to watch your breasts be sucked. Del will help us out."

"No," she whimpered.

"You change partners all the time. Why does it matter?"

Del approached her and pressed his body close to Shanna's. Ali didn't say a word, just lifted her breasts up to him.

Just before he bent to her, Del sent her a smile that said he was ready for scorching hot sex.

"It just matters," she whispered. "Please no."

Lifting dark eyes to Ali, Del waited for a cue.

Ali had what he wanted for now. He shook his head.

With a wry grin, Del contented himself by placing a chaste kiss on the curve of her breast. But to show he wasn't going to be dismissed, he took a seat on a nearby pillow and sent a scorching stare her way.

In truth, Ali knew they had to play along, just in case their black-mailer was in the room. But he wanted nothing more than to get Shanna alone. *Soon*, he promised himself.

Turning her back toward him, Ali watched her stage smile collapse. She looked at him with a mixture of hurt, anger, and relief. Apparently, swapping partners did matter to her. And he sensed that the sooner he got her to admit that about dance, the sooner she'd settle into having one man in her life.

Impatient to touch her, Ali tore down the zipper of his leather pants and freed his stiff cock. "Suck me."

He kicked a pillow under her knees. Shanna hesitated, then sank down, bent her head, and consumed him.

Oh, hell. Her mouth was a silken oven, soft and scorching and robbing him of breath. She damn sure knew what to do with that tongue of hers, caressing the length of his staff, curling it around the head. She sucked deep and hard, all the way to the back of her throat.

His heartbeat rattled in his chest. His ears buzzed with the excitement. Faintly, he was aware of male groans and a "fuck, yeah," from the audience. But focusing beyond Shanna's hot mouth was growing impossible.

As wonderful as it was, it had to stop. They had a show to put on for these guests—and a potential blackmailer. A blow job was all well and good, but not blackmail-worthy, compared to Kristoff's show.

With a groan of regret, Ali cupped her cheeks and lifted her mouth from his cock. Then he helped her to her feet. In four steps, he had her bent over the huge, cushioned bed, her breasts pressed to the silk comforter. A few seconds later, he was sheathed and deep inside her.

She gripped him like no one ever had, like every contour had been formed just to clench around him perfectly.

He seized her hips and tunneled deeper. Then set a ruthless pace.

She cried out. The sight of her all spread out under him, her hands still cuffed at the small of her back, her pussy taking every inch he had…hell, he wasn't going to last long. And he didn't want to go off alone.

"I ache to play with your clit and feel you orgasm around me…" He hadn't even finished the sentence before he slid a pair of determined fingers right over the button of her nerves.

With his other hand, he gripped her hips tight. He thrust inside her repeatedly, dragging the head of his cock right over that sensitive spot that had her muscles tensing, shaking.

In moments, a low, feminine groan split the air. Almost there…

"Come for me," he demanded. "Come!"

With another brush and press of his fingers over her clit, she screamed. Around them, the audience groaned. Several stroked their own cocks…even Del.

Then the rippling walls of her sex contracted, tightened, gripping and coaxing him, blotting out all other thoughts. Ali closed his eyes and focused on her. He shouted through clenched teeth as he followed her into ecstasy.

More than one groan of satisfaction split the air within moments. Ali didn't care. All he knew was that underneath him was the woman he would not let go of. They had seen to business.

Now it was time for the real pleasure—and hopefully, the future—to begin.

8

A pleasure cloud. Heavy limbs, light head. A gentle throb between her legs pulsing as it slowly abated. Alejandro's embrace providing warmth, even as he gripped her as if he'd never let go. Ah…

Shanna could happily stay here, connected to him for a while. A long while. There were reasons she shouldn't, she knew. She just couldn't remember them now.

Then Alejandro slipped free of her body and broke her sensual haze. She lifted weighty lids to watch him walk past her and snap the curtains shut between them and the audience. Del remained on their side of the drape, and Shanna was suddenly conscious of her nudity and Del's dark eyes on her.

"Keep them the hell out of here," Alejandro growled in low tones.

Del clapped his gaze on his buddy, who was now buttoning his pants and wearing a sly smile. "You got it. Tomorrow?"

Ali smiled. "Maybe the day after."

What were they talking about? It should be obvious, but her brain was so clouded by satisfaction that thinking was just a lot of effort right now.

Del's laugh barely registered when Alejandro turned and stalked across the floor to her. In seconds, he uncuffed one of her wrists, grabbed her up in his arms, and headed for the stage door.

"What...? Where are you—?"

"Alone." He said the word like a vow. "No one except you and me, being us together."

Just in case others could hear, she whispered, "But the blackmailer—"

"If he was here tonight, he already got what he came for. Del will call me if they captured something on the security cameras. Now, this is about us."

"But you said we would stay all night, if necessary."

He stopped. "Is that what you want, for me to fuck you again for an audience? Shall we invite more people in this time?"

Sarcasm. Anger. And she understood. Something inside her rejected the notion of more audience time, too. "No."

"Good. I'm done sharing you with other hungry male eyes." He pushed through a door, out into a bright hall, past the open door to security. Laughing and clapping ensued from the crew inside the office, and Shanna buried her head in his neck.

"I'm naked!" she shrieked.

"They just watched us on the cameras. They are not seeing anything they have not yet seen. Which is another reason I want you all to myself."

Shanna didn't have the chance to speak again before Ali opened another door and let it slam behind him. Now it was dark, and Southern California's summer evening sky simmered all around them in a velvet hush. Frogs and crickets hummed in the sultry breeze. The lights of the city beyond the hill twinkled and winked as far as she could see.

"It's beautiful out here."

"That I would rather look at you should tell you how I feel about *your* beauty."

Shanna snapped her gaze up to Ali's. No smile. His stare was full of gravity—and rising need.

"Alejandro, maybe we should talk about—"

"No. Tonight is about you and me. No conversation, no people, no blackmail, no cameras. I need to feel you like I have never needed before."

She gaped, totally unable to deny the breathless rush of joy at his words. Did he…care about her?

There was no time to ponder the answer before he spirited her into his cottage, through the intimate cocoon of the hushed night, straight to his bed. In the shadows, she could make out its straight lines and modern flare. It was big, dark, exotic—just like the man.

Then his mattress was at her back, and he grabbed the empty cuff dangling from her wrist, and Shanna expected him to attach it to his bed somehow so he would have her at his mercy.

Instead, he attached the cuff to his own wrist.

They were joined. Together. Bound.

"Alejandro?"

He didn't answer. Instead, he tossed the handcuff key somewhere on the floor, far out of reach, then covered her mouth with his own.

Shanna expected his ravenous hunger, a hard-edged *boom-fast-now* kind of touch. She was shocked instead by his soft insistence. His kiss was seduction itself. Thorough, unhurried. Slow, deep. Unabashedly intimate, as he conveyed his every want, spoke with his soul, communicating only using his mouth.

It was impossible not to fall under his spell.

A new ribbon of desire tied her stomach in knots as he trailed hot kisses across her cheek, down toward her neck. He exhaled against her neck, close to her ear, stirring sensitive skin. She shivered as his lips caressed her, branded her. He swept a fingertip down the arch of her throat and nipped at her lobe.

"Necesito tocarle, su cara, su piel. Su corazón."

Shanna had no idea what his words meant, but they melted her. In that moment, whatever he wanted, she wanted, too.

"Tell me…"

He didn't right away. Instead, he swept his mouth over hers again. The tangle of breaths, lips, tongues became a deliberate kiss of endless hunger. Eloquent, shockingly sexual as the fingers of his free hand sifted into her hair, curling possessively around the strands. Sizzlingly intimate as he tore his mouth from hers to stare, penetrating her with eyes like burning coals in the pitch of night. Ensnared, Shanna could not look away.

"I said that I need to touch you, your face, your skin. Your heart."

Something both shocked and joyous burst inside her. She gasped, and Alejandro swallowed the sound with another drugging kiss.

With every brush of his lips, every glide of his hot palm, every male moan poured into her mouth he ripped past her barriers until she opened completely to him—parting her lips wider to accept more of his possession, clutching one hard shoulder with her free hand to keep him near, spreading her thighs to invite him inside. She sighed when his narrow hips fit right into the curve of her body as if he'd been made to fill her.

"Yes." She arched under him, unable to hold anything back.

He nestled his free hand under the curve in her back, keeping her breasts and the damp heat of her skin right against him.

"Yo le tocaré toda la noche. Cada parte de tú sabrás el se siente de mí."

"Ali…please."

The way he touched her, as if he had not another thought in his head except pleasing her… She burned inside her skin, yet she knew only he could save her. He would shatter her into a million pieces first, then remake her into a new woman. A warning bell went off in some distant part of her mind, but his fingers gripped her hips, fitting her directly against the hard column of his erection. He wound down her body and brushed soft lips against the side of her breast.

"I will touch you all night long," he translated. "Every part of you will know the feel of me."

She had no doubt Alejandro would keep that promise.

He suckled her nipples over and over, lavishing attention on her until they stood red, swollen, so sensitive that nothing more than his breath on her induced a shiver. All the while, his fingers free from the cuff whispered across her skin. Her back, her thighs, her buttocks. Even her knees, calves, and toes. Alejandro put that hand on every inch of available skin, finally drawing her leg up high on his hip so he could toy with the sensitive underside of her knee.

Gently, he rode her clit with his erection. Not pushing or grinding. Not bruising. Instead, a soft nudge of delicious pressure in a hypnotic rhythm, one that took her higher and higher.

The seed of pleasure under her clit sprouted and bloomed. Shanna panted, trying to resist the searing pleasure for just another moment. She dug the fingers not bound by the cuff into the hard flesh of his back, pressing down his body, far down, until she gripped his ass in her hand.

Moonlight spilled past the open blinds, swirling in on the evening breeze as he whispered, *"La piel estas rosácea, mi amor. Eres maduro y listo, sí?"*

"Tell me, Ali!" She moaned. "Please…"

"Your skin is rosy, my love. You are ripe and ready, yes?"

"Yes. Yes, now!"

He pressed against her again, nudging her clit with his cock. The cream of her arousal spread all over his flesh, and the next time he rocked against her, the bead of nerves he teased leaped at the slick pressure. Blood rushed south, pooled between her legs, gathering need, pleasure, and anticipation right where it impacted her most. She clawed, cried in his arms.

"Who is here, Shanna? Who is in this room?"

"Us. Just us."

"Apenas tú y mí. Ninguna audiencia. Ninguna cámaras. Nosotros." He breathed as he gathered the crooks of her knees into his arms. "Just you and me. No audience, no cameras. *Us.*"

The way it always should be. The thought ran through Shanna's mind unchecked, unchallenged, unstoppable as Alejandro paused, probed, then on a long glide, he penetrated her.

His hard flesh filled her sex, sank deep, deeper, then deeper still. Making love face to face…totally different than being dominated by him for an audience. The slick rasp of his engorged shaft raked against her sensitive walls. A jolt of pleasure coiled, tightened, intensifying, growing faster than she could assimilate.

"So tight, my love," he murmured as he drew back and brought their cuffed hands up to her breast. Her palm cupped her flesh as his thumb caressed her nipple. It was as if they were seeing to her pleasure together, and it drove Shanna mad with delirious need.

All the while, the slow steady pleasure of his thrusts made her into a wild woman. She writhed, lifted her hips, arched—anything to reach more of him, lure him deeper still into her.

Alejandro went willingly, every lingering slide of his erection inside her lifting her arousal higher. Her pulse pounded in her ears. Heat suffused her body. She could barely breathe. And she didn't care.

For the first time in years—maybe in her life—she didn't just feel; she was wholly alive, driven by something more than a statue of faux gold molded like dancers she wanted to someday sit on her mantle. She lived for now. She lived to feel the man growling words in a language she didn't understand but adored as he strained to fulfill every promise of pleasure boiling in her body.

Alejandro gripped the hand joined to his by the cuff and laced their fingers together. He squeezed her hand tight as their breaths merged, their cries mingled. "Come for me."

The request from his mouth became a demand from his body as he thrust straight into her core again.

Shanna splintered into a million pieces, blinded by the brilliant pleasure bursting inside her. In the next moment, he followed her into the white-hot rush of shattering pleasure. Oh, god. He was all over her, everywhere…inside her. Shanna doubted she could wash his possession away with a mere shower. It seemed unlikely that time and distance would completely free her from him.

She feared she'd given a piece of herself to Alejandro she'd likely never get back: her heart.

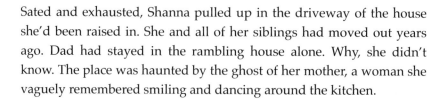

Sated and exhausted, Shanna pulled up in the driveway of the house she'd been raised in. She and all of her siblings had moved out years ago. Dad had stayed in the rambling house alone. Why, she didn't know. The place was haunted by the ghost of her mother, a woman she vaguely remembered smiling and dancing around the kitchen.

She should have gone home first. Showered, changed, had a cup of coffee before coming here. If she had stayed in Ali's bed, he would have offered her all that and more. Instead, she'd pleaded the need to use the bathroom and persuaded him to unlock the cuffs joining them. She'd waited a few minutes, until she was sure he'd drifted back to sleep, then dressed in one of his shirts and a pair of long sweatpants, then sneaked out. Not that it mattered. Ali was with her, in her, in a way that had nothing to do with the fact they'd had unprotected sex and everything to do with the fact she cared far more about him than she should.

The chilly California air of the early morning hadn't helped to sort out her head. She was in love with a man who would never mean to stand in the way of her dance dreams, but how could Alejandro not, as consuming as he was? She'd barely driven two miles from *Sneak Peek*, and she'd begun to feel the withdrawal of his warmth, his acceptance and tenderness.

Dangerous. She was the Bitch of the Ballroom because she'd adhered to strict discipline and a ruthless dedication to perfection. She intended to win that long-coveted trophy, damn it. When the music was high and the lights down low, the judges didn't care what was deep in her heart. She'd do well to remember that.

Still, those moments in Ali's arms… For the first time in years, maybe ever, she'd felt adored, and not because of what she might achieve or what competition she might win. She didn't have anything to prove in that moment. Alejandro cared about her. He proved that in amazing, pleasure-drenched ways every time he touched her.

Now, she clutched a bag of bagels and cream cheese, along with a portable carafe of coffee she'd purchased at a bakery, and let herself into the house.

Shanna followed the smell of burned toast with a poignant smile.

She sauntered into the kitchen and looked at her father, older now, gray at the temples, his reading glasses askew, but still vital and well built for pushing sixty.

"Bagels?" she offered.

Her dad plucked charred bread from the toaster with his fingertips, then dropped it on the counter with a curse.

Then he skewered her with a stare. "Sure. As soon as you explain why you're wearing men's clothes, are rosy with whisker burn, and smell like sex."

Certainly nothing off about his eyesight.

"I do things beyond work and practice at the dance studio."

He sent her a pointed stare over the top of his glasses. "I never noticed it until today. You've always been very single-minded about winning."

"I still am. What happened last night won't happen again." She passed him the bag of bagels, hoping it would distract him.

He ignored the gesture and arched a sharp brow, as if he disapproved. But Shanna couldn't shake the impression that he was suppressing a smile.

"I suspected it would happen someday. Maybe it's the female way. Who is he?"

Shanna frowned. "What do you mean, 'the female way?'"

He shrugged. "Women follow their hearts, which usually lead them to some man or another, who may or may not respect their desire to keep pursuing their goals."

Exactly. No doubt, he'd have complete disrespect if she ultimately made that choice. Her brothers, too.

"Which is precisely why Alejandro and I are…done."

"Alejandro? Do I know him?"

Shanna shook her head. "Argentinean. He owns a nightclub. We met at the benefit for the Catholic orphans charity last weekend."

God, it was weird to be discussing her love life with her father in the kitchen of her childhood home at seven in the morning. She needed coffee for this.

"Hmm." Her father hesitated. "What does he think of your dancing?"

"I assume he's okay with it. Not that it matters." Shanna sipped the caffeine-laden brew and let it sink into her hazy brain.

He reached for the carafe of coffee and poured a steaming mug. "A hindrance, is he? Resenting your practices?"

"No." Not unless she was avoiding him.

"Latin men are notoriously jealous. He can't handle your time with Kristoff and the way your partner has to touch you?"

Shanna had to laugh. "No, he knows way too much about Kristoff to be jealous."

"So you're just worried he'd be a general distraction?"

"He would. The other night, I was headed for a sensible dinner and an early evening to bed. Big day of practice the next morning, which is vital with the competition coming up. He came by and just assumed I'd go out for ice cream with him."

"Ice cream. That's a huge problem." Her father sipped his coffee, seemingly deep in thought.

Somehow, Shanna got the impression he was laughing silently at her.

"It is! I can't afford to blow off sleep and eat a gallon of ice cream to satisfy some romantic notion of his. And then he tells me personal stuff, about his childhood and friendships. He blurts out his views that commitment is absolute and infidelity is inexcusable. Why tell *me*? The whole incident is taking up my thoughts that should be directed to the competition, which is tomorrow. And last night, he kept me up half the night…"

Realizing she'd nearly spilled the details of her sex life, Shanna flushed, then continued with a safer topic. "The man is just consuming. Him just *being* steals my attention and leads my thoughts astray. Every trick I've used in the past to ward off would-be Romeos doesn't work with him. He just doesn't give up and won't go away."

"And you're so tempted to let him into your life that it frightens you." It wasn't a question. He seemed to *know* that's exactly how she felt.

"How…?" She grappled to find the right words. "You know?"

"Your mother had a life before we married. Did you know she was a prima ballerina?"

A prima ballerina? No clue. "I knew she flitted around the kitchen and she was graceful…"

But her mother had died years ago. In some ways, her mother was as great a mystery to her as she would be if Shanna had never met her.

"American Ballet Theater. She was set to star in the season's *Giselle*.

To this day, I'll never know what she saw in a cocky weightlifter coming fresh off a gold medal high. I had to have been a complete ass. But she claimed to love me. God knows the sun rose and set on that woman, as far as I was concerned."

Shanna frowned, sensing that she would not like what came next.

"You married her and—"

"Encouraged her to stop dancing. Made sure I got her pregnant with your brother so she had to stay beside me. I was a hugely selfish bastard where her time and energy were concerned. If I could take it back somehow and let her take her rightful place on stage…"

Mouth gaping open, Shanna stared at her father. *This* was the man who had driven her for years. Nothing she'd ever done was ever good enough. Second place was first loser. Quitting was the professional equivalent of a noose.

"I don't understand."

"I know." He sighed heavily and sat on one of the little wooden chairs they'd had forever. "I pushed you and pushed you. I don't think I realized until just now that I did it because I wanted to make up for what I did to your mother. She never said that she regretted her decision. But I'd catch her every so often holding her toe shoes with a wistful look on her face. I suspect she always wondered what could have been. I didn't want you wondering, too."

Shanna gaped, shock ricocheting through her. Her father had intentionally killed her mother's dance dream? And regretted it like hell. For years, he'd driven Shanna, fueled her ambition. As a child, she'd wanted to follow one of her brothers into their sports, but he'd specifically signed her up for dance class after dance class. Now she knew why. But…

"You sound as if you're encouraging me to continue with Alejandro. Why change your mind now?"

He stirred his cooling coffee. "In retrospect, I don't think your mother really regretted her decision to leave dance and marry. After she was gone, I realized how short her life had been cut and that I'd prevented her from fulfilling her dream. I regretted standing in her way. I beat myself up a lot over it. But you know, most of my memories are of her smiling. Your mother used to have this one little grin when she was particularly happy. A little lopsided, with a dimple in her left cheek and a twinkle in her eye. When I think about that smile now, I know she was at peace with her life." Her father paused, looked up at her. "Until this morning, I'd never seen that smile on you. But there was a moment when you got out of your car. I was watching through the window. I saw that smile on your face. I'm guessing Alejandro put it there."

He had. When she pushed aside her tumult about tomorrow's competition, happiness sneaked in, again and again. The thought that, after last night, she might never see Alejandro again, gouged her with deep shards of pain. And it shouldn't. Their relationship had been short. Intense, yes, but nothing to build a lifetime on?

Why did she feel like she was selling them short?

"He sounds like the kind of guy who wouldn't demand you give up your dream," her father said. "If he can make you happy and give you the freedom to pursue what you want professionally, why aren't you grabbing onto him with both hands?"

Yeah, why not? "With him as a distraction, I may never win."

"Would you rather lose a competition or the man you love?"

"It's not that simple, Dad. If I…divide my time, I won't be as dedicated. If I never become a champion, you won't think I'm weak?"

"Would it really matter if I did?"

Shanna paused. Thought. Alejandro's love or her dad's approval? No choice. "It would bother me if you weren't proud, but I'm an adult." She drew in a deep breath as her realization became an admission. "I should be doing what makes me happy."

"Yes, and you need a man's love more than Daddy's blessing."

She nodded. "Jason, Ash, and Kyle would make fun of me if I chose to be with Alejandro."

Her dad rolled his eyes. "They'd make fun of you no matter what you did. They're convinced that's their prerogative as big brothers."

In spite of the weirdness of the conversation, Shanna laughed. "You think?"

The smile faded as something occurred to her. "I'm not sure matters with Alejandro will be as simple as me expressing my feelings. Let's say I've played very hard to get. He may not be talking to me after I, um…sneaked out on him this morning."

"Why don't you send him tickets to tomorrow's competition? I bet he shows. I want to meet the man who managed to see beyond your Bitch of the Ballroom act."

"You're coming tomorrow?"

He reached across the table and squeezed her hand. "I wouldn't miss it for the world. Whether you're crowned champion of the ballroom or of Alejandro's heart, I'm proud no matter what."

9

aiting in the darkened corner of the ballroom's dance floor, Shanna drew in a deep breath, smoothed her hair, straightened her sleeve, shifted her weight. And scanned the crowd —again.

Nothing.

"You must not fidget."

If she hadn't been so nervous, she would have laughed at Kristoff. Why not just tell her she shouldn't breathe? "I know. Sorry."

"You are nervous?" her big, blond partner stood behind her and whispered in her ear. "Do you fear losing?"

The competition? Not as much as she thought. They would lose, of course, and during her largely sleepless night, she'd come to accept that. Kristoff had only been living his personal life, and he'd tried to engage in his kink of choice in a responsible environment. It wasn't his fault someone had it out for her and had circumvented *Sneak Peek's* rules to hurt her. But Alejandro? She absolutely feared losing him. In fact, she suspected she already had.

Shanna had delivered the tickets to *Sneak Peak* in person this morning. Del had greeted her at the door. Actually, greeted was a strong word. Met was more accurate. Reluctantly, in fact. His behavior had been considerably cooler than their last meeting. When he said he'd give the tickets to Ali, she added that she hoped he would visit her before the show so they could talk. Del had merely given her a terse nod, then shut the door in her face.

Clearly, she'd hurt Ali enough to seriously piss off Del.

Alejandro hadn't come to see her before the competition. Another scan of the ballroom…there sat her father, who waved. She smiled back, but she still didn't see Alejandro's coffee-dark hair, swagger, or sin-laced smile.

Had she pushed him away one too many times? The painful thought tightened her stomach into impossible knots. Throwing up didn't feel out of the question.

"Shanna, you are nervous about the routine?"

No. She and Kristoff were ready. Beyond ready. They knew these dances. They had perfected their chemistry and rhythm on the floor. The blackmailer's footage would keep them from winning, but they would give their best showing. She couldn't ask for more than that.

"Or do you regret that you were unable to replace me with a new partner in time for this competition?"

Scowling at his bitter tone, Shanna glanced over her shoulder at Kristoff. Mouth pinched, eyes tight, shoulders stiff. Damn, he looked nervous. Petrified. What was that about? He was never wound up before a competition. Maybe he was rattled about the video potentially circulating the judges' table? After all, this threat affected his career, too.

As Kristoff continued to watch her with narrow, burning eyes, and she replayed his question in her head, Shanna finally understood.

"I'm not replacing you." She dropped her arm to her side and reached for his hand. She gave it a friendly squeeze. "I never auditioned anyone else. You were right about the partner swapping; it was stupid."

He shot her a suspicious stare. "Why the change?"

"I used to bury my guilt about dropping someone for the sake of winning. It never worked. You made me see how pointless it was." *With a little help from Ali and Del.*

"You do not seek to replace me? Truly?"

She smiled. "You're stuck with me."

Kristoff leveled his mega-watt smile at her. "For days now, I cannot stop from worrying you plan to replace me." He squeezed her hand. "Thank you. I am happy now."

"We win or lose together, okay? Besides, maybe we haven't been winning because we've forgotten that dancing isn't all serious. Maybe…we just need to have fun with it tonight, see what happens."

Kristoff hesitated, then teased, "Who are you and what have you done with my partner?"

Despite her nerves and her worries about losing Ali, Shanna had to laugh. If nothing else, she'd cemented one important relationship tonight. And damn if it didn't feel good.

"If we were alone, I'd slug you for that."

"There is the Shanna I know and adore," Kristoff muttered.

Just then, the music ended, and the announcer reminded the crowd of their competitors' names and number. Shanna drew in a relaxing breath. *In. Out.* They were next.

"Before we go on, I must tell you something."

"Kristoff, we're about to be announced."

"This is true, but—"

"Couple number one hundred three, Shanna York and Kristoff Palavin from Los Angeles, California."

The crowd's cheer wasn't as enthusiastic as Kristoff would like, Shanna knew. She should care, she supposed, but right now, she couldn't get past the fact that Alejandro had chosen not to use the tickets she'd left him.

Which meant he'd given up on her, she feared for good.

Forcing a smile as the onlookers clapped, she walked onto the dance floor, Kristoff beside her, cradling her palm in his. They struck their pose and waited.

Doing her best to focus on the next three minutes, Shanna plastered on a smile and projected it to the crowd. The music burst over the quiet, Shanna arched, kicked, and turned.

There sat Alejandro.

His face gave away nothing, but the grin that shaped her mouth was her first real one of the day.

He's here. Here!

And he looked incredible in a black suit, white shirt, and a satiny charcoal tie.

She knew he looked even better out of the suit.

Before she whirled around to face Kristoff again, she flashed Ali a look she hoped communicated just how thrilled she was that he'd come.

Over the next two minutes, forty seconds, she and Kristoff poured their souls into the dance. And he was spectacular, as if some light had been turned on inside him. Relaxed yet crisp. Strong. God, he played to the crowd. He really was incredible. Shanna responded, acting the part of the seductive female to his commanding male in the cha-cha-cha.

No doubt in her mind, they sparkled, shined, brought the *WOW* to the dance floor. Shanna couldn't remember the last time she'd enjoyed dancing so much.

When the music ended, she knew they had done their best. Yes, she'd love to win tonight, but if it wasn't in the cards, they would spend a year living down the scandal and practicing their butts off. They would conquer this trophy next season.

The crowd stood, cheered, their enthusiasm catching. Never before had she felt so liked by the crowd, so connected to them as she and Kristoff bowed.

She turned her head slightly to see Alejandro. He, too, stood and clapped, then bent to whisper into the ear of a small but striking middle-aged woman who shared his eyes. His mother.

Then he turned his attention back to her, fixing burning hazel eyes on her, and Shanna felt the zing and sizzle all the way to her toes.

Damn, she loved that man.

"You and Alejandro?" Kristoff asked as they left the dance floor. "You have a…thing?"

"What?"

"You looked at him as if you cannot wait to devour him, as if you are all his. Or as if he is all yours. Is that true?"

Shanna swallowed a lump of nerves. God, she hoped Alejandro being here meant that he'd forgiven her for running away and being afraid to believe in them... If not, she wasn't giving up. No more switching partners for her when things got difficult—not professionally or personally.

"That's my plan."

"In fourth place..." the announcer droned, and Shanna listened long enough to realize her name hadn't been announced, then clapped politely.

This was usually the part of the event that made her most nervous. How many times had she stood at the corner of the stage, trying not to pass out, praying she would not be disappointed by failing to grab the trophy again, only to hear her name announced long before the first place winner's? How many times had she trotted out her plastic smile, like third place thrilled her, while feeling crushed inside? Too many.

But tonight...she almost *wanted* the announcer to call her name now, so she could finish this dog and pony show and talk to Alejandro. His face still gave away absolutely nothing, not anger, not joy. Had he forgiven her and come to be with her? Or had he simply come because she'd given him free tickets and his mother liked to attend? No clue. That man could probably play a mean game of poker.

"In third place..."

Again, not her name. Another polite clap. Another clandestine glance at Alejandro. He raised a brow at her, but his expression remained utterly, frustratingly unreadable. Forget the contest results. Not knowing how Ali felt about her was killing her.

And what did that say about how much she loved him? She was well and truly hooked.

"In second place..."

Not her name again. The couple beside them swept out on the floor, and Shanna could see the woman's forced smile hiding disappointment and the crushing blow of defeat.

But wait...if second place had been announced, and there were no other couples out on the floor...

"In first place, the California Dance Star Latin dance ballroom champions, couple one hundred three, Shanna York and Kristoff Palavin of Los Angeles!"

Kristoff squeezed her hand as he led her out onto the floor. "We did it! We did it!"

They had. Finally! Alejandro was clapping for her. His mother, too. The whole crowd, including her father, who enthusiastically whistled like he was at a football game. It was bad form in ballroom, but she smiled, glowed, and grinned from ear to ear.

Tonight, she was finally a champion.

But how had it happened, given the blackmailer's threats?

"What about...you know?" she said to Kristoff through her smile. Maybe the threatening bastard hadn't followed through?

Before he could answer, the emcee came forward with their trophy. Kristoff grabbed it with one hand and hoisted it up in the air, along with their joined hands. Together, they bowed.

Professionally, she had never been happier than in that moment.

"Ms. York and Mr. Palavin are now eligible to compete in the upcoming World Cup Latin competition."

Wow, a huge dream come true. And yet... Her life would be incomplete, her triumph hollow, if she didn't have Alejandro to share it with.

The emcee took the trophy from Kristoff. The lights dimmed, and as champions, she and Kristoff danced. But her mind was on Ali, the way he watched her, his face shuttered but his posture relaxed. What was the man thinking?

Soon, others crowded onto the floor. With the spotlight no longer on them, Shanna all but forced Kristoff to tango Alejandro's way.

Kristoff resisted. "I must tell you something."

"Later. Okay?"

"But—"

"Give me fifteen minutes."

Before he could reply, they reached the edge of the dance floor. She turned to Alejandro's mother.

"Mrs. Diaz? Hi, I'm Shanna York." She held out her hand.

"*Ella es su novia?*" his mother asked Ali sharply.

"*Mamá...*" He sighed. "*Sí.*" Then he whispered something in her ear...and her entire face changed, lightened, glowed.

She turned to Shanna with a beaming smile and said in accented English. "Thank you for the tickets. Congratulations on winning, *nuera.*"

Nuera? Damn she was going to have to learn to speak Spanish at the first opportunity. "Thank you. Have you had the pleasure of dancing with my partner, Kristoff?"

She shook her head and risked a shy peek at Kristoff. "He is one of my favorites."

"I'm sure he'd consider it a favor. He gets tired of dancing with me and would love your company." Shanna turned to her partner. "Kristoff?"

Her partner smiled charmingly and took hold of the older woman's hand. "Shall we dance?"

Off they went. Shanna watched Kristoff handle Ali's mother with aplomb as he led her into a waltz. The problem was, with Kristoff engaged, well-wishers and competitors were headed her way.

Her father approached first with a proud gleam in his eyes and big hug. After she quickly introduced him to Ali and basked in her dad's pride, Shanna kissed his cheek. Then she grabbed Alejandro's hand and dragged him backstage, down a poorly lit, winding hallway, into an empty office. She had no idea who it belonged to—and didn't care—but she shut the door behind her and locked it.

"Hi." She smiled. "You came. Thank you."

God, could he hear her heart pounding like an up-tempo song at full blast?

"You sent tickets. This competition meant a great deal to you." Shanna heard the edge of anger in his voice, glimpsed it in his tight jaw.

"Not as much as I thought. I know that now, thanks to you." She bit her lip, wondering how bad it was going to hurt if he didn't want to hear what she had to say. "I'm sorry about…the other morning. You know, leaving you alone. For everything. Please tell me you don't hate me."

"I do not hate you."

His face still gave her no inkling about her true feelings, but Shanna considered not hating her a decent start. She rushed to Alejandro, threw her arms around his neck, and kissed him like there was no tomorrow.

Then again, unless she convinced him of her sincerity, there might not be a tomorrow for the two of them.

He kissed back. Oh, did he ever. And he tasted *so* good. Like brandy and a hint of cinnamon. Hot. And a few moments later, hungry, insistent as his mouth devoured hers. He threw his arms around her, banded them tight around her middle, as if telling her without words that she wasn't going anywhere again. She melted, might as well have become a puddle at his feet.

Long minutes and a pair of damp panties later, she broke away, breathing like she'd run a marathon. And unable to restrain a hopeful smile. "Does that mean you forgive me?"

"For leaving me in my own bed, alone? Hmm, I may need more… persuading." A smiled toyed at the corners of his lips.

"Does tonight work for you?" She cupped his cheek in her hand, looked right into those killer hazel eyes, and threw caution to the wind.

"I may require more nights. Many of them."

Hope burst in her heart, so explosive she could hardly breathe. "Ali, I am so sorry. What I did was insensitive. I know it. I knew it then. I was just…scared. But I'm not anymore. And I want you to know that I care about you. A lot."

He quirked a dark brow. "Care. In what way?"

Shanna knew she had his attention. Not only did she feel it against her hip, she felt it in his gaze, in the way his arms tightened around her.

"How much, *querida*?" he prompted again.

She swallowed down the tangle of anxiety and need and anticipation threatening to kill her courage. "I love you."

Those three words had barely cleared her lips before Ali stepped around her and, with an impatient arm, wiped every piece of paper off the flat, faux-wood desk and onto the floor. A moment later, her back was against the cool laminated surface and every inch of his body covered her completely, from the bunching shoulders beneath his elegant coat to the hard abs that rippled with every breath.

"Say it again." His voice was thick with demand.

"I love you."

"And you mean this?"

"Except my dad, I've never said those three words to a man. Ever."

Finally, expression warmed Alejandro's strong, square face. Happiness, hunger, adoration...love.

"Te amo, querida." He dipped his head for a long, sweet kiss. "I love you, too."

Then he kissed her again, long endless moments where Shanna felt blissfully lost in passion. Alejandro's endless caress shimmered want in every crevice, corner, and nerve ending. She wanted the moment to last forever.

With a moan, he lifted his head, his hazel eyes snapping with a hunger like she'd never seen. "What I wish to do to you...with you, to show you how I feel... How do I get you out of this infernal costume so I can make love to you?"

"I want to," she breathed the words against his mouth. "I want that so much...but I was sewn into this costume. If you take it off, we won't get it back on, and I have nothing else to wear."

He cursed in Spanish, something that sounded melodious but was, no doubt, foul.

"I'll make it up to you."

He smiled, something sharp and greedy with his signature charm.

"We're leaving now. You will come to my bungalow and stay all night?"

"Yes." And the next, and the one after, and the one after that, if he'd have her.

"You will not leave?"

"In the morning? No."

"Ever?"

Was he saying... "Are you asking me to...move in with you?"

He clenched his jaw. "No."

Her stomach plummeted. "Of course not. I misunderstood."

"My *Mamá*, she would be very disappointed if we lived together. Just before you sent her to dance with Kristoff, a brilliant move, by the way, she asked if you were my girlfriend."

"You said yes." A smile crept across her mouth.

"I did, then I whispered in her ear. Do you recall?"

"Yes, what did you tell her? And what is a *nuera*?"

"I told her I had other plans." Alejandro grabbed her hand, kissed it, then whispered, "*Nuera* means daughter-in-law." He took a little black box from his pocket. "Interested in the role?"

Shock burst inside her, breath-catching and sweet. "You're proposing?"

"Yes."

"Aren't you supposed to be down on one knee?" she teased.

"I would rather be on top of you, always." He winked. "Will you marry me?"

"*YES!!!!*" She clutched Ali tight as he opened the box. She fell in love all over again. "Yes!"

"Good. I wasn't taking no for an answer."

"It's beautiful," she breathed as he stood up and slipped the square solitaire on her ring finger. Tears gathered in the corners of her eyes, slid down her cheeks. Probably ruining her mascara—and she didn't care. "When did you buy this?"

His cheeks flushed a dull red. "About four hours ago. But I have known that I love you for far longer than that."

"Me, too. I was just too afraid that love meant giving up my dream. I'm sorry. Never again."

"Together, we can face anything. Shall we tell my mother and your father?"

"Yes. Just... I want another moment alone with you." She squeezed his hand. "This is the happiest night of my life! The win, the engagement... Wow, almost too much good stuff to take in. I feel so complete."

He brought her against him for a lingering embrace. "Me, too. I will be here to share your triumphs for the rest of our lives. But..." he frowned. "What happened to the blackmailer? He threatened to circulate Kristoff's video to the judges to prevent you from competing and winning."

"I know. I've been scratching my head, too. Maybe he changed his mind?"

A pounding on the door interrupted their closeness and musings. Oops…someone wanted their office back, and they'd made an absolute mess.

Ali opened the door with an apology on his lips. "We are very sorry…"

But instead of an event manager standing on the other side, it was Kristoff.

"What?" Shanna asked. "Is something wrong?"

"I must talk to you."

She'd promised to talk to him in fifteen minutes. She supposed those were pretty much up. "Okay."

Kristoff paced; he looked oddly hesitant. "You are happy we won, yes?"

"Of course! Aren't you?"

He nodded. "Very."

"I don't know how, given your footage and the threat but—"

"I did that."

"Did what?"

Grimacing, he confessed, "I created the video. Before you force me from *Sneak Peek*…" He risked a glance at Ali. "The people in the video consented to be filmed. They are my…how should I say, boyfriend and girlfriend. We are together, and they agreed to help me."

Shanna had no idea Kristoff was in any sort of relationship, much less with both a man and a woman. Whatever floated his boat, but… "You're telling me you filmed the clip and left it for me with the blackmailing note? *You* staged this? Why the hell… I worried until I was sure I had no stomach left for days!"

"This, I know. I apologize. But, um…before I invest more years in being your partner, I must know if you will stay with me. If I pretended like the news of my relationship reached the judges, I wondered what would you do, keep me or dump me."

"So the blackmail…it wasn't real?"

"No." He grimaced. "Please do not hate me."

A moment of anger surged through her…then died. He would never have needed to test her if she hadn't spent years partner swapping to feed an ambition that, in the long run, had nearly consumed her spirit and happiness.

"I don't hate you. Just don't, um…surprise me again."

"Now I know where I stand, so…never." He snatched up her left hand, noted the ring there, and grabbed her in a bear hug. "Engaged? Congratulations! You are happy, yes?"

"Incredibly so." She sent Ali a warm smile, and he caressed her back in return.

"I think all will be good now," Kristoff pronounced.

"Not just good." Ali brought her closer to his side, and she rested her head on his shoulder. "It's going to be perfect. I'm going to be so happy."

"Are you sure?" Ali teased.

"I'm a champion with a great dance partner and a wonderfully hot fiancé. Oh, yeah." Shanna sent him a saucy smile of challenge. "Don't believe I'll be happy? Just watch me."

He slid his arms around her, and his kiss promised a passion that left her reeling. "Oh, I will."

NAUGHTY LITTLE SECRET
Standalone - Sexy Stranger / Office Romance
By Shayla Black
Available in eBook and print!

Her boss. Her friend. Her secret lover?

After divorcing her never-home husband, Lauren Southall plucked up her courage, dusted off her power suits, and returned to corporate life. Two years later, there's just one six-foot three, testosterone-packed problem: her ex-husband's good friend and her current boss, Noah Reeves. Lauren aches for him. But she can't possibly measure up to the silicone-packed professional cheerleaders he dates. So she hides her desire behind a professional persona and fantasizes.

For ten years, Noah Reeves has waited to make Lauren his. Once her divorce was final, he tracked down and hired the brilliant, dedicated woman. But when he's with her, it isn't spreadsheets and profit margins on his brain. Problem is, she's never seen him as anything but her ex-husband's pal. Now that she's finally a free woman and with him forty-plus hours a week, well… he'd love to persuade her to throw in her nights and weekends. So Noah decides to romance her by day. By night, he becomes a mysterious stranger devoted to her pleasure… and discovers she's hiding a naughty little secret of her own.

EXCERPT

When Lauren rounded the corner of her desk, she moved to sit in her chair…and found something in it. A white envelope. Thick and textured. Nothing written on the front, but definitely something inside, judging from the bulge of neatly-folded paper inside.

Given the fact it was on her chair, she assumed someone set it here for her. Safe assumption, right?

Shrugging, she opened the envelope, withdrew the lone page inside, and unfolded the thick paper.

You. Me. Naked skin. Shared fantasies. A whole night.

Soon. Lauren blinked at the typed note. Read it again. And nearly stopped breathing. Someone here wanted her? Someone who'd gone to the trouble of writing her a note and leaving it in her chair. No hint of a signature or his identity. And maybe the situation should have creeped her out…but she didn't sense menace behind the words, just desire. She looked around the sea of cubicles with new eyes. Who? Gary was too straightforward. Most of the other men here were older, happily married, or gay. Except Noah, and he had little Miss Pom-poms to keep him warm at night. Maybe it was simply someone who worked in the building. Tender Forks shared this building with several other businesses. Security was relaxed. Maybe it was one of the consultants across the hall? The possibility didn't excite her.

"Lauren?"

The object of her fantasies stopped just behind her, his deep, sin-inspiring voice seeping into her. His warm breath cascaded down the back of her neck. She couldn't help it; she shivered. "You find that report?"

"Report?" she repeated numbly.

She couldn't seem to get her mind off a whole night of naked skin and shared fantasies and inserting Noah in the picture.

"This it?" He took the piece of paper from her hand and lifted it to read.

Lauren reached out to grab the page back, but it was too late. His dark expression told her he'd already read every word.

"Did someone give this to you?"

She could feel herself flushing every shade of red. "I found it in my chair. Someone left it there."

"Interesting note."

She couldn't tell whether he was pissed she might be hooking up with someone in the office or so amused he was about to laugh his ass off. He was a master negotiator. His face never gave away anything unless he wanted it to.

"I—I don't know who left it."

"Well, you don't have to guess what he wants."

The flush spread wider, seeping heat through her body. "No, that's clear."

He quirked a dark brow at her. "Worried? Do you think this is someone psycho? I can beef up security."

Gnawing on her bottom lip, she cast a brief glance up at Noah. Those gorgeous blue eyes were too much to look at, her desire too deep to conceal from him. She looked away.

How perfect. One man wanted her—a man who clearly understood how much she loved surprises and wished for a lover. But the man she ached for stood right in front of her, asking questions and offering to protect her like a brother. Damn, he chased everything else in a skirt. Why not her?

"I'm fine. You need that appetizer report, right?" She moved to round the corner of her desk, toward her computer.

Noah grabbed her arm, his grip gentle but unyielding. "Talk to me. Are you scared?"

With a rueful smile, she worked to set him at ease. "I probably should be. But this is the most admiration I've had since my divorce. Whoever it is, I don't think he means any harm."

Slowly, he released her arm and sent her a long stare. "You want naked skin and shared fantasies?

Lauren sighed. "What red-blooded woman doesn't? I appreciate your concern, but—"

"Can you handle skin and fantasies?"

She shrugged, wondering if Noah cared even a tiny bit that some other man wanted to hold her. "According to him, I'll find out soon. Guess I'll let you know then."

WHAT TO READ NEXT!

Seductive, Angsty Contemporary Romance
Reed Family Reckoning

If you missed the eldest of the Reed Family siblings finding his seductive happily ever after:

MORE THAN WANT YOU – Maxon and Keeley's story – FREE!
I hired her to take down my enemy. Now I'm determined to have her for my own.

And if you're excited to find out how Reed Family friend Trace turns his fling into forever:

MORE THAN DARE YOU
I dared her to spend a hot, no-strings night with me. Now I'm determined to keep her forever.

Sexy Bedtime Stories
Forbidden Confessions: First Time

If you want more steamy, first-time encounters, check out:

SEDUCING THE INNOCENT - Kayla & Oliver's story
How far will she go to persuade her brother's best friend to stay?

SEDUCING THE STRANGER - Calla & Quint's story
How deep will she fall after one night with a hot stranger?

Forbidden Confessions: Protectors

Want a little suspense with heart-pounding attraction? Meet hot protector, Rand Garrison.

SEDUCED BY THE BODYGUARD
What will he demand in exchange for keeping her safe?

Erotic Stranger/Office Romance

NAUGHTY LITTLE SECRET
Her boss. Her friend. Her secret lover?

High-heat, High-octane Romantic Suspense
Wicked Lovers World
Ready for a super-sexy, nail-biting world of suspense, danger, and
love? Join the tough-as-nails, former military operatives of the EM
Security team. Meet sniper Pierce "One-Mile" Walker…

WICKED AS SIN
*She begged him to rescue his enemy from death. In exchange, he
demanded her body…*

OTHER BOOKS BY SHAYLA BLACK

WICKED LOVERS: SOLDIERS FOR HIRE

Steamy, High-Octane Contemporary Romantic Suspense

FREE! Wicked as Sin (One-Mile & Brea, part 1)

Wicked Ever After (One-Mile & Brea, part 2)

Wicked as Lies (Zyron & Tessa, part 1)

Wicked and True (Zyron & Tessa, part 2)

Wicked as Seduction (Trees & Laila, part 1)

Wicked and Forever (Trees & Laila, part 2)

Wicked as Secrets (Matt & Madison, part 1)

Wicked and Bare (Matt & Madison, part 2)

REED FAMILY RECKONING

Sultry, Angsty Family-Drama Contemporary Romance

SIBLINGS

FREE! More Than Want You (Maxon & Keeley)

More Than Need You (Griff & Britta)

More Than Love You (Harlow & Noah)

BASTARDS

More Than Crave You (Evan & Nia)

More Than Tempt You (Bethany & Clint)

More Than Desire You (Xavian & Corinne)

FRIENDS

More Than Dare You (Trace & Masey)

More Than Hate You (Sebastian & Sloan)

NOVELLAS

More Than Pleasure You (Stephen & Skye)

More Than Protect You (Tanner & Amanda)

More Than Possess You (A Hope Series crossover) (Echo & Hayes)

DOOMSDAY BRETHREN

Sexy Paranormal Romance

Tempt Me with Darkness (Marrok & Olivia) (October 24, 2024)

FORBIDDEN CONFESSIONS

Sexy Bedtime Stories - Contemporary Romance

FIRST TIME COLLECTION

Seducing the Innocent (Kayla & Oliver)

Seducing the Bride (Perrie & Hayden)

Seducing the Stranger (Calla & Quint)

Seducing the Enemy (Whitney & Jett)

PROTECTORS COLLECTION

Seduced by the Bodyguard (Sophie & Rand)

Seduced by the Spy (Vanessa & Rush)

Seduced by the Assassin (Havana & Ransom)

Seduced by the Mafia Boss (Kristi & Ridge)

FILTHY RICH BOSSES COLLECTION

Tempted by the Billionaire (Savannah & Chad)

Tempted by the Executives (Marcus, Kate, & Josh)

Coming Soon:

Tempted by the Bosshole (Bella & Nathan) (January 12, 2024)

THE WICKED LOVERS

Sizzling Contemporary Romantic Suspense

Wicked Ties (Morgan & Jack)

Decadent (Kimber & Deke)

Delicious (Alyssa & Luc)

Surrender to Me (Kata & Hunter)

Belong to Me (Tara & Logan)

Wicked to Love (Emberlin & Brandon)

Mine to Hold (Delaney & Tyler)

Wicked All the Way (Carlotta & Caleb)

Ours to Love (London, Javier, & Xander)

Wicked All Night (Rachel & Decker)

Forever Wicked (Gia & Jason)

Theirs to Cherish (Callie, Thorpe, & Sean)

His to Take (Bailey & Joaquin)

Pure Wicked (Bristol & Jesse)

Wicked for You (Mystery & Axel)

Falling in Deeper (Lily & Stone

Dirty Wicked (Sasha & Nick)

A Very Wicked Christmas (Morgan & Jack)

Holding on Tighter (Jolie & Heath)

Devoted to Wicked (A Devoted Lovers crossover) (Karis & Cage)

THE DEVOTED LOVERS (Complete Series)
Steamy Contemporary Romantic Suspense
Devoted to Pleasure (Shealyn & Cutter)

Devoted to Wicked (A Wicked Lovers crossover) (Karis & Cage)

Devoted to Love (Magnolia & Josiah)

THE UNBROKEN SERIES
(co-authored with Jenna Jacob)
Scorching Ménage Contemporary Romance
Raine Falling Saga (Complete)
The Broken (FREE Prequel!)

The Betrayal

The Break

The Brink

The Bond

Heavenly Rising Saga

The Choice

The Chase

The Confession

Coming Soon:

The Commitment (August 22, 2023)

THE PERFECT GENTLEMEN (Complete Series)

(co-authored with Lexi Blake)

Steamy Contemporary Romantic Suspense

Scandal Never Sleeps

Seduction in Session

Big Easy Temptation

Smoke and Sin

At the Pleasure of the President

MASTERS OF MÉNAGE (Complete Series)

(co-authored with Lexi Blake)

Sizzling Contemporary Romance

Their Virgin Captive

Their Virgin's Secret

Their Virgin Concubine

Their Virgin Princess

Their Virgin Hostage

Their Virgin Secretary

Their Virgin Mistress

STANDALONE TITLES

Naughty Little Secret (Sexy Stranger/Office Romance)

Watch Me (Steamy Romantic Suspense)

Dirty & Dangerous (Sizzling Ménage Romantic Suspense)

Her Fantasy Men (Sizzling Reverse Harem Contemporary)

A Perfect Match (Sweet Opposites-Attract Contemporary)

THE HOPE SERIES (COMPLETE SERIES)
Steamy Contemporary Romance

Misadventures of a Backup Bride (Ella & Carson)

Misadventures with My Ex (Eryn & West)

More Than Possess You (Echo & Hayes) (A Reed Family Reckoning crossover)

SEXY CAPERS (COMPLETE SERIES)
Steamy Contemporary Romance

Bound and Determined (Kerry & Rafael)

Strip Search (Nicola & Mark)

Arresting Desire (Lucia & Jon)

HISTORICAL ROMANCE
STANDALONES

The Lady and the Dragon (Sexy Georgian Privateer Romance)

One Wicked Night (Sexy Regency/Forbidden Love Romance)

STRICTLY SERIES (COMPLETE DUET)
Sexy Victorian Historical Romance

Strictly Seduction (Madeline & Brock)

Strictly Forbidden (Kira & Gavin)

BROTHERS IN ARMS (COMPLETE TRILOGY)
Angsty Medieval Romance

His Lady Bride (Gwenyth & Aric)

His Stolen Bride (Averyl & Drake)

His Rebel Bride (Maeve & Kieran)

BOXSETS/COLLECTIONS

ABOUT SHAYLA BLACK

LET'S GET TO KNOW EACH OTHER!

Shayla Black is the *New York Times* and *USA Today* bestselling author of nearly ninety contemporary, erotic, paranormal, and historical romances. Her books have sold millions of copies and been published in a dozen languages.

As an only child, Shayla occupied herself by daydreaming, much to the chagrin of her teachers. In college, she found her love for reading and started pursuing a publishing career. Though she graduated with a degree in Marketing/Advertising and embarked on a stint in corporate America, her heart was with her stories and characters, so she left her pantyhose and power suits behind.

Shayla currently lives in North Texas with her wonderfully supportive husband, her daughter, and two spoiled tabbies. In her "free" time, she enjoys reality TV, gaming, and listening to an eclectic blend of music.

TELL ME MORE ABOUT YOU.

Connect with me via the links below. You can also become one of my Facebook Book Beauties and enjoy live, interactive #Wicked-Wednesday video chats full of fun, book chatter, and more! See you soon!

Website: http://shaylablack.com
VIP Reader Newsletter: http://shayla.link/nwsltr

Shayla Store: https://www.shaylablack.com/bookstore/
Facebook Book Beauties Chat Group: http://shayla.link/FBChat

facebook.com/ShaylaBlackAuthor
instagram.com/shaylablack
tiktok.com/@shayla_black
twitter.com/ShaylaBlackAuth
bookbub.com/authors/shayla-black
pinterest.com/shaylablacksb

NEW YORK TIMES BESTSELLING AUTHOR

SHAYLA BLACK

Steamy. Emotional. Forever.

BOOK BEAUTIES
Facebook Group
http://shayla.link/FBChat

Join me for live,
interactive video chats
every #WineWednesday.
Be there for breaking
Shayla news, fun,
positive community.

VIP Readers
NEWSLETTER
at ShaylaBlack.com

Be among the first to get
your greedy hands on
Shayla Black news,
juicy excerpts, cool VIP
giveaways—and more!

Shayla Store
Books & Merch
at ShaylaBlack.com/bookstore

Get signed Shayla Black
print books, cool bookish
merch, and early access
to Shayla's latest eBooks.